BELANOPEK?

Creatio Ex Nihilo

To Karen —
Bonne lecture!
Complimenti —
Belanopek
Paris 29. Août 2025

PETER BEALE

A Song of Methuselah – Volume Five

Peter Beale
18 Rue de Montpensier
75001 PARIS, France
beale.publishing@gmail.com

Printed Worldwide
First Printing 2024
First Edition 2024

'And when you pass your nine hundredth birthday you are not what you used to be.'

- Isaac Bashevis Singer

BELANOPEK?

Dreamland - 1

From his helmet to the soles of his iron-studded boots the guard stood over two-metres tall. He wore chainmail, a long sword belted at his waist, and carried a razor-sharp spear. Snowflakes drifting down from out of a black and frigid sky glinted on his armour. In front of him, clutching an envelope in both hands, was a small boy dressed in rags, scarcely taller than the guard's knees, who now looked up at him and said:

"Is this where the Princess lives?"

"It is," the guard said, amused by the serious demeanour of the boy.

"I am to take this envelope to her," the boy said.

The guard smiled.

"If you give it to me, I will see that she gets it," he said.

"I cannot do that," the boy said. "My master told me I must give it to her myself."

"Do you not see these gates, boy?" With his thumb the guard pointed over his shoulder at the immense wooden gates in front of which he was stationed. "This is Tre Kronor Castle. These are the gates to the King's palace. Nothing and no one enters without my authority. Now be a good lad, give me the envelope." He held out his hand.

The boy shook his head and took a step backwards.

"I gave my master my word," he said.

"Enough!" The guard's voice was no longer friendly. "Who is this master to contradict a Royal command?"

"I cannot tell you his name."

"What insolence! You will tell me his name or -" the guard tried to grab the boy's arm, but he ducked away.

"You will make me very angry," the guard said. "Do you want to be arrested for disobeying an order?"

"I only take orders from my master," the boy said. From under the rags he wore he took out a very large toad and put it on the ground.

"Mind," he said to the toad and pointed at the guard. Like an amphibian tank, its wart-covered body swelling up, the crested eyes of the toad fixed on the guard as it shifted its stance to face him.

The guard laughed. "A toad? You think to threaten me with a toad?"

"I wouldn't laugh," the boy said.

As swift as a bolt of lightning the guard slashed his spear at the toad. But, in the timeless second before the toad was cut in half, it spat a great gob of toxic poison from the parotid gland behind its eyes onto the guard's foot. The guard screamed as the poison burned through his boot, through the skin and tendons and bones of his foot, all the way through the iron-studded sole.

"I told you not to laugh," the boy said. "I can always get another toad; yet I doubt you can get another foot."

Which is when the narrow wicket gate built into the palace gate opened and a knight stepped out, dressed in black velvet with an ermine cloak and a grey wolf ushanka on his head to keep out the winter cold. "What is this commotion?" he said.

The guard being in no condition to answer, it fell to the boy to say, "I have an envelope for the Princess."

"She is sleeping and cannot be disturbed," the knight said. "Give me the envelope and I will see that she gets it when she wakes up. I am Lord Oxenstierna, her guardian." He held out his hand for the envelope.

"Please excuse me, my Lord, but I cannot give it to you," the boy said. "My master bade me give it to the Princess in person."

"Who is this master?"

"It is forbidden for me to say his name," the boy said.

"Then we have a problem", the knight said. He knelt in the snow the better to look the boy in the eye…

3

…which is when he woke up. All he could remember was feeling cold.

Paris Now.

"Belanopek? Strange you should ask. A woman came into the shop a couple of days ago - Tuesday, wasn't it, George?"

"Wednesday," George said.

"Right, Wednesday, asked the same question, did we know fact from fiction regarding the entry on him in Google?"

"Bloody cheek," George said.

"Yeah, but understandable. Difficult to believe he was born in 1896 and is still alive. And working. I doubt she was satisfied with what I said but she told us something interesting. Apparently, her parents knew him back in the '50s, when he was driving a taxi in Paris. Never heard that one before. It seemed unlikely, but so does so much else about the man. He had a place up the street, you know, in a garret on the seventh floor. No lift. I confirmed to her that he bought paints and brushes right here from my old man when he was alive - before I inherited the shop. Well, bought is perhaps the wrong word since he apparently never had a penny to his name."

Chapter One

One
  Two
    Three
      Four
        Five
          Six
            Seven
              Eight
            Nine
          Ten
           Eleven
            Twelve
             Thirteen
              Fourteen
              Fifteen

The student always counted the stairs. The stairs were at the end of a narrow hall tiled in black and white. Made of wood, worn by time, they climbed an oblong stairwell, the walls painted beige, lit by a distant skylight seven floors above. There were fifteen steps between each floor. For the first three flights the stairs were carpeted, dark blue with a magenta stripe to left and right, brass stair rods holding the carpet in place.

Then, floors four and five, jute, six and seven, uneven bare worn wood. Everything threadbare, old, scarred. Smelling faintly of cat piss, wood polish and Dettol.

After fifteen steps a landing, with an apartment door left and right. The doors were painted to match the carpet for the first three floors, then plain oak with traces of polish. Screwed in the middle of each door a brass label holder for the tenant to put their name. Some were engraved business cards, some handwritten. The rotation of tenancies could be accurately calibrated by how faded the labels looked. The more faded the label, the older the tenancy. The apartments on the first three floors were distinguished by having their own bathrooms and toilets. Above, facilities were shared, with a bathroom on the half-landing of Four and a toilet on Five, another bathroom on Six and a toilet on Seven.

The entrance door to the building gave directly onto the Rue des Beaux-Arts, outside which the two small children of the concierge, Émile and Marie-France, would play where they could be watched by their mother whose miniscule loge was to the left as one entered, basically a thin railroad flat with one window at one end, a skylight at the other and a glass-paneled door to the lobby. There was no father. He died in the Great War.

Ier Gauche: was Maître Léon Legrand, Avocat à la Cour, his card almost illegible, he had been there so long. *1er Droite:* the building's owners, two spinsters, one 78, the other 80, Mesdemoiselles Espinasse, from Auvergne. Despite their age, they confidently ran the bar/tabac to the right of the front door, a gift from a generous uncle. Over the years, this establishment made so much money under the counter that they prudently lent it to those in need, one of the needy being the building's former owner, Monsieur Alphonse, overfond of betting on the nags at Longchamp and Chantilly. When this worthy was unable to pay back his debt plus accumulated interest it fell to Maître Legrand to suggest to the ladies that in lieu of a lawsuit he be allowed to negotiate with Alphonse title to the property and the apartment on the first floor. His success included a generous reduction in his own rent from the new proprietors.

Sixteen
  Seventeen
    Eighteen
      Nineteen
        Twenty
          Twenty-one
            Twenty-two
              Twenty-three
                Twenty-four
                  Twenty-five
                    Twenty-six
                      Twenty-seven
                        Twenty-eight
                          Twenty-nine
                            Thirty

2ème Gauche: In exquisite calligraphy the card on the door read **B.S.** Equally anonymous, the tenant was rarely seen and when seen one was unsure of the tenant's gender, hidden, summer and winter, under multiple shawls, greatcoats, and hats. What was not anonymous was the smell, a mixture of unwashed flesh, rotted socks, faded cologne and cat piss from an unknown number of cats living there. The stink crept under the door, across the landing to *2ème Droite:* M. et Mme. Descourtis. A faded couple, like a bleached watercolour, not given to complaining, who countered the stench by the involuntary farting of their ancient beagle. They had acquired the dog as a puppy and enjoyed his scampering down the stairs for an evening walk along the Quai Malaquais overlooking the Seine. Now, nearing the end, he had to be carried downstairs to do his business and they were lucky if he made it to the corner of the Rue Bonaparte.

Thirty-one
  Thirty-two
    Thirty-three

Thirty-four
Thirty-five
Thirty-six
Thirty-seven
Thirty-eight
Thirty-nine
Forty
Forty-one
Forty-two
Forty-three
Forty-four
Forty-five

3ème Gauche: the pink card of the delicious Mlle. Zoffany, whose many admirers led some to whisper it would be better she installed a revolving door. She always had a ready smile for her *voisin de palier* in *3ème Droite*, Jacopo Zucchi, for the shared initial of their respective surnames, which smile invariably drew a frown from Zucchi's mistress, Marina di Spilimbergo, the erstwhile vedette of the Moulin Rouge.

Forty-six
Forty-seven
Forty-eight
Forty-nine
Fifty
Fifty-one
Fifty-two
Fifty-three
Fifty-four
Fifty-five
Fifty-six
Fifty-seven

Fifty-eight
Fifty-nine
Sixty

The doors of both apartments on the fourth floor bore the same name printed in block letters, **LAMBERT**, since they were occupied by the same family. *4ème Gauche,* housing the patriarch, Jean-Claude Lambert and his wife, Marie-France; *4ème Droite,* their unmarried children, Jean-Charles, 38, Marie-Louise, 35, Jean-Yves, 30, and Marie-Claire, 27. All six were living on the dwindling capital of what had once been a substantial fortune made in the slave trade by an ancestor no one was allowed to mention. Instead, they spent their time squabbling with the tenants on the fifth floor for the use of the bathroom and/or the toilet.

Sixty-one
Sixty-two
Sixty-three
Sixty-four
Sixty-five
Sixty-six
Sixty-seven
Sixty-eight
Sixty-nine
Seventy
Seventy-one
Seventy-two
Seventy-three
Seventy-four
Seventy-five

9

5ème Gauche: G. Facchini, Mosaiste, an engraved card with his business address underneath, 2 bis Rue du Valois; across the landing, *5ème Droite,* handwritten, M. Laurent Doumeng, a retired bookseller, much given to smoking a pipe. Both widowers, who often shared a table in their landladies' bar, where, over a pastis or absinthe, they speculated out loud on the advantages to be had for the Espinasse spinsters to give up their long-preserved chastity and join their tenants in matrimony.

Seventy-six
   Seventy-seven
      Seventy-eight
         Seventy-nine
            Eighty
               Eighty-one
                  Eighty-two
                     Eighty-three
                        Eighty-four
                           Eighty-five
                              Eighty-six
                                 Eighty-seven
                                     Eighty-eight
                                         Eighty-nine
                                           Ninety

6ème Gauche: DEMAILLY, Delphine, Comptable/PAULIN, Pauline, Astrologue, a lesbian couple living with their pet parrot, Coco, a cockatoo, which spent its time squawking and screaming if it failed to get the attention it constantly needed; *6ème Droite,* the dim initials B.T., which never changed although the current occupants were called Mme. Anna et Mlle. Nathalie Steinem, an attractive widow and her nymphomaniacal daughter.

Ninety-one
Ninety-two
Ninety-three
Ninety-four
Ninety-five
Ninety-six
Ninety-seven
Ninety-eight
Ninety-nine
One hundred
One-hundred-and-one
One-hundred-and-two
One-hundred-and-three
One-hundred-and-four
One-hundred-and-five

One hundred and five steps to reach the seventh floor. If he had a clear run it took him one minute and forty-five seconds, top to bottom. More going up.

On the seventh floor were the maid's rooms, six in all. Numbered 1 to 6, painted on the doors, with no brass label holders. Small, dismal, and cramped, the sloping ceilings punctured by dormer windows. In the summer you roasted, in the winter you froze.

Only two were occupied by real professional maids: Marie-Laure, 56 years old, who looked after the owners, and Gaby, 39, recently from Guyana, who 'did' for the Lamberts. The other four were rented to a miscellaneous assortment of local workers. A waiter in the Café des Beaux-Arts at the bottom of the Rue Bonaparte, the man who sold newspapers in front of the Café Flore and the Deux Magots, the Madame-Pipi, who presided over the toilets Chez Lipp.

And the student. His gift from Mme. Steinem for services rendered.

Southwest from his room, with the dormer window open, an abstract mosaic in varied hues of zinc-grey formed a patchwork vista of rooftops as

11

far as the eye could see, pierced by the church towers of Saint Sulpice and the Eglise de Saint Germain des Prés, the dome of the Panthéon, and, on the horizon, the Eiffel Tower. Under all those multiple roofs were buildings just like his, packed with the teeming anonymous multitude of people who called Paris home.

It is one of the curiosities of urban life in a dense city like Paris that the more people are crammed into a building the less likely they are to know one another. A brief nod of the head if you crossed someone on the staircase or in the street. Perhaps a muttered 'bonjour' to a tenant of long standing. Even sharing a landing was never reason enough to invite your neighbour to cross your threshold, leave alone those on the floors above and below. No. It sufficed that you eased your way in and out of your abode with the least contact possible, averting your eyes from the transgression of prying into another life, thus avoiding any knowledge of the trials and tribulations commonly suffered, and, above all, taking no responsibility for their solution. Avoiding the concierge was another magnitude of difficulty - particularly if you had not paid your rent. It was a favourite theme of the two widowers when they chanced to meet in the Café-Bar Espinasse.

"*Bonjour Monsieur Doumeng.*"

"*Bonjour Monsieur Faccini.*"

(Never Hullo Laurent, Hullo Gaston.)

"*Vous allez bien?*"

(A rhetorical question met with a grunt and a shrug.)

"*Ça va. Est-vous?*"

"*Comme d'hab.*"

"*Qu'es qu'on boit?*"

"*Pastis?*"

A nod.

Both men sit at a table they always occupy facing the street. They stare through the window at the odd person passing by. They can vaguely hear a street organ and the Whup! Whup! of a carpet being beaten in a courtyard nearby. It never consciously occurs to either that in the nearly twenty years they have lived in the building neither has so much as seen inside the apartment of the other, let alone shared a drink in there.

Without an order given, perhaps by habit (or telepathy), two pastis in tall narrow glasses arrive on a tray with a carafe of ice-cold water and a bowl of olives. It is brought to them by the older of the Espinasse sisters, Mademoiselle Victorine, who dilutes the anise-flavoured, dark, transparent yellow liquor into a milky soft yellow by adding the water until told to stop. If, by divination, the requirement calls for absinthe, then it falls to the younger sister, Mademoiselle Géraldine, to bring the chartreuse green spirit, a distillation of alcohol, wormwood, anise and fennel. First, she pours an ounce of absinthe into the appropriate small glass. Then she places a flat silver spoon pierced with holes over the rim of each glass. On it is a sugar cube. With great care she slowly pours ice-cold water onto the sugar, just enough to saturate the cube, which is then allowed to sit and dissolve, with more water slowly added until, at the nod of her customers, the desired dilution is found. As the water hits the liquor, there is a swirl, the *'louche'*, which releases the absinthe's herbal bouquet. When all is at rest, the sugar dissolved, the louche dissipated, she makes a quick twirl of the spoon in each glass. *Voila!* The drinks are served.

"Merci."

"Merci."

The two widowers raise their glasses in salute. Very little is said as they sip their drinks. Then they see the student on his way out of the building, as always dressed in black corduroys, a black turtle-neck sweater, and a black astrakhan hat on his head. Open-toed sandals. No socks. He turns right, heading for the corner where the Rue des Beaux-Arts joins the Rue de Seine, on his way to the Sorbonne.

"You know he was in the war?" Monsieur Faccini says.

"Really? He looks very young. How do you know?"

"The concierge told me."

A nod. Of course.

Chapter Two

One shop in from the corner is an artist's emporium in the windows of which is a cornucopia of paint brushes, tubes of oil paint and gouache, crayons, watercolours, pencils, pens, ink, erasers, painter's smocks, easels, palettes, palette knives, turpentine, varnish, gum arabic, chalk, charcoal sticks, glue, frames, mattes, panes of glass, scissors, anglepoise lamps, drafting tables, drawing boards, sketch-pads, tracing paper, blank canvases of every size, portfolios, satchels, even straw hats for painting in the sun. The shop's walls are painted off-white and the floor is made of polished wood in long planks, 60 centimetres wide. Hanging everywhere, everywhere, are paintings, drawings, lithographs, posters. No two days offering the same display.

The owner of the shop, Monsieur Auguste Phillipon, is a taciturn man, balding, slight to the point of being undernourished, needing a shave, wearing a soiled grey apron tied with a string around his waist, his beady eyes framed by steel granny glasses sitting astride a bird's-beak of a nose, the fag-end of a short, wide, unfiltered Gitanes on his lower lip. From the high stool where he sits behind his desk at the back, every day, morning and evening, he morosely watches the student stop to stare in the window of the shop. He never comes in. Never buys anything. Goes on his way. It gets on Phillipon's nerves.

Unaware of the opprobrium caused by his window-shopping, the student continues walking south for 600 metres where the Rue de Seine crosses the Rue Saint-Sulpice and changes its name to the Rue de Tournon. In the boulangerie on the corner, he buys a croissant with the few centimes remaining in his pocket. Eating slowly, he continues to the end of the street,

14

turns left on the Rue de Vaugirard, walks past the former home of Marie de Médici, the Palais du Luxembourg, then another 80 metres to turn right and enter the gates into the park at the Porte Odéon, to walk around the octagonal pond and cross the 23 hectares of the Palace gardens to the exit on the Rue Auguste-Comte. A diversion, taken for the pleasure of walking in the calm glory of such a beautiful place. Then a brisk left where Auguste-Comte hits the Boulevard Saint-Michel, gently downhill another 600 metres to go right on the Rue Soufflot and left on the Rue Victor Cousin to the doors of the Faculté des Lettres of the Sorbonne. After school he returns home down the Rue Saint Jacques to turn left along the Seine until he reaches the Pont des Arts, and then left again up the Rue de Seine and right into the Rue des Beaux-Arts, to pause as always and look into his favourite window. A daily roundtrip total of 5 kilometres, 300 days a year, 1500 kilometres, the combined distance walking from Paris to Warsaw. Poland. His mother's birthplace. Origin of his Slavic cheekbones.

One day it got to the point where, seriously irked, Monsieur Phillipon, standing in the open doorway of his shop, felt compelled to accost the student.

"What do you want?" he said, the stub of the Gitanes bobbing on his lip.

"Nothing. I'm just looking."

"It's annoying."

"I'm sorry."

"You never come in. Never buy anything."

"With what?" Turning his pockets inside out the student showed he had no money.

"No kopecks," he said.

Phillipon grunted. Turned in the doorway. Pointed to a tall rectangular cardboard box at the back of the shop.

"There," he said. "Take what you want."

Inside the box was the unsaleable detritus of his trade: broken crayons and pencils, dried out tubes of paint, split brushes, stained drawing paper, odd lengths of string. Bits and pieces. Junk.

The student peered through the doorway. Hesitant.

"I can come in?" he said.

"Yes, yes. Get on with it." Phillipon retreated to his stool, watched while the student edged into the shop looking around in awe. When he got to the cardboard box he squinted his eyes to look inside and could not believe his luck. "I can really take what I want?" he said.

"Not if you keep asking questions. Can't you see I'm busy?" From where he sat perched heron-wise, Phillipon frowned at the youth.

Without further ado the student picked up the entire box and strode to the door.

"What are you doing?" Monsieur Phillipon sat up straight.

"What you told me to do, taking what I want."

"Everything?"

"Oui. Merci! Don't worry, I'll bring the box back." And off he went, leaving Phillipon to shake his head.

Thus began a strange collaboration. Every few days the student would stride into the shop, pick up the box and bring it back empty. It went on for weeks until Phillipon could no longer conceal his curiosity.

"What on earth do you do with all the stuff you take?" he said.

"Well, you know, I make…things."

"What do you mean, things? What things?"

"Pictures. Images. I make stuff I like…you know?"

"You mean paintings?"

"Well, yes, I suppose you could call them that."

"Show me.'

"What…?"

"Your pictures. Show them to me."

"Do you want to see them?"

"Yes."

"Really?"

"Yes. Really. What is it with you? You think I have the time to waste my breath debating with you?"

"Well…it's just that nobody has ever asked to see them."

"*Mon Dieu!* Do you never stop talking? Go. Bring me something to look at."

"Well…there's a lot of stuff…"

"Go!"

The student went. Climbed up 105 steps to his room on the seventh floor. Selected a few items. Put them in a large, dilapidated portfolio which he hiked over his shoulder by a strap. Then walked 105 steps down and back to the shop. And there, not without some trepidation, offered up his work for examination.

"*Alors?*" Monsieur Phillipon sniffed, got off his stool. Removed his spectacles to give them a quick polish on his apron. Settled them on his nose. Squared his shoulders. Gave the student a stern look.

"What have we here?" he said, opening the portfolio.

Ten pieces, on thick parchment, in mixed media, mainly gouache, a waterfall of colour and light. Without comment, Phillipon held each piece in front of him. He took his time. Went through the entire portfolio twice. The student held his breath.

"So," Phillipon said again. "Extraordinary. Let's see…"

Whereupon he went to a selection of mattes, chose one and a frame to go with it, put matte and frame on one image, set the framed artwork on an easel and stared at the result for the longest time.

"Extraordinary," he said. "Extraordinary. It looks like a picture. Of what, I don't know. But it is splendid. Marvelous. How did you get such colour, such light? *Mon Dieu*, I am tempted to say you have painted the air, the very air. How on earth did you make these?"

"In the shower," the student said.

"The shower?" Phillipon looked up at him, astonished.

"I need hot water to melt the dried-up paint. There's none in my room. When I get the chance to use the bathroom, down on the sixth floor, it becomes my studio. I press the parchment paper to the tiled wall of the shower stall and hose it down with the hot water. Then I make marks with some lumps of that gum arabic I found in your box and then I press paint out of the tubes. Because the paper is wet the colour runs. It runs around the gum arabic. It makes a pattern. If I need more paint, I use more. If there is too much, I squirt it off with the hot water. The colours mingle and spread. When it pleases me, I stop. I must be careful peeling the wet paper from the wall because it can easily tear. I dry the paper on the radiator in my room or out on the roof tiles if it is a sunny day. The drying makes a texture that I like."

"What are these black marks?"

"When it's dry, I make those little marks with indian ink and a fine nib pen. I like to think they look like the footprints of tiny birds left wandering about on a foreign landscape."

"How long does all this take?"

"Not that long. I can usually make six or seven before I run out of hot water. The other tenants get mad when there's none left. Because they complain I only paint late at night when they're all asleep."

"Six or seven a day! My God, how many have you got?"

"I don't know. I don't keep count. But dozens, maybe even hundreds."

"Unbelievable. Let me try another."

One after the other, Phillipon tried mattes and frames on the different pictures. He stared at them. Shook his head.

"Incredible," he said. "How much do you want?"

"Want?"

"Yes. They're for sale, right? What do you want? What's the price?"

"I've never thought of it."

"Never thought?…You don't have a penny in your pocket and you never thought of selling these?"

"Who would want to buy them?"

"Let me worry about that. But first you must sign them."

"Why?"

"So people will know who made them."

"What shall I put?"

"Your name of course." Seeing the puzzled look on the young man's face, Phillipon added, "You do have a name?"

"Yes. Pyotr."

"Pyotr what?"

"Szépség. It means '*belle*' in French

"Pyotr Belle? What sort of artist's name is that? No, no. That won't do. We will have to find a better name."

Which they did.

BELANOPEK.

From the first three letters of his surname in French and the absence of kopecks in his pocket.

Monsieur Phillipon made him practice writing the name hundreds of times until the signature looked natural. Then he conjured up a pricelist, took 50% of all sales after deducting the cost of the mattes and frames. And off they went. Sales were brisk. The student was happy. For the first time in his life he could look forward to supplementing his meagre bourse from the University and having enough money to pay his rent at the end of each month and eat more than a measly croissant when he was hungry. Before falling asleep at night, he was careful to include Phillipon in his prayers.

It did nothing to alleviate his nightmares.

Dreamland - 2

The small girl muttered in her sleep.

She was on a battlefield in Saxony with her father, the King. She could feel his hand on her shoulder. "What day is today, Christina?" her father said.

"Wednesday."

"And the date?"

"September 17, 1631."

"Good girl." He squeezed her shoulder. She was four months shy of her fifth birthday. They were standing on a terrace in front of a hamlet called Podelwitz, ten kilometres north of Leipzig.

"What do you see," the King said.

"The enemy in the field between us and that little town, Breitenfeld, over there on the right." She pointed.

"How many are there?"

"37,000."

"Who is the Imperial commander?"

"Field Marshal Johann Tilly."

"And on our side?"

"23,000 Swedes and 16,000 Saxons."

"Tilly is a formidable foe," the King said. "He has won battles at Mingolsheim, Wimpfen, Høchst, Heidelberg, Mannheim, Stadtlohn, Lutter, Magdeburg…"

"But he will lose here because he does not know about our new guns," the little girl interrupted. She had to crane her neck all the way back to look up at her father.

From high up he smiled down at her.

"No. Nor does he know how many we have." Squeeze. A shiver of pleasure went down Christina's spine. "And we have more cavalry. Whose battle flag do you see on our left flank?"

"Count Gustav Horn."

"Opposing him?"

"I see the arms of Prince Egon of Furstemberg."

"And on our right?"

"Count Johan Banér."

"Opposite?"

"The banner of Graf zu Pappenheim."

"What will be their opening move?"

"They will attack the Saxons."

"Why?"

"The Imperials have spies. They must know the Saxons are our weakest link. Most are untrained conscripts and militia, with very few muskets."

Behind them, on horseback, the armoured escort of the King's personal bodyguard, each of them the veteran of untold battles, exchange nervous glances. Unspoken, why bring a child onto the battlefield?

Without turning around, the King, speaking in the German tongue, said, "Hören Sie gut auf mich, mein Herren. Der Apfel fällt nicht weit vom Baum. Heed me well, gentlemen. The apple does not fall far from the tree. One day she will be your King. Pray to God your sons have the wit and courage of my daughter."

Just then a single cannon fired from the Imperial line. The arc the cannonball made ended with a thump into a hillock in front of the Saxon position. "They're getting anxious," the King said. "What time is it?"

Nearly noon, his equerry said, holding the bridle of Streiff, 18 hands, 870 kilos of muscle, the King's giant Oldenburg chestnut war horse, impatiently pawing the ground with its steel shod hooves, uncaring that the

King had paid one thousand riksdalers for him, ten times the value of any such beast.

"Streiff wants to charge," Christina said, standing on tiptoe to pat the stallion's muzzle. The horse eyed her. Lowered its great head to nibble at her hair. They were friends.

"You bring Papa back safely," she told the horse.

And opened her eyes in her bedroom to see Lord Oxenstierna and a small boy with an envelope bending over her.

"I am to give you this envelope," the boy said.

Waking stiff and cold, he remembered that line.

I am to give you this envelope.

Chapter Three

It didn't take long. On the occasion of her fiftieth birthday, Mlle. Demailly woke up to the warm embrace of her companion, Pauline, singing ever so softly across the pillow they shared:

"Joyeux anniversaire,

Joyeux anniversaire,

Joyeux anniversaire-rreee, ma petite Delphine, joyeux anniversaire !"

Followed by a long, long kiss.

At just under 75 kilos Delphine Demailly was scarcely petite. But she was well made, kept in shape by trekking up and down the ninety steps to the sixth floor with hardly a pause to take breath. Her Pauline, razorblade-thin, 42 kilos, hardly dented the mattress they lay on.

From under their bed where she had hidden it the previous evening, Pauline pulled out a carefully wrapped present. *"Regarde ce que j'ai trouvé pour toi,"* Pauline said. "Look what I've found for you."

It was a picture. One metre square matted and framed.

"Before you open it," Pauline said, "tell me what is your favourite colour?"

"Green!"

"Of course! Because today is the fifth of May and you are a Taurus. Green is your colour. Green, grounded in the energy of the Earth, binding you to nature and growth, right? Go on now. Open it."

The wrapping is torn off. The picture glows. It is like peering into an emerald green well from the high walls of which waterfalls tumble down to a distant circular turquoise pool.

23

"*Mon Dieu!*" Delphine Demailly cannot believe her eyes. "What does it mean?"

"It doesn't mean anything. It's a mandala. A guide to a sacred space."

"Who on earth made this?" Squinting, Delphine can just make out the letters in the bottom right-hand corner. She spells it out.

"B.e.l.a.n.o.p.e.k. Belanopek? I've never heard of him. Who is he?"

"You'll never guess." With her thumb Pauline points at the ceiling. "That boy, the student."

"He gave this to you?"

"No. I bought it from old Phillipon. They have an arrangement. The boy paints and Monsieur Phillipon sells. He is his dealer. You should go in there and take a look before there are none left. Phillipon says he sells them before the paint is dry."

"Where will we hang it?"

Incongruous in a frilly nightie, Delphine lumbers out of bed clutching her picture. She looks around the small apartment. The only wall space suitable is where a tiny crucifix hangs above their bed.

"He won't mind," she said (crossing herself just to be sure), as she takes down the crucifix and hangs up the painting.

"There. Look Pauley. Isn't that perfect? I cannot begin to tell you how happy I am. Thank you so much."

Pauline smiled. "Don't thank me. Thank the boy," she said.

Which is when somebody knocked on their door. The two women looked at each other, neither one dressed to receive a visitor. Then Pauline shrugged. "This early in the morning they get what they deserve," she said. And opened the door.

It was the boy. Dressed in black as usual. The student from upstairs. The painter.

He blushed at seeing the two women in their nightgowns.

"Yes?" Pauline said, her question at his intrusion slightly mocking, but also intrigued. Nobody in the building ever paid a visit to a neighbour.

"Please forgive me..." the student stammered

"What have you done that I should forgive?" She couldn't help mocking him which made him blush even more.

"Are you Mademoiselle Paulin, the astrologer?"

"I am."

"I need your help. I don't know how to properly say this, but I seem to be living inside a dream."

"An astrologer does not interpret dreams, Monsieur. We predict the future by the relative position of the Sun, the Moon, and the other planets. If it is your karma to live in a dream it is not something I can change."

"*Arrête de le taquiner,*" Delphine said. "Stop teasing him. Instead of debating on the doorstep, why don't you ask the young man to come in?"

Pauline did. He had barely crossed their threshold before he saw his painting above their unmade bed. For the longest moment he stared at it. "Thank you," he said.

"It is not for you to thank us," Delphine said. "It is for us to thank you. It is my birthday today and that picture is the finest birthday present I have ever received. Your picture has transformed this room. We had no idea you were such a talented artist."

More blushes.

"Now sit down while I make breakfast and you tell Pauline your problem."

No one argued with Delphine Demailly. The boy sat where told at a table in a nook off the kitchen. Breakfast was a freshly baked baguette, cheese, saucisson, red wine and coffee.

"So? Begin," Pauline said.

Dreamland - 3

Eyes wide open in curiosity, the little girl sat up in bed and opened the envelope. It contained an unsigned broadsheet and a smaller envelope, sealed in wax, with her name written on it. She broke the seal. Inside was a single sheet of paper. She immediately recognized her father's handwriting. She read:

My child,

If you read this, I am dead and you are now King in the eyes of God, the Court, and the people of Sweden. Just as we do not choose the time of our death, so too we must accept the fate of our birth. Yours is to be my heir and to accept the burden of ruling our land. No tears. Rejoice.

Be just in your dealings with men both high and low. Listen to the council of Lord Oxenstierna and to that of your mother, Queen Maria Eleonora, but above all, as leader of our Protestant faith, listen to God the Almighty in your heart and in your prayers. Let His light shine on your path and guide your steps.

My faith in you is absolute. You honour the House of Vasa. There are great things to be done that require the courage and duty of those who rule. Carpe Diem!

Your loving father,
Gustavus

Dry-eyed she re-read the letter, folded it and put it back in its envelope. Dry-eyed, she looked at the boy and Lord Oxenstierna. Dry-eyed, she looked beyond them to a window which looked out to the land over which she must now reign. Dry-eyed she unfolded the broadsheet, read it to herself, then read it out loud:

"Like a ray of light flashing through the fog No rider sits in the saddle.
The fleeing beast, steams, reeks,
Its white is dipped in scarlet red.
The saddle bloody, bloody the mane,
All Sweden saw the horse
On the field of Lützen that same day
Gustavus Adolphus lay in his own blood."

"The King is dead," she said. She is just six years old.

"Long live the King!" said the nobleman, dropping to kneel in front of his Sovereign.

The boy stared in amazement…

Chapter Four

Amazed, the two women stare at the student.

"I am that boy," he said. "Every time I fall asleep, I find myself living this dream. I am in Sweden during the Thirty Years War. I can't get away. It's a nightmare."

"Perhaps it's one you should embrace?" Mlle. Paulin said. "It is not given to everyone to live two lives. *Ne t'en fais pas.* No worries. Let us see what the stars have to say. When were you born?"

"I don't know."

"How can you not know when you were born?"

"I know where but not exactly when."

"Explain."

"My mother was on a ship in the coolie trade out of San Francisco bound for China. This is in 1896. She was pregnant when she got on board and, in sight of Hawaii, it was obvious she was going to give birth. The captain of the vessel thought it prudent to have medical help and put ashore on the island of Molokai where there was a leper colony, and it was the doctors from there who helped in my delivery. The only record of my birth was in the ship's log in mid-December of that year: *Born, a boy, to Frau Dr. Szépség.* No date. Nothing else."

Pauline Paulin sniffed. "Where was your father in all this?"

"I- I never met him. Unknown."

"Brothers? Sisters?"

"One brother, two sisters."

"Surely they know when you were born?"

"Perhaps they did. Unfortunately, they are dead."

"All of them?"

"Yes. My mother too."

"Mon Dieu! So, you are an orphan."

"Yes."

"No matter. The period governed from November 22 to December 21 is Sagittarius, the ninth sign of the Zodiac. You are in luck. Your element is fire. Your ruling planet is Jupiter, domiciled in Sagittarius. Jupiter is the Great Benefic. Everything it touches is expanded. No wonder you think your dream is real."

Dreamland - 4

That night, when at last Christina fell asleep, the boy was led to a chamber deep inside the castle, given some food and water and shown where he should rest. The door to his chamber was left ajar and he could hear what Lord Oxsentierna said to another man when he was questioned.

"So, you believe the boy?" the man said.

"Yes, of course. He didn't invent the letter."

"Strange way to confirm the King's death, don't you think?"

"No. You see conspiracies behind every rumour, Lennart. Accept it - the King is dead. Christina reigns. There can be no question of her just succession. It behooves all of us to support her in these perilous times."

"The astrologer was right then. He should never have led the army."

"Rubbish. How can you believe such quackery? We're not living in the dark ages, you know. When he wakes up the boy will give us the details. Enough said. You will take command. I'll have your appointment proclaimed at once and ..." the voices faded away as the two men walked off. The boy tried to stay awake, but his eyelids refused to stay open. His sleep was dreamless.

The next morning when he opened his eyes, he found himself being examined by another boy not much older than himself.

"So, you are awake at last. I am Magnus. Magnus de la Gardie. I am ten years old. I am the most handsome, witty, seductive Prince in all Her Majesty's realm. Some say I am conceited, vain, brash and impudent. And stupid - mostly said by friends; my enemies are more polite. I have come to take you for a bath and to get you out of those filthy clothes before your examination."

The speaker, tall for his age, well built, wore an ivory-coloured padded doublet with long sleeves, a fine sleeveless leather jerkin over it, and a pair of black hose ending in embroidered purple slippers. He had profound ice-blue eyes with golden hair down to his shoulders. About his waist he wore a belt with a scabbard and dagger. He now smiled.

"We will be friends," he said. "What is your name?"

"Pyotr."

The boy sat up from the pallet on which he had been lying.

"In Swedish?"

"Petrus - I think."

"Like in the Bible. So, Petrus, give me your hand."

The two lads shook hands with some formality and Magnus led Petrus to be washed and dressed. Then, before Christina and Lord Oxenstierna and the assembled congress of the Riksens Ständer - the Diet of the Four Estates of Swedish society, made up of the Nobility, the Clergy, the Burghers and the landed Peasants - Petrus, groomed and suitably accoutered in a dark brown velvet suit with a lace collar, gave his account of that terrible day.

"First I must tell you why I was there," he said. "My father was an assistant to Johannes Kepler, the mathematician and astrologer of Generalissimo Albrecht von Wallenstein, leader of the Imperial forces. Although he had already defeated King Gustavus at the battle of Alte Veste, Kepler warned him of difficult times ahead. He was ignored. Since he could not make the journey to Lützen with the latest horoscope he had sent my father. My father took me with him to help and told me to be brave. We were hiding in one of the three windmills on the Imperial side overlooking the Flossgraben canal which you Swedes would have to cross in order to attack. There was a thick mist mixed with smoke from the many burning buildings that made it difficult to see. You could hear the cannon and other guns firing over the sound of buildings crashing down and the thunder of the charging cavalry under Graf zu Pappenheim. I was frightened by the noise and then I got separated from my father when he went to help a wounded soldier. I looked for him everywhere but couldn't find him and so I moved from hiding place to hiding place trying to get away from the fighting. There were bodies lying all over the ground with great gouts of blood coming out, both men and horses, smelling of piss and shit like the worst outhouse and…" his voice faltering, the boy began to cry.

"Be brave, Petrus," Magnus said.

Petrus looked at him, nodded, wiped his eyes, glanced up defiantly at the serried ranks of courtiers looming over him and addressed himself to the only person his size, Christina, who smiled at him with eyebrows raised in query. Go on? He took up his tale.

"Suddenly in that din I heard a shot from very close by, a scream, and out of the foggy smoke saw an enormous white warhorse stumble and pitch its rider to the ground. He had bullet wounds but was still alive. The riderless horse bolted, and a great cry went up from the Swedish side. Then out of the fog I saw a mighty Prince loom up who shot the man on the ground in the head. He knelt to make sure he was dead and from the dead man's hand took an envelope. He was looking at the envelope when he in turn was cut down with a spear thrust into his back. As he fell he saw me crouching in some bushes not two metres away and held out his hand with the envelope. Take it, he said. Show it to no one until you deliver it. Bubbles of blood were coming from his mouth. Never say who gave it to you. Now run. Run for your life, boy. Then he died. I ran. It has taken me six weeks to get here."

"And your father?" Christina said.

Petrus shook his head.

"Dead," he said.

Chapter Five

"It's incredible," Mlle. Paulin said. "How is it you know so much history of the Thirty Years War? And in such detail?"

"I don't. It's a dream. There was no assembly. I checked in the Bibliothèque National. Oxenstierna wasn't even in Stockholm. After the King was killed, he stayed in Germany from 1633 to 1636, as Commander in Chief of the Protestant forces armed with plenipotentiary powers which were almost regal."

"But the letter?"

"It exists in my dream. No such letter has ever been found."

With her forefinger, Delphine Demailly pushed up the tip of her nose. "Does it not occur to you to wonder if historians really know all they pretend to? It seems inconceivable to me that Lord Oxenstierna, the Queen's appointed Regent, would not see his ward for three years. Her father, the King, is dead, killed in battle. Think about it. She's six. He would go straight to her side to protect her and ensure the succession. Maybe the historians are wrong, and your dream is true. Does not Nerval say 'our dreams are a second life?'"

This discourse goes on for a year. By which time he has again walked the distance from the French capital to that of Poland. And is a year older with the beginnings of a moustache and a straggling rim of whiskers growing on his thin pale cheeks. He is unsure of the benefits to be gained by continuing to study at the Sorbonne but, despite his art, still cannot afford to abandon the meagre comfort of his bourse. He is also unsure of the advice of Pauline Paulin who alarmed him by introducing the term *Anareta* into her discourse about the planets.

"It's from the Greek," she said at their most recent meeting. "Roughly translated it means 'destroyer'; a planet in your sign that has a deeply malefic effect on your life. The question is do we have such a bad planet in the eighth house of your natal chart and if we do what are we going to do about it?"

"How do you know if it's there?"

"I don't. But with Jupiter, who knows?"

"I thought you said Jupiter was beneficent?"

"Oh, it is. But there is always a negative side. Like black and white. Good and evil."

"What has that to do with my dream?"

"Whether we like it or not, anareta can change our lives? With or without our consent. It is the dark side of the zodiac and of our personal horoscope. If you think about it, the world is divided into opposites. Duality in the world is the source of all our uncomfortable problems. Big and small. Fat and thin. Full and empty. Good and bad. Yes and no. Our anaretas bring them out, starting from the most innocent of fairy tales that depict the good maiden and the evil witch, all the way through to contemporary life with the polarity in religions, sexuality, politics and finally in us not being able to accept death as a natural part of life."

"I don't understand."

"The eighth house in our chart always speaks of our deepest, darkest fears. Yours is your dream. If you let fear lead the way, it will slowly eat you up. Your negative reaction and negative thoughts will inevitably lead to a negative conclusion. Whatever your anareta is, it is through change that you must shape it and find meaning and purpose to its role in your life. No matter if it is Jupiter, and it's dark role in this scenario. Dreams are telling you something and you must learn from them. You must seek to meld all that is positive and negative into a Unity so you can become one with your shadow and finally live unmolested in your dream."

"Do you think he understands?" Delphine asked Pauline, when the boy had left.

"No," Pauline said. "But the seed is planted."

Delphine nodded. "For a 29-year-old, he's very naive, not to say innocent - particularly if he fought in the war. There is something there he has not told us." Delphine lumbered up from the couch on which she had been sitting. "I'm going to have a shower. Coming?"

Chapter Six

"While you were out, your friend came by," the concierge said. "He will be in Polidor at 9 this evening."

Pyotr had few friends. Well, that's not accurate - he had one friend. Many acquaintances, but just one friend. They were of the same age. Someone whom he could trust, who would listen to him, empathize with his deepest concerns, offer intelligent advice, and never share what he learned with any third party. Like himself, a war veteran. His friend's name was Markus. A German. He was reading History and Law at the University. They habitually met at Polidor on the Rue Monsieur le Prince, which had good food for little money, four-course dinner, 5fr50, including wine, perfect for impoverished students from the nearby Faculté de Médecine and the neighbouring intelligentsia, equally broke -Verlaine, Benoît, Gide, Valéry, Joyce - the list went on. After the war there was no shame in being poor. Being hungry, yes.

"I'm going to have the *blanquette de veau* with rice," Markus said before he was even seated. It was what he always ordered.

Pyotr said, "You're late. I've been waiting for half an hour."

"So? You always fuss about such little things."

"I am not fussing. I'm making an observation."

"Then permit me to make one too - get rid of the beard and moustache. You look like a goat."

He sat down where he always sat down, with his back to the wall commanding a view across the dining room to the front door and the street, helped himself to a glass of wine from the carafe Pyotr had on the table, and said, "You still paying your rent fucking the widow Steinem?"

Markus was one of that rare breed who, no matter how long you hadn't seen him, carried on a conversation as if he had momentarily stopped to greet someone or just come in from an errand. This time he had been away for six weeks. Where? Don't ask. No one who knew him ever did. It was one of those things. He was there and then he was not there. Even mid-term he would go missing and when he showed up again not even his professors dared ask him where he went. He had been a student at the Sorbonne before the war and returned to finish his doctorate. The thin boy returned as a thin man, thinner if that were possible. But somehow the war had given him substance, a gravitas not usually found in a student, leave alone in the staff, most of whom escaped military service by grace of their age. Despite being richer than most of the students, he lived in the newly opened Cité Universitaire, on the Boulevard Jourdan, next to the Parc Montsouris, in the 14th arrondissement. Now, sipping his wine, watching the pretty girls scattered at tables throughout the restaurant, he nods. "You know your problem?" he said. "You don't let life happen. You want everything planned, in its place, secure, safe. No pointy corners."

"You call screwing La Steinem safe?" Pyotr laughed. "You haven't met Nathalie, the daughter."

"Ah, there's a daughter? How come you've never mentioned her? What's she like?"

"A sexual maniac. You can't go to the bathroom without the little nympho trying to get in."

"So, mother and daughter, congratulations. What are you complaining about?"

"I am unaware I was complaining about anything."

"It's the look on your face. I know you. Something is bothering you."

"Do you believe in astrology?"

"Astrology? No. And neither do I believe in Father Christmas. What's the problem?"

Pyotr told him.

Dreamland - 5

"Petrus, now that we've adopted you," Magnus said, "I think you should know something about our family. We live in Makalös, the Great House, they're building over there on the Norrström," he pointed out of a window to the river, "there, south of Kungsträdgården, across from the Royal Palace. My mother, Ebba Brahe, should never have married my father. She was in love with the King, betrothed to him in fact when they were both 14, but his mother, Christina of Holstein-Gattorp, thought she was not royal enough, not highborne enough, so she married my father instead and today we are richer than the Crown." Magnus shrugged. "I was born in Reval, capital of our dominion of Estonia where my father, Jacob, is the governor. They've already had 10 children. I'm the fourth. My elder brother, Pontus, died earlier this year. He was only 13. My sisters, Christina, Sophia and Brita, and my brother, Gustaf, all died almost as soon as they were born. I have two living sisters, Maria, who is 6, and a new Christina, who's a baby, and two brothers, Jakob, who's 4, and another Pontus, who's 2. So I'm the oldest now."

Magnus paused. Thought. Sniffed. Said: "I wouldn't want to be a woman having babies every year and watching half of them die before they are one year old. I used to cry when we buried them, but now I don't. I'll show you their tomb when we get home. If you think about it, it's just as well she didn't marry the King or she would be a widow now and have to wear black, a colour she hates."

Petrus nodded. He was an orphan with no siblings, whose mother died giving birth to a still-born baby. To be part of such a large family like de la Gardie was something he had never imagined. And when, as happened that

38

afternoon, he met Countess Ebba Brahe, he saw immediately that she was expecting yet another child, witness her swollen stomach swathed in an emerald-green robe protruding between the wings of a dark magenta cloak. The meeting was on the third floor of the still unfinished mansion where Countess Brahe was taking the architect, Hans Kristler, to task for delays in construction, cost overruns and a paucity of qualified workmen. "I am tired of always hearing the same excuses, Minherr," she said. "When we contracted with you to design and build this palace you promised it would be done in two years. Here we are at the end of the third year, and we are not even halfway there."

"With respect," the architect said, "I actually said it could be built in two years provided the initial plans, approved by your Ladyship, were not modified."

"Utter nonsense," the countess said, "I may have asked for a few details to be altered to improve your plans, but that in no way condones these delays."

"If by a 'few details' your Ladyship is referring to change orders moving the living quarters to the ground floor after they had been built on the piano nobile, and replacing them by the reception rooms and festivities hall, and moving the dancing and music rooms to the third floor instead of the library, and the stores and armoury to the fourth and fifth floors instead of the cellar where they belong, to be replaced by some larders resulting in the housekeeping facilities being built separately outside, next to the stables, and the resultant modifications to the facade, not to mention the relocation and in some cases the reconstruction of already finished stuccoed plafonds, the columns of certain loggia, and redesigning the galleries for the paintings..." here Herr Kristler paused for breath. "I can detail more if you..."

"Enough!" The countess cried. "On ne saurait faire d'omelette sans casser des œufs." And - off the Austrian architect's puzzled look - instantly translated to a German metaphor: "Wo gehobelt wird, da fallen Späne. You can't make an omelette without breaking eggs. No more of your tricks. Just get it done."

It took four more years to finish and when done the five-floor building, built of brick and stone with a copper roof, unrivalled in all of

Sweden, humbled the surrounding area and made Petrus proud that he could call *Stora Huset*, the Great House, his home. By then he was 10 years old.

Chapter Seven

By then the carafe was empty and Markus ordered another to go with their meal.

"How come you haven't told me this before?" he said.

"Too embarrasing."

"How long has it been going on?"

"Couple of years," Pyotr said.

"And you're sober when you fall asleep?"

"More or less."

"How soon after you're asleep do the dreams start?"

"I don't know. All I know is when they end because they usually wake me up."

"And then?"

"I go back to sleep."

"To dream?"

"No. I have a trick. I imagine a car's windscreen wipers going left to right, left to right, and that puts me back to sleep. Out like a light in no time."

"But in the morning you still remember what you dreamt?"

"Yes, obviously, or I wouldn't be sitting here telling you all this."

"You're a lucky sod, you know. I can never remember my dreams. It's like childhood, try as I might, I cannot remember anything before I was five years old. I've seen pictures of course, of me in a pram on Sylt or playing in the snow with my sister, but can I remember doing that, no. The first real memory I have is being held tight in the arms of my Nanny when there is a very loud bang, a window shatters and she tries to cover my ears so I can't hear someone screaming."

"I can remember my Chinese Amah when I was two, waking me up because God had sent us a beautiful morning," Pyotr said.

Both men nod, each aware of an unanswered echo. Each memory in limbo, no before, no after. Across the restaurant a family of tourists got up to leave, mother, father, 3 small children, boy, girl, baby.

"You think they'll remember their parent's treat of a meal in Polidor?" Markus said.

"Where is your sister now?" Pyotr said.

"Married."

"Oh."

"Two kids. Lives in Hamburg on the Alster. Husband killed on the Somme. Left her a packet. Why? You interested?"

Pyotr smiled. "What happened to that girl, the waitress?"

"Karla? She's around. Going to marry an American from what I hear." Which is when the waiter brought them their food. Of a common accord all conversation was suspended while they ate - but not their thoughts. Markus thought, he always brings up Karla.

Pyotr thought, he's still hooked.

Chapter Eight

As was their habit at the end of each month, in their office on the first floor, the two sisters, heads bent forward in concentration, sat across from each other at a massive mahogany partner's desk, its veneered surface covered in large leather-bound ledgers containing the accounts of their tenants.

From where she sat, Victorine, if she looked up, could see on the wall behind her sister's head the faded sepia portraits of their parents, Jean-Joseph Espinasse and his wife, Victorine-Louise, after whom she was named. The portraits covered the outline of pictures removed by the departing bankrupt, Monsieur Alphonse, when the sisters took over his property at the turn of the century. That 25 years later they hadn't bothered to redecorate his apartment reinforced the cliché of Auvergnats being miserly, not that they gave a fig for clichés. Some people can't tell the difference between a respect for money and being stingy, Géraldine was wont to say.

From where she sat she could see the grand piano beyond her sister's left shoulder on the lid of which were a multitude of silver-framed photographs of the two girls growing up, dominated by a telling image showing them dressed in dark blue pinafores over dark blue pleated skirts worn below the knee, made of an itchy wool, thick dark blue stockings and black buttoned ankle boots, in boarding school, in Chambéry, run by the Sisters of St. Joseph, two of whom in their black robes and white wimples loomed slightly out of focus behind the girls. A place they hated, to which they had been confined following a calculation made by Jean-Joseph that it was cheaper for his daughters to be brought up in a convent school than at home. Behind his back people termed such pettiness *'pingre'* - an adjective difficult to translate but easily imagined as the man who always finds a reason to leave the table just before the bill arrives, who somehow never pays for his round in the pub but is forever on to you because he paid for your coffee in the café a month ago. Whatever. From where he hailed, deep in the Massif Centrale, earning a substantial living shipping coal and wood from Montluçon to Paris on barges down the Allier, nobody could say his girls would not get a handsome dowry when they married. Make that if they married, which of necessity required a husband.

Unfortunately, fate dictated otherwise. Victorine was born in 1845, and Géraldine in 1847, and in 1848 the beginning of an endless series of republican revolts against the monarchs of Europe started in Sicily and quickly engulfed France, Italy, Germany and the Austro-Hungarian Empire. A staunch republican, Jean-Joseph, supported the revolution, applauded when King Louis Philippe was forced to abdicate and cheered when Alphonse de Lamartine proclaimed the Second French Republic, cried for vengeance when Prince Louis-Napoleon Bonaparte staged his coup d'état in 1851, proclaiming himself Emperor Napoleon lll, only to ally with Britain in the Crimean War against Russia from 1853 to 1856, ally with Italy in the Franco-Austrian War of 1859, foolishly involve himself in establishing a monarchy in Mexico, and even more foolishly getting himself captured leading the French troops in the Franco-Prussian War of 1870 in which France was so humiliatingly defeated - which defeat Jean-Joseph took as a personal insult. Adding injury to insult, German troops occupied Paris, only leaving in 1873 upon completion of payment by France of 5 billion francs in indemnity for starting the War! So much strife and so many dead young men reduced the field of available suitors for his daughters, upsetting his plans for unloading them once they were out of their teens.

Fate then struck a second blow with his own death, age 51, of the smallpox, which he contracted when visiting his invalid brother, a Lieutenant recovering from a bayonet through the gut in the military hospital, Val-de-Grâce, rife with the disease infecting many of the 14,000 wounded returning from the Battle of Sedan. Distraught, Victorine-Louise took her own life by throwing herself into the Seine at the Pont Neuf, the oldest standing bridge in Paris.

Mais jamais deux sans trois, as the saying goes. Fate, in the shape of their Tonton, a jovial uncle from Clérmont-Ferrand, who celebrated becoming the legal guardian of the girls by inviting them to work for him in his bar-tabac (deflowering them both shortly after they arrived in Paris), then did away with himself when he caught yellow fever on a trip to New Orleans in 1905, leaving his wards the legacy of dispensing tobacco and alcohol to the citizens of the Quartier Latin which, in time, made their fortune. But time, as always, also blurred the past.

The daily drama of Great Events oft recounted and furiously debated, polarizing kith and kin, alienating countless French families around their own dinner tables, became something quaint, the faded wallpaper of memory, forever overtaken by the latest headlines which grow dim in hindsight even as they are being read. By way of contrast, entering into the ledger who had and who had not paid their rent on time was an excellent factual exercise.

Since Géraldine had the calligraphic gift of a fine copperplate script, it fell to her to make the entries her sister dictated as she went through the monthly pile of accumulated cheques and cash submitted by their tenants, a ceremony with its own protocol. 14 line items. An efficient clerk could have whipped through the task in fifteen minutes. Not if you were an Espinasse. *"Bon?"* said Victorine.

"Prêt," said Géraldine, adjusting her pince-nez, a book of receipts at her left hand, pen freshly dipped in the inkpot, poised over the page in the ledger marked *Novembre* 1924.

"Legrand, chèque," said Victorine. *"Mille cinq cent cinquante francs."*

Géraldine carefully writes *Legrand - 1550 fr (mille cinq cent cinquante francs)* and fills out a receipt which she puts in an envelope with the recipient's name. "I still say he swindled us," she says.

"Yes, as you've remarked every month for the past fifteen years."

"Don't pretend you don't think as I do."

"Even if I do, it doesn't change the agreement we made with him."

"Which you signed."

"So did you."

"Only because you made me."

45

"You know as well as I do we wouldn't own this building if it wasn't for him. Let's drop it or we'll never get done. Next: *Deuxième - Descourtis, chèque, deux mille francs.*"

The pen dips into the ink. *Descourtis,* Géraldine writes, quietly mouthing the name, *2000 fr (deux mille francs.)* "They should really put down that poor dog."

"Not going to happen." Victorine opens the drawstring on a small leather bourse. Looks inside. "Babette Seidenfeld," she says. "Thirteen Louis."

She counts them out one by one.

B. *Seidenfeld - 13 Louis d'or (Treize L).* The pen stops.

"Only thirteen?" Géraldine says. She looks across the desk at the thirteen gold coins, each with a dimension of 23mm, a weight of 7.6 g, a fineness of 0.917 and a gold content of 0.2255 troy oz. with a value of 154 francs each. "Did you see in the paper the franc has gone down again against gold? Why can't she pay in francs like everyone else?"

"Because she is a Jew. Because of all the pogroms. Because she doesn't trust the banks and certainly not this government or the value of the franc. Can you believe we're at 35 francs to the dollar? If trouble comes and she has to flee again, she and her coins can go in an instant."

"How many has she got left, do you think?"

Victorine shrugged. "More than you and I will ever have. Did you send her the note from the sanitation people about her cats?"

"It's still in the hall in her pigeonhole. The concierge says she hasn't been down in months to collect her mail. Maybe she's dead."

"You and your imagination." Victorine sniffed. "This bourse didn't walk in here by itself, you know. Anyway, Madame Vionnet likes it when we pay in gold."

The girls were among the very first clients of Madeleine Vionnet when in 1912 she opened her boutique in the Rue de Rivoli. The simplicity of her bias-cut dresses, flowing loosely to the contours of the body, neither bust nor waist made evident, creating an androgynous silhouette to go with an ultra-short garçons hairdo, became the symbol of their emancipation; no men in charge of their lives, they were free to do as they alone wished. When the First World War upset everything and the maison had to close, for years they continued to wear what they had bought, giving proof to Madame's maxim 'that in the long run, quality, like a Rolls Royce, never goes out of fashion and is more economic than anything bought because it's cheap'. Then, in 1923, when the house reopened at 50, Avenue Montaigne, there they were again, among the first customers through the door, at ages 78 and 76, forever giving the lie to the mythical stinginess of the Auvergne.

"*Troisième* - Zoffany, cash, *deux mille deux cents francs.*"

Zoffany - 2200 fr (deux mille deux cents francs). "Her laundry bill will have to be adjusted the way she goes through bedsheets with all those men she has up there -" Géraldine huffed - "two hundred francs is not nearly enough. I'm putting a note on her receipt."

Victorine shrugged. "Zucchi," she said, "*chèque, deux mille francs.*"

Zucchi - 2000 fr (deux mille francs).

"Can you believe the way his woman dresses?" Géraldine said. "Under her fur coat she hardly wears a thing. In this weather!"

"You're just jealous you don't look like that. Quatrième - Lambert, *chèque,* for both apartments and their *chambre-de-bonne, trois mille huit cents francs.*"

Lambert - 3800 fr (trois mille huit cents francs). "Are you sure that check will be good after the last one bounced?"

"Have faith. Somehow, they always manage."

"They'd manage a damn sight better if the parents gave those kids a good boot in the pants, idle bastards the lot of them lounging about all day."

"They're scarcely kids."

"That's my point, they're not kids anymore. They're all in their thirties and forties. They've been to the best schools. They should be working instead of scrounging off their parents. Mme. Lambert's worried sick if anything should happen to the old man because she knows damn well none of them could replace him. He must be nearly 70, out the door, off to work every day, rain or shine. Bloody kids should be ashamed. Always complaining there's not enough hot water."

"Cinquième," Victorine soldiered on, "Facchini, cash, *mille huit cent cinquante francs*. You know he and Doumeng want to invite us out for dinner?"

Faccini - 1850 fr (mille huit cent cinquante francs).

"Again? What did you say?"

"I said I'd ask you."

Géraldine laughed. "We must be a million years old. Bit old to go out on a date, don't you think? Still, they never give up, I'll give them that."

"Doumeng, *chèque, mille huit cent francs*. It might be fun."

Doumeng - 1800 fr (mille huit cent francs).

"You're such a flirt, Victorine. If you want to go, go."

"Not without you."

"Where will they take us?"

"No idea."

"Okay. I'll think about it." Géraldine could never say no to her sister. "Shouldn't we be getting on instead of you dreaming? I thought you wanted to get this done."

"*Bien. Sixième,* Demailly-Paulin." The way Victorine said it made it sound like one person. "*Mille cinq cent quatre-vingts francs.* Cash."

Demailly/Paulin - 1580 fr (mille cinq cent quatre-vingts francs).

"I saw them shopping for groceries. They were holding hands and looked so happy." For a bleak moment Géraldine glimpsed how empty her life was.

"Cheer up," Victorine said. She knew all too well what her sister felt. Thank God, we have each other, she thought. "Now then, the Steinems and their maid's room, *deux mille francs*, cash."

Steinem - 2000 fr (deux mille francs).

"Maid's room, my eye. You know that boy's enjoying them both?"

"Really, Géraldine!" Victorine pretended to be shocked.

"Be a laugh if they both got knocked up."

"Géraldine!"

"Well you must admit it's quite scandalous. Reminds me of Tonton back in the day. He'd applaud."

"Enough," Victorine said." Septième. Chambre 2. We have a note from Didier. As soon as the Café des Beaux-Arts pays him, he'll pay us for his room."

"That's the second month in a row he's said that. So now he owes 900 francs. Do you believe him? I know times are hard but where will you draw the line?"

"We…Where will *we* draw the line, Géraldine? Didier's been here for a quarter century. Could you really throw him out?"

"We could rent that room in the blink of an eye."

"Maybe. But that's not who we are. Next : Madame Pipi, Chambre 5, cash, *quatre cent francs.*"

Mme.P - 400 fr (quatre cent francs.) "How come she can pay, and Didier can't?"

Victorine ignored the question as she sorted through a small hill of coins, making little stacks of 10 francs, until she finally reached a total: *"Trois cent quarante francs, Chambre 6,* Moïse Polydore, cash, plus a note - *Je vous dois soixante francs."*

Moïse P 340 fr (trois cent quarante francs.)

"We'll never see the 60. He'll just deduct it from what we owe him for the newspapers in the bar."

Religiously, prior to any early-morning customers, Moïse would come into the bar before he began his newspaper round, take down the newspaper sticks and remove yesterday's papers for today's edition, help himself to a packet of Gauloise in the tabac and drink the coffee that would be on the zinc counter waiting for him, nod, mutter "Mesdames" with a bob of his head to the girls, and leave. His 'facture' for doing this, balancing what he took for what he gave, was incomprehensible, the cost of an essential cog in a well-run establishment.

"Fair enough," Victorine said. "What's the total?"

"Just a second." Géraldine finished writing the last receipt, then added up the numbers she had so carefully entered in the right-hand column of her ledger.

"Voila!" she said: *21,520 francs.*

For a moment they looked at each other, sharing the same thought - is it enough? Enough to pay the tradesmen - the plumber, the electrician, the chimney sweep, the carpenter, the roofer for the tiles blown off in the last storm. And the utilities - the gas, the water, the electricty? And the insurance? And the taxes - the *taxe foncier*, the *taxe d'habitation*, the window tax, the tax on revenue and the tax on profits and all the other taxes that the State cooked up? In truth the property barely made ends meet. A truth they both knew.

"You know as well as I do, we should raise all the rents," Géraldine said, ignoring the fact that since the end of the war there was a moratorium on all increases to supposedly aid the returning soldiers. "We must be the cheapest house in the entire Quartier Latin. Do you have any idea what people say about us behind our backs? 'Like the dresses they wear, they're so out of date they'll become fashionable one day.'"

"Who cares what people say," Victorine said. 'We're not going to change, and neither are our rents. The other day, that broker, Pierre what's-his-name, told me in the bar that his son has qualified as a teacher, with a starting salary of 898 francs a month, which will go up after a year to 1300, and, provided he works hard, is lucky and ambitious, maybe in 20 years he can hope for 4000. If - a big if - by the end of his career he becomes a professor in the University. Apparently, a policeman gets 1260 francs and a postman not even a thousand. And that's before taxes. How on earth anyone can afford to live in Paris is a mystery. Thank God we have the bar," Victorine said. She stacked the checks prior to taking them to the bank, swept up the cash into the cash-box and put the box into a small safe behind her, while Géraldine rang for their maid, Marie-Laure, to take the receipts down to be put in each tenant's pigeonhole in the hall rack. Every month the same routine.

"By the way," Géraldine said, "have you seen the painting in the concierge's lodge?"

Chapter Nine

The concierge's name was Spangerro, Mme. Marie Spangerro, but like all the women in her profession she was only called by her maiden name, Marie. Nobody said Bonjour Madame Spangerro, they said Bonjour Marie, with no implied familiarity, as they went out the front door or collected their mail or asked for an errand to be run when they saw her sweeping the hall or washing the pavement in front of their building which she did every morning. *Bonjour, Marie - si vous avez un moment,* (always *vous,* never *tu*), if you have a moment, could you post this package for me/pick up my prescription at the pharmacy/take these to the dry cleaners/etcétéra and so on - *Merci, Marie.* An assumption that what was asked for would be done without any consideration, not even a tip. Forget please. You had to be a woman of character to accept such a role, a woman who gave with no thought of reward.

Imagine then her surprise when one day, while dusting the tiny sepia photograph of her long dead husband, Lulu, that hung over the mantelpiece that faced the glass-panelled door to her loge, she saw the student struggling through the lobby with a pile of unframed pictures and went to help him carry them down the street to Monsieur Phillipon's shop and watched while they were matted and framed and was then asked to choose one?

"*Moi?*"

"*Oui, Madame, vous,*" Monsieur Phillipon said.

"But I know nothing about art."

"It is prescisly for that reason we would have your opinion. Never mind knowing, is there one that you see that you like?"

51

Without hesitation, she pointed. "That one!" she said.

It was an abstraction of what appeared to be the bottom half of an enormous plane tree, back-lit, light shining down through thick branches and leaves, with a dark green bench just visible in the deep-purple, blue-black shadows cast on the ground. "What is it you like about that one?"

"I am not sure how to say this. It is not so much what I like, but rather what I feel."

"And what do you feel?"

"The sun on a hot summer day, me sitting under there in the cool of the shade, bare feet, no cares, *un jour de fête.*"

"Bravo! How perfectly put. You are a poet, Madame." Monsieur Phillipon said.

"Hélas, I am only a concierge, Monsieur."

"As I, Madame, am only a tradesman."

"And I am just a student," Pyotr chimed in, raising his eyebrows in a glance of inquiry to Phillipon, who intuitively nodded agreement.

"It is yours to take home," Pyotr said, waving at the picture and bowing. "*Complimenti, Belanopek!*"

For a moment the poor woman was at a loss. Then, gathering her wits, she said with considerable dignity, "I cannot afford it."

"It is a gift."

"Thank you. Sadly, I cannot accept it. It is something far beyond my station. People would laugh at me. I would be called pretentious. Or worse." For the longest time, frowning, she stared at the picture. And Time, an alchemy of infinite plasticity, slowly transformed her features and she appeared to relax and then smile. "But even if I did say yes, where would I put such a huge picture in my tiny place?" she said.

"I know just the spot," Pyotr said.

It sat on the mantelpiece as if by right, filling the entire wall behind it. When her children came home from school and saw it for the first time they were mystified, even a little afraid.

"*C'est quoi?*" said Marie-France. What is it?

"*Notre jardin,*" her mother replied. Our garden.

"Mais ou et Papa?" Émile said. But where is Papa?

His mother smiled. *"Il se cache derrière l'arbre,"* He's hiding behind the tree. And just like that it became their magical garden, expanding their tiny flat into a landscape that transformed the imagination. Eating at the kitchen table, Emile would look up and say, *"Tu sais, quand j'étais derrière l'arbre j'ai vu Papa."* To which Marie-France would enquire, *"Qu'est qu'il t'a dit ?"*

"Qu'il nous aime, d'être sage et d'écouter Maman."

And Marie, drying dishes at the sink, would feel tears welling up and use the dish cloth to surreptitiously wipe them away.

Of course, news of the picture went up and down the street, from concierge to concierge, who all found an excuse to visit Marie. In no time Phillipon was besieged with enquiries by these ladies, none of whom had the wherewithal to buy one outright, and it is to his ingenuity, and that of the nighttime industry of his artist, that demand was satisfied by a system of credit that allowed the pictures to be sold for a modest price and paid for incrementally even as their new owners carried them home in triumph. The Greek critic, Christian Zervos, published a short article about L'Art Concierge and the unknown painter Belanopek, in his new magazine, Cahiers d'Art, which led to an influx of curious visitors going up and down the now aptly named Rue des Beaux-Arts, ringing the doorbells marked Concierge, and asking to view the pictures. So it was that when Victorine called on Marie, she found a small group of Scandinavians outside the Lodge peering in to see the picture, one man being so bold as to offer to buy it. On seeing Victorine, Marie shooed them away and said, *"Bonjour, Madame."*

"Bonjour Marie," Victorine said. "May I come in?"

"Yes of course, please come in."

Stepping over the threshold, Victorine came face-to-face with the painting and entered another world. The vast canvas took her breath away to the point she hardly heard Marie say, "Please sit down," offering her a kitchen chair in front of the picture.

"Thank you," Victorine said, and sat down. She considered herself to be something of a connoisseur and had assembled an interesting collection of academic landscapes, but she had nothing remotely like this.

"Extraordinary," she said, echoing Monsieur Phillipon, "it gives that young man a dimension I never suspected he had."

"Have you seen the other ones?" Marie said.

"You mean you have more?

Marie laughed. "In this small space? No. No, I meant my colleagues down the street. They all have one. You should go and see."

"Mon Dieu," said Victorine, wondering how any concierge could afford the frame, leave alone the picture.

As if reading her mind, Marie said, "He gave me mine, but they had to buy theirs. Old Phillipon gives them credit."

Which gave Victorine an idea.

That evening, when Pyotr got back from the Sorbonne, he found a card in his pigeonhole inviting him to come into the bar when he had a moment. The card was signed *V. Espinasse.* The landlady. Trouble. It couldn't be about the rent of his room unless Mme. Steinem had somehow forgotten to pay it. Impossible. So it was going to be another complaint about the hot water. Pyotr shrugged, squared his shoulders, crossed the lobby back out into the street, turned left, and entered the bar already half-full of students from the Beaux-Arts making their usual racket. Victorine and Géraldine were behind the long zinc counter serving drinks, their backs reflected in the equally long mirror framed in mahogany running the length of the wall on which it hung. The globes of vintage bar lamps were doubled in the mirror and reflected off the lacquered ceiling. As he approached the bar he saw himself mirrored between the two ancient women, incongruous in their old-fashioned clothes, one in mauve, the other chartreuse, each with the standard long dark-grey barman's apron fastened at the waist with a fine braided cord. "Good evening," Pyotr said.

"Ah, *Monsieur le Peintre,*" said Victorine, with a smile. "Thank you for coming." She dried her hands on a cloth, came around the bar, shook hands and escorted him to a vacant table. "What would you like to drink?"

"Me?" Pyotr was still standing, taken aback by so much attention.

"Yes. Please sit down. We have a proposition for you. But first a drink. Champagne, I think."

A bottle of Veuve Clicquot Brut was brought to the table by Géraldine and for the first time in his life Pyotr found himself in a little bubble of fame and good fortune being toasted by his landladies.

"So," Victorine said. "You don't come in here very often, but what do you think of this place?" She waved her hand to indicate the four walls, the ceiling, the four-bladed fans up there, the golden glow from the lamps, the wide, polished oak floorboards, the antique coat racks either side of the front doors, the big windows half-curtained horizontally, the floor-to-ceiling paneling, its cracked veneer yellowed with age by the countless pipes smoked around the pot-belly stove that stood in the middle of the room.

"It is like being in a time capsule," Pyotr said.

"Exactly!" Géraldine said. "Nothing has changed since we first arrived in Paris and now it's all falling to pieces."

"Nearly fifty years ago!" Victorine said.

"You weren't even born then," Géraldine said.

"We were in our twenties and now we're nearly eighty. Just think, fifty years from now it will be 1978, when you will be as old as we are now," Victorine said. "Can you imagine that?"

"No." Pyotr found it difficult to imagine next week, never mind 50 years. Even saying 1978 sounded improbable. He'd probably be dead, he thought.

"What we want is for you to do something to this place, that will make people say - Extraordinary! I wish I'd been living back then." Victorine said.

Pyotr was stunned. He blinked.

"Me?" he said.

"Yes, you. Do something modern," Géraldine said. "Like your paintings."

"The summer vacation starts in August. Do it then." Victorine said.

August was a month away. The Gods of Change held out their hands. He was at a crossroad. He looked around the bar. Choose wisely Pyotr? He nodded. As much to himself as to his benefactors.

"You are sure?" he said.

"Yes!" the sisters said in unison.

"But I must have carte blanche?"

The ladies nodded.

"I will put a piano in."

The ladies nodded again.

"And I'll need paint?"

Nods.

"And hot water?"

"Yes!"

It was the excuse he needed to quit the Sorbonne. And, for a reason he could not explain, his dreams abruptly ceased.

Chapter Ten

It was in the grocery shop on the corner of the Rue Mazarine and the Rue de Seine, that Monsieur Léon Legrand, the elderly lawyer, overheard a conversation between the two *gouines,* the lesbians who lived on the 6th floor. It was not his intention to eavesdrop but hearing that the bar was to be redecorated by the student living on the 7th floor, he could not help himself and said, "Please excuse me, Mesdames. I do not wish to intrude, but I could not help overhearing what you were saying. Is it then true? The bar in our building is to be renovated?"

Thus addressed, Pauline Paulin and Delphine Demailly, neither of whom had ever spoken to Monsieur Legrand (although they knew who he was - l'ancien, the ancient one on the first floor, dressed in musty old clothes from the Edwardian era, striped, grey trousers, spats, high stiff wing collar, cravat, double-breasted waistcoat, frock-coat), nodded.

"Yes," Pauline said. "There is a notice on the front door."

"But what a dreadful idea," Monsieur Legrand was appalled. "How could the Espinasses agree to this?"

There was no answer to his question and, ignoring him, the ladies continued their shopping.

Monsieur Legrand determined to find out why such a decision had been taken without his opinion. Not one to delay, on his return to the building he first looked at the offending notice taped to the front door of the café. Instead of the familiar *'Fermeture Annuelle: 1 Août - Réouverture 15 Septembre'* he saw *'Fermeture pour Décoration: 1 Août - 15 Septembre'.* Then, when he peered into the bar, neither Victorine nor Géraldine were there. And when he went up to the first floor to knock on the door of their apartment - no answer. He went back down to ask the concierge, something he should have done in the first place. All this on his gammy knee which made him very cross.

"Bonjour Marie," he said, when she opened her door. *"Avez-vous vu les propriétaires ?"*

"The owners?" Marie said. "No, I have not seen them today. Did you look in the bar?"

"Yes. They're not there."

"If they're not in the bar maybe they are in their apartment?"

"I've looked. They're not there either."

Marie shrugged. She found Monsieur Legrand to be tiresome. A tiresome nosey parker when he wasn't banging on about his various ailments. "Have you tried the cellars?" she said. "They were expecting their wine merchant to make a delivery. Or would you rather I tell them when I see them that you are looking for them?"

"Yes. Perhaps that would be best," Legrand said. "Tell them it is important I speak to them about the bar." He was about to tell the concierge why it was important. Then reconsidered. One did not voice a critique to a *domestique.* "Merci," he said, and abruptly turned away to limp up the stairs to his flat, leaving Marie to shake her head.

Quel con, she thought.

Legrand's flat was like the man himself, Edwardian. Dusty, heavy old-gold damask curtains, behind matching fringed pelmets, (uncleaned in a quarter century,) covered the three tall windows of the drawing room facing the street. Thus filtered, daylight only just managed to illuminate the brocaded, plum-coloured couches and the brown leather club chairs that sat on multiple Persian rugs on either side and in front of a large fireplace dominating one wall, with a cushioned inglenook, whose velvet, buttoned seat matched the plum colour of the couches. Tall standing lamps and wall sconces, like so many sentries, cast down pockets of light on faded pictures in gilt frames and Regency-striped wallpaper that had come unglued in corners around the glass-fronted bookcases which marched the length of the room on the opposing wall, filled with leather-bound volumes in buckskin, Morocco green and midnight-blue. Balzac, Hugo, Flaubert,

George Sand, Émile Zola, Dumas, Maupassant, Stendhal, Marcel Proust, the stalwarts of the 19th century, standing there, mute, no longer read. A grandfather clock in a corner, ticked loudly enough to act as a metronome that put Legrand to sleep every afternoon when he took his siesta on a moth-eaten emerald-green velvet chaise-longue next to the grand piano after lunch. Beyond the drawing room, through mahogany doors 4-metres tall, lay a dining room - that once upon a time sat 18, but was now rarely used - and a study crowded with long-unopened files from his legal career, packed into folders, filling all the shelves and the entire surface of an antique roll-top desk behind which was a high-back swivel chair, buttoned in calf-skin, wonderfully patinated by time and the lawyer's backside. A kitchen and butler's pantry led off from the dining room, and, down a short hallway, a large and two smaller bedrooms, only the large one ever being used, with a view into the pocket garden at the back of the house. Plus a tiled bathroom complete with a showerhead the size of a colander. Over 180 square metres, commodious accommodation for a single gentleman.

He used to have a manservant, but since the war did without, paying a maid when he needed one. And it was a maid, Marie-Laure, who found him in his shirtsleeves when she knocked on his door to tell him when he opened it that her mistress, Madame Victorine, was home and open to receiving a visitor. Putting on a burgundy velvet smoking jacket smelling vaguely of camphor, Monsieur Legrand followed her across the landing to be greeted by Victorine, seated in her salon taking a cup of hot chocolate, holding out the back of her hand to be kissed. "Monsieur Legrand!" she said. "What a pleasure! Marie told me you would like a word. Please sit down. Will you have some tea, or would you prefer a *chocolat chaud?* My sister will join us in a moment. Tell me, how is your knee today?" Like every landlady worthy of her calling, Victorine knew of all the *'malheurs'* afflicting her tenants as recounted to her in private over a glass of Cognac by Docteur Armand Blanche, the affable general practitioner who lived three doors down and made house calls a profitable duty.

"It is an inflammation of the anterior cruciate ligament," Legrand said with some authority, flexing and rubbing the offending knee. "Blanche told me to rest and put ice on it."

"You poor man. It must be very painful. How did you hurt yourself?"

"I don't really know. Coming up the stairs a few days ago it made a sound like a loud pop and my knee began to swell."

"How awful!"

"Yes. It is. But it is not about my knee that I wanted to see you. I have learned that you plan to redecorate the bar. Is this true?"

"Yes. About time, don't you think? Ah - here is my sister -" as the lady in question swept in, swathed in a bright yellow ruffled silk moiré gown - "Géraldine, Monsieur Legrand, is enquiring about our plan to redecorate downstairs."

"About time," Géraldine echoed her sister. "The place is an old-fashioned relic. I can't fathom why we didn't do it ages ago."

"But surely you would want to preserve something so authentic?" Monsieur Legrand said, sitting bolt upright as if to reinforce his words. "Authentic, pas des vulgarités d'aujourd'hui."

"Authentic!"

"Authentic!'

Simultaneously from both sisters, a double-barrelled expression of astonishment.

"Yes," Monsieur Legrand persevered. "All this tearing down of what is traditional in the name of 'modernité'." He made the word sound like a disease. "I would think it wise for you to reconsider your plans."

"What has got into you, Monsieur Legrand?" Géraldine said quite sharply. "You know as well as I do our uncle bought all that rubbish in the puces, the flea market, because it was a cheap way to furnish the bar."

"And most of it is falling to pieces now," Victorine said. "Besides, what is it to you? You hardly ever set foot in the place, so I am more than surprised that you question our plan."

"I am merely voicing the concern of those of us who live in this building," Legrand said, taken aback by what he thought of as insubordination.

"Don't tell me you've canvassed our tenants?" Géraldine was shocked.

"No." Legrand said. Until that moment it had not occurred to him. "But I fully intend to. It is only right that we have a say in the matter."

"Right?" Now Géraldine was angry. She raised her voice. "How dare you question our rights, Monsieur!"

"Beware, Madame! I am a lawyer."

"Indeed, Monsieur Legrand? Is that meant as a threat?" Victorine said, her voice a whisper. "Perhaps you would like to retire and reconsider your words?" In the silence that followed Victorine rang for the maid.

When Marie-Laure showed herself, Victorine said, "Please show Monsieur Legrand to the door."

Legrand, expressionless, stood up, straightened his spine, looked from one sister to the other, fractionally bowed his head, said *"Ce n'est pas fini, Mesdames,"* and, limping, followed Marie-Laure out of the apartment.

When the door closed behind the lawyer, Geraldine said, "What on earth was that about? Bloody man. Did you hear what he said - 'it's not finished.' What do you think he meant?"

"Nothing probably," Victorine said. She sighed. "He's old. His knee hurts. He'll realise it's a storm in a teacup and apologise."

How wrong can you be? Legrand, approaching ninety, found the energy for one last legal joust. The first the Espinasses sisters learned of this was when they ran into their second-floor tenant, Monsieur Descourtis, in the post office on the Boulevard St. Germain, where he was the Sous-Directeur. After exchanging the usual pleasantries and asking how his beagle was doing and learning that soon, hélas, it would be time to put him down, they were surprised when he pulled out a printed leaflet from a satchel he was carrying and said, "Have you seen this?" It was addressed simply:

CHER COLOCATAIRE

Fellow tenants, I, the undersigned, Léon Legrand, Court Appointed Attorney to the Tribune of Paris, draw your attention to the following illegal sign affixed to the front door of the bar on the ground floor of our building:

'Fermeture pour Décoration: 1 Août - 15 Septembre'.

After consultation at the Marie of the 6th Arrondissement, 78 Rue Bonaparte, Paris, the proprietors/licensees of said bar have failed to obtain the necessary permits from the Mairie for any modification, renovation, or redecoration to the facade or to the interior of the premises. Without such authority no work is authorised until appropriate plans have been submitted and approved by the Building Department of the Mairie and the Préfecture and the Architect in charge of Historical Buildings.

In addition, the following infractions have been noted and, until cured, the bar cannot be reopened:

Item - SNC: *Société en Nom Collectif 'VC Espinasse'* – non-conforming.

Item - *Permis d'Exploitation,* Licence IV - out of date.

Item - Licence for the Sale of Alcohol - out of date.

Item - Préfecture Posted Opening and Closing Hours - not enforced.

Item - Signage & Fixture of Prices for Alcoholic Beverages - missing.

Item - Obligation to Sell Tobacco at the prices listed in the Journal Officiel – not enforced.

Item - Sale of tobacco to minors under the age of 18.

Item - Deficient interior layout - the tobacco stand is neither visible from nor adjacent to the threshold of the front door as required by law.

It is proposed that a meeting be called to discuss the above at a date and time convenient to all. If you approve, please sign below, and append your apartment.

Signed: *Léon Legrand, Avocat à la Cour,* Apt. *1er Gauche*

Signature: _____ Apt._____

"We all got one," Monsieur Descourtis said. "He put them in each tenant's pigeonhole in the hall."

"Well, well," Victorine said, returning to him his copy of the leaflet. "A declaration of war. The old boy has more spirit left in him than I thought."

"What will you do? It is serious, non?" Descourtis said.

"Non, Monsieur Descourtis," Géraldine said. "It is the foolish gesture of an old man one step from his grave, who doesn't realise that right now, outside his window, all of France is celebrating the greatest Art Deco Exhibition in the world. Hundreds of thousands of visitors are here in Paris to see what our artists and artisans can make. Have you seen Melnikov's Soviet Pavilion, or Le Corbusier's Pavillon de l'Esprit Nouveau ? Or even that gigantic Citroën sign on the Eiffel Tower? Let him sue. He'll be laughed out of court."

Chapter Eleven

In the year 1900, a period of transition between centuries and wars, the ingénue, Marina di Spilimbergo, age 19, started as a *danseuse* at the Moulin Rouge after a casting audition before Josep Oller, the jovial Catalan who founded the cabaret in 1889. Twenty-two years later she was still doing the Cancan when Oller died and was buried in the cemetery of Père Lachaise, mourned by all his 'Girls'. By 1925 the cabaret was run by a businessman, Monsieur Francis Salabert, who put in a man to watch the money, Pierre Foucret, and a man to run the show, Jacques-Charles. All three thought a 44-year-old woman somewhat old to be kicking her legs in the air and doing the splits every night in frilly white knickers, a garter belt, and black stockings to the rousing music of Jacques Offenbach. If the truth were told, so did she. Her safe-haven was a fellow-Italian, Jacopo Zucchi, a stage-door-johnny, there every evening, rain or shine, to bring her flowers, take her to dinner after the show and home to bed after the last bottle of wine. He was five years her junior, a costume designer from Milan, who could have had his pick of any of the showgirls twenty years younger, as she teasingly reminded him on every birthday, like today, the seventh anniversary of their tryst.

They took the Métro, Line A, from Pigalle to the Rue du Bac, and the weather being fine, walked arm-in-arm under the stars down to the Seine, turned right along the Quai Malaquais, to the corner of Rue Bonaparte and into the Café des Beaux Arts for a snack and nightcap. Served by their co-tenant, Didier.

"Alors, les amoureux?" Didier said when they were seated. *"L'œufs mayo, frites, Bordeaux?"*

Routine. It was what they always ordered. Perfect hard-boiled eggs, freshly made mayonnaise, hand-cut French fries, a carafe of the blended claret the house ordered by the hectoliter. And Fleur de sel. Sea salt. From his station behind the bar, dressed as custom demanded in a white shirt, sleeves rolled up to his elbows, black waistcoat, long starched white apron down to his laced black shoe-tops, black bowtie, white towel dangling on his forearm, Didier, smiling like some overfond uncle, watched his customers tuck in. What luck, he thought, to find love at their age. A lifelong bachelor, for whom it was anathema to even imagine waking up next to a woman, the long, long shapely legs of Mademoiselle di Spilimbergo, in his line of sight where she had them crossed under the table, made him nod his head in appreciation and wonder if he had perhaps failed to make the right choice in life. Which was when, out of the corner of his eye, he saw the tall, stooped figure of Monsieur Legrand, wearing a top-hat, pass in front of the bar to turn up the Rue Bonaparte and remembered the petition. He pulled it from his back pocket, unfolded it, flattened the creases, put on his spectacles to read, again, a document that made no sense to his republican mind. Bloody lawyers sticking their nose into other people's business. If the Espinasse sisters wanted to redecorate their bar, why, *putain de merde,* shouldn't they? He was so engrossed in his thoughts he failed to see Monsieur Zucchi signalling for a fresh carafe of wine by holding up the empty one.

"Didier!"

From where she sat at the cashier's till, Madame Arthur, the ever-vigilant doyenne of the bar, barked at the waiter, making him jump. "*Arrête de rêver.* Stop dreaming. Attend to your customers." And with her unshaven chin she indicated Zucchi.

Quick to respond, Didier brought a fresh carafe to the table with his apologies. "I was reading this," he said. "Have you seen it?"

"I have already signed my copy," Monsieur Zucchi said.

"You mean you approve?" Didier was shocked.

"Of course not! I crossed out everything and modified the first paragraph." From his coat pocket, Zucchi took out his copy of the petition and pointed. "Here, take a look."

'To Léon Legrand, Court Appointed Attorney to the Tribune of Paris, I, the undersigned tenant, draw your attention to the tripartite motto of the French Republic - *Liberté, Égalité, Fraternité* - affixed to the facade of all public monuments as a reminder of the fundamental democratic virtues that define French society. Liberty means individual freedom to do as he or she wants without harming others. Equality means all citizens are equal irrespective of caste, race, religion, or gender. Fraternity means brotherhood.

In the small republic that is our building on the Rue des Beaux Arts should we not aspire to live peacefully by such virtues instead of bringing frivolous lawsuits?'

Signed: *Zucchi, J* - 3ème Droite

Chapter Twelve

It was the custom for the Lamberts to dine *en famille*. A family tradition done in a precisely regimented way. Well before Monsieur Lambert returned from work, which he did every day for lunch and for dinner, Madame would be in the kitchen supervising Gaby, just as she did when they went to the marché to do the shopping. She ordered; Gaby carried. Fresh bread from the boulangerie on the Rue Jacob next to Michaud's, the restaurant at No. 60, where she never failed to stop for a chat with Mme. Michaud to reminisce about the time the Seine overflowed its banks in 1910 and flooded the street. Now the place was jammed with young foreigners - Hemingway, Dos Passos, Scott Fitzgerald, James Joyce, *va savoir?* A shrug. Never heard of any of them. Then for vegetables, to the grocery shop on the corner of the Rue de l'Échaudé and the Rue de Seine, fish from the poissonnier under the arch in the Cour du Commerce-St. André, and meat or poultry from the cheeky boucher on the Rue de Buci tossing out compliments like flower bouquets - 'Alors, mes Belles Dames! Profitez, profitez-en!' - and butter, cheese, eggs and crème fraîche from the crèmerie on the Rue Grégoire de Tours - a daily circuit that took them an hour and a half without leaving the 6th, their *quartier.*

Once home, after climbing the sixty steps to the 4th floor, before going into her apartment, Madame would say, '*Gaby, dite aux enfants de se préparer* - Go tell the children to get ready' and the maid would cross the landing to knock on the opposite door to relay the message to whomever opened it. Jean-Charles, Marie-Louise, Jean-Yves, and Marie-Claire would then stop whatever they were doing - usually nothing of importance - to get dressed. Three-piece suit and tie for the men at lunch, smoking jacket and cravat for dinner. Day dress for the ladies at luncheon, formal gowns in the evening. The children would first meet their parents in the salon for an apéritif before going into the dining room where Gaby had laid the table for six: sets of solid silver Christofle forks to the left, Christofle knives to the right, Christofle knife rests, Christofle spoons for soup, the luxury of Christofle tableware Madame had been given as a bride 40 years ago, endlessly used, washed and polished. Set on a lace tablecloth from her Grandmother's house in Rouen. With Limoges china and Baccarat glasswear - always the correct lineup whether they were drinking Bordeaux, Burgundy or Champagne.

Equally correct, the menu: soup, followed by fish, followed by meat or game, then salad, cheese, dessert. Always. In that order. *Comme tout le monde.* Twice a day. *En famille.* With enough left over for Gaby to eat in the kitchen.

Madame, like many of her bourgeois contemporaries, lived with a well-thumbed copy of Ali-Bab, her practical gastronomic bible, at her elbow. As instructed, the menus changed with the seasons and with what was available in the marché.

Madame and Gaby, dressed in identical aprons, took turns chopping the vegetables to make the basic stock for the soup in a large tureen in which a whole raw chicken, including the bones and skin, was set to simmer in water with chopped celery, carrots, onions, parsley, thyme, bay leaves, peppercorn and salt. Endlessly replenished, blended with cream to make a potage to aid Monsieur's mastication due to his ill-fitting dentures, it also served as a base for stews, ragouts, goulash, and, when cold, salmagundi.

The main meal was lunch, with something lighter in the evening to aid the digestion. This Monday they had started with a *Petite marmite,* followed by a *Barquettes de ris d'agneau, morilles et foies de volaille, Timbale de filets de soles, Palombes rôties, Salade de laitue à la crème,* cheese, fruit and a pudding glacé. Tuesday, they had vichyssoise to start, then oysters, *Filet de sanglier rôti, Lasagnes gratinées aux épinards, Salade d'endives,* cheese, *Bombe glacée chocolat-crèmes pralinée et Chantilly.* Wednesday saw a *Potage crème veloutée de soja,* then *a Soufflé aux crevettes,* then *a filet de lièvre sautés, sauce béarnaise, and Grouses rôtis, pomme de terre Léontine, salade de céleri,* cheese, *Mousse à la Chartreuse glacée.* Thursday, *Potage crème de lentilles,*

Langoustines provençales, Rôtie-de-Boeuf, Macédoine de légumes, Chaud-froid de volaille truffé, Salade de chicorée à la crème, cheese, *Bombe glacée marron-vanille.* Friday, as good Catholics, was reserved for fish: Fish soup, *Sole Colbert, Bar au beurre, Foie gras truffée en aspic, Salsifis au mirepoix,* cheese, *Bombe glacée kirsch-cerise.* Saturday, *en fin de semaine,* it was raining and cold, so they had a *Potage purée de marrons* to warm up the arteries, then a *Vol-au-vent,* a *Brochet farci rôti,* a *Civet de pré-salé aux pommes Duchesse,* a *Coq au vin, Courgettes farcies,* cheese, fruit, and a *Glace panachée* to finish. Sunday they went to church.

Their church - founded in the 6th Century by Childebert 1, the son of Clovis 1, the first King of the Franks - was the Church of Saint-Germain-des-Prés on the eponymous Place at the junction of Rue Bonaparte and the Boulevard St. Germain. The Lambert pew, on the left, three rows from the altar, had seen seven generations of the family, sitting, kneeling, rising, praying, giving thanks for the generosity of their ancestor, the never-to-be-mentioned slave trader whose munificent donations for the restoration of the church in the 18th Century led to him being buried in a plot in the garden of the Bishop's Palace adjacent to the Church in the Rue de l'Abbaye with a *Te Deum* sung in his memory on the first Sunday after Lent every year.

Mass was from 10am to noon and no sooner finished then the family repaired across the Place to the Deux Magots for refreshments before going home for a late lunch. This was the most important meal of the week as it was the one meal where Monsieur did not have to go back to work after the last spoonful of dessert, but could instead take a well-deserved *sieste* on the sofa in the salon.

This Sunday started with a *Potage crème de chou-fleur,* then *Langouste à la Parisienne,* followed by a *Salmis de Bécasse, pommes allumettes,* and *Faisan rôti au becs-figues, salade verte,* cheese, fruit, *Parfait au café.* Between each course, conversation. No talk of business, money or politics, subjects Madame banished from her dining table. Art? Yes. Music? Yes. Literature? Yes. Fashion? Yes. The opera? The weather? The traffic? Yes, yes, yes. Gossip? *Bien sûr!*

"I had a letter from Cousin Lucy," Marie-Louise said. "She's met a man she thinks she will marry."

"She always thinks that" Jean-Yves said. "Who's it this time? You know as well as I do, without a dowry nobody will marry her."

"Must you be so unkind, Jean-Yves?" Madame said. "Lucy is a perfectly charming girl from an excellent family."

With no money, Jean-Charles thought, but kept his opinion to himself.

"What on earth made the priest go on about pickpockets?" Monsieur said, but nobody seemed to listen.

Marie-Claire said, "I think I met him."

"Who?" Jean-Charles said.

"The man she's going to marry. Remember at the Vidal's in Rambouillet? The deputy? You were there, remember?"

"The little fat chap? You can't mean him."

"Yes. He's rich enough not to care about a dowry. He lusts after her body."

"Marie-Claire!" Madame pretended to be shocked.

"You should have seen the way he looked at her. Positively drooling."

"I can't stand men who slobber after women," Jean-Yves said.

"Really?" Marie-Louise said. "What about you and what's-her-name? Rosalind? At the cocktail in Danton's?"

"I was not slobbering."

"The way you were kissing her neck when you thought no one was watching looked pretty slobberly to me."

And so on…the desiccation of petty peccadillos of friends and family. With the coffee and before Monsieur retired, Madame, though a firm believer in keeping up appearances, was well aware of the family's dwindling fortune and determined to introduce her children to the novel idea that it was about time they earned a living (a subject recycled *ad nauseam* since they graduated from college) when the maid came in to say there was a gentleman at the door. Her announcement was met by a round table of blank stares.

"On Sunday?" Monsieur said.

"Without an appointment?" Madame said.

"Who is it?" Jean-Charles said.

"The old man who lives on the first floor, Monsieur Legrand," Gaby said.

"He climbed up here?" Jean-Yves said, impressed.

"Why?" Marie-Claire said.

"He wants to know if you have signed his petition?" Gaby said.

"What petition?" Monsieur said.

"The one I gave to you, Monsieur. Remember, it was in your pigeonhole? About the bar?"

More blank looks.

"Why didn't you tell me you had a petition, Jean-Claude?" Madame, his wife said.

"Because I haven't read it, Marie-France, that's why. Is it too much to ask that I have a day of rest? I can read it on Monday."

"Not if the poor man is on our doorstep. Gaby, please ask him in. We will adjourn to the salon."

Monsieur Lambert groaned, mentally saying goodbye to his siesta.

When Monsieur Legrand, out of breath, was shown into the salon he was momentarily taken aback. It was the first time he had climbed to the fourth floor, and the first time he had visited the Lamberts in their apartment. If he was surprised by the quality of the furnishings and the excellence of the art on the walls and the rugs on the floor, it was seeing the entire *famille Lambert* arrayed in their Sunday best staring at him as if he were a ghost that made him flustered.

"What an unexpected pleasure it is to see you, Monsieur Legrand," Madame Lambert said, with that generosity of welcome inbred to any hostess worthy of the name. "Please, do sit down." She waved her hand at a handsome armchair and the old man doddered across the room to sink into it with a sigh. "I do not believe you have made the acquaintance of our children. This is our eldest, Jean-Charles -" and here she stopped to study their guest. "Are you alright, Monsieur Legrand? You have gone quite pale?"

"It is the stairs…" Legrand said, closing his eyes, taking a deep breath. "Please, excuse me."

"Do not apologise," Monsieur Lambert said. "If you are not used to it, 60 steps will undo the strongest man." A slight exaggeration perhaps. Lambert looked from the bowed figure of Legrand to his wife, eyebrows raised in silent query.

"Maybe we should call for Doctor Blanche?" Jean-Yves whispered to his sister, Marie-Claire. Their mother glared at them. Whispering in company was the height of bad manners. Marie-Claire shrugged her shoulders. *Quoi?*

It was Marie-Louise who intuited the problem. "Perhaps Monsieur Legrand has not had lunch?" she said.

"*Mon Dieu!*" Madame Lambert said, an image instantly forming in her head of an ancient bachelor dining on stale scraps and fish bones. "Of course! Gaby!" she called, and when the maid showed herself, she was instructed to quickly prepare some soup and bread, put it on a tray with a glass of wine and bring it immediately to their guest here in the salon.

"No, no, really, I am quite alright," Monsieur Legrand protested, but when it was in front of him the way he spooned up the invigorating soup and swallowed the wine gave the lie to his words. "Excellent!" he said when finished, looking around as if expecting applause, while swiping the bottom of the soup bowl clean with the last piece of bread. "Most excellent! Many thanks, Madame, many, many thanks. I feel so much better." Taking a silk handkerchief from the breast pocket of his coat to wipe his mouth.

"*Un petit digestif?*" said Monsieur Lambert after this performance. Not waiting for a reply, he unstopped a bottle of Cognac to pour a generous dose into a ballon for Legrand to swirl, sniff, taste and swallow.

"Excellent!" Legrand said again, and having exhausted his supply of adjectives, raised his glass to toast the company. "To your very good health. Merci!" Swallow. Burp. "*Pardon!*" A dab on the lips with his handkerchief. "I apologise for disturbing your Sunday, but it was the only day I thought I could find you and the other tenants at home."

"Oh?"

"Yes. It is for my petition. It is a matter of some urgency. You have received one I hope?"

The Lamberts looked at one another. How to reply without giving offence? Yes, the petition has been received, but, no, it has not yet been read. Madam rode to the rescue.

"I am always the last one to be told," Madame Lambert said. "My husband prefers me to lead a quiet life." She lied without effort. "What is your petition about?"

"The bar."

"What bar?"

"The bar downstairs in our building."

"What of it?"

"Have you not heard? The Espinasses intend to redecorate!"

"About time!" In unison, the combined voices of Marie-Claire, Jean-Yves, Marie-Louise and Jean-Charles, delivered their verdict. Monsieur Legrand was aghast.

"Surely you do not approve?" he said.

"*C'est une poubelle.* A garbage can. We never go in there," Madame said.

"Well, not never," her husband said. "We go for New Year's Eve at the invitation of the sisters." Legrand stared at him; incomprehension written all over his face.

"Every year the Espinasse sisters invite us in to celebrate," Madame clarified. "We feel obliged to go. Otherwise, it's full of those noisy students, getting drunk, throwing up all over the floor. No wonder they want to redecorate."

"So, you will not sign my petition?"

"Hélas! Non."

Poor Monsieur Legrand had to be escorted by Gaby, firmly holding his arm, as he tottered down the stairs to his apartment on the first floor, his hopes dashed.

Paris Now.

As usual I waited on the sidewalk while George locked up. Long white beard, grey-white hair down past his shoulders, wearing a fine pink paisley shirt with red buttons over tailored blue jeans and black Gucci moccasins. Trim and slim.

"What're you looking at?" he said.

"You're looking very dapper," I said.

"Yeah? And you look like a right poofter." George was from the East End of London and still used some of the old vernacular. Both my beard and hair were shorter than his but equally white. I was slightly taller, same build, wearing a turquoise shirt embroidered with flowers and pale beige chinos. We held hands as we walked up the street to what we considered our bar for our apéro, George a Negroni, mine a Vodka sour. It's the place we had met for the first time *en drague*. As usual, Jack Lang was at his customary table, by the window where he could look out without being seen. Since he had the place put on the list of Monument Historique, he'd become quite possessive of what he thought of as his 'salon', always escorting *Academicians* from the *Institut* on the Quai in for a jar and a literary *tête-à-tête*. To give him his due, without his efforts, the developers would have long since gutted the bar when the building was sold and converted into a boutique hotel after the last tenant, a Jewish lady on the second floor, died, aged 108, and the City's extermination squad were called in to remove the 23 cats who had been living in her apartment.

There was no question the bar deserved its qualification, its pale silvery Art Deco interior still as immaculate as when it was painted 50 years ago. To this day nobody really knows how the artist achieved the effect of an ever-receding landscape made by hundreds of black, grey and white panels set like a hidden corner of the Alhambra plunked down in the middle of Paris. Depending on the time of day, on how much light came in the front window if it was sunny, or on how many lights were switched on when it grew darker, the room mysteriously seemed to change shape. Every visitor tried to explain how this chameleon-like malleability was achieved.

And the furniture! Priceless. George and I loved the streamlined lacquered ebony Art Deco bar, its zinc top and mirrored front providing the perfect décor for the countless trysts of the many people who had sat on the zebra-striped bar stools arrayed along its length. Eileen Gray, who used to live around the corner for 71 years in the same flat in the Rue Bonaparte, designed the sofas and chairs and Carlo Bugatti did the tables and the piano. Every piece should have been in a museum. It's hard to believe there was nearly a lawsuit brought against the owners of the building for renovating the bar; even harder to imagine that at one time such a sophisticated space was invaded by art students!

But - there's always a but - like every other fashion, the vogue for Art Deco has come and gone and today, more private club than bar, the place is a quiet memory of what it once was. A blessing for those of us who appreciate the labour that goes into making fine things in an increasingly depressing landscape where throwing paint at canvas is considered art and the childish scribblings of so-called street artists sell for millions. Thank the Lord for the Belanopeks of this world. Too bad my father didn't keep a single one of his pictures while he had the chance.

Chapter Thirteen

"*J'arrête,*" Pyotr said.

"What do you mean?" Monsieur Phillipon said. "You can't just stop."

"I have to. I'm done. There's nothing left in my head." Between painting the bar and making pictures for Phillipon to sell, another year had gone by, and Pyotr was exhausted. Drained.

"What about all these orders I have? What am I going to tell my customers? That I have nothing to sell?"

"Say you're sorry. Belanopek is dead."

"Sorry!" Phillipon snorted. "This is very unprofessional. Something you will regret!"

"Yes. Probably," Pyotr said. "Sorry." He turned to leave the shop. Then, just in time, remembered his manners and held out his hand. "Thank you, Monsieur, for your faith in me. It has given me the confidence I lacked."

Taken aback, Phillipon had nothing to say, shook hands and watched the artist walk off up the street.

"Just like that?" Markus said when he told him. They were back in Polidor having a beer.

"Yes. I feel bad after everything he's done for me, but I can't go on pretending I'm an artist. I'm too old for these games."

"What will you do?"

"I don't know. I'll think of something." Pyotr said. He looked around as if to make sure nobody was listening. "I'm also going to move," he said.

"Out of your room? Leave La Steinem? Are you mad? Where will you go?"

"I've found a place in Montparnasse. Dirt cheap. One of the old ateliers of Eiffel, for his workers when they were building the tower."

"You're always broke. How will you pay the rent?"

"The two old ladies gave me enough for painting the bar. When that's gone, I don't know, maybe I'll write a novel." Pyotr shrugged. "I'll find a way."

"Write a novel? The worst paying job in the world - you are mad. You're going to leave the heart of Paris where you live gratis, and get to fuck a beautiful woman into the bargain, to go and live in some dump in the suburbs where you know nobody and have no work? You're not just mad, you're -"

"Free," Pyotr interrupted.

Standing in the middle of the decrepit atelier with his one suitcase at his feet containing all he owned, Pyotr could not help thinking that perhaps Markus was right. He was mad. From the termite-ridden floorboards, to the water-stained ceiling six metres above his head, where long strips of paint were interwoven by multiple spider webs, to the huge, filthy, cracked windows facing north and the miniscule stained toilet under a staircase going up to a mezzanine with a free-standing claw-foot bathtub and a platform for putting a bed, with no heat, one electric light bulb which did not work and a front door with a broken lock and no key. Yes, mad. There was also no kitchen. Only solution. Roll up your sleeves and get to work.

It took him a month of hard labour to gut the place and another two months to replaster and paint the walls, sand and replace the floorboards, working 14-15 hours a day. Even the concierge, Madame Lucette, was impressed. She introduced him to a friend, Henri, a sign painter from Belleville, who did restoration work all over Paris, and Henri helped him with tools, ladders, scaffolding, the plumbing and tiling for a bathroom and rewiring for electricity, installing a kitchen and a wood-burning stove, in exchange for his labour on other jobs. When Markus turned up to inspect the place after one of his mysterious forays out of the country, he too was impressed.

"*Sagenhaft,*" he said, staring up at the vast pristine emptiness of the renovated atelier, flooded with light coming through the newly glazed, washed and painted windows. "Amazing - it's like being in a chapel. I would never have thought you capable of doing this. But why no furniture?"

"No money left," Pyotr said. Shrugged. He was sleeping on a mattress on the bare boards of the mezzanine. "All this cost more than I thought it would."

"Then you're in luck. I have money, more than I need," Markus said. "We'll trade. I'll give you money and in exchange you can stick another bed in here and I'll stay with you when I come into town. I'm fed up with the Cité and their fussy rules about no co-mingling of the sexes."

"Done," Pyotr said.

In celebration, Markus insisted they go to Le Select on the Boulevard Montparnasse, to down a few and see if they could pick up any girls. When they got there the place was jammed with tourists, inside and out, and they had to wait for a table which made Markus grumpy. Lighting up a cigarette from the stub of one just finished, he said, "Bloody tourists. When I think about what we went through in the war...why?" Looking at the crowd. "What was that about? People go around as if it never happened."

"That was nearly eight years ago, Markus."

"So?"

"You don't think they have the right to forget? All that shit? All that misery?"

"You know what happens when you forget? What did Santayana say? 'Those who cannot remember the past are condemned to repeat it.' You were in Heidelberg, right?"

"Briefly."

"Did you know a fellow called Goebbels there? Got a PhD in Literature?"

"No. I was doing medicine."

"Well, he's in bed with a guy called Hitler. Prisoner in the war. Actually an Austrian, but calls himself the Führer now, head of the Nazis, the National Socialists. Tiny party with a few thousand members. Came in ninth in the elections we've just had, with only 12 seats in the Reichstag."

"Never heard of them."

"Well you have now and believe me, when you hear them, listen carefully. They will scare the shit out of you and all these cheerful people in here. Hitler was let out of jail last year after serving just eight months of a five-year sentence for treason in his role in a coup d'état the Nazi tried to pull off in Munich. They've made a film of their rally in Nuremberg, *Symphonie des Kampfwillens*, which ends with the march of the SA, the *Sturmabteilung*, their stormtroopers. Paul Warndte's poem is their battle-cry: *'Was wir verlosen haben/ Darf nicht verloren sein!'* What we have lost/Will be regained! It's a herald of things to come for people who want to forget. Mark my words."

"I wish you'd stop playing Cassandra," Pyotr said.

"Who said I'm playing? You know what the so-called allies are doing, forcing Germany to repay 132 billion gold marks in war reparations?"

"No."

"The country's bankrupt! Forget the principal, we can't even pay the interest - and even that is borrowed from the American banks!" From a pocket he pulled out a well-thumbed notebook. "You know the only nation *not* invited to the Treaty of Versailles? - Germany! You know the only nation condemned to pay reparations? - Germany! You know the only nation cursed with the so-called 'War Guilt Clause'? - Germany!" With his forefinger he stabbed his notes. "Here, Clause 231 - I'll read it to you: *The Allied and Associated Governments affirm and Germany accepts the responsibility of Germany and her allies for causing all the loss and damage to which the Allied and Associated Governments and their nationals have been subjected to as a consequence of the war imposed upon them by the aggression of Germany and her allies.'* And who are these allied and associated governments? France, England, Russia and the United States - the first three easily as guilty as Germany in starting the war and the Americans only coming in in April 1917 when the so-called peace-loving President Wilson asks Congress for 'a war to end all wars'!" Markus had no idea he had raised his voice - so loud people in the queue were staring at him.

"Come on, Markus," Pyotr said quietly, "tone it down or you'll start another war." Markus glared at him, then turned to glare at the people staring. Fortunately, this was the moment the maître d'hôtel intervened to say their table was ready and they followed him into the brasserie. Seated, they were handed menus and asked what they wished to drink and by the time they finished ordering Markus had calmed himself.

"Forgive me, Pyotr. Sometimes I get carried away," he said. "But I meant it about Goebbels. He's the brains behind Hitler. The man has a real genius for propaganda. He's the one constantly reminding the Germans of their humiliation, stoking their anger, exploiting the perceived weakness of the Weimar republic, labelling its supporters 'November criminals' for signing the treaty, calling them 'backstabbers' in league with the Jews, and intent on re-establishing the Kaiser hiding in abdication in the Netherlands."

"But surely they approve of Germany being a democracy now?"

Markus laughed. "Christ, you're naive. Nothing short of a totalitarian dictatorship will satisfy these bastards. Even if it means another war."

"I don't believe it."

"Believe what you like," gloomily Markus studied his notes. "You know what the exchange rate of the mark to the dollar was in 1914? 4.2 to one. I had saved about 100,000 marks by then, so I was quite well off, with enough to buy a nice house, a motor car or travel anywhere in the world. You know what I could buy with that after Versailles? Not even a loaf of bread!" Abruptly he pulled his wallet from his coat pocket and fished out a wad of money. "You seen one of these?" A banknote, issued by the Reichsbank. *Eine Billion Mark.* One Thousand Million Marks. Seeing it beggared belief. "You know what this was worth a couple of years ago? 1923? Not even a dollar. And today? Nothing. Not even worth the paper it's printed on. Have you the remotest idea how this has affected the average German family? Yes? No. I can see by your face you haven't given it a thought. Just like the majority of these morons in here, a bunch of ostriches with your heads stuck in the sand. You read what Keynes wrote, John Keynes? Of course not. He's an American economist. Listen to this." With his finger he pointed to a paragraph outlined in red ink: "*'The Treaty includes no provision for the economic rehabilitation of Europe - nothing to make the defeated Central Powers into good neighbours, nothing to stabilise the new States of Europe, nothing to reclaim Russia... it is an extraordinary fact that the fundamental economic problem of a Europe starving and disintegrating before their eyes, was the one question in which it was impossible to arouse the interest of the Four Powers.'* You know the only thing they focused on? Reparations! Can you imagine, bloodthirsty ghouls like Clemenceau and Foch call the Treaty 'a capitulation, a treason'. Foch actually said as the Treaty was being signed 'This is not peace. It is an armistice for 20 years.' Sadly, Hitler is going to prove him right. And 20 million people died because of this lunacy - 20 MILLION!"

"Markus! Your voice..." Pyotr said.

"Sorry. It just makes me crazy. The irony is that not a single major battle took place on German soil, in fact no allied soldier stepped foot in the country until after the armistice was signed. And yet the country is ruined. Two million German soldiers died so that their countrymen could be completely humiliated and here we are in Paris having an Art Deco exhibition to forget the one million seven hundred thousand poilus killed *pour la Gloire* and the one point three million Russians slaughtered so that there could be a revolution to murder the Tzar and his family," Markus shook his head. "It's crazy, it really is crazy. Ask yourself this, are we humans so stupid that we think war is a rational way of solving problems?" It was then he noticed the bottle of wine on the table. "Thank God!" he said, actually looking up as if the Lord himself were peering down through the ceiling. "We're saved."

Later Pyotr said, "If it's so bad, why go back, Markus?"

"Because Berlin is my home. Because I have found a way to play the game. Because someone must stop these lunatics from taking over the world again."

"And if you can't?"

"I'll do what everyone else does."

"What?"

"Go to America."

"America?"

"Yes. Why? You don't approve?"

So, Pyotr told him. His dreams had started again.

Dreamland - 6

A heavily gloved hand, gripped by the talons of a hooded falcon, outlined against a brilliant blue sky. The hood is removed from the falcon's head. It is a peregrine falcon, who's startling yellow eyes scan the horizon before it flexes its wings and takes off from the glove. Effortlessly, the raptor soars in a climbing spiral until it is a dot in the sky.

Far below, a strutting white dove, cooing to itself on a tree limb, glides away in search of food.

Nearly a mile up, the falcon sees the dove etched against the green grassland as it innocently flies along. Instinctively adjusting the attack angle of its wings, the falcon dives. At over 200-miles per hour it closes its wings, stoops, and aims...the sleeper mutters a warning, waves an arm, rolls over...into a driving snowstorm. Night. Deep in a Swedish forest, the thunder of hooves on ice growing louder and louder, as armoured warhorses mounted by a savage barbarian horde brandishing burning torches burst through the blizzard. At their head, the striking figure of Gustavus Adolphus, King of Sweden, his long hair and beard caked white with flakes, yelling, "Would that we're in time, Oxenstierna!"

"Fear not, my Liege. I see the lights of your castle. Your heir will surely wait to be born into his father's arms."

There ahead, through the storm, the night fires and flares in the watchtowers of the huge, grim bulk of Tre Kronor Castle can be seen and the excited shout goes up - "THE KING! THE KING!" - over the wail of a new-born baby.

Inside, in the Queen's bedchamber, the exhausted mother, Queen Maria Elenora, scans through the crowd assembled around her four-postered bed, doctors, midwives, ladies-in-waiting, until the doors are abruptly thrust open to reveal the travel-stained figure of her husband. All eyes in all the anxious faces turn to look at him. Understanding instantly, the King strides into the room, takes the crying infant - now swaddled in a long white shawl - from the hands of a midwife, looks intently into its tiny monkey face, bends down his head, his hair and beard a curtain completely shielding the child from view, breathes in deeply and then deliberately breathes out into the baby's face. And the baby stops crying!

Gustavus smiles. Looks at his Queen. "Thank you, Madam, for our lovely daughter," he says.

"You are not disappointed?" Maria Elenora cannot hide her anxiety.

Gustavus, looks at the baby. "She is our blood. She is a Vasa." He bends to kiss the Queen. "She will rule as a Vasa." He surveys the room. Sees Oxenstierna in the doorway. "Now, my Lord, assemble the Court!"

In the Great Hall of the castle, under the war banners captured in his many campaigns, the King gazes out over the assembled buzzing multitude. Lit by hundreds of candles and huge logs burning in two giant fireplaces, the rude appearance of his warriors clashes with the finery of the Court nobles, the clergy, the foreign Princes and their retinue, ambassadors and their pages, the colourful dresses of the Ladies-in-waiting, the scurrying servants bringing meat and drink. At a signal, a fanfare of trumpets silences the many voices. Chancellor Oxenstierna now steps forward bearing the blue-and-gold colours of Sweden on a long black staff which he bangs on the wide, wooden floorboards. In his powerful voice, rising in volume, the Chancellor says, "My Lords - My Ladies - People of Sweden - Pray silence for His Majesty, KING GUSTAVUS ADOLPHUS!"

A roar goes up from a thousand throats!

Oxenstierna bangs his staff again. As the echoes fade in the rafters, all sound dies away. Silence.

Gustavus steps forward. "Hear me!" he says. "Good my friends, my countrymen, my many allies, you Noble Princes and Ambassadors who grace Our Court and shower upon us your many attentions - hear me all! I bring you news dear to our Swedish hearts: through the Grace of God, our noble Queen, Maria Elenora, has this night given birth to Our heir -" the King turns to where a midwife stands behind him carrying the baby, takes the child into his hands, holds her aloft for all to see - "Behold! KING...CHRISTINA!"

Consternation! A great babble of voices sweeps the hall. And at this precise moment, with the ingrained timing of a master, Chancellor Oxenstierna drops to his knees to kiss the hem of Christina's swaddling clothes. Rising, he says, "LONG LIVE THE KING!" The trumpets blare and the crowd, surging forward, take up the chant: 'LONG LIVE THE KING! LONG LIVE THE KING!'

Petrus would always remember that date: Tuesday, December 8, 1626. And now, 18 years later, Thursday, December 8, 1644, in the Riksdag. The great day of Christina's majority, her birthday. Where, before the assembled States, she receives their oath of allegiance after the Regents, led by Lord Oxenstierna, have turned over to her all authority to rule the Swedish Empire. There will be no coronation, that will have to wait because of the war with Denmark. Nevertheless, for the first time, seated on a silver throne - the gift of Magnus standing proudly behind her - Petrus sees his childhood companion in all her glory. Dressed simply, no make-up, no jewellery, with only the emblems of office in front of her, rising to speak to the ranks of noblemen, priests, farmers and peasants. Her's is not the voice of a young girl. It is the voice of a monarch appointed by God. Petrus shiveres, goosebumps on the muscles of his forearms. For the first time he understands the enormous gulf that now separates him from the girl he knew as a child.

In hindsight it could hardly be otherwise. Two six-year-olds may well play together. But when one of them has inherited an empire which included Finland, Estonia, parts of Norway, Germany, and Russia, and all of Sweden, there is an immediate distance. To which the little girl's thirst for knowledge and acute attention to her many tutors (a discipline recommended in writing by her father, the King, in the event anything untoward happened to him while he was off fighting wars!) led to a lifelong interest in the arts, sciences, medicine, philosophy and theology; the mastery of foreign languages of which she spoke 6 by the time she was 8 - Swedish, Finnish, Latin, French, Dutch and German - 3 more which she taught herself by the age of 12 - Greek, Italian and Spanish - and a further 3 while still in her minority - Hebrew, Arabic and English. Chancellor

Oxenstierna himself presided over her political education, giving her a detailed grounding in state affairs, encouraging her even as a child to meet and converse with foreign envoys in their own tongue. At 14 she was receiving direct briefings on government affairs and by the time she was16, in 1640, she regularly attended Cabinet meetings and those of the Council of State. It was this body that, on her majority, officially proclaimed: 'Her Majesty is a King, she must be respected as a male!' And, as if to the manor born, it is manly the way she takes to riding, fencing and even military strategy - right down to dressing as a man whenever she feels like it - and you have a person so prodigiously gifted that you could be excused in your pride for having once been that person's playmate.

Petrus was at the Assembly in his role as equerry to Magnus. Although four years his junior, he had grown into his role naturally following a lengthy apprenticeship as page and scribe in the entourage of Lord Oxenstierna, who valued the boy's loyalty to his adopted country, the fact that he could read and write and that German was his mother tongue, a useful attribute when sent on delicate missions to the ever-quarrelling Princes of the Lutheran coalition of armies facing the Hapsburg Catholics and their allies.

Oxenstierna, as supreme controller of all Sweden's interests in Germany, had to conduct the intricate diplomacy necessary to sustain the war-effort. He must determine strategy; he must allocate available resources to this army or that; arrange for and control recruiting, taking care that the military enterprises did not cheat the Swedish crown. He must settle bitter disputes regarding the assignment of quarters; compose the often-violent jealousies between generals, for which disputes, over quarters, provided an inexhaustible store of inflammable material; he must flatter the vanity, appease the pride, and curb the disintegrating ambitions of commanders who were also near-sovereign princes. The task of ensuring the proper functioning of the vital apparatus of "contributions" was in itself a full-time occupation. Every day confronted him with the question of how the armies were to be paid, and by whom. How to persuade financiers, in Hamburg or Amsterdam, or among German adventurers doing well out of the war, to make the necessary loans? How coax the entrepreneurs to shoulder, for just a little longer, the cost of keeping their troops in a state of no more than simmering mutiny? How to reconcile the fundamental principle that war must pay for itself, with the no less fundamental principle that the economic life of Germany must be preserved in sufficient health to permit the financial bloodletting without which the war could not go on? And at the same time, as Lord Chancellor and Regent for the Crown, it fell to him to organise the postal system, to fix tolls on rivers, to regulate trade and fairs, to establish a new ecclesiastical organisation for the occupied lands, to see to the provision of scholarships for deserving students out of ecclesiastical revenues, to personally specify exactly how much wine, how much meat, how much bread, must be provided from the archdiocese of Mainz, what taxes should be paid by householders, craftsmen and stock-farmers, how the salt-trade should be regulated, and how to insure those tolls which Sweden levied on the Baltic ports were paid. He also had to determine in the most minute detail the wage-scales for civil servants, the official emoluments of the Regents, the best types of taxation for the easing and maintenance of fiscal burdens, the framing of budgets and the correct minting-policy to be pursued. A summary of tasks nigh on impossible for one man - leave alone a girl just turned 18!

Before the ceremony began, watching the delegations filing in, Magnus said to Petrus, "Have you seen what that little minx, Ebba, is up to?"

"No," Petrus said. Ebba Sparre was a recently appointed 15-year-old 'hovfröken', maid of honour, to the Queen.

"Oh yes you have," Magnus said. "You can't stop staring at her."

Petrus blushed.

Magnus grinned. "Wait till you take her over the fences, then you'll have something to blush about."

"You?"

"Of course! Noblesse oblige. But let me tell you something, there's nothing you and I could teach her that she hasn't already done."

"Magnus!"

"What? You're shocked?" Magnus cuffed Petrus on the chest. "Not half as shocked as Christina will be when she cottons on. It won't be long I wager, as I'm sure they're already bedmates."

"Christina?"

"Yes, Christina. Our darling Queen has fallen for her. She will be an aptly named Lady-of-the-Bedchamber, mark my words."

Anxious to change the subject, Petrus said, "I don't see the Queen's mother."

"Nor will you," Magnus said. "They've got her locked up in the castle at Gripsholm. She's out of her mind most of the time. You know what she said of Christina at birth? 'Dark and ugly, with a great nose and black eyes. Take her from me, I will not have such a monster.' Imagine if your mother said that of you?"

"She wanted a son."

"Who doesn't? But she's weird. Remember when we were kids accidents were always happening to Christina? Falling down the stairs, a beam mysteriously dropped on her cradle, and that time she supposedly fell on a stone floor and broke her collarbone? Her shoulder wasn't even set right. Accidents, my arse. You know after Lützen, Maria Eleonora kept Gaustavus's embalmed body for two years in a dark chamber next to her bedroom and forced Christina to sit in there with her night after night while it rotted away? How'd you like to do that? Then she had a golden casket with the King's heart hung above Christina's bed? Not to mention all those dwarfs and jesters she's obsessed with. I'm telling you she's out of her mind. Hysterical. She hates Sweden. She can't even speak Swedish properly. No wonder they've locked her up."

"Still. She's the mother. After all, if the King married her she must have had some merit?"

"He married her when she was a beautiful German princess courted by half the nobles in Europe. Then she goes and has a child who dies at birth, another that lasts a year, a third that's stillborn, and a fourth she hates. It's driven her mad. Thank God she was not allowed any influence in raising Christina. Oxenstierna and my father made sure of that. The King decreed she should get the princely education deserving of the male heir to the throne and look at her -" Magnus gestured to where the Queen was seated - "I would say a damn good job was made of it."

It was not for Petrus to disagree. But looking at the solitary figure sitting on her silver throne, he could not help but wonder if she was happy.

Chapter Fourteen

"**H**appy?" Markus said. "What has happiness to do with being a Queen? Or a King, or whatever she was? This is a pretty weird dream you have. Has it occurred to you that you are projecting a version of yourself into these so-called dreams? Is it coincidence that Petrus is Pyotr by another name and has a best friend called Magnus and not Markus? And loses his father? You want me to go on?"

"I had no idea you were an expert on dreams," Pyotr said.

"I'm not. And nor is anybody else. We don't even know where in the brain dreams originate or what purpose dreaming has for the body or mind. It's all illusory. Black mumbo jumbo from the Dark Ages."

Maybe to you, but not to me, Pyotr thought.

And not to Mlle. Pauline either when she bumped into him the next day, shopping for garlic and leeks in the open-air market on Boulevard Raspail with a thunderstorm rumbling menacingly overhead.

"Just the man I've been looking for," she said. "Soon after you decamped from our building - you cannot imagine the scandal you left behind! - I found something incredible. Unfortunately, I don't have it with me, so you must come over to see it at your earliest convenience."

"What is it?" Pyotr said.

"Something that corroborates your dreams."

"Which I am told are illusory mumbo jumbo."

"Rubbish. Who told you that? Everybody dreams. It is the body's way of making sense of the impossible. Awake we constantly monitor our senses through the filter of self - what we believe we know by what we have been taught or experienced. It is only when we sleep and all external stimuli are blocked, that the part of the brain that recognises self, shuts down. Come over for supper and I'll explain. Wait till you see what I've found -" Pauline raised her eyebrows in query, a mischievous grin on her face, just as a flash of lightning and a growl from the heavens announced the approaching storm.

It poured. And it was still belting down when a bedraggled Pyotr, dripping water on all 90 steps as he climbed to the sixth floor, knocked on the door of Pauline's apartment at the appointed hour for dinner. The door was opened by Delphine with the cockatoo screeching *QUI-EST-LÀ? QUI-EST-LÀ?* in the background.

"*Mon pauvre homme!*" Delphine said. "You're soaked! Off with your clothes or you'll get sick." Despite his protests, Pyotr found himself bundled into a rough linen chemise that came down to his knees and an enormous padded dressing gown with a dragon motif on the back, while his hat, shirt, coat, trousers and jacket were hung to dry next to the pot-bellied stove that separated the dining alcove from the kitchen where Pauline was making a daube in a terracotta pot with beef braised in wine, vegetables, herbs and garlic.

"Give it another hour," Pauline said. "Sit, have some wine and look at this:" Pyotr sat where directed, stretched his bare legs out to the warm snug comfort of the stove, and studied the inscribed manuscript he was given, closely watched by the two women.

Pause. Time suspended. Acutely aware he was meant to say something, Pyotr didn't know what to say.

"Know what that is?" Pauline finally said.

"My guess is, it's a horoscope," Pyotr said, holding it at arm's length. "Whose?"

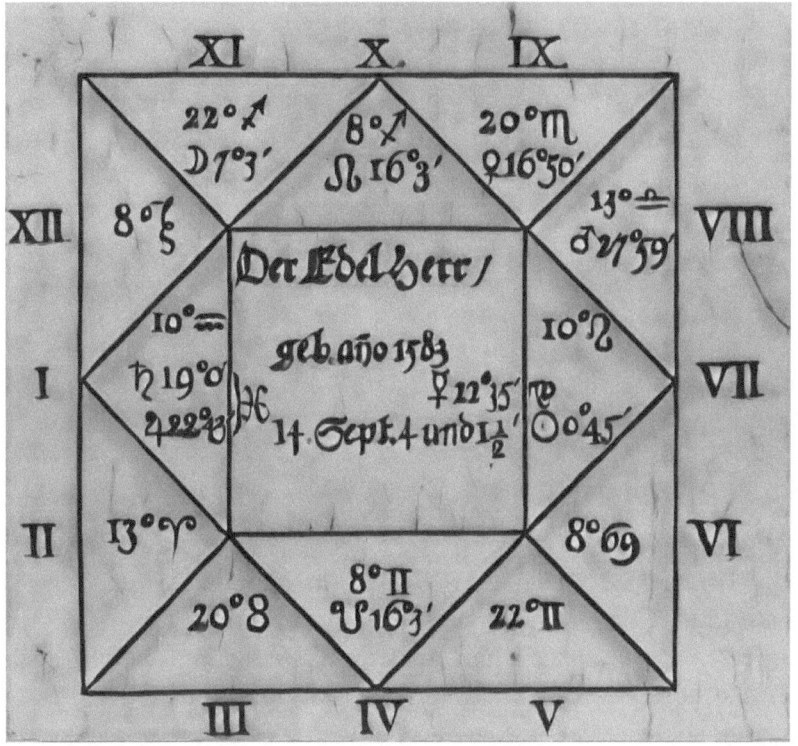

Pyotr shrugged. "I don't know. This inscription in the middle - *der Edel herr* - is in German. It means *the noble gentleman*. And *geb* is probably an abbreviation of *geboren - born;* and *ano* of *anno*, of the year, 1583. Then the day, September 14. So we have a noble gentleman born on September 14, 1583. I would guess this number 4 is the hour he was born, and the 1 and a half minutes is the exact time. Is that feasible? Who records a birth down to half a minute?"

"Johannes Kepler."

"Kepler!" Pyotr was stunned. He looked at what he held in his hands as if it was suddenly on fire. "This is by Kepler?"

"Yes. And guess who the noble gentleman was?"

Pyotr, face blank, could only stare.

"Wallenstein!" Pauline said. "Exactly as Petrus recounts, that is the horoscope his father was given by Kepler to bring to Graf Albrecht von Wallenstein in Lützen on the fateful day of the battle in your dream."

Pyotr was dumbfounded. It took him a moment to finally mumble, "Incredible. It's incredible."

"So much for mumbo jumbo," Pauline said.

MAMBO JAMBO! MAMBO JAMBO! her parrot screeched, rocking on its perch.

"Tell him the rest," Delphine said.

"I found it in the Bibliothèque Nationale where they have a vast trove of Christina's personal papers," Pauline said. "Back then many notables had horoscopes cast, not out of superstition but because they believed that they were a pragmatic aid in making decisions - and to this day, many still do."

"What does it mean?"

"To start, look at the date. Wallenstein is born on September 14, a Virgo, an earth sign, with Mercury in ascendant, his ruling planet, personal in the way it reflects individual motivation. Virgos are famous for being meticulous perfectionists, good at dissecting information and objective analysis, holding emotions in check, careful with their words, good at reaching sound conclusions to complex situations. Since Mercury governs the mind, communication, and logic, it gives the ability to question, analyse and resolve."

"And these numbers around the edge?"

"Those are the twelve stations for the signs of the Zodiac. Where they fall in any chart is dependent on your place, date and time of birth, and where exactly the stars and planets are aligned at that moment. We know Wallenstein's birth date, and at the Bibliothèque I found out he was born in a town called Hermanice, in the Kingdom of Bohemia. Numbers 1 through 6 -" here Pauline took the manuscript from Pyotr and tapped each number as she spoke - "are, broadly speaking, internal and personal. 7 through 12, are external; the interaction of you with the outside world. As you can see, he has Jupiter and Saturn in his first house. Jupiter symbolises openness to all that life can bring. He is easy to live with and people flock to him. He is admired which can lead to complacency. Fortunately, Saturn is there. Saturn means discipline in everything and everybody it touches. He will be the first to understand and appreciate this. And with Aquarius in the ascendant here" - she tapped the chart again for emphasis - "to add physical power, this could very well be the natal chart of a born leader. The second house is about possessions, money, material things. Wallenstein has Aries in the second house, which means not being passive, always having something to do, chasing something he wants. It's not surprising he was one of the richest men in the Hapsburg empire. Here, in his third house, he has Taurus, which can mean he is stubborn and needs to learn to communicate with others whose opinions may differ from his own. The fourth house is the house of home and family. Having Pisces in the fourth indicates Wallenstein's deep emotions for his family and friends. The fifth house is about innovation, personal pleasure, what makes one feel good. With Gemini in the fifth, Wallenstein can show off his knowledge and put his incredible mind to work on the myriad fronts that confront him. The sixth house is to do with health and wellness and having Cancer in the sixth indicates qualities of nurturing and caregiving, essential for a military leader, mindful of the troops in his command but also of his own comfort and safety. Here in the seventh, we have Virgo and the Sun. Since the seventh is about committed and legal bindings like marriage or business partnerships, Virgo in the seventh is seen as positive as it prioritises the well-being of others. Since he is born a Virgo, this is significant. However, the Sun is adversely placed as you can see. This could mean a troubled marriage or something far more serious in his relationship with his peers. The eighth house is the house of sex and death, with feelings associated with rage, jealousy, fear and despair. Having Libra and Mars in this house is conflicting, Libra being about life and Mars about accepting decay and death. And then here in the ninth we find Scorpio and Venus. He is attracted to women who are dynamic, powerful. But having Venus in the ninth has numerous negative implications, and ruled by Scorpio, may indicate a disputatious marriage of conflict. Leo in the tenth is a need for recognition in his profession, since this house is about self-respect, honours, knowledge, and dignity. It governs his public image and reveals an ambitious individual. Here, in the eleventh house, we have Sagittarius and the Moon - a very fortuitous coupling, since the eleventh is the house of money and good luck. With Sagittarius ascendant it denotes fortune, industry and influence, a great faith in God, and in his own destiny. Having the Moon dependent makes him optimistic, expansive, and innately positive in his quest for power. Wherein lies a danger: by temperament he may be too impulsive. *Not* looking before he leaps. But here, in the twelfth house, he has Capricorn, a definitive sign, that by working hard, with a clear conscience, he will succeed."

Pauline gave the manuscript back to Pyotr, who took it, a dazed expression on his face.

"I know it's a lot to digest," she said. "Bearing in mind that what I've just told you is the barest summary."

"Wait till she gets into planetary degrees," Delphine said.

"But -" Pyotr struggled to formulate his thought "- the part I don't understand is what would Wallenstein make of it? He gets this -" Pyotr waved the manuscript - "on the eve of battle. Does he look at it and say to himself 'All things being equal, I'm a lucky commander. Overall I have a green light to go. By working hard I know I'll win?'"

"In essence, yes. Remember he has had horoscopes cast for him all his life. His familiarity with them would allow him to look it over and, short of a warning, it would confirm what he knows about himself. After all, he has already beaten Gustavus at Alte Veste. That simply confirms he could do it again. Anyway, I think the daube is ready now. Let's eat before Delphine dies of starvation."

"And while we eat you can tell us your latest dream," Delphine said.

Hours later, when Pyotr left to walk home in his now dried clothes, the rain had stopped and all he had to do was make sure he skipped the puddles on his way back to the 14th, his mind so preoccupied he failed to see he was being followed.

Chapter Fifteen

"You'll never guess…"

"What?"

"I saw him?"

"Him? Who?"

By way of answer, with her teaspoon, Nathalie Steinem, pointed at the ceiling. She was having breakfast with her mother on the terrace, the most attractive feature of their flat on the sixth floor. In bright sunshine, the air smelled fresh after the previous night's storm.

"Lui!" She knew her mother knew whom she meant.

"You're sure?"

"Of course. I followed him. He's living in the 14th. I was coming home from the club last night and saw him come out of the front door here. He didn't see me and walked off up Bonaparte, the Rue de Rennes, left on Raspail and all the way up to a block from Denfert. I lost him there because I had to hang far back so he couldn't see me." This was not quite true. She had seen him turn into the Rue Boissonade and then into a walled courtyard which she could not enter, but from the street she saw lights turned on in an atelier on the first floor, and his silhouette against the tall windows. She saw no reason to give these details to her mother.

Madame Steinem studied her daughter. Why do children always think they can dupe their parents? Nat was a clever girl, sometimes too clever for her own good. But she was a hopeless liar. All those fibs and fabrications when she was secretly seeing Pyotr. At the time it amused her - mother and daughter sharing the same lover. It was inevitable. She recalled how they first met. Walking in the Luxembourg gardens. Nathalie saying oh look, there's our lecteur d'Anglais, and being introduced to this tall young Englishman, with a much-travelled face, and eyes that had already seen too much of life, and a smile of genuine pleasure when they shook hands. Before the first word was spoken, she knew. And she knew he knew. Despite that, the formalities. The song-and-dance of social custom. When she proposed they have a drink, his frank admission that on his modest bourse from the University he could not afford the pleasure. It is my pleasure to invite you, she had said. And the three of them went to the Carrousel next to the bandstand to drink kirs and listen to the music. And when that stopped his ready replies to her questions. And when she learned he was looking for somewhere cheap to live, what came out of her mouth?

"You must come and stay with us!"

"You are very kind, but that is not possible."

"Why is it not possible?"

"I could not intrude on your family."

"What family? There are just the two of us, Nathalie et moi. My husband died in the war. We would welcome a man in the house." But still he refused.

Which is when Nat said, "*Peut-être la chambre de bonne*?" And that's how he ended up in the maid's room, one floor up, directly above our flat. And the dance began. She could feel herself smiling as she remembered.

"What's so funny?" Nathalie said.

"Life," her mother replied.

Afterwards it was child's play to find him. Lunch on the terrace of La Rotonde, where Boulevard Montparnasse met Boulevard Raspail, combined the delights of an alfresco meal with those of a strategic lookout post. She had scarcely finished an order of a dozen oysters from Arcachon when she saw him strolling along with a friend on the opposite pavement, two aloof observers of the social scene. Inevitably, as all *flâneurs* do, the pair crossed over to idle past the café-brasserie, to see and be seen. And in the serendipitous choreography of such encounters, their eyes crossed hers. *Quelle surprise!*

"Anna! What a delightful surprise! Allow me to present my friend, Markus." She raises her hand to be kissed. Invites the gentlemen to be seated. They protest. She insists. Inevitably they accept and soon, over a dry Chablis, they too are sampling the oysters from Arcachon.

After the usual pleasantries, between molluscs, Pyotr said, "What brings you here, so far from the 6th?"

"And you? What are you doing here?" Anna said. She always answered a question with a question.

"I live nearby," Pyotr said, waving vaguely toward the intersection.

"Yes, I know. My daughter told me."

"Nathalie? How could she -"

"Know? She saw you and followed you home. Simple."

"Oh."

"Oh? Is that all you have to say? Given what went between us?"

"No. Not really. It's just that -"

"Have I upset you, Pyotr?"

"No. Well, simply put, I suppose I needed to -"

"Escape? Leave, without so much as saying goodbye?" Anna's eyebrows went up a *soupçon*. "Is that what they do in England?" She was smiling. Pyotr blushed. Stammered. Markus watched the exchange like a spectator at Roland Garros, head going from side to side, Borotra versus Lacoste.

"Your friend does not know how to end an *affaire*," Anna said to him.

"*Pauvre homme*," Markus said. "But let's not spoil the occasion with talk about endings. I much prefer beginnings." Now he was smiling. "I propose a toast. To beginnings!" He raised his glass and Anna did the same. The dance began again. A ménage à trois? Why not? Which had Nathalie wondering why her mother was so cheerful when next she saw her. In the interim, Pyotr was dreaming.

Dreamland - 7

"The young man is waiting, Your Excellency."

"Show him in," Graf von Wallenstein said. He was lying in great pain on a couch in his palace in Prague. Ever since Lützen, before that in fact, his health made it impossible for him to ride a horse, and now, so pained by gout he could scarcely sit up, he must receive an emissary sent by that two-faced wizard, Oxenstierna, to re-negotiate for Sweden what had already been determined. He slowly moved his leg, still affected by a spent musket ball fired at him by a Hessian cavalier from less than four paces on that fateful day. To prevent Lützen's capture, Wallenstein had the town burned. Acrid smog blanketed the field, and the two armies pummelled each other blindly all day long, at one point volley-firing muskets at five paces, their King slain on the field, struck in the head, side, arm, and back by bullets. Darkness, he remembered, brought an end to the fighting, leaving both sides on much the same ground they had occupied that morning. Tell that to the dead. And now their Queen was a child.

His equerry ushered in a youth, tall, handsomely dressed in grey satin, with a black velvet doublet, a black velvet beret on his head, sporting a grey feather. "Your name?" Wallenstien said.

"I am called Petrus," the youth replied with a bow.

"Forgive me for not getting up. You are the one who saw Gustavus die?"

"I am."

"I admired him, you know. A great man. But it is well for him and for me that he is gone. There's no room in Germany for both of us. You claim a victory, but if truth be told, Lützen wasn't a matter of who won or lost, but of who retreated last." Wallenstein winced as a nerve in his calf twitched. "We pulled back that night, abandoning the field, leaving the Swedes to have Lützen, a technical Protestant victory, but a pyrrhic one. Your advance on Leipzig had been blocked; you lost more men, more battle flags, and your king." Wallenstein sniffed in disapproval. At the age of 49, Wallenstein had already led a longer life than most men of the period, mainly spent fighting battles for the emperor all over central Europe. He longed for peace, understanding belatedly that serving the empire and serving the emperor were not the same thing. He studied his young guest. "Tell me, this child, the Queen, what's she like?"

"Remarkable," Petrus said.

"It's a pity she's so young," he said.

"Sir?"

"Your master, Lord Oxenstierna, is a devious man. He uses his position as Regent as if he alone ruled Sweden. He is no more Protestant than I am Catholic. He rebuffs my offer that hostilities between our armies be suspended, and that instead our forces should be used in combined strength against anyone who attempts to disturb the state of the Empire and to impede freedom of religion. Why has he sent you here?"

A good question to which Petrus had no ready answer. His brief was ambiguous, Oxenstierna having hinted that Wallenstein was no longer in favour with Emperor Ferdinand. 'There's a rumour he'll be accused of treachery. I want you to sniff around,' Lord Oxenstierna had said. 'Find out how much support he has.' Unsure what to say, Petrus did what he always did, he told the truth.

"My brief is vague, Your Excellency," he said. "Lord Oxenstierna is of the opinion that you are no longer in favour with Emperor Ferdinand. Apparently he is wary of your ambition and suspicious of your attempts to negotiate peace."

Wallenstein smiled. "Frankly put, young man!"

"My Lord also wants me to find out how much support you have."

"Well, you can tell your master that I have as much support as he has, and that if he wants to accuse me of disloyalty, he'd better have the proof to back it up." For a moment, lost in thought, Wallenstein closed his eyes.

Petrus nodded, not sure if he was being dismissed. He looked at the many mementoes and decorations that adorned the room, awarded to this man lying in pain on his couch: Duke of Friedland, Prince of the Holy Roman Empire, Duke of Mecklenburg, Duke of Sagan, Lord High Admiral of the Imperial Navy, Generalissimo of the Imperial Army, the titles were many. To make space for his palace, Wallenstein had razed 26 houses, six pastures, and two brickworks. Four huge courtyards were created to make way for a layout that included period gardens, the Avenue of Sculptures, an Astronomical corridor depicting allegories of the four continents and zodiac emblems, stables for a platoon of horses and the large Riding School. One garden in the Italian style had an aviary, a grotto, and a fountain by Adrian de Vries. A loggia, monumental in its conception, with three arcades on doubled columns, recalled the Baroque style. The total value of interior furnishings was said to be 70,000 gold pieces, while another account claimed 134 000 gold pieces were invested in jewels and tableware made from precious metals. Nothing in Sweden was comparable. When Petrus looked back, he found Wallenstein eying him. Sitting up with difficulty, the duke said, "I am no traitor. I am a loyal servant of the emperor. I have fought for him all my life. I have shed blood for him. I have sacrificed everything for him. And what does he give me in return?"

Uncomfortable, Petrus could only stare. Wallenstein sighed.

"He fears me, Petrus. He is jealous of my wealth. He fears that I will become too powerful and challenge his authority. But I have no such designs. I only want what is best for the Empire."

"I understand, Your Excellency," Petrus said.

"Do you? Do you understand what it's like to be constantly doubted and mistrusted? To be seen as a threat by those you have sworn to serve?"

"I'm just an emissary, Your Excellency. I'm not here to judge." Petrus said.

Wallenstein sighed again. "No, of course not. You're just a pawn in Lord Oxenstierna's game. A game that could cost us all dearly if it's played poorly." Petrus nodded despite himself.

"Well, no matter." Wallenstein settled back into his pillows. "You're here now. What is it again that Lord Oxenstierna wants?"

"He wants me to find out how much support you have among the Imperial troops."

Smiling wryly, Wallenstein said, "Ah, I see. And what will he do with that information?"

Embarrassed, Petrus said, "I'm not sure, Your Excellency,"

Holding Petrus' gaze, Wallenstein said, "But you suspect, don't you? You suspect that he will use it to try and undermine me, to try and weaken me in the eyes of the emperor."

Petrus looked away. "I don't know, Your Excellency. Lord Oxenstierna is a wise man. He has the best interests of Sweden at heart."

Wallenstein snorted. "Always Sweden and the Swedes! What do they care for the Empire? What do they care for the people of Germany? All they care about is power. And they will stop at nothing to get it."

Petrus, uneasy, unsure of how to respond, could only look at his feet. "Enough said. Thank you for coming, Petrus," Count Wallenstein said. "You may go now. And tell your master he will not find me an easy mark."

Upon his return to Stockholm, Petrus immediately reported to Lord Oxenstierna in his study, seated as always behind a large wooden desk, surrounded by books and papers. "So, what did he say?" Oxenstierna asked.

"He was in obvious pain, my lord," Petrus said. "The gout. He could barely sit up. But he was still as sharp as ever."

"I wouldn't expect anything less from the great Wallenstein." Oxenstierna smiled wryly. "How were you received?"

"With the greatest courtesy."

"Of course."

"He asked me about the Queen. He seemed genuinely interested in her."

"Interesting." Oxenstierna raised an eyebrow. "What else did he say?"

"He regretted that she was so young."

"Thank God. No opportunity for him to offer marriage to one of his princelings."

"He wants peace, my lord. He offered to suspend hostilities between our armies and join forces against anyone who threatens the Empire's stability and freedom of religion," Petrus said.

"And what did you make of that?"

"I'm not sure, my lord. On the face of it, his desire for peace seems real and he says he has all the support he needs, but at the same time he claims to be constantly doubted and mistrusted. To be seen as a threat by those he has sworn to serve."

"Good heavens! He actually said that?"

"Yes. He was quite frank. He also said he was no traitor, that he has always been loyal to the emperor, but mentioned that the emperor might be jealous of his wealth and suspect him of being ambitious."

"Ambitious?" Oxenstierna echoed. "He used that word?"

"His exact words were 'challenge his authority.'"

"What did he mean by that?"

"He didn't give me any specifics, my lord. But he did say that serving the empire and serving the emperor were not the same thing. He quoted Aristotle's paradox - 'The past does not exist except in memory; the future does not exist except in hope. There is only the present.' Ask yourself this, he said, 'how thick is the present?'"

Oxenstierna rubbed his chin thoughtfully. "How thick is the present, eh? He's right. Ferdinand is a two-faced bastard who would sell his own mother for a whore if it gave him an advantage. Wallenstein's a shrewd man. He knows how to play both sides. He's a wily and dangerous opponent, but he could also be a valuable ally. We need to figure out which one we're dealing with."

"What would you have me do, my lord?" Petrus asked.

"For now, nothing. The cards will fall as they are dealt. Thank you for your report, Petrus. You've done well. You must be tired after such a long journey. Get some rest. Just remember, be very careful. Wallenstein's an old fox. Don't let him outsmart you."

"No, sir. The last thing he said to me was 'tell your master he will not find me an easy mark.'"

Chapter Sixteen

When Petrus woke up the following morning it took him a moment to recognise where he was - not in 17th century Stockholm, but in 20th century Paris. And he was not Petrus, he was Pyotr. Looking at himself in the mirror as he shaved, he wondered if he was going mad. Downstairs in the atelier he heard voices.

Markus talking to Anna. Anna laughing at something he said. Momentarily, Pyotr felt a flush of jealousy as he remembered how they had said goodnight to him and gone off together to the alcove where Markus made his bed. He'd fallen asleep to the rhythm of their lovemaking. Still half-dressed, he opened the door of his bedroom on the mezzanine to look down at the lovers where they sat having breakfast. On hearing him, Markus looked up. "You are a first-class idiot, Pyotr," he said.

"I can see that," Pyotr said. "And good morning to you too."

Anna smiled. She was wearing a shirt of Markus' and nothing else. "Come down and have breakfast with us," she said. "The gods have sent us a glorious day."

It was so. A bright light, diffused through the huge windows facing north, bathed the atelier in a golden hue as Pyotr stumped downstairs. "And you can stop looking so grumpy," Markus said.

"Markus!" Anna said. "*Sois gentil.* Be kind."

"Well he is. Look at him. You'd think he'd lost his favourite teddy bear."

"Fuck you," Pyotr said.

"Stop this at once!" Anna said. "You are both behaving like children. Sit down, Pyotr. I will say this once or walk out of here never to see you again. What I gave you, I gave freely and wanted very little in return - a few kind words, some kisses, a cosy bed, to love and be loved in return. Obviously not enough, because you moved out. What do you care who I give myself to?"

"That's not -" Pyotr started to say, interrupting Anna. Then he stopped, not sure how to go on.

"Not what?" Anna said. "The truth? I'll tell you the truth. Maybe I should have loved you more, or not at all."

"That's not what I was going to say. It's not important about you and me or you and Markus."

"Then what is?"

"Remembering."

Anna and Markus stared at Pyotr, then looked at each other, then back at Pyotr.

"Have you gone mad?" Markus said.

"Yes," Pyotr said. "Probably. Well, a little anyhow."

"Is it that dream?"

"That and something else."

"What?"

"What you said in the restaurant the other day, that it's all illusory. I can't shake it off. The war; what happened in the war to all of us. And now? The whole world is coming to gay Paree for the Exposition. We have this capacity for collective amnesia. Like you said the war is scarcely over and the last victims from the pandemic have just died and all we want to do is forget."

"Maybe it's how nature protects us?" Anna said.

"Why talk about it?" Markus said. "You're just going to spoil breakfast."

"'Those who cannot remember the past are condemned to repeat it.'"

"Don't you bloody quote Santayana at me."

"Markus, stop it!" Anna said. "Sit down, Pyotr. I'll get you a cup." She said it as if it were her house. Pyotr sat while she went to the kitchen. Presently she came back with a cup and some toast. Neither man had said a word in her absence.

Anna sat down, looked at each of them. To Pyotr she said, "Don't worry. I'm not moving in here. You deserve your space. I have mine." To Markus she said, "And you're moving there with me."

"But…" Markus began.

"No buts," Anna said. "Why make things complicated? There's only my daughter and plenty of room. Ask Pyotr." Anna smiled at him. What a woman, Pyotr thought.

Her daughter? Markus thought, a gleam in his eye. "Okay," he said. And couldn't resist adding, "You really are a first-class idiot, Pyotr."

Pyotr nodded agreement.

"You had an idyllic life in your hands," Markus went on, "and now you end up broke and alone in this dump with just your dreams for company."

That same afternoon Markus moved his few things over to Anna's apartment and Pyotr, free, went to bed happy in his solitude, little dreaming what life had in store for him.

Chapter Seventeen

Nor did life wait. The very next morning, when he returned from a fruitless round looking for work, the concierge accosted him in the entrance lobby. "There's a young girl who came by to see you. Insisted she was expected. Suitcase and all."

"Name?"

"Wouldn't say."

"Where is she?"

"Well, I wasn't going to let her in, was I? Told her to come back when you were here."

Which is when a young girl coming into the lobby behind them said, "Pyotr?" He turned to find Nathalie Steinem, Anna's daughter, smiling up at him. "Surprise?" she said. And kissed him.

"What on earth..." Pyotr managed to say. She giggled.

"Carry my case upstairs," she said, with much the same authority as her mother. "I'll explain."

But of course, no explanation was necessary. Hardly had the door to the atelier closed behind them, then they tore off each other's clothes and it was as it had always been back on the seventh floor of the Rue des Beaux Arts.

"At least we don't have to sneak about," Nathalie said, sated, naked, lying on her back gazing with an almost proprietary satisfaction at the vast pristine space of the atelier.

"Aren't you meant to be in school?" Pyotr said.

"That's what that lecherous man said."

"What lecherous man?"

"The one my mother brought home."

Pyotr laughed. "You must mean, Markus?"

"Is that his name? I didn't like the way he looked at me."

"Do they know you're here?"

Nathalie laughed. "I doubt it. They probably haven't come up for air since they went into Maman's bedroom."

"You know you're going to catch cold lying there naked like that?"

"Not if you lie on top of me."

Later.

Nathalie said, "Maman said you stopped painting to write a book. Is that true?"

"No," Pyotr said. "I mean, no, not a book, but trying to write something."

"About what?"

"Two guys sitting on the ground under a palm tree in the Medina in Marrakech. It's hot as hell, flies and dust everywhere. "

"What are they doing?"

"Nothing. Just talking."

"Can I see?"

"There's not much to see. But if you're interested, get dressed and you can read it for yourself."

Dressed, seated at the kitchen table, this is what Nathalie read:

NO MAN'S LAND

The Medina, Marrakech. The sun is directly overhead. Under a palm tree two men are talking:

Archibald: (Sighs) I'm weary of all this retelling of history. It's all so tiresome.

Balthazar: (Muttering) - the faded wallpaper of memory...

A: What's that mean?

B: I heard it somewhere. But you were there, weren't you? You should know.

A: It doesn't mean I understand.

B: Maybe not, but you were part of it.

A: (Nods.) The Zeitgeist. Forever overtaken by the latest headlines... dimming even as they're read.

B: God, the garbage that's spewed up across the dining table.

A: Ah, those exquisite dinner tables. Once a haven of unity, now a battlefield... opposing ideologies clashing in silence across the tablecloth.

B: Weaving, unasked, through the weft and wrap of our consciousness...all these once great events fade away. Fading into an abyss...

A: The abyss, you mean. Our memories, feeble as ever...edited to justify what we did. Struggling to forget the weight of our past atrocities.

B: (Whispering) In the war to end all wars? Our war. The Great War. What? What is great about such an unbelievable horror story?..All sorrow forgotten, lost.

A: A chronicle to the stupidity of human cruelty... obscured by time's relentless march.

B: And the sick? Who now remembers them and the pandemic? The countless lives lost? More soldiers dead than on the battlefield? The anonymous fragility of life... slipping away, slipping away...

A: Maybe it meant something?

B: (Whispering) What? Memories of shattered dreams?...memories obscured by the illusion of progress?

A: So we're trapped to wander, Balthazar, trapped in this cycle... condemned to repeat the absurdity of our absurd history.

B: There is a pattern...a theatre of the absurd...

A: (Bitterly) In which we all play a part. We think we strive, we think we fight, only to trot across the same tragic stage, time after time, night after night.

B: What's the point if our actions dance to the tune of hope and despair?

A: Call it collective amnesia, our curse, our destiny... In this forgetfulness, we confront the absurdity of our existence that defines our very lives.

B: What then? Must we either embrace the void or find meaning in defiance, rebel against the absurd?

A: Perhaps…if only for a fleeting instant.

B: And what? Maybe, just maybe, get a glimpse of meaning?

Then nothing, just a blank page.

"That's all?" Nathalie said.

"For now, yes," Pyotr said.

"Weird. Why are they called Archibald and Balthazar? I've never met anyone with those names."

"Well, you can't expect me to call them Fred and Charlie."

"Why not? Fred and Charlie at least sound real. I can easily imagine them sitting on the ground under a palm tree. I'm pretty sure no Archibald or Balthazar would do that."

"Yes, but can you imagine Fred and Charlie exchanging ideas on our collective amnesia?"

"Collective amnesia? Because they're too stupid to remember? No. In fact it all sounds phoney. *C'est bidon.* Nobody would say: *In this forgetfulness, we confront the absurdity of our existence that defines our very lives.*"

"I know. It's very stilted. It's just an outline. I'm still trying to get used to writing. What I'm trying to do is dramatise my thoughts."

"Maybe you should stick to painting."

"That's not very kind. The fact is that I think we do suffer from collective amnesia regarding terrible events. We want to forget the War, the flu, the pandemic, the horrible things we do to each other or are done to us. How else do you deal with the death of 100 million people?" Pyotr couldn't hide his distress. "Let me ask you a simple question. What memory do you have of it all?"

"That's not fair. I'm only sixteen."

"So what?" Pyotr spread his hands. "Just think. You were born in 1909, you've lived through the whole thing, here, in Paris. It's been the background to your entire life. To be asked what it is you remember is a bit like me asking you if you can remember the oxygen you breathed last night"

"You know you're weird?" Nathalie said.

"Weirdness has got nothing to do with our failure to remember the past. It is not simply a matter of repeating history, but of how we are trapped in it. That's what I mean about the absurdity of human existence. We are condemned to relive the same mistakes, over and over and over. And we forget that we do this. In fact we want to forget." He said it with such a sense of resignation and despair that Nathalie stared at him. He was crying. "What happened, Pyotr?" she said.

He told her. Something he had never told anyone else.

I was scarcely older than you. Drafted into fighting for the Kaiser in a stupid war, bogged down in the endless trenches we dug, covered in filth, ticks, flies and mud. You could never get clean. Never! And the smell! Old sweat, unchanged socks, stained underwear, rancid food, piss, shit, and blood.

One day we were trapped in the confines of a ruined farm. You could look out through iron bars in the shattered windows of stables attached to what had once been a long-barn on top of a hill on the northeast side of a village called Vauquois, thirty-five kilometres west of Verdun. We'd been fighting for three years on a 450-mile front which stretched from the coast of Belgium to the Swiss border. A war of attrition. You know what that is? Each side gained or lost a little terrain, sometimes just a few metres, while the deaths piled up. Mathematically the odds of surviving such a stupid war were slim to none with one in every three soldiers sent to the front already dead.

It had been snowing. As far as you could see through the bars was a field of deep snow all the way to the horizon, pretty enough in moonlight sifting through high clouds, sending shadows across the snow as the odd snowflake drifted down. Below there were undulations in the snow and, even if they could hardly be seen, they were the enemy trenches. Above the trenches were lumps covered in snow. One lump moves, they are soldiers, our targets. As usual their barrage starts at 0400 in the morning when the French 75mm field guns open up with their predictable delivery of 5.3-kilogram impact-detonated high-explosive shells raining down on our trenches. They fire at us from a distance of 8000 metres at a sustained rate of 15 rounds per minute per gun of which they have 4000 in service, each with a highly trained crew divided into 4-gun batteries comprising 170 men and 4 officers. Plus 6 horses to pull each gun and its first limber and another six horses for each additional limber and caisson, a total of 160 horses and their attendant grooms. Thus 170,000 soldiers and 4,000 officers and 160,000 horses have to be woken up, fed, supplied and in position for the daily bombardment of 15,000 shells per minute, a logistic nightmare to supposedly clear the field and enable their troops, 200 metres away, to climb the ladders out of their trenches, traverse no man's land in sleet and snow and knee-deep mud, and charge uphill through barbed wire - into the furious chatter of our machine-guns. Complete and utter insanity.

Ask any one of our junior Unteroffizier and they could have told your Général Joffre the facts. As soon as the bombardment starts, we move deep underground to the safety of a warren of tunnels we have cut in the rock under the farmhouse and when the bombardment stops, which it has to in order for the poilus not to kill each other, we come back to our positions, take up our weapons and mow them down. We are deployed in a succession of defensive machine-gun nests such that a relatively small number of guns allows us to protect a large part of the line, enfilading fire ensuring our safety against an enemy attack.

We are an elite force, the Sturmtruppen. Today we are going to try a novel tactic in an attempt to break the status quo and gain us some much-needed mobility. We have been issued with new lightweight machine-guns, the MP18, firing 9mm Parabellum rounds at a rate of 450 rounds per minute, with a 32-round magazine. After the enemies' initial assault has been beaten back the idea is to counterattack down the hill, get into their trenches before they have time to regroup, avoid enemy strong points, bypass them and cut them off from their supplies, and, by concentrating our superior firepower, break through their lines and move into their vulnerable rear to overrun their batteries and command posts. Like all good ideas it is simple, so simple I was sure it would not work, the Gods of War having long ago mastered the art of the unforeseen. While waiting for the off I flatten the snow on the window ledge in front of me and with the fingertip of my gloved hand I draw a circle. Hauptmann Manfred, our Captain, is standing next to me and as I finish drawing the moon's face in the snow, he softly says, 'Punkt, Punkt, Komma, Strich -Fertig ist das Mondgesicht.'

Downhill to our left we can hear the unmistakable chatter of a Vickers heavy machine-gun which must mean Tommy has joined the Frogs. I look at

112

Manfred and he draws a line across his throat. 'Verdammt Englander,' he says. The Brits have a reputation. In '16, on the Somme, a company of ten Vickers fired continuously for twelve hours a total of a million rounds, swapping the barrels of their guns every hour due to the heat, wear and tear of constant use, changing the loaders and gunners throughout the day, and, by so doing, preventing any chance of a German counterattack.

Suddenly a star shell climbs into the sky, its magnesium flare explodes, followed by another and another until the whole front below us is brightly lit as the lights drift down on their little parachutes. 'Here they come, Pyotr,' Manfred says. Someone blows a whistle and abruptly our machine-guns open up and the slaughter begins. Manfred and I have been in more engagements than we can count, losing runners and loaders by the score, but neither of us has so much as a scratch. It is highly unusual for a Captain to be at the sharp end of an attack, but soldiers are superstitious and in our unit he and I are always together, professional killers covering each other's back. We fired in short bursts as we were taught when we were recycled to Saarbrücken to train with these new guns. Keep your finger on the trigger and the whole magazine is gone before you can think. You don't so much aim the gun as spray it, hosing down the enemy like washing a car. And that is exactly what it feels like, a power hose of lead pouring down on the enemy caught tangled in our wire not fifteen metres away, the macabre scene lit only by the muzzle flashes of guns reflecting off snow as the flares fade. Desultory rifle fire opens up. Another whistle blows.

As their attack falters, we charge out of the barn, go over the top into them. It only takes minutes but feels like hours. Time stretched. We punch our way down into their trenches, past torn bodies, headless, limbs cast aside, a leg here, a hand there, a stench of shit and piss and the contents of torn guts - what were entire human beings blown to pieces by the staccato hammering of our machine guns. There is no fear, the adrenal rush so great it makes the work seem effortless, our job blinding us to any rational thought that these men we are killing are just like us, fodder, raw meat, to be chewed up and fed into the gaping maw of our War. When we stop it is because there is no one left to kill. Manfred and I look at each other. We are literally knee deep in corpses, ours and theirs. We have to walk on them to move down the trench. I open my mouth to clear my ears, to stop the echo of gunfire and it is only then that I hear the silence. Momentarily all is quiet, still, silent. The snow falls on us. Our guns feel hot in our hands and you can see the snowflakes melt on the barrels. At the back of my

113

skull, all I can feel is a deep pain from the endless concussion of the enemies'
shells. "Man . . ." I begin to say. "Christ, you're hit, Manfred. Look at your
shoulder!"

The blood is pumping out in little spurts, and he leans against the slippery
mud wall of the trench.

"I can't feel a thing," he says. Which is when we both hear a voice say,
"Hans?"

It is a young British soldier, badly wounded, but still alive, lying in the
mud not two metres away, looking up at me. "Is it you? Why are you with Jerry?"
he says. Then he adds, "I can't move. Give us a hand, Hans."

"He said your name?" Manfred says, suddenly suspicious. "Wie kann -?"

And tries to bring up his gun to point at me. - which is when I shoot him
in the head. And then the Brit decides to go for his gun, so I shoot him too. I am
that man. I am a killer. I have killed my Captain and my friend, the boy next
to whom I sat for five years in a boarding school for orphan children in England.

Pyotr nodded. He had stopped crying. "I don't know why I am telling
you all this," he said. "If you weren't there living it, no words can come
close to the absolute hell we went through. Did I want to kill them? No, of
course not. It was a reflex to protect myself. Which is an absurd excuse, as
if I were more important than they were. It perfectly reflects how stupid
war is and how meaningless we are. We never seem to learn."

Nathalie was still staring at him. "Hans?" she said.

"It was what I was called in school." Pyotr said. "My uncle insisted."

Then she said something unexpected: "So, instead of crying and being
miserable, why not just accept the absurdity for what it is, absurd?"

"What?"

"Face it. You're absurd. I'm absurd. We're all absurd, if nothing has
meaning in a meaningless world," Nathalie shrugged. "Why bother?"

Now it was Pyotr's turn to stare.

"Why are you staring at me like that?" Nathalie said. "You think
because I like to fuck, I don't have a brain? If you're going to wallow in
existential dread you'll have to do it on your own or I'm not unpacking my
bag. Choose."

Pause.

As the thought sank in. 16. Beautiful. Intelligent. And so erotic.

Slowly, slowly a smile spread across Pyotr's face.

She unpacked.

It was Markus who brought the news to Anna that her daughter had moved in with Pyotr. He had gone to the atelier in the Rue Boissonade to recover two books he had forgotten to bring away when decamping to the Rue des Beaux Arts, and it was Nathalie who had opened the door to him.

"She has greatly improved the place," he recounted, "with coloured rugs and cushions, and flowers everywhere. She's teaching Pyotr how to write."

"Surely he knows how to write?" Anna said.

"Not really," Markus said. "I mean he obviously knows how to spell words and write a sentence, but that doesn't make you a writer. If you think about it, he has scarcely had an education. Apart from a few tutors when he was a child in Asia, and then boarding school in England before he was called up, what's he done? Nothing. Instead of university he gets bombed and shelled in a trench from the age of seventeen onwards for four years, poor chap."

Anna nodded. You think you know somebody because you've slept with them. But you don't. She couldn't imagine Pyotr in a trench.

Paris Now.

"Here's a thing on the subject of Belanopek. The other day, browsing the stand of one of the *bouquiniste* on the Seine, George came across an old copy of 'Documents', Georges Bataille's short-lived magazine. It had this in it:

A MYSTERY

The riddle of P. A. Belanopek's life is a tapestry woven with threads of fantasy, embroidered with fabrications, laced together by an uncompromising artistic brilliance. Born on the leper's island of Molokai, Hawaii, in 1896, to aristocratic parents from Budapest in the Austro-Hungarian Empire, his early years were marked by privilege and diverse cultural infuences. However, tragedy struck with the untimely demise of his parents, leaving him an orphan in an English boarding school at the outbreak of World War I.

As the war engulfed Europe, Belanopek's Austro-German parentage obliged his return to his Prussian uncle in Bad Oldesloe, Germany. This stern man promptly enlisted the young boy in his private regiment to fight in the ranks of the Kaiser's forces, thrusting him into the brutal trenches to face the horrors of war. The innocence of his youth was shattered as he witnessed the carnage, and his involuntary killing of a schoolmate, fighting for the British, has left a profound scar on his soul.

Surviving the war, albeit wounded and emotionally scarred, Belanopek found himself recovering in a Parisian hospital. The aftermath of the confict cast a shadow over his existence, as he grappled with the horrors he experienced. Emerging France struggling to rebuild, he lived in extreme poverty, and the harsh realities of an expatriate's life.

But, as often happens, this crucible of adversity allowed Belanopek's artistic spirit to blossom. Turning to painting as a means of catharsis, he found solace and the courage to vanquish his phantoms in the ephemeral beauty of the invisible, in shadows and reflections and the fleeting nature of existence, the core themes of his early artworks.

He is known by his frst name, Pyotr, and only uses his surname to sign his work. His artistic aspirations have evolved, transcending mere catharsis. The experience of war has imparted a unique perspective on life for him, inspiring a profound appreciation for the beauty that surrounds us, particularly the clouds that adorn the skies that he, memorably, calls 'God's Canvas'. He delves into what he refers to as the concept of "Virtualism," using his artistic vision to capture the ethereal and ever-changing beauty of clouds, their transient shapes refracting the 'virtual' essence of non-existence.

Belanopek is an idiosyncratic, arcane visionary, not bound by the realm of academic reality, the 'virtual' part of his artist's life extending into the domain of fiction, inspiring tales, adding further layers to his shadowy persona, a continuum of his belief that who made something is of no importance, compared to the thing made. This Delphian artist's journey has taken him to foreign lands, where he has honed his craft informed by influential figures. His linguistic *talents facilitated connections, opening doors to various cultures and societies. To date his popular appeal has left its mark, captivating a wide audience with his unique approach to portraying transient beauty. Yet, even as his artistic fame continues to grow, he remains elusive, his near-manic insistence on privacy ensuring that the true details of his life remain elusive. This is the mystique that surrounds him. His work is there, in front of you; his whereabouts a tantalising puzzle, testament to the enduring allure of a life shrouded in enigma.*

Written in 1929. Bataille has a curious way of expressing himself, don't you think? *Mais c'est quand même intéressant, je trouve.*"

Chapter Eighteen

"You know you talk in your sleep?" Nathalie said. Even though it was nearly midday, she had only just woken up to take in dark clouds and rain running down the window facing west onto the mezzanine where Pyotr had his bed. Across the pillows, Pyotr opened his eyes to look at her. "In some funny language I can't understand, Swedish or Norwegian or something."

"Swedish," he said.

"I didn't know you spoke Swedish," she said.

"I don't. It's all a dream," he said.

"Aren't you meant to be at work?"

"Later."

Nathalie knew he had a job washing dishes in a restaurant on the Boulevard Montparnasse. Now she sat up, her curiosity piqued. "What do you dream about that makes you speak a language you don't know?"

Pyotr's gaze remained fixed on her. "It's strange, really," he began, "hard to explain. The dreams are like bits and pieces of a distant past, or perhaps another life altogether. I hear the words and phrases as if I were there, but the memory of them when I wake up doesn't make sense. I have no idea, no comprehension of their meaning, or even if they have meaning."

Nathalie's face was a mixture of fascination and concern. "Do you think they have a connection to your past, to the way you were brought up? Maybe to your heritage? Perhaps another life, some forgotten ancestral link?"

Pyotr's brow furrowed. "I don't know. It's possible, I suppose. My family's history is such a tangled mess, who knows what's in there." He let out a half-hearted chuckle. "Though it could just as easily be my mind's fancy, my subconscious conjuring up stuff. I don't think anyone knows what the mind hides away?"

Silence.

"So?" Nathalie said.

"So? So what, so?"

"So, are you going to tell me what you dreamt?"

He did.

Dreamland - 8

It was in November, 1645, that Christina honoured Lord Oxenstierna. Standing before the whole Senate, she acknowledged his conduct of the Peace of Prague in the complicated negotiations with the emperor and his allies (which, let it be said, in no way conformed to his wishes, but to hers.) As a mark of her favour, Christina conferred upon him the title of "Count," a rank so rare in Sweden that it belonged to only three families; and that the dignity should not be barren, she gave him at the same time a considerable domain which contained the entire district of Brömsebro where the treaty had been signed.

"My Lord Chancellor," she said. "Although other titles of honour have their value, it cannot be doubted that the title of Count is highest of all. Finding myself, by the grace of God, in a position to reward good and faithful service, I confer upon you this dignity, the first in the kingdom. I can say with truth and without injury to anyone else, that during the thirty-four years you have served my grandfather, my father, and myself, you have performed every duty entrusted to you in a manner worthy of a great minister of a great king."

"Laying it on with a trowel," Magnus muttered from where he stood in the crowd next to Petrus.

"Perhaps it hardly becomes me to speak thus of my father," the Queen went on, "but everyone knows that he made Sweden greater than she had ever been before, and he, therefore, deserves from us the name of Great. I will not dwell on your own actions, lest I offend your modesty. God and your own conscience are your witnesses that you had the full approbation of a great king whose good fortune it was to have you for his minister. It is

120

not the least of your merits that, although you laboured with him and assisted him with your advice, you still respected the King as your master."

"Crafty," Magnus whispered.

"When it pleased the Most High to take my father from me," the Queen said, fixing her Minister with a knowing look, "you, as Regent, ruled in my name with intelligence and forbearance, and, upon my majority, turned over to me all authority to rule the Swedish Empire."

Unblinking, ramrod straight despite his age, the Lord High Chancellor stood as still as a statue, staring at the Queen. Petrus wondered what he could be thinking. "What is it Cardinal Mazarin said of you?" The Queen paused theatrically for her audience to register the rhetorical question, then went smoothly on with the answer, "That if all the ministers of Europe were on a ship, the helm would be handed to you, my Lord. And it is with the greatest gratitude that I here publicly acknowledge your great skill in steering the good ship of Sweden into safe harbour. Pray kneel now, Lord Oxenstierna, and rise as Count of Södermöre!"

With care, Oxenstierna knelt on the kneeling stool before him, and with a ceremonial sword the Queen tapped him first on the right shoulder and then the left. Handing the sword off to an attendant, she then, in an unconventional but most natural manner, held out her hand to the aged nobleman and said, "Come, let me help you up."

A telling gesture, much commented by the murmuring Court.

"What a woman!" Markus said in admiration. He and Petrus drifted to the fringe of the crowd where they could talk without being overheard. "She never fails to surprise me," he continued. "Did I ever tell you what happened the very night after her coronation?"

The way he told it was like a play.

A SIGN: MID-SUMMER, STOCKHOLM HARBOUR - CLOSE TO MIDNIGHT, IN THE STRANGE HALF-LIGHT OF THE SUN JUST BELOW THE HORIZON.

A tavern door slams, and two young sailors stagger across the wharf to where a small sailboat is tied. Quickly they climbed aboard, cast off the mooring lines, set the sails and beat into a light wind, headed out across the harbour to the open sea.

In silhouette, the figure at the tiller calls to the one at the sheets. "Thank God, I'm out of that white dress. *This* is freedom." And laughs as a wave slaps the bow. "You looked so beautiful…all the men did nothing but adjust their codpieces." More laughter, as the boat heels over in a little gust.

"I think I'm a bit drunk." The helmsman shivers. "It's cold out here."

"Me too. There's the light of Brumsviken! I see the islands - what do you think?"

"Twenty minutes and then a hot, hot…"

"Sauna!" They both say together, squealing in delight.

A SMALL ISLAND, LATER

As the boat scrunches ashore on a shingle beach and is hauled up above the waterline by the two laughing sailors, they suddenly notice another beached boat. They stop laughing, look at each other, perplexed. "Who can be here at this hour?" the helmsman said.

"I smell wood-smoke…it's…look, it's from your sauna."

And effectively, from the chimney of a tiny, log cabin outlined against the sky above the beach, smoke climbs upwards in one long, thin spiral.

A WOODEN SAUNA, LIT BY ONE LAMP AND THE GLOW OF EMBERS IN A STONE HEARTH, AS THE DOOR OPENS AND THE TWO SAILORS COME IN TO THE SHOCK OF SEEING THE FABLED, MUSCULAR, SWEATING, NAKED BODY OF MAGNUS STRETCHED OUT ALONG A SLATTED PINE BENCH.

Without moving a finger, Magnus opens one eye. "Ah!" he said, "the navy has arrived…a few sheets to the wind, eh?"

"This is presumptuous, even for you, my Lord Magnus!" The helmsman's voice would have frozen the Bering Straits. "You are not of royal blood. Why are you trespassing on my land?"

"Who knows?" Magnus said. "If I am going to trespass on the Queen's person, it might as well be on her land. Since what is going to happen between us will happen sooner or later, I prefer sooner. Come, stop your masquerade and crown your celebration on the staff of life." With a flourish, he indicates his tumescent member.

Christina laughed. "You've got a nerve. How can you be so sure?"

"The Gods dictate these things," Magnus said.

"And if you give me the pox?"

"Then half the ladies in your Court have it. Ask her." He nods at Ebba, blushing behind the Queen.

"So the Queen comes after her maid?" Christina said.

"Blame not the maid," Magnus said. "Queens tend to keep a man waiting while they make up their minds and this fellow (now in full erection) cannot wait."

"Then let us be mindful," Christina said, pulling off her sailor's jacket. "But first put out the light."

"You know what I did then?" Magnus said to Petrus. "I got off the bench, picked up the lamp, put it on the floor and crushed it with my bare foot!"

"You did what, Magnus?" Christina said.

It startled both men, neither having noticed the Queen approaching.

Chapter Nineteen

"That's when I woke up," Pyotr said.

By then there was a break in the clouds, and it had stopped raining. A weak sun began a slow descent in the West, casting a golden hue across the atelier.

"Mon Dieu! You're so lucky. I can never remember my dreams," Nathalie said, "and now I'm starving."

"Me too," Pyotr said. "There's not much in the kitchen, but I'll try to make us something."

He was lying. They had eaten every scrap of food in the house. They were broke. Neither moved from where they lay, and Nathalie found herself smiling in the warm unspoken complicity they shared.

"We can always go to my mother's," she said, nestling into the curve of Pyotr's arm. Pyotr chuckled, his eyes tracing the contours of her face.

"You think?"

"Oh, she'd feed us. *Elle n'est pas rancunière, tu sais.* She doesn't carry a grudge just because you did it with her and now you're with me."

"What?"

"Have I shocked you?" Nathalie grinned, tracing patterns on his chest with her fingertips. "I meant to ask you, is there a difference? You know, when you're in her, and when you're in me?"

"What!" Pyotr tried to sit up.

"O la la, now you really are shocked. Lie down," she ordered, a thread of thought unravelling. "I'm just curious. Sometimes I wonder if a penis can think. Or is it all random?"

124

Pyotr was speechless. He sank back into the pillow.

"I suppose that's the beauty of following it," Nathalie said. "You never know who it will meet or what will happen. Everything is ruled by uncertainty. Look at us."

"And you call me weird?" Pyotr said.

"Each of us is unique," Nathalie went on, ignoring him, "but coming" - she laughed at her own pun - "together makes something harmonious, right? I think so. Anyway, if you can't tell the difference, what's the point? It's all pure chance, a bit like your paintings," she said, her words light, a brushstroke, curious. "I've often wondered, how do artists like you choose colours, decide which ones to use?"

"Seriously?" Pyotr rested his head against his hand. "In my case it was the other way around, the colours chose me, since I had to use whatever I found dumped in old Phillipon's box. They have a way of conjuring up unspoken feelings that words can't reach, like they speak in a language of emotions; you don't so much choose them, you listen, you feel."

Pause. Silence. It started to rain again.

Nathalie gazed up at the ceiling, her thoughts adrift. "So if you could color your feelings right now," she said, "what would they be?"

"Deep indigo," Pyotr said, "for the quiet surface, carmine red for the fire below, the simmering pulse under us."

Nathalie wrinkled her nose. "That's such a cliché. What about in these mysterious dreams where you speak Swedish?"

Pyotr frowned, remembering. "Ah, the dreams…thick white, slashed on with a palette knife, imperial purple, a bit of emerald-green hidden in corners, a dance to the unknown, the mystical…"

Nathalie's eyes danced. She rolled off him. "*Comme toi* you mean, unknowable and mystical; you the canvas full of tall stories waiting for an audience?"

Pyotr said nothing, reached out, his fingers gently brushing a strand of hair away from her face, then continuing down her nose, her lips, her chin, the hollow of her throat, down and down, breasts, ribs, belly, down and down, a canvas of endless possibilities. Their eyes met, locked. Words dissolved, leaving only a tangled complexity, the air between them choked with passion. Finally, blinking, Nathalie broke the spell. She said, "You know something, I think maybe life is just an unfinished canvas with big empty spaces. We don't know what's going to go in them but we keep adding stuff, mixing colours, and experimenting until we either fuck it up or create something beautiful, even if it's not always perfect."

Pyotr could only stare at her. 16, he thought again. Beautiful. Intelligent. Erotic. "Yes, maybe," his fingers stop short of their target. "Like you say, a work in progress, but I have to get out of bed right now or I'll be fired for showing up late."

As more and more frequently when broke, he had joined the queue of the destitute, out-of-work, out-of-luck, famished workmen outside the Dingo Bar at 10, Rue Delambre, a narrow street in the 14th behind *Le Dôme*. Jimmy, the barman, a former lightweight boxing champion from Liverpool, vetted the lineup of those hoping to be picked by M. Vapetto, a large toad-like figure ensconced in his booth at the back of the bar next to the toilets, who daily distributed the jobs as 'plongeurs' in the big cafés on the Boulevard Montparnasse: *La Rotonde, Le Select, La Coupole* and *Le Dôme*. No one knew how such a crapulous individual came upon this sinecure, but if you needed the work that's where you went, and you gave him his cut of the daily pittance you earned whether you liked it or not since the restaurants paid him and not you. They had an *'arrangement'* with *Le Vap,* as he was called, which ensured, in an ever-changing economic landscape, that they were guaranteed labour from 6 o'clock in the morning when the cleaners went in, to well past midnight when the last dishes were washed and the shutters went up.

A *'plongeur'* was the lowest of the low in the hierarchy of a restaurant, working a minimum 12-hour shift with only a 30-minute break between lunch and dinner, standing at a metal sink washing dishes, glasses, pots and pans, in an endless round of service, enveloped in boiling water, steam, scrubbing brushes, liquid soap that took the skin off your hands, garbage bins which were always full and a constant stream of abuse from the cooks and the waiters yelling at you for something you didn't have. Most plongeur never looked up from where they were working, intent only on swiping left-over food as the plates came in and tossing back the dregs of wine in unfinished glasses.

The pains started soon after the first hour bent over the sinks. First in your lower back, then your legs and finally your feet. The din made your head throb. As the hours went by, it grew worse. No amount of stretching, rubbing or bending seemed to work - only suffering. After 12 hours even the most hardened were reduced to sweating wrecks. And there was no point in complaining if you needed the money, something Jimmy took pains to point out to Pyotr on the first day he showed up for work.

"From your accent you're a Brit, right?" Jimmy said.

"Close enough." Pyotr said.

"Show me your hands," Jimmy said.

Pyotr held out his hands for inspection.

"You've not done this before," Jimmy sniffed. It was not a question. He eyed Pyotr.

"The bizzies lookin' for you?"

"No."

"It's bums' work, won't even keep you in bifters. You sure?"

"Yes."

"You got gloves?"

"No."

"Ask me, you'll need 'em with hands like that. We'll get you kitted out. The price will be deducted from your pay. Oh, and no geggin' in on what cut Monsieur V takes. He'll get a real cob on if he hears about it, an' you'll be out on your ear, got it?"

Pyotr nodded.

"Good lad," Jimmy said. "End of each week you'll owe me a bevvy."

Most nights when he got home after work, Pyotr was so tired he hardly had the strength to undress before falling asleep and he brought the stench of the restaurant kitchens into the bedroom. Nathalie endured the smell and the comatose state of her mate for the first few days after she moved in, and then took her problem to her confidante, the concierge, Madame Lucette. This worthy lady, who had at first viewed the girl with some suspicion, was delighted to be consulted. It came about in the most natural way. Seeing Nathalie airing the stinky sheets and pillowcases on the clothesline in the backyard every morning, Madame Lucette, naturally curious as is every concierge worthy of the name, enquired what was going on? *"Qu'est-ce qui se passe?"* she said, coming into the yard wiping her hands on her apron, *"c'est quoi ce cinéma?"* Nathalie told her.

The concierge shook her head. *"Ma pauvre. Il faut savoir souffrir sans se plaindre,"* she said. "Your man has been in the war. He has no *métier*. He tries to earn a few *sous* to put food on your table. Instead of grumbling you must help him and in the process help yourself. It is like this. When he comes home you must be up to greet him, with a warm bath already drawn. You must help him to undress and then wash his hair and his shoulders, and his back. *Doucement.* Gently. Very gently. Then you put him in his pyjamas and take him to bed, where he will love you and fall asleep in your arms and the clean scent of fresh soap." This from a woman who had only ever known one man, whom she married days before he was called up and got himself killed on the bloodiest day in French military history, 22nd August 1914, in the Ardennes, along with 26,999 other French soldiers, four times more than died at Waterloo. "Ah, you smile? You think this will not work? Try it and see."

Nathalie tried. It worked.

From then on Nathalie found herself adopted by Madame Lucette, a relationship she embraced, much like the one she had had with Marie with whom she had often been left as a small child when her mother was out. It got so that whenever Pyotr was at work, she would trot down the stairs to the Concierge's lodge to lend a hand if there was something that needed doing, have a chat and share a bite, Madame Lucette knowing the girl only ate whatever scraps Pyotr brought home. This was survival in a land of plenty, where, if you had the money, anything could be bought, and if you didn't, you starved. With the food came talk. What about? Everything.

"Je me sens vieille," Madame Lucette said one morning. *"Bientôt le trou."*

"Don't say that!" Nathalie said.

"Why not? It's true. One of these days I'll be in a hole in the ground." She shrugged. "You know, when I was born in '75, life expectancy for a woman in France was about thirty-five, and now it's fifty. It says so in the Journal. 50. Exactly my age next month."

"You don't believe what they write in the newspapers, do you?" Nathalie said. "Pyotr says half of it is lies and the rest is fiction."

"Rubbish. Numbers don't lie. Back in the eighteenth century, 50% of all children died before they were ten. Now it's closer to 5%. That's progress. Goes to show how much medical care and medicines have improved. But there's no magic pill to prolong life. That's why I always say enjoy it while you can!" For a moment Lucette's eyes went to the faded sepia photograph of her long dead husband in his soldier's uniform hanging over the fireplace. "Imagine. In my fifty years I have seen the advent of the automobile, the telephone and the aeroplane. Fifty years from now it will be 1975 and you will only be sixty-six years old and probably live to eighty. Think of all the new things you will see that nobody has even invented."

And all the men I haven't yet met, Nathalie thought - and was amazed when Madame Lucette said, as if divining where her mind had gone, "I hope you're being careful?"

"Careful?"

"You know what I mean. With him."

Nathalie blushed.

"You're too young to get knocked up."

"Don't worry, I use a diaphragm. My mother got me one when I was fourteen."

"Wise woman. Nothing can blight a life like having a kid too soon."

"Are you sorry you have no children?"

"No. I thank God. I would hate to bring up a child without a father."

"It hasn't hurt me."

"Oh, pardon, *chérie*, I'm clumsy. I didn't mean it as a criticism. You must miss your Papa."

"Not really. I was five when he went off to war. Maman never said anything when he didn't come back. I can hardly remember him."

"Even so. Be careful."

When Pyotr came home that night Nathalie told him what Madame Lucette said. They were in bed after his bath and she had him in her hand and he was just getting hard and her words had no effect at all until he was in her doing all the things she liked, on and on, and got her arching her back reaching for a familiar crescendo, when he suddenly stopped. Just like that. For the longest moment. Still in her, hard, unmoving.

"Don't stop," she said.

'I'm practicing," he said.

"What?" she said.

"Being careful," he said.

Chapter Twenty

Nathalie walked out of Pyotr's life the same way she walked in. Packed her suitcase and left. No explanation. No letter. No excuse. Pyotr came home from work one night and she was gone. It fell to the concierge to tell him. "*Mon pauvre Monsieur.* She has gone. It was inevitable, was it not? Someone so young! How can she know her own mind? *Ne t'en fais pas.* I have made a fine daube for us. Come. Sit. Eat with me."

Over a delicious lamb stew and a pitcher of Côte du Rhone, this generous woman consoled her lodger, serendipity worked its magic, and it was only the next morning, when waking up with him in her bed, that it occurred to her she was the same number of years older than Pyotr as Nathalie was younger. She could see no significance in this fact, but it made her smile. And it was her smile Pyotr saw when he opened his eyes.

"Well, here we are," he said.

"Disappointed?"

"No. You?"

"No. You are only the second man I have ever known. I never thought it would happen again." An image of the sepia photograph of her husband flashed across her mind. She made the sign of the cross. "Thank you."

Pyotr never imagined this chance coupling would lead to him writing screenplays in Hollywood. But it did.

It happened one night Pyotr came home to find Lucette in the atelier that she now shared with him entertaining a friend. "This is Alice, Alice

Guy," she said. "Don't mind us, we're just gossiping. Your bath is ready. When you finish, come down and join us for a glass of wine."

Having bathed, Pyotr put on a dressing gown over his pajamas and joined the ladies. "Alice thinks you are very handsome," Lucette said, "and that you should be in the movies."

Pyotr laughed.

"It's true," Lucette said. "Didn't you say that, Alice?"

"Yes," Alice said, "but I also said you should fatten him up. He's too thin."

"I agree." Lucette said. "Exactly my feeling. But they like him thin at the Grand Chaumiere." The Grand Chaumiere was an art school on the Rue de la Grande Chaumiere where she occasionally modelled to make a few francs, and she had taken Pyotr with her once when Ossip Zadkine spotted him. Zadkine was a sculptor who also taught art at the school and had often lusted after 'La Divine Lucette' as he called her, always trying to lure her to his studio on the Rue d'Assas. He thought Lucette had brought Pyotr along as a gift for him, but bore no grudge when being informed of his error. *'C'est votre amant!'* he said. *'Formidable! Quel bel homme. Vraiment. Giacometti va être jaloux et Modi dingue.'*

"Anyway, Alice has just come back from America," Lucette went on, "and she was telling me of the dreadful night her entire studio in New Jersey was burnt to the ground and she lost everything, including all her films!"

"Her films?" Pyotr said, looking at Alice.

Alice nodded. "I've made a few," she said modestly.

"A few! She's made hundreds. She invented the cinema." Lucette said. "You must have seen some - *'Madame a des envies', 'La Naissance et la Vie de Christ', 'Le Fou et son Argent', 'La Femme Collante', 'Au Bal de Flore'* - I can't possibly remember all of them!"

"Mon Dieu," Pyotr said, now staring at Alice, "you made those? Of course, I"ve seen them. I had no idea they were made by a woman. What a privilege it is to meet you." He made a gracious bow. "I am fascinated. How did you get into that business?"

"Pure luck," Alice said. "I was a secretary in a company that was sold to Gustave Eiffel back in 1895 -"

"Incredible!" Pyotr interrupted. "Did you know this was his atelier when he was building the Tower?"

"I know," Alice said. "Lucette told me. Eiffel was trying to stay out of jail back then and survive the Panama Canal scandal, so he put the company in the name of the manager, Léon Gaumont, and I ended up working for him. We sold cameras and lenses and all kinds of accessories and to demonstrate what they could do, Gaumont had his cameraman shoot endless scenes of workers leaving the factory, horses pulling ploughs and donkeys going around and around threshing grain. You can imagine how boring that was once you'd seen it five or six times. I suggested we should tell little stories with a plot, like small, photographed plays, and somewhat to my surprise, Léon let me try, and the audience loved them. Pretty soon every picture house was showing moving pictures instead of repetitious panoramas. There is nothing in making movies that a woman can't do as easily as a man. The only problem is making men understand that. Lucky for me, Léon did, and he made me head of production from 1896 to 1906 and, when I married my head cameraman the following year, sent us off to America to run Gaumont over there."

"Where she founded her own company, had two kids while making hundreds and hundreds of films, as screenwriter, director, producer and even actress in some of them. She made the first film with an all-black cast. Before Hollywood, her company was the most important one in America. Tell him, Alice. Stop being so humble," Lucette said.

Alice blushed. "*Voyons,* Lucette, please - you will embarrass me," she said.

"How did you two meet?" Pyotr said, looking from one to the other.

"Chance," Alice said. "We were both born in Saint-Mandé. We were playmates before my mother carted me off to Chile. I'm a year older, I think, right Lucette?"

"Yes," Lucette said. "You're 1873, I'm '74."

Extraordinary, Pyotr thought, two lives and two such different trajectories. Extraordinary, Alice thought, I once had everything and now I'm divorced, alone and penniless and she gets to live with this lovely man.

Extraordinary, Lucette thought, she's so famous and has done so much and I am unknown and done nothing.

"The strangest thing," Alice said, "after I finished each one of those films, I would look at them and wonder who made them. Colette, who's exactly my age, has written *'Ne fallait-il, pour en arriver là, que trente ans de ma vie? Je finirai par croire que ce n'était pas payer trop cher.'* And her husband, Willy, used to sign her work, just as my husband, Herbert, did mine. God, the way women are treated! Of course it's *'trop cher'*. Why do we put up with it? Sometimes I feel like a doormat."

"Don't say that!" Lucette said. "It's amazing what you've done."

"It is," Pyotr chimed in. "But…May I ask you a question?"

"Of course," Alice said.

"How in heaven do you invent hundreds of stories?"

"Easy. Whatever comes into your head, like dreams; movies are illustrated dreams."

Lucette laughed. "Dreams? Wait till he tells you about the one he's living in!"

Dreamland - 9

'I am a pageboy, carrying a beautiful, elaborately painted wooden box, attending King Gustavus, dressed in black satin, with a blue silk sash running diagonally from his shoulder to an elaborate bow at his waist. We enter the antechamber outside Christina's bedroom, a high-ceilinged, darkly-curtained room, lit by candles, where several ladies-in-waiting in attendance to the Princess immediately drop into a deep curtsey before the King. "Is Kerstin asleep?" the King asks.

"No Papa," Christina says from the other side of her bedroom door. "Come and see me."

Christina's bedroom is undoubtedly the strangest bedroom for a 5-year-old girl ever seen. It is festooned with war banners, maps, swords, pistols, assorted arms and bits of rusting armour. She sits up on gold and pale blue pillows with a gold quilt spread across the bed beneath a silk and brocade canopy in the colours of Sweden. Two enormous candelabras on either side of the bed bounce light off her ash-blonde hair. As the King enters, he pauses to look at his daughter and in the smiles they exchange there is an evident delight and complicity shared by them, a loving bond that, for a moment, makes me jealous. "So, daughter," the King says, "why are you not sleeping?"

Christina giggles, as if this were a well-known game. "I am waiting for you," she says. "You promised me a surprise."

"And you shall have it," the King says, clambering onto the bed, making himself comfortable next to her. "Come, Petrus, put the box between us." I do as instructed.

Christina's eyes are sparkling. "Oh, Papa, what's in it?" she says.

135

"Be patient, my child. First inspect the outside."

With her nose practically glued to the wood, the small girl examines the box, the top and each side of which is divided into eight painted panels, each representing a different city in flames, with its major architectural features surmounted by a flag and coat-of-arms writhed in smoke. In the centre of the lid is an equestrian painting in a gold-framed medallion of the King on a snorting white war-horse. "Now," Gustavus says, "let's see what you can identify."

"That's easy, Papa," Christina says. "In the middle, this is you on old Streiff." She taps the lid. "Then this is the flag of Mainz" - tap - "this is Neumark" - tap - "this is the shield of Nuremberg, this of Bohemia, this Bavaria, and this Franconia" - turning the box in her hands as she speaks - "and this Swabia...and this one Saxony. Oh, Papa these...these are your victories! Here is Leipzig, and Meissen and Prague - Prague? You haven't taken Prague yet, have you?"

"That's why it's not burning."

And, effectively, the only city not on fire in the panels is Prague - which is the moment Queen Maria Eleonora chose to come into the room. "This is quite unsuitable for a little girl," she says. "You will only excite her unnecessarily."

"OH, Mama!" Christina says.

"'Tis a pity, Madam, that you do not have the same grasp and interest in the affairs of state as our daughter," the King says. "You should be proud of her knowledge. What child would know a fraction -"

"She's a child. She should be playing with dolls!" the Queen interrupts.

The King snorts his contempt. "*These* are her dolls!" he says, flipping open the lid of the box to reveal the serried ranks of an exquisite hand-carved, hand-painted set of miniature soldiers. Christina squeals.

"OH, Papa, how beautiful!" she says. "Can I touch them?"

"Of course!" Gustavus says. "Let us take them out. See, these are our colours and these are the colours of the Habsburg and their allies..." the quilt becomes the battleground of an imaginary war with the rival toy armies aligned and arrayed behind specific features, with the King's blue sash used as a river. "Let this represent the Rippach, see how it goes here, between these hills, with a bend towards the west where you are? Upon this escarpment -" he pinches the quilt to make a hill - "are our cannon and because we command the high ground we can fire down directly on Wallenstein and his troops…"

Ignored, the Queen sadly leaves the room.

Now I, Pyotr, see it, the vast panorama of war. I crouch next to my father in the shadow of the windmills on the bluff commanded by Count Wallenstein, the richest nobleman in Bohemia, Generalissimo of the Armies of his Imperial Majesty, the Emperor Ferdinand. There in the distance is a highway, bisected by the Rippach, leading to the cities of Lutzen and Markranstadt. Wallenstein's forces occupy deep trenches on this side of the road, planted with musketeers supported by batteries of cannon, plus small fieldpieces on such eminences as can be found. Three hundred paces away are five brigades of infantry, flanked by cavalry - in all 70,000 men.

Across from us, at a slight elevation, Gustavus Adolphus has his artillery to his front facing our trenches, with two lines behind formed of small squadrons of horse interspersed among divisions of infantry. He has troops of musketeers placed strategically among the cavalry, holding the flanks on either side of the river - in all 45,000 men.

Time stands still the better to enjoy a fine day dawning and, as a breeze clears the morning mist and reveals the disposition of the rival armies, my father sends me off on a scouting mission behind the enemy lines. Nobody suspects a young lad in rags among the other non-combatants, particularly one with a basket of bread loaves for sale, and I wander at will unchallenged, making conversation and giving change to hungry soldiers with pennies to spend. No one seems in a hurry to start the fight.

Presently I see the King as he rides between the lines to review his troops surrounded by his aides and courtiers and even a prelate or two, chattering amongst themselves, much as if they were on their way to a picnic. I draw closer.

Now he dismounts and kneels before his men. His head goes back, his hands stretch out to the sky above. In a clear voice, he says, "Hear me, our

God," as row upon row the army kneels before their King, while overhead the blue and gold banner of Sweden waves and snaps in the breeze.

To this day I hear his voice, the words so enunciated you would think he kneels in church not on a battlefield: "This contest, long delayed, whose decisive consequence all Europe awaits, now pits our noble force against a worthy foe. Matched in renown and ability, our daring must be cooled by council lest our fired blood, lusting after victory, overmatches our smaller numbers against these well-entrenched Imperialists. Tomorrow, one leader, hitherto invincible, must acknowledge his defeat and to his victor bow. Doubtful victory can but be earned by hard labour and bloodshed. Let every private here share the emotion that inflames our bosom."

A pause. Not a soldier moves. In the distance I hear a sweet bird sing.

"Hear me, O God!" the King says. "I do not lightly or wantonly involve myself and my faithful people in this new and dangerous war. As You are my witness, I do not fight to gratify my ambition. But the Emperor has wronged me most shamefully. He has supported my enemies, persecuted my friends, trampled my religion in the dust and stretched his revengeful arm against my crown. I am fully sensible of the dangers to which my life will be exposed. I have never yet shrunk from them, nor do I ask to escape them now. Providence has wonderfully protected me, my country, and my men, but if at last I should fall, I commend you, my comrades, to the protection of Heaven."

Another pause, as the King lowers his head to look directly into the eyes of a trooper kneeling in front of him. "Be just, be conscientious, act uprightly," he says, "until we meet again in eternity. God be with us!"

Then, from the assembled troops, like rolling thunder, his words are echoed in a roar: "GOD BE WITH US!"

Now the King stands to survey those around him. "To you Chancellor Oxenstierna and my councilors of state, I address myself first. May God enlighten you and fill you with wisdom to promote the welfare of my people and the care and education of my legal heir, Princess Christina, until her maturity. You, too, my brave nobles, I commend to divine protection. Continue to prove yourselves the worthy successors of those Gothic heroes whose bravery humbled to dust the mighty pride of ancient Rome. To you, ministers of religion, I recommend moderation and unity; be yourselves examples of the virtues you preach and abuse not your influence over the minds of our people. To you of the Guilds and the Peasants Estates, I give my especial thanks for your unfailing support, and I entreat the blessings of Heaven on you; may your industry be rewarded; your harvests prosperous; your stores plenteously filled and may you be crowned with all the blessings of this life."

A pause.

"I now ask that all non-combatants withdraw from the field."

I am among the last to leave and just hear the King say, "To you men who will now fight with me I offer my warmest prayers to Heaven. We are in good company. Look at the banners of our great commanders..." and as he recites the names, each noble mounts up and, preceded by his fluttering standard, rides to his allotted command "...Field Marshall Gustavus Horn...the Rheingrave Otto Lewis...Count Thurn...the Elector Ottenburg...General Banner...the Prince of Bandissen..."

And in my dream, I hear the small voice of Christina in her bedroom "...General Teufel...Field Marshall Åke Tott...the Count von Falkenberg...Baron Knyphausen..." moving the toy soldiers to their designated place on the quilt watched closely by her father until there is nobody left, which is when the King says "...the Prince Christina Vasa!" taking from his pocket, where he had concealed it, the carved figure of Christina mounted on a beautiful black pony and placed it on the quilt at the head of the Protestant army and in my mind I again heard the tremendous roar of the troops: "GUD VARE MED OSS! GOD BE WITH US!"

"So my ferocious warrior - are you ready?" the King says. "Fire the cannons! We march to war!"

And the little girl, quite unafraid, with drums beating and trumpets blaring, kicks her heels into her pony. Holding a burning taper, she rides behind a battery of massive cannon touching the flame to each gun port, igniting the powder, while the troops cheer each thunderous explosion. The cannons belch smoke and flame. Swords flash. The cavalry charges a hedgehog of pikes. Men and beasts are shattered; walls are blasted; buildings are burned; shot-torn war-banners are shredded; over the anguished yells and screams of the wounded and dying, the bark of command: CHARGE!

FIRE! STAND! STEADY! AIM! FIRE! The sleeping child rolls over in bed; in her mind's eye a map of the endless campaigns fought by her father; she silently mouths the names: Minden, Neuberg, Callemberg, Magdeburg, Halberstadt, Stettin, Damm, Stargard, Camin, Wolgast…and always, always, the blue and gold banner of Sweden moving forward, relentlessly moving forward to a relentless drumbeat.'

Out of breath, Pyotr stopped talking. Now it was Alice's turn to stare. "My God," she said, "I could have used you in Hollywood. Forget about writing novels, man. You should write screenplays. I know exactly who you should meet, my old *scénariste*, Louis Feuillade. He's written more films than even I have made."

Paris Now.

"That didn't work out, right, George?"

"Yes. Feuillade was dead. Died at his place in Nice in February 1925, and about a month after that Belanopek was stuck in the nick. No fault of his - in fact a complete balls-up by the cops, accusing him of having something to do with that old lawyer falling down the stairs and breaking his neck. It was all over the papers back then."

Le Petit Journal, Mars 2, 1925
Mort dans la Rue des Beaux-Arts - un faussaire accusé !

A retired lawyer, Maître Léon Legrand, 92, was found dead this morning on the landing of the 5th floor of the tenement in which he lived by a maid, Mlle. Marie-Laure, on her way down to work from her chambre de bonne on the 7th floor of the same building. The police were immediately called, and it was the médecin légiste who established that death was due to a broken neck. How it was broken is a matter of conjecture. Mlle. Géraldine Espinasse, a co-owner of the property, gave her opinion - 'Ask for yourself, he obviously fell down the stairs, but then also ask, what was he doing up there, since his apartment was on the 1st floor?' Inspecteur Tropois, of the Commissariat de Police, Rue Bonaparte, in charge of the inquiry, must answer this question.

"Like all professions having to do with violence and death," he said, *"it is of the utmost importance to maintain a sound distinction between the nervous and the mental systems. It does not help to speculate. The victim was found dead on the 5th floor. Alors? The usual investigations will be made. Answers will be found. It would appear to be a banal accident. But if it were not, rest assured, the culprit will be unmasked and apprehended."* A search was then made of the apartment of feu Maître Legrand, where it was discovered that he kept a daily journal in which he recorded in meticulous detail his many contacts and conversations. Here it was learned of his petition to the co-tenants of the building about the illegal renovations planned for the bar on the ground floor and his frustration at being repulsed, leading to his threatening a lawsuit against the owners and their so-called artist/décorateur, Belanopek, a foreigner, no papers, an undoubted forger, obliged to hide his true identity under a nom-de-pinceau. This man, it was discovered, had recently moved to a new address in the 14th arrondissement and it was there he was apprehended, and held en garde-à-vue in La Santé Prison, where executions by guillotine of those found guilty of murder are conducted on the pavement at the junction of the Boulevard Arago and the Rue de la Santé.

Chapter Twenty-one

"It is beyond obscene!" Victorine Espinasse struck the open newspaper where it lay on the counter of the bar, with an image on the front page of Pyotr, manacled and chained, held at the elbow by two gendarmes. "How can they dare insinuate he had anything to do with this? He wasn't even here when that old fool fell down the steps. I'm going to go to the station and give this macaroni- brained *Inspecteur* a talking-to."

"I'll go with you!" her sister said.

"And I," said M. Faccini.

"Me too!" said M. Doumeng.

All the regulars in the bar volunteered their support and led by the two old ladies, this motley crew stormed up Rue Bonaparte to confront the *Inspecteur*. Of course, having no appointment, they were kept waiting. And waiting. Outside it began to rain. And still they waited, seated on the hard wooden benches provided, in the stale air of the police station, combining the pungent fug of stale second-hand cigarette smoke, disinfectant, human sweat and urine wafting up from two drunken tramps lying in a holding cell. As inevitably happens, sitting there on the hard bench, they had time for second thoughts.

"Is this wise?" Geraldine whispered to her sister. "The press asking questions about illegal renovations?"

"I have the same apprehension," Victorine said. You do not come from the Auvergne for nothing. A long heritage of caution, of not rushing into the unknown, of the conservative measurement of risk, in-bred over centuries of war and conquest, had taught the lesson - the hammer head seeks the tallest nail. Much better to crouch down. "Anyway, we've waited long enough," she said, standing up. "We'll send a letter of complaint."

And just as they had followed her to the police station, the regulars followed her back to the bar where they arrived damp, but ready for a drink.

"Comme des moutons," M. Doumeng said to M. Faccini.

Faccini shrugged. *"Vous avez autres choses à faire?"*

"Non."

"Alors..Pastis?"

It was left to Didier, the waiter, on his return from work at the Café des Beaux-Arts, to contact Pyotr in jail after Marie-Laure told him the news when she bumped into him on the 7th floor.

"Le pauvre," Didier said. "What are they doing to get him out?"

"Nothing really," Marie-Laure said. "Writing letters is just saving face. They're more concerned about who pays for the funeral and having to relet his flat."

"Typical," Didier said. "Do you know where Pyotr is being held?"

"La Santé."

"Putain. Has he been charged?"

"I don't think so. Not yet. He's *en garde-à-vue.*" Marie-Laure sniffed. "You can't just waltz in there, you know. You're not his lawyer. You have to have a reason."

"Clean clothes," Didier said, and, off Marie-Laure's incomprehension which showed clearly on her face, added, "you're allowed to bring them clean clothes."

It worked. Didier turned up with an ironed old shirt and pair of pants and the guards let him in to see Pyotr. To his surprise he found Pyotr unchained and in good spirits when he was brought into the parloir. "Five minutes," a guard said.

Pyotr smiled. "So you found me," he said to Didier.

"Marie-Laure told me you were in here," Didier said. "You okay? How are they treating you?"

"*Pas mal.* Somehow, they found out I was decorated after Verdun," Pyotr said. "There are a lot of veterans here and they came to see me. The news got to the Governor and so he came to shake my hand, called me a hero, and offered me a private cell, but I told him I was fine bunking with the lads. Compared to the trenches, better than a suite at the Ritz. It made him laugh, but he's stuck me in solitary for my own protection he says."

Didier couldn't imagine that there was much to laugh about in prison.

"I'm glad you came," Pyotr said. "I know Lucette has been trying to see me -"

"Lucette?" Didier said.

"My woman. They wouldn't let her in. She will be worried sick. Could you find the time to see her and tell her I am okay and not to worry, I'll be out soon?"

"Of course," Didier said, but couldn't help thinking what made Pyotr sure he would be out soon. He asked: "How do you know you'll be out soon?"

"Well, I wasn't there, was I? In fact, I never met the bloke, so how could I push him down the stairs?"

"Easy to say. Can you prove it?"

"I've told them where I was working. All they have to do is find Le Vap. He'll confirm it."

"Le Vap? The guy in the Rue Delambre?"

"Yes. You know him?"

Didier nodded. Like every waiter looking for work he'd had dealings with Le Vap. The idea that he would vouch for Pyotr...? Talk about optimism, Didier thought, but didn't say. Instead, he said, "You know Jimmy, the boxer?"

"Of course. How do you think I got any work?"

"Bien. At least he's straight. I'll go see him; maybe work something out. But it will take time. You going to be okay?"

"Three meals a day and a roof over my head for free?" Pyotr laughed. "I even have time to think. If it wasn't for Lucette -"

"One minute," the guard interrupted.

144

The two men stood up from where they sat, shook hands, kissed each other on both cheeks and, as he was being led away, Pyotr turned back to Didier and said, "Don't forget, Lucette."

"That's what he said," Didier told Jimmy. "Bugger's in jail on a suspected murder charge and all he's worried about is the girlfriend." They were talking out in the street where they could not be overheard. "Gave me the address and all. I went by to see her, turns out she's the concierge where he lives. Banging the concierge, can you believe it? Anyway, her worry is that he'll lose his loft if he doesn't pay his rent and how's he going to do that if he's locked up? You think Le Vap will give him an alibi?"

Jimmy snorted, then dropped his voice. "Can't, can he? The way he runs his business everything's under the table, no books, no records, no tax." He glanced back at the Dingo to make sure no one was coming out of the bar. "It's got to be done on the q.t. Who's the copper on this thing?"

"Tropois. Rue Bonaparte."

"Okay. I'll ask around, see if he's on the take. Most are, but it will cost a few bob. And there's no guarantee it will be quick."

"Merde."

"You can say that again."

In the end it took two months. Yopi, the Dutch wife of the American owner of the Dingo, Louis Wilson, knew the *patron, M. Pléget,* of the newly-opened brasserie, *Le Select,* on the corner of Rue Vavin and Boulevard Montparnasse, who had a client who was the *Commissaire* in charge of the police station on the Rue Bonaparte. A quiet chat here, a quiet chat there. The suggestion that perhaps an error had been made. The man was a war hero, etcetera, and working in the *Quatorzième* when the accident occurred, so how could he have been in the *Sixième?* etcetera. The charges were dropped. Lucette, Didier and Jimmy, were waiting for Pyotr when he walked out through the metal door of the prison at the entrance on the Boulevard Arago. *"Mon Dieu,"* Lucette said. "You look like you've been on holiday. I do believe you've put on weight!"

It was true. Pyotr smiled, hugged and kissed her, then the men, then did it all over again. "The Governor insisted I eat with him and tell him war

stories. One way or another we got around to my dreams and Christina…"
Here he goes, Lucette thought, putting off the moment when she would
have to tell him he no longer had an atelier to live in.

Dreamland - 10

'On the battlefield near Lützen, in the trenches, a line of Wallenstein's musketeers crouched under the shot-torn and tattered Double-Eagle Imperial Flag of the Habsburgs. They are commanded by the Imperial Gefreyter, desperately peering through the half-light of smoke, fog and cannon fire. Of a sudden, a break in the gloom reveals the swift dash of a troop of armoured riders under the Swedish banner galloping across his front. Before they are again swallowed up, he is yelling "Fire! Fire at him yonder! That man must be of consequence to be so brave - or so damn foolish!" A volley rings out. The hard-charging Gustavus is hit. His left arm is shattered. "It is nothing!" he cries. "Follow me!" Streiff gallantly lunges forward. A great cry goes up. Standing behind the Gerfreyter, Graf von Saxe-Luendorf cannot believe his eyes. "It's the King! He is shot! He bleeds!"

"Fire!" the Gefreyter screams, as another volley rolls out. "Fire!" And before the smoke and fog roll back, he can see the King, hit, and hit again, as he falls from the saddle and the blood-spattered, white stallion gallops away. From ten thousand throats a vast moan of despair rises up over the sound of battle.'

Pyotr stopped.

"Mon Dieu," the Governor said, "I see it as if I was there! Go on, man. What then?"

"My throat is dry," Pyotr said.

"Christ in heaven!" the Governor said. "Here. Give him something to drink."

A convict, pressed into service as a waiter, poured wine from a carafe into Pyotr's empty glass. Pyotr, with a nod of thanks, raised his glass to the Governor, took a hefty swig, and continued:

'All the nobles and great figures of state attended the King's funeral, lining the roadway outside Riddarholmen Church in Stockholm, for 300 years the final resting place of the Kings and Queens of Sweden. The church bells toll the death march over the silent assembled company waiting in the snow, as in the distance, to the sound of a single snare drum, the funeral cortège comes into view. The King's body, in its catafalque, lies on a black gun carriage drawn by 6 black horses with muffled hooves, followed by Streiff, riderless, led by Magnus on foot. Winding behind them is a long procession of mourning citizens and peasants bearing torches. At their head is a little figure leading the way: Christina! All eyes are on her. Dressed in pure white furs, carrying in her up-turned hands a purple cushion, across which lies the great dead King's Sword-of-State, she moves in and out of the torch-light to a murmur growing ever louder, until it becomes a roaring chant - "LONG LIVE THE KING! LONG LIVE THE KING! LONG LIVE THE KING!" The words echo into the church.

"I was only six when my father died," Christina says. "He was thirty-eight and had been fighting continuously since he was seventeen. I miss him so much." She is now eight and dressed as a boy in a smart black velvet suit, with lace cuffs and collar to match, and a velvet cap with a long black feather on her head. She is playing in the Palace Garden, waving a wooden sword at her 10-year-old, roly-poly cousin, Karl Gustav, who is using his wooden sword as a fly swat to ward off a swarm of midges. "Be careful!" her mother, Queen Maria Eleonora, calls from where she is standing at a safe distance, attended by Count Oxenstierna.

"En garde," Christina says, taking up a fencing pose, right foot forward, left arm raised.

"How can you fight me?" Karl Gustav says. "You're a girl."

Girl or not, they come to blows, the wooden blades shedding splinters, as first one and then the other gains the upper hand, the skirmish only coming to an end when Oxenstierna shouts, "Enough!"- at the precise moment Christina lunges, the tip of her sword nicking Karl Gustav!

"I am the King!" Christina exults. "Die, Prince Wallenstein!"

"Ahhhh!" Karl Gustav hams an elaborate death scene. "I am stabbed! I bleed!" He staggers, drops his sword, clutches his chest, and writhing, falls to the ground. It is a worthy performance.

"For God and Sweden," Christina says, putting her foot on his chest, her wooden sword at his throat.

"Ohh!" her mother exclaims, while Oxenstierna politely appluads.

From where he lies on the ground looking up at Christina, Karl Gustav says, "Now it's my turn to win."

"You know that's impossible, Karl-Gustav," Christina says. "I am the King! I cannot die!"

"No, it's not!" Karl Gustav says. "Look what happened to your father."

For an eternity Christina stares at him, her face now white, then she bursts into tears, throws down her sword, and runs away.'

"Parbleu!" the Governor said. "Now I need a drink."

Chapter Twenty-two

Léon Legrand was buried in the tomb he had reserved for himself in the Eighth Division of the Cimetière de Monparnasse attended by no family members, only the Espinasse sisters, Marie Spangerro, the concierge, and the maid, Marie-Laure. It was a brisk Saturday morning, cloudy, with rain in the offing, and the attendant priest fairly raced through the ceremony. As the coffin was lowered into the ground to disappear beneath clods of dirt swiftly shovelled on to it by the gravediggers, a tearless Mademoiselle Victorine invited the party, including the priest, to adjourn to the near-by tavern, *Il Vaut Mieux Ici Que D'En Face*, located appropriately on the Rue Froidevaux, the cemetary's southern boundary. Gathered around the pot-bellied stove in the main saloon, they all followed Victorine in ordering a bouillon laced with vodka to ward off the cold, an egalitarian moment if ever there was one, a maid and the concierge sharing a drink with their *patrons*.

"Who will remember him this time next year?" Geraldine Espinasse said. She didn't expect an answer. And she didn't get one; the question floating there, as her audience ingested their broth along with the unspoken thought - who would remember any one of them a year after they were gone? It fell to the priest to make the sign of the cross.

"Strange that he had no family," he said.

"Actually, it's not strange," Marie said. "He never married, poor man, so how could he have children or grand-children to grieve for him?"

"Siblings? Cousins? Surely there must be somebody?" the priest said.

"He outlived them all," Victorine said. "Not surprising, given he was born in 1830, the year Louis Philippe became King."

150

At least he didn't get his head cut off, thought Marie, who, in her heart-of-hearts, was a royalist, but she kept the thought to herself unsure if her sentiments were shared by the other three ladies.

"Does it happen often?" Marie-Laure asked the priest.

"What? That someone dies alone? More often than you think," the priest said. "Just last week I buried a woman alone who had been shot by her husband because she was always drunk and insulted him - a gamekeeper in the Bois de Boulogne, carrying his gun on his shoulder when he came home. They have him in custody, with his trial coming up in a couple of weeks and they wouldn't let him out to bury her."

Le Petit Journal, May 12, 1925

Témoignage à la Cour d'assises de Seine-et-Oise.
(Court testimony from the defence lawyer.)

The wife of the gamekeeper had, as it is commonly said, a drink too many in her nose, perhaps even a bottle. Naturally, her husband was not happy coming home from work. 'Madame,' he said, 'it is not very pleasant for a husband to find his better half in such a state.' And to frighten his wife, he aimed his unloaded gun at her and said, 'Maybe I should shoot you.'

'Fire away, you big coward,' she cried, taunting him.

'You watch it, or you are going to make me angry,' he said, pretending to cock the rifle. Which only made her repeat, 'Go ahead if you can, you phony coward.' At this, the gamekeeper began to feel a little annoyed.

And then to hear his wife say, 'See, you don't dare, you miserable fat coward!'

At this third insulting exhortation from his wife, the good man had another idea; he took his loaded revolver from its holster on his belt, pointed it at her, saying 'I'm a coward, am I? And fat and miserable? Well, see how you like this!' And fired three times killing his wife who fell down quite dead.

These are the facts. They are not disputed. This, indeed, is what happened. But in fairness, let it be said, no wife has the undisputed right to insult her husband in such grievous terms.

The Versailles jurors, despite their reputation of being severe in the application of the law, acquitted the gamekeeper and the public applauded. Released, and free to leave the court, our man went home without saying a word.

Marie-Laure showed her copy of the newspaper to Gaby after the two maids, working overtime, had finished clearing out half a century of accumulated rubbish, ancient cobwebs, box files full of legal papers yellowed with age, riddled with silverfish, and the droppings of rats and mice, in the old attorney's apartment. Gaby had bad eyesight and it always took her a while to read, but when she got to the end of the article, she said, "I would do the same."

"They'd hang you."

"No, not shoot her. Insult him. Men can insult us as much as they like, and nothing happens to them. But if we do it - BANG! - dead. She's better off wherever she's gone, up or down, doesn't matter." *Pragmatique, les Guyanaise.* *"Bon.* I think we're finished here. I wonder who the new tenant will be?"

It was the same thought that the owners had. "What a mess," Victorine said, arms akimbo, surveying the empty flat, whose fissured walls and floorboards bore the faded outline of the pictures and carpets that had once adorned them, a large, mottled mirror over the fireplace in the living room reflecting the patina of cracked paint and peeling varnish on doors and windows, and the unmistakable, ingrained smell of old body odour. "We'll never rent it like this."

"You know what we should do?" Geraldine said. "Ask him to come back and redo this place." She meant Pyotr.

The message was conveyed, he agreed, and moved back into the same chambre de bonne on the seventh floor he had previously occupied since he had nowhere else to live.

The news was greeted joyously on the sixth floor by Pauline Paulin and Delphine when they bumped into him running down the staircase. They wanted to know everything that had happened to him - including every little detail of what Pauline called his real second life with Christina. No, not here on the staircase. Over a nice dinner. Tonight.

For Pyotr it was a homecoming, down to him dressed in his black corduroys and black turtle-neck sweater, leaning back into the cushions of the club-chair he occupied, glass in hand, the two ladies leaning forward in anticipation of the story he would tell them after they had all enjoyed Delphine's canard à l'orange, 6 duck legs, trimmed of excess fat, sprigs of thyme, 4 blood oranges, peeled and sliced into disks, baby watercress, the whole sprinkled with sea salt and black pepper, roasted on a rack in the oven, with *pomme de terre grenaille rôties au four,* and on the side a fresh salad. Plus cheese and wine. And Pauline's special chocolate mousse.

"Before we start," Delphine said, "what was it like - in jail, I mean."

For a long moment Pyotr looked at Delphine, surprised by her curiosity. Finally, he said, "I will tell you and then I don't want to talk about it again. There is no privacy. You are not a person anymore, just a numeral. They take your watch so you cannot tell the time and you no longer know day from night. Your cell is 4 metres long, 2 and a half metres wide and 3 metres high. There are no windows, just a grill in an iron door. You must use a toilet out in the open. The lights are turned off at 10 and on again at 6. You get 1 hour a day to excercise, which means walking around and around a small yard on your own. All night there's noise from other prisoners shouting and guards on their rounds looking in at you through the grill. You smell, your mattress smells, your cell smells, the other prisoners smell, and all the guards smell of sour sweat, piss, rats, and disinfectant. And garlic. Once a week you get to shower. But no amount of washing gets rid of the smell. In fact, it was like being in the army without the bombs falling on your head." Pause. "I'll say this though, you spend four years in the trenches, trust me, in comparison prison's easy - a roof over your head, a bunk to sleep on and three meals a day." A shrug. "Easy. And I was lucky. Every inmate I met declared he was innocent, but I *knew* I was innocent, and it was only a matter of time before I'd get out. Even the Governor thought so but put me in solitary for my own safety from some of the nutcases in there. In solitary there are rules. The rules are rigorously enforced. You are not allowed to talk in the presence of a guard; it is forbidden if the lights are on. A guard is usually there, somewhere on the floor, footsteps coming and going. You cannot see them, and the convicts cannot see each other even though the cells are side-by-side." Another pause. "You talk, you suffer the consequences. This can mean an extended sentence. A deprivation of food. A curtailment of visiting rights. So? What's left? Not much, except time to think."

Solitary Confinement: Day 1

Why?

Why me? It doesn't matter why; it is why it is. Why? Me? Because it doesn't matter. It doesn't matter why, it is. You. No, you, me. Here. Me. Now. Yet, what have I done?

What have I done? Nothing. Done nothing. I've. Done. Nothing - but stay alive To end here? Sit, must sit. Alive yes why. Why? What for? In this place? What for...for nothing. Nada. My papers, my non-existent papers, vos papiers, just because I'm a foreigner. Permis de séjour? Permis de bullshit. Lucette - she was right, must have papers God, the stench in here. With me. It's not...keep calm...it's not...calm...fair. It's not. Get used to..Think. God, it's dark. Dark. Think. Slowly. Slow down. Think. Say it. Slow. Fairness has nothing... fairness to do with fairness has got nothing to do with this. Accept it. Fairness has got nothing. To do. With this. Never had. Okay. Nothing. Think. Postulate. Non-verbal they are non-verbal. Thoughts. Back there down the dark corridors. My brain black blacker than this black cell with no light eyes closed dark. Curious. They do not have sentences, thoughts don't. Nor. Grammar. Incorrectly so. Of course I'll get out. They do not translate. Never thought of that before. If I've done nothing...how can they keep me? Because. What? Stacked, they are, and yes also multi-dimensional, what did the fellow say? Because what? I'm innocent. Lucette knows. She'll tell them. Atoms, is all it is. Atoms. Who would think, under her black smock, the gift she had for me. That body. 50 years old and the figure of a girl. And I'm stuck here. Why? Me? Why? Can't think properly. Can't see my hands. Poor, poor, Lucette. No way. None for her she can't find the rent for the atelier if she could see this rathole she'd weep, cry. Not even a window, not even that. Lie down, must lie down now. Must...in the castle they'd be pissing themselves...my home who'd believe this once a castle, fall about pissin' and in the palace too and...they shuld see me now...dead, they're all dead all dead gone...nobody there nobody sees me...how far is the wall? Not quite to my fingertips...bunk to wall an arm length not even...Pips and Bobeli would laugh, smaller than my crib in the nursery...my sisters, they'd laugh, the nursery…twenty times the size of this cell…bunk is okay, hard, better than the trench…better…same smell of piss though, sweat stale, same stale sweet sweat smell…me, must be. Me. Did I sleep? Must have. Black in here. Eyes closed. Even darker. Atoms. That's all we are. In English just talk to him so I was using this sings to write something up with thinking about and when I was walking for example are use notes or Notes was not to be disturb of my sentence but then would write something crazy I even had a project then Nat would ride write something crazy I even had Anna and Rachel..Rachel? who what that is that's how torch look but then you cut it that help but then you cut it that's how much you do but then you can make it more beautiful You did win I'm doing it now I'm gonna show you show me that you said in your message did certainties like lost long last lovers help about unwanted speculation where in the pencils in dark Lucette no nor Nathalie imagine homelands is a week from sleep good then that sound loud as you ever heard, shaking your ribs, mending your spine to octaves beyond the edge sword invoice but fuck they come from for the thunder all I know is that I didn't. I really didn't want to do that but how could I know he would be there you must've been. I'm sure as frightened as me how are you? God I never heard no sound. Good night God you scared scared like I am scared I- I- I think numb I'm numb. What's up at what purse that you endeavour, endeavour to say, but the sound cuts off cut you cut you off like thunder the cannons shells in the dark exploding spine bending explosions can't hear here I noticed we are free we offered somewhere close concussed maybe no, the song imagine the bullets rewrite his face just think last month I have never ever confessed so don't the fear the fear of jelly is my stomach shaved your legs shaved to find the flea, my feet, shaved, and how and how trusting you and he was to me, his face bony and hair black the tough boy, my friend why why why were you in front of me?

Then:

Hey, you, English. Are you awake?

Silence.

This is not how you imagined life in France, I wager.

Silence.

I know you're awake. Buried in your thoughts, right? You can talk, you know.

At night no one will turn you in.

Silence.

Your first day, but it feels like an eternity. Am I right? Yes, of course I am. Take me for instance, I'm in the cell next door to you, an innocent man locked up, ninety-one days in solitary and counting. You want to know why I'm here. Let me tell you. That son of a bastard pig coming round to sniff at my woman day after day soon's my back's turned got what was coming to him, you can believe it. Not my fault he croaked, fucking swine. How was I to know he had a heart problem? Didn't stop him taking down his pants, did it, fucking asshole. And she let him.

Silence.

Can you believe it, she lets this fucker do her. And not just the once.

Silence.

You going to say something? No? Bastard. Alright, have it your way. Shut the fuck up, see if I care. Give it a few days, you'll be glad enough to talk, you'll see, they all do.

Silence.

Solitary Confinement: Day 2

You want to know how I caught them? Pure luck. I'm out the door early like always, down the hill, nearly at the Yard when I remember the bolt cutters I was meant to bring back. The railyard back of St.Lazare where I work, you know? Fucking foreman, little prick, Rachid, always bitching, he'd fire me if he knew I'd borrowed them. Anyway, I go back and get the cutters and I'm trying to be quiet, not wake up the missus when I hear this noise. Can't make it out and I'm about to leave when I hear it again, familiar like. It takes me a moment and I get it, the fucking springs under the mattress, used to piss me off they did when we were at it. And I'm hearing this and nearly out the door before I say fuck! she's at it! and sail back in, straight into our bedroom and there's this fucker, Maurice, lives on the top floor, runs the drygoods place on the Rue Blanche, giving her one. Belted him with the bolt cutter, didn't I. And he croaks!

Silence.

A crime of passion, the lawyer said. He got that fucking right, he did. And what does the judge do? Gives me ten for manslaughter and tells me I'm lucky not to get topped.

Silence.

Injustice! I'm telling you. It is not fucking fair. It's not. They know damn well I didn't mean to kill him. Fucking the wife, What did they think I would do? Kiss the bugger? Say thank you? I can't shake it off, what those two did, but I must stay cold in my head or I'll never get out. They know I didn't mean to kill him.

Silence.

Solitary Confinement: Day 3

Injustice, you know this word? Let me tell you it is fucking not right. It curdles the blood in my veins if you want to know. I didn't run off. Went straight round to the station to tell them what happened. And the fuckers arrest me! I'm locked up for what the pigs call a crime. Can you believe that? I can't shake it off. It makes me angry and I end up stuck in here.

Silence.

You don't have to talk, it's okay. Just listen. Each day is a test of your patience and resolve. Fucking food never changes, place smells of shit. It's like the war all over again, a different kind of war. You were there I'm told. The Somme, Verdun? Right? We fight for this fucking country and end up in here. It's not fair.

Silence.

You can ask them for books, you know. I think I've read every book they've got. Keeps me sharp, but being in fucking isolation is beginning to gnaw at me. The trenches were hell, I don't have to tell you, but this...this sitting in the dark is different.

Solitary Confinement: Day 4

My wife showed up one day. In the visitor's room, sweet and smiley. All the bitch could talk about was how thick and putrid the air was and that the stench of body odour, stale urine, and sweat was not good for her health. She had a court order for our apartment to be put in her name. Also she wanted a divorce. I lost it and tried to grab her through the bars, choke the bitch. And I would have if the warden hadn't whacked me with his club. Why I ended up here in solitary. Can you believe it? The bastards want us to know just how fucked we are.

Silence.

You know your silence is beginning to piss me off. Fucked if I'll bother talking to you if you can't open your gob.

Solitary Confinement: Day 5

"What? What did you say? Your cell is too small? Really? That's the first fucking thing comes into your head? Putain de merde. And it's maddeningly quiet and you can't believe you're in here? After five days you can't think of anything else to say? Say merde and be done with it.

I said that?

Yes, you fucking did. Just now. Told you didn't I? They all talk, everyone, but it's the first time I heard someone say their cell was too small. You a fucking architect, or something?

I can't just sit here. I need to prove I'm innocent.

HYSTERICAL LAUGHTER.

Merde!

That same evening, the prison Governor, Alphonse Prud'homme, had dinner with the prison doctor, Dr. Léon Bizard. Over a carré d'agneau with a full-bodied Côte du Rhone to wash it down, they discussed the new prisoner. "I have had many intelligent men incarcerated here, mon cher Docteur," the Governor said, "but none like this man. From his file it is evident he was born into an aristocratic family with immense wealth, only to lose everything, including his parents and siblings, in the cataclysm of this war we have just endured. You would think he must reflect on the cruel and capricious nature of fate, his thoughts filled with profound loss and trauma, n'est ce pas? Eh bien, pas du tout. No, far from it. Instead, he discusses the theories of this young Swiss physicist, Einstein, who would have us believe we are not flesh and blood but made of something invisible called atoms."

"Oh, you may well believe it," Dr. Bizard said. "The fellow's got a Nobel Prize for Physics. It is fascinating. Hard to believe he was nominated ten years in a row before finally winning. Apparently, he was so far ahead in his field that the Swedish Academy had difficulty appreciating the significance of his work. Some even say he should have won four Nobels by now."

"Well, you're better read than I am, and I can't claim to have any real understanding of the matter. But back to our man. You have seen him, yes?"

"Yes. Twice in the past week. He was mistreated by the gendarmes when they brought him in, so I gave him something for his pain and I had a chance to talk to him after he was deloused and in uniform. As a survivor of the war, he may be grappling with what we in the profession call survivor's guilt." Dr. Bizard paused to sip his wine. "The horror of the battlefield is not easily imagined by those of us who were not there. His is a confusing story in which he kills his boyhood friend with whom he was at boarding school for orphans in England. His involvement in the war, fighting on the German side, is a source of inner turmoil. The memory of that night, when, in a suicidal attack on the British lines, he kills this man fighting for the Allies is agonizing, the weight of betrayal and the emotional toll of taking a friend's life, overwhelming. His memories of the trenches, of what happened when he was wounded, what he witnessed, I think will haunt him for the rest of his life."

"Betrayal?"

"Yes. Fate betrayed him. Never could he imagine his friend in the opposing trench. Of the millions fighting, what are the odds? Now he questions who he is and where he fits in a drastically altered world accusing him of pushing a man he never met down the stairs of a building when he wasn't even there to do it."

"Did he tell you about his dreams?"

"Dreams? No. What dreams?"

Dreamland - 11

Christina, 12-years old, is in the Palace classroom, seated on a bench next to her cousin, Karl Gustav, gnawing the end of a pencil as usual in fear he would be asked a question he could not answer, which was usually the case. Both of them watch their teacher, Professor Messenius, who is using a large astrolabe to illustrate his lecture on celestial navigation while at his feet his 4-year old son, Arnold, is intent on interfering with the lesson. Looking on from where they sit side-by-side on a bench at the back of the classroom, are Magnus, Petrus and Lord Oxsenstierna, with the theologian, Johannes Matthiae, Christina's personal tutor, appointed by her father to make sure she was raised as a Prince, seated on a chair in one corner studying his ward. His task has not been easy and with each passing year becomes more difficult in direct proportion to Christina's development and growing maturity. He was aware that he no longer thought of her as a child but as a young adult. Looking at her attired in the same manner as Karl Gustav, with the same black waistcoat under a knee-length dark brown velvet coat and black leather riding boots, was like looking at two youths of the same gender, if anything Christina the more manly.

"Arnold," Professor Messenius now said, "It is impossible for me to demonstrate the relevant position of the Earth, the Sun and the planets if you keep playing with those levers."

The boy stops for a moment, glances up at his father, smiles in familiar complicity. "But I like doing it," he says, wiggling the lever in question, watching the stars and planets whirl about in concentric circles. The spectators titter.

"It's what they do anyway," Christina said.

"What is?" Professor Messinius said.

"If I understand you correctly, we have a heliocentric solar system, with the Earth and planets orbiting a stationary Sun as stated by the ancients, Pythagoras, Aristarchus and Heraclides and confirmed by Galileo observing with his telescope the moons of Jupiter orbiting that planet and not the Earth, then what Arnold is doing is an accelerated version of what we think we know," Christina said. Silence in the classroom.

"It would be wise if we bought a telescope," Christina said, turning to Lord Oxenstierna. "I would like to see the planets. Please order it done."

"That would not be wise," Johannes Matthiae said.

"In what way?" Christina said.

"It will upset the Church. They still believe that Earth is the centre of the cosmos."

"Along with all that other rubbish about an invisible man with a long white beard living up in the clouds?"

"Christina! That is blasphemy. May God forgive you."

"Why? If He made me, He made me as I am. Able to think for myself. And I don't for one moment believe He would have me accept the dressed up nonsensical folderol preached by our clerics to ignorant peasants. There is nobody living up in the sky as you can see for yourself if you go to the window and look up."

"You will burn in hell saying that. Is that what you want?"

"No. Because there's nothing down there either. It's all made up. A fairytale to frighten the gullible. You know it as well as I do."

"Christina!" Wildly, Matthiae looked to the others for support.

"Christina, be mindful of what you say!" Lord Oxenstierna said. "What is said in this room will stay in this room, but one day you will rule this land. You will be the head of the Protestant faith. An example to all, as was your father. To survive a king must be modest in thought and discreet in speech."

"But to rule," Magnus said, "one must be seen in the image that the public projects of the monarch: regal, autocratic, glamourous, willfull, mysterious and above all, powerful. Powerful! A reality kings have understood since the beginning of time."

"And just!" Professor Messenius said.

"What?"

"You left out the most important quality, the characteristic that has distinguished every great king" - turning to Christina - "they must be just! They cannot abide injustice! And to be just you must always, *always!* recognise the truth. Without the truth, there is no justice! The monarch's absolute authority is not capricious either; rather, it is grounded in the imperative duty of a noble leader to embody the collective interests of the entire nation under their governance. A truly heroic ruler must steadfastly resist becoming a mere instrument of any faction, instead prioritising the pursuit of justice. This commitment must be seen through the ruler's public display of just actions, adhering to the principle that a prince should always maintain perfect neutrality. The ruler's sole focus should be on dispensing justice based solely on the facts of each case and the merits of each subject, compelling all to fulfil their duties through fair punishments and rewards, and, most significantly, by setting a virtuous example."

Messenius was speaking so fast and vehemently spittle flew out of the corners of his mouth.

"To uphold this dedication to the common good rather than partisan interests, the ruler must actively seek broad consultation. Emphasising accessibility, the prince should grant everyone the opportunity to approach and engage with them openly. Like the sun, whose rays illuminate all, the ruler should avoid isolation, steering clear of being confined by either ministers or favourites."

Raising an eyebrow, Magnus muttered to Oxenstierna, "Are we talking the same language?"

Glaring at them, Messenius said, "The legacy left to us by King Gustavus was his unfailing attachment to the truth - which is why he will be revered as a great and just king forever!"

What has any of this to do with the astrolabe, Petrus thought?

Chapter Twenty-three

"Can we eat now?" Pauline said. She was rewarded with a blank stare from Pyotr.

"You've been talking for an hour. If you go on any longer you will ruin the delicious meal Delphine has cooked for us."

"Sorry," Pyotr said.

"My fault," Delphine said, turning to the stove. "Lucky I turned the gas down. No worries. Cooked slowly, the duck will be all the better for it." It was. They ate in silence, interrupted only when a wine glass needed to be filled. When finally, the meal was finished, down to the last spoon of chocolate mousse, they sat back content. Then Delphine said, "It's interesting that your dream is not sequential. The dates skip around; Petrus, Christina and the others age accordingly as your dream goes backwards and forwards in time."

"Why is that interesting?" Pauline said.

"If it was linear," Delphine said, "it could have been learned from a history book and the text recollected in a dream even if reading the book had been forgotten. The fact that it skips about seems relevant to me, the fragmentary episodes much closer to how we remember life. Nobody recalls their life like entries in a diary. We pluck things out." She looked at Pauline. "Remember how we met?"

Pauline blushed. Delphine laughed. "One evening we were waiting in line to go to the bathroom during the interval at the Comédie-Française," she said to Pyotr, "and Mademoiselle here, then a complete stranger, was obviously bursting so I let her go ahead of me. Unfortunately, not soon enough, with the result you can imagine."

"Delphine!" Pauline said.

"*Quoi? C'est vrai.* It's true. You peed in your pants."

"You don't have to mention it!"

"Why not? If it wasn't for that we wouldn't be here today. Serendipity has no rules, as I am sure you know, Monsieur Pyotr."

Serendipity: the gift of chance finding unintended good, Pyotr thought, but what of its opposite? As a pustule of memory squeezed into focus: the MP18 light machine-gun firing into the face of his friend from school. He suddenly felt sick.

"Are you alright?" Pauline said. "You've gone white."

"Put your head between your knees if you're feeling nauseous," Delphine said. "Get some blood into your brain."

Pyotr shook his head. "Sorry," he said. "Just a thought." Eyes closed, he took a deep breath. "It will go away."

Pause.

When he opened his eyes he found the two women anxiously looking at him. "Sorry," he said again.

"When do you start the renovation downstairs?" Pauline said, to change the subject.

"When the sisters agree to the plan I have made," Pyotr said.

The carefully drawn plan lay open across the partner's desk. Géraldine and Victorine Espinasse studied it as Pyotr explained what he wanted to do. "As you can see it is the mirror image of your apartment," he said. "Everything is flipped, but the ceiling height, 4 metres, is the same throughout. The entrance door leads into this dual-aspect hallway that connects the living room and dining room overlooking the street and two of the dwelling's three bedrooms. This corridor," he tapped the plan, "connects to the kitchen, then to the bathroom fitted with an old-fashioned iron bathtub, a shower and a lavatory. The corridor also connects to a utility room and boiler room, as well as a separate lavatory. Chevron parquet, in poor condition, extends across the hallway and into this parlour or lounge, the ceilings of which are adorned with fine mouldings and corner embellishments sculpted with foliage motifs. The lounge includes a fireplace of brickwork and pale sculpted marble that stands against the wall as you can see, separating the lounge from the dining room. I propose demolishing this wall which is not load-bearing and combining it with an open-plan kitchen. These two rooms would then offer a total reception space of around 50m² flooded with natural light from these five double-glazed windows." Tap. "This whole space – the kitchen and dining area – would then be big enough for large feasts for families and guests to be enjoyed in comfort. These old, paneled doors currently separate the rooms from one another. These two will go, and the others will be stripped down to raw timber and varnished pale grey to create a warm atmosphere in the apartment. The interior will be brightened up with flooring of large, pale travertine tiles with small square black marble inserts in the corridor, the dining area and the open-plan kitchen. I propose reducing the three bedrooms to two, each with a large en-suite bathroom and built-in wardrobes in the walls. The space gained will allow for an office or library here." Tap. "It will all take about three months to do, fingers crossed."

"What happens to the chimney and fireplace if you take that wall out?" Géraldine said, tapping in turn.

"Nothing," Pyotr said. "They remain but are turned into a free-standing tiled stove going from floor to ceiling like we had at home when I was a child. You see them in Sweden based on German models found in royal castles in the 16th century. It will be made of a lot of bricks and mortar, consisting of clay, sand and water. These are heavy materials, so the body of the stove will accumulate heat and radiate it for several hours using the smallest amount of wood in order to work. It will have five internal flues which will give it exceptional efficient energy. I have some tiles for you to choose from." Here he pulled sample tiles out of a satchel lying on the floor. "They're from the porcelain factories of Rorstrand and Marieberg and as you can see, they are very beautiful. I particularly like the majolica." Tap. "The tiled area also affects the efficiency, so usually a squared stove makes more heat than a rounded one. Having five internal flues means that the heat keeps radiating for about twenty hours after the fire has died down."

Victorine fingered the tiles. "I like this blue and white one," she said. "If all four faces of the stove are covered in tiles, imagine how much light will be reflected around the room."

Géraldine looked at her sister. "I know what you're thinking," she said.

"Same as you," Victorine said. "Which bedroom do you want?"

And so it was that the sisters decided to move into the renovated flat, enlarging the office to accommodate the partner's desk. Once done, installed in style, they asked Pyotr to do the same conversion to their old apartment. It took him another three months of hard work and he was just putting on a last coat of paint when Marie, the concierge, put her head around the door to announce the arrival of Lucette with an old lady who was looking for him. It was his Great-Aunt Tilly.

Augustine, Grand Duchess of Austria-Hungary, Princess of Romania-Bukovina, Baroness of Reichenau, Countess of Saxe-Meiningen, stared at her grand-nephew through a broken lorgnette she wore on a silver chain entangled with the many necklaces around her skinny neck. "I heard you were a painter," she said, "but had no idea they meant housepainter. Really, Pyotr, this is scarcely becoming a member of our family."

"Ah so you do know each other?" Lucette said.

"Unfortunately, we do," Great-Aunt Tilly said. "I held him in my arms when he was a tiny *bebelus,* a baby."

Pyotr smiled. "How did you find me?" he said.

"With great difficulty and the help of the Red Cross," she said. "Apparently you're a British Citizen now, God knows how?"

"I hope He does," Pyotr said.

"What happened to your friend, Markus?"

"You know Markus?"

"Everyone knows Markus. When I met him In Berlin last year, he said he was sharing your *atelier* until you two had a row over some woman. Doesn't surprise me. Bloody men -" this to Lucette - "can't keep it zipped up. Never could."

"How long have you been in Paris?" Pyotr said.

"I've just arrived."

"Where are you staying?"

"I was hoping with you as I am penniless, but this lady tells me you no longer have your *atelier* since they put you in jail for throwing a man down some stairs. Another woman I suppose?" She peered past Pyotr into the newly decorated flat. "But this looks big enough for both of us," she said.

Pyotr laughed. "*Ma pauvre Tante*. Alas, I have neither the atelier nor this apartment, but live here on the 7th floor in a chambre de bonne. I am not a housepainter by choice but by necessity, as I too am penniless. I do whatever jobs I can find. Let's go to the bar downstairs for a drink and we can talk in peace once I get out of this *salopette*." Suiting action to his words, Pyotr took off his paint-splattered dungarees and in rumpled black corduroys escorted the ladies down the stairs, out into the street and into the newly renovated bar.

"My goodness!" Great-Aunt Tilly said, on stepping into the place. "What a wonderful space!"

"He did it," Lucette said with considerable pride. "He designed and painted the whole thing!"

"*Necrezut!*" Unbelievable, Great-Aunt Tilly said in Romanian, looking at Pyotr with fresh interest. "Where did you learn to do this?"

Pyotr shrugged. Since nobody understood what he did he saw no reason to explain. "It's nothing special," he said. "What would you like to drink?"

"Vodka," Great-Aunt Tilly said. They sat at a table, an ice-cold bottle was fetched, drinks were poured. "*Sănătate!*" the old Lady said by way of a toast.

"*Skol!*" Pyotr saluted her. They drank. Another round was poured. "Now tell me," he said, "how is it at home? Is there anything left?"

"Since Carol ran off with that girl, it's been a disaster -" Great-Aunt Tilly turned to Lucette - "Prince Carol, our heir-apparent, much to the disgust of the King and Queen, married a commoner, Zizi Lambrino, and wanted to give up his rights of succession. This morganatic marriage has been annulled but, guess what? They have a son, also called Carol. Just to complicate matters, in short order our randy Prince marries again to a Princess this time, Helen of Greece and Denmark, a girl chosen by his mother. And, of course, another son is born, Michael, who will be our future King when Ferdinand falls off his throne."

On and on she went, conjuring an almanacks list of monarchs and their various wives, mistresses, concubines and assorted progenitor, breeding incestuously in castles and palaces of extraordinary, detailed splendour when they weren't murdering each other or otherwise deposing of fortunes earned by right and might, that it gave Lucette a headache. "My palace in Bucharest is now a convent for unmarried mothers, and my chateau in Chernivtsi, overlooking the Prut, is a branch of the City Council. All my paintings are deemed national treasures and hung in museums, and my jewellery sold at auction to supposedly reduce the National Debt - when in fact the paintings are often seen hanging in the newly confiscated homes of whatever gangster got himself elected and they're riding around in motor cars bought with my money. There's no point in complaining since the person you complain to will not be in office the following week, either shot dead or on the run with whatever they could steal." Great-Aunt Tilly finally ran out of steam when she realised the bottle of vodka was empty. "Here in Paris you've been celebrating the Exposition Internationale and a few kilometres away, in the middle of Europe, the world as we know it is coming apart," she said. "I am so tired. Is there somewhere I could lie down?"

Since there was no way she could walk up 105 steps to the 7th floor, Pyotr took the problem to Marie who spoke to Géraldine who consulted Victorine. "If she doesn't mind the smell of fresh paint," Victorine said, "make up a bed for her in the new apartment. There's furniture in the cellar she can use." Subsequently, Magda, Great-Aunt Tilly's Polish maid, turned up, and a bed was made for her in the office, and then, a Hungarian cousin, István, fortune-still-intact, occupied the second bedroom and paid the rent. The house was full again.

Chapter Twenty-four

One evening, accompanied home to Rue Boissonade by Pyotr, Lucette said, "Do you think your Aunt minds the fact that I am only a concierge?"

"No." Pyotr said. "If anything, she's jealous you have someone in your life and she doesn't. She may look old and faded now, but when she was young half the royal bloods in Europe were after her. And not just for her fortune. She was absolutely stunning, turning the head of the Tsar himself until Nicholas married Alexandra Feodorovna. When the Bolsheviks executed them it broke her heart."

Said casually. Lucette stared at Pyotr, once again baffled by the gulf between them. The great names and places of history so liberally sprinkled throughout his life enjoined with the prosaic simplicity of a woman like herself, who had never left Paris, not even on holiday. Why me? She thought. As if reading her thoughts, Pyotr said, "I am the lucky one. You are God's gift to me." He smiled. Took her to bed. Made love. Fell asleep. Dreamt…

Dreamland - 12

O n the 21st anniversary of the death of Gustavus, November 6, 1653, Petrus stood in the nave of Riddarholm Church gazing up at sunlight streaming through stained-glass windows to where, in the rafters, it fell on dusty war-banners of long-forgotten battles of long-dead kings whose tombs lay below, amongst which was the sarcophagus of Adolphus 1 in its crypt, just visible in the gloom, a stone effigy, hands piously clasped on its breast, the Great Sword-of-State lying parallel to the body, as choirboys raised their voices in the Te Deum accompanied by an organ.

A priest, Father Allerts, was standing by the crypt, one hand rubbing the marble, the other raised in salute to Petrus, when a veteran soldier and the publican from the tavern across the street, brought in a wreath. "They should be here any minute," Father Allerts said.

"I don't need them to remember him," the soldier said. "I was there. I saw him fall. I don't need a wreath to remember Lützen. We won that terrible day to avenge him. Look,"- pointing with a finger for the benefit of the publican - "there's his banner. Shot to pieces. I was the first to get to him. Who are you? I said, not recognising him with all the blood pumping out from his many wounds. I was the King of Sweden, he said. My brother, I am done. Look to your own life now. And then he died. It is why they invite me here - to tell how I held him in my arms."

"And then?" the publican said.

"Then it was terrible. All life was lessened in value with his death. If the most sacred life is so easily pinched out, then death held no terror for us other ranks." Tears rose in the eyes of the old soldier to make their way

170

down his scarred face. "With what fury did we rush on the enemy, every regiment of ours, Uplanders, Smälanders, the Finns, the East and West Gothlanders, showing no mercy to even the bravest amongst our foe, until they were entirely beaten from the field or lying dead in it. I am not ashamed to weep in memory of how the spirit of Great Gustavus led us anew. Would that it were so today."

"Shhh!" the publican said, "the walls have ears."

"I'm not afraid. I only say what most believe," the soldier said.

Petrus glanced at Father Allerts who shook his head and raised a finger to his lips. Say nothing. Stay silent. With a slight nod, Petrus acknowledged the warning. Looking at the soldier, hearing his voice, who could doubt his sincerity? How many times had Petrus heard this same lament, told with the same conviction, until you had to believe every veteran soldier in the Swedish army was kneeling there that day as the King died? Father Allerts moved closer to whisper in his ear. "Why disillusion an honest man?" Said with the same priestly tact he used when giving absolution. Petrus was about to reply when the great doors at the far end of the nave creaked open and a procession entered, each person bearing a wreath.

"Father Allerts," the publican said, "may we stay until the Queen comes?"

"If I get the pint you promised me. Be still now. Step back into the shadows." And it was from the shadows that he recited the names of the courtiers as they paraded past like so many beads on a rosary. "Here comes the Queen's tailor, Johan Holm."

"Who is rich beyond belief," the publican said. "They say he is familiar with her figure."

Father Allerts glared at him. "And that handsome lad is Klas Tott, the old Field Marshall's son."

"On whom she heaps more than gifts," the publican said.

"And now, Bulstrode Whitelock, Cromwell's man, the English Ambassador."

"Carrying no wreath, but a smirk. A regicide in the Court of the Queen. He looks too jolly to have seen Charles beheaded."

"A king's murderer…here?" the old soldier whispered.

"Shhh!" Father Allerts said. "Look now, there's Dr.Bourdelot, the Queen's French physician." Carrying a small but very pretty wreath in one hand, Dr. Bourdelot has a lorgnette in the other through which he examines everyone, paying particular attention to Ambassador Whitelock.

"Her pet monkey, you mean" the publican said. "Another intimate of the Queen's person, who sneers at our Swedish manners."

"He's a catholic. And here are two more: the Papal Envoys, Monsignori Malines and Casati." Wearing the Jesuit cassock bound at the waist with a cincture, the two Italian priests stride up the nave like natives coming home.

"Are they the Queen's friends...her father's enemies?" the old soldier said.

"All Europe wants to bed our Queen," the publican said. "To mate the Crown of Sweden to their distant cause. And she, in 'intellectual pursuit', fills the Court with these bright popinjays on whom she spends our millions."

"Hold your tongue!" Father Allerts said, "or you'll have it torn from your mouth. Be quiet, I say. Look, here comes an old war-horse, Field Marshall Horn himself...and with him, General Wrangel."

"Great men...brave men, both," the soldier said.

"But now belittled by the Queen publicly declaring they used religion as a cloak throughout the Thirty Years War to conceal their territorial ambitions. They must disgorge what they have taken," the publican said.

"What! No bounty? Dear Lord, does she envy her dead father's soldiers?"

"Yes!" the publican said. "It must be hard to be one's father's daughter brought up as a son with the thumb of Oxenstierna pressed down on your neck."

"Good heavens! Look!" Father Allerts pointed. "Magnus de la Gardie."

"Ready to explode!" the publican said.

Effectively, Magnus, alone, strides up the aisle looking both depressed and humiliated - and angry enough to explode. Almost negligently he drops the wreath he is carrying on the pile accumulating around the crypt. He is attired in the height of French fashion, wearing a doublet and matching cape in pink over heavily padded hose in mauve, with netherstocks in turquoise showing above silver-buckled pumps in contrast to everyone else's mourning.

"Just look at him," the publican murmured, "the former favourite, intended King of Sweden, with the prize in his hand, married off by the Queen to her own cousin just to shut up the gossips! What a ninny! Who does he think he is?"

"A great man by the look of him," the soldier said.

"A man undone," the publican said, "Countess Ebba Brahe's son, whelped tis said by Gustavus, lying there stone cold."

"All talk and slander, you should be ashamed," Father Allerts said. "But, softly now, here comes the Queen Mother and…" he stopped as everyone turned to watch the entrance of Maria Eleonora, followed by the Countess Ebba Brahe de la Gardie, and Countess Ebba Spaare, all dressed in mourning. The assembled nobles bow.

"Fie! I cannot believe it!" Father Allerts said. "The Queen's friend!"

"Ebba Spaare? The Queen's whore, you mean," the publican said. "She calls her Belle. And, unblushing, parades her in our narrow streets…oh, stand back, stand back, they come this way."

As the trio shrink deeper into the shadows, Magnus now sees Petrus and comes over to stand next to him. "What are you doing here?" he said.

"Watching."

"For Oxenstierna?"

A nod. Yes.

"Or should I say, spying?"

"Say what you like. Why on earth are you dressed like that?"

"You think he cares how I'm dressed?" With his chin Magnus indicated the sarcophagus. "Every year we do this. It's boring."

"What's boring, my son?" Countess Ebba Brahe said. "Did you have to dress like a peacock? Why did you come here?"

"You may well ask, Mother," Magnus said, "I don't know."

"The Queen does not want to see you since you are no longer satisfied to be in her Court…"

"What Court? Look at them." Magnus waved a hand at the growing multitude cramming into the church. "Why would anyone wish to belong to this gang?"

"Sush, my child.." the Countess said.

"Why?" Magnus said again. "No one wants to talk to me."

"They probably want to, but they don't dare. Dressed like that, who can blame them? Tell him, Petrus. He listens to you."

"Your Mother is right," Petrus said. Then stopped and listened as a growing volume of voices outside the church attracted everyone's attention. "She comes. The Queen is coming!"

All eyes are on the door as Christina enters alone. She is dressed in black, a black velvet mantle trimmed in black bear fur, a large veiled black hat with a black bear fur crown and brim, with a black plume and a diamond aigrette, a long black gown in velvet with a black ermine collar, a long necklace of pearls depending a silver crucifix. Slowly, with dignity, with respect for the Church and the occasion, she enters, measuring everyone present. She pauses. A moment of absolute stillness passes. It is as if all the light in the church is concentrated on her, leaving everything and everyone in nebulous darkness, holding their breath. Then slowly, slowly, she moves up the nave followed by a page carrying a wreath, and as she walks, she smiles or nods or simply raises an eyebrow to those present, thereby indicating the different degrees of friendship, enmity or indifference in which she regards them individually. She is a month shy of her 28th birthday.

"No suite...no guards...no escort...no chamberlains?" Father Allerts whispers in disbelief. "No fear of her loyal subjects...she must believe everybody still loves her."

"Because she loves herself," the publican said quietly.

"Is that true?" the old soldier said.

"Quiet, man! Lower your voice," Father Allerts said. "She only believes what she wants to. But, by God, look at her! She is the...Queen! She draws every eye, even those unwilling to acknowledge such majesty!"

"I grant you that. She is...majestic! I would follow her," the soldier said.

174

"To your doom," the publican said. "It's all playacting and she's the star. Any fool can see that."

And at that moment, mid-nave, Christina stops. She has just caught sight of Magnus. For a moment she cannot believe her eyes. Then, despite herself, she laughs. "Magnus! Dear God! In church?" With a black silk handkerchief, she tries to stifle her laughter. "Magnus, Magnus, you'll be the death of me. What are you pouting about, standing there in that extraordinary costume?"

"I'm in mourning," Magnus said.

"Have you lost someone?" Christina said, her eyes flicking to her father's crypt.

"Yes, I have. I've had a great loss!"

"So? With your luck you'll inherit…"

"No," Magnus interrupted her, "apparently Tott will."

"Jealous, Magnus? Surely you can do better than believe in rumours. Try and say something pleasant."

"How long are we going to keep up this farce?"

"Have you finished?"

"I was already finished -" Magnus choked on his emotions; his voice dropped - "when you left me." Said so quietly Christina had to come right up to him to hear what he said.

Touched by his words, she whispers, "You did love me?"

"What a question!" Magnus said. "Shame on you!"

"I'm sorry, Magnus, I treat you badly," Christina said, her voice intimate, shutting out the world. "If you only knew how all these dead and half-dead great ones depress me. Look at them: the great Horn, the great Wrangel, Oxenstierna, if he had bothered to come. Using the reflection of my truly great father to enlarge their imagined stature. It was not like this when we started."

"Do you remember, after your coronation…?"

"Oh Lord, Magnus, I remember many things," Christina said dreamily, drowsily, her voice slowly fading, "many, many things, before and after that, some with more favour than others…"

"Christina!" Maria Eleonora, the Queen Mother, interrupted. "Have you forgotten why we are here?"

"Bless you, Mother," Christina said, turning from Magnus to face the challenge. "We've been doing this for the past twenty years. How could I possibly forget?"

"What are we waiting for, my child?"

"The Chancellor, Mother! Little Kerstin must always wait for the great Oxenstierna, even when she knows he won't come."

"That is so thoroughly Swedish," Maria Eleonora said.

"You are right, Mother. Perhaps you can tell him that us German Queens do not have time to wait. He will listen to you. You are of the same generation: Old!"

Late in the evening of that same day, in the privacy of his chambers in the palace on Högvaktsterrassen, behind a stout door with his escutcheon carved into the stone lintel under the dictum *An nescis quantilla prudentia mundus regatur?* Count Oxenstierna debriefed his spy. He listened intently to what he was told, then said, "Thank you. Your thoughts on these matters, Petrus? Speak freely."

"The people are unhappy, my Lord," Petrus said. "Discontent among the public, the clerics and the elite is rife. They whisper behind closed doors, speaking about a dark truth. The Queen's political theory and religious philosophy, while seemingly liberal, emphasises the issue of Divine authority and the legitimate use of her power, making people afraid to speak out in public."

"My fault as much as hers," the Count said loyally.

"People believe whatever rumours are current. This malaise, where everything is unknowable, only gives rise to more rumours and theories of conspiracy."

"It's what I fear," Lord Oxenstierna said. "Can you be more specific?"

Petrus nodded. "Allusions are made to the Privy Purse and the missing monies that should be there after the Treaty of Prague. Specifically, the public are upset at the extravagance of the Court. All these foreigners - Chanut, Descartes, Isaac Vossius, Bochart, Nicholas Heinsius, Christian

176

Ravius, Salmsius, to name a few - here at Her Majesty's invitation, but at the public expense, to philosophize, to act and dance in ballets and theatres to which the public are not admitted, living in luxury while the poor can't afford a loaf of bread."

"It is her ideal to improve herself and the nation," Oxenstierna said. "She believes a commitment to personal learning is essential for the success of a political reign."

Petrus looked dubious. "Do you believe that?"

"It is the duty of the prince, no matter how busy the prince is, to put aside several hours of retreat each day. This time must be used to reflect on his conduct, to correct his faults, and to ask for strength and grace from God, without which nothing valuable can be done. It is what I have taught her."

"With respect, I fail to see the connection," Petrus said.

"The ruler must not only develop a personal intellectual and spiritual curiosity," Oxenstierna said, "but must also act as a patron of the arts in the conduct of government. In this she is right. It is necessary to know how to use cultured people as if they were open books, living libraries. You esteem them, reward them liberally, employ them and consult them on what they know. In sum you exploit them. This, too, I taught her."

Was he defending her or was he defending himself? Petrus thought. What he said was, "I see."

"I wonder if you do?" his Lordship said. "What do you think she will do next?"

Chapter Twenty-five

Death revisited the tenement on the Rue des Beaux-Arts when a worried Monsieur Doumeng reported the absence of Monsieur Faccini. "I have not seen him for several days," he told Victorine Espinasse.

"Did you knock on his door?

"No. I felt it more appropriate that you do that."

Marie-Laure was summoned, told to fetch the passkey for 5ème Gauche, and ordered to climb up the 75 steps, knock on the door of the apartment, and, if there was no answer, to let herself in and report back. Which she did. "Il est mort," she said.

And he was. Dead. In his bed. As before, the médecin-légiste was called who diagnosed a heart-attack. As before the spinster sisters made the funeral arrangements. As before the funeral was sparsely attended in the Cimetière de Montparnasse, and, as before, the attendees repaired across the Rue Froidevaux to partake of a *post-enterrement* drink in the saloon of the tavern *Il Vaut Mieux Ici Que D'En Face*.

"I wonder who'll be next?" Géraldine said.

"We must be getting to the top of the list," Victorine said.

"We're too old to die now," Géraldine said. It was a game they played to allay their fears of the unspoken void awaiting everyone, their biggest fear being the one left behind when the other was gone.

"I propose a toast," Monsieur Doumeng said, "to the indelible mosaics our departed friend has left in every Grand Passage in Paris. A hundred years from now, when we are all forgotten, they will be a reminder that he

178

was once here! Salut!" The glasses went up. They drank. The glasses were refilled.

"It is curious, is it not," Doumeng went on, "that the names of the rich entrepreneurs who built the Passages have vanished with time, and the only ones remembered are the artisans who decorated them." The remark struck a chord with Pyotr. No one remembers who paid for something - only who made something. He carried the thought up to his tiny room on the 7th floor.

Inevitably he was asked to redecorate the late Monsieur Facchini's apartment. Imagine his surprise, on opening the door for the first time, to find a pristine open-plan layout, light and airy, with whitewashed walls and ceiling, and Facchini's trademark mosaics laid on the floor of each room as if they were so many oriental carpets. "There is nothing I can do to improve his apartment," he said, when next he met the sisters in the bar. "Clean it thoroughly, and I'm sure the first person who sees it, and who can afford the rent, will snap it up."

This proved to be true. An American writer, a poet, who had served as an ambulance driver in the war, obsessed with trying to find a prostitute he had once loved, Marie Louise Lallemand. Do you know her? It was the first question he asked of anyone, and it was the question he asked Pyotr when he met him coming down the staircase. Gaby, who cleaned his rooms and emptied his trash, found a note scribbled on a piece of paper. It read '*Bon Dieu! may i some day do something truly great. amen.*' She showed it to Pyotr to translate since he spoke English.

Paris Now.

"Cummings, right George, e.e. cummings?"

"That's the bloke," George said. "My hero. Nobody writes like him today. All through the '20s and '30s he was going back and forth between America and Paris. He really loved Lallemand, you know. '*true lovers in each happening of their hearts/live longer than all which and every who;* ' Where 'which' and 'who' are nouns. Imagine writing that! He never found her after the war, but, by Christ, he loved her." George pointed outside. "Funny to think he lived just down the street. He must have walked past this shop a hundred times. Belanopek was lucky to cross paths with someone like that."

"They say he walked twenty kilometres a day."

"Cummings?"

"No. Belanopek. If it's true, that's 7,300 kilometres a year. You know what that is? That's from here to Caracas."

Chapter Twenty-six

Pyotr walked. Mostly to work, whenever and wherever he could find it, but if free on weekends, he crossed the Seine by the Pont des Arts, then walked through the Cour Carrré of the Louvre, to make a left on the Rue de Rivoli to the Palais Royal, leading to the Rue Vivienne and the triple sequence of covered galleries, the Passage des Panoramas, running from the Rue Saint-Marc to the Boulevard Montmartre, built in 1799, the first one built in Paris, with specialist stamp shops and Stern, the stationers, to enter the Passage Jouffroy, past the waxwork museum of the Musée Grévin, to the Passage Verdeau and its antique bookstores, to come out and turn left on the Rue du Faubourg-Montmartre, then up the steep climb of the Rue des Martyrs, to the even steeper Rue Dancourt, which changed names and became steeper still in the Rue des Trois Frères, where it peaked below the Basilique du Sacré Coeur, and did a a long left-hand downhill turn to Rue Burq, then Rue Caulaincourt, down two long flights of steps to Rue Lamarck, Rue Duhesme, and a left on Rue Letort to the boulevard Ornano and the porte de Clignancourt, to the Rue des Rosiers and the flea market. 6.5 kilometres there, 1 hour and 20 minutes if you did not stop. Two or three hours wandering the Puces, hands in his empty pockets, browsing the largest second-hand market in the world, jammed with the poor speaking every known language, haggling with 1,500 merchants in as many stalls in the Marchés Serpette, Biron, Vernaison, Dauphine, an endless list of names, and then another 6.5 kilometres home, to climb 105 steps to his room on the 7th floor and bed. Saturday and Sunday. Rain or shine. For fun.

Lucette came with him a couple of times if she felt her custodial duties permitted it, but for the most part begged off, sensing he enjoyed the solitude of a flâneur going at his own pace.

For work, when they needed polyglot ushers in the Olympic stadium in Colombes during the 1924 Olympic Games, Pyotr crossed the Seine by the Pont Royal, turned left along the river bank to the Place de la Concorde, walked past the Obelisk in the centre, to the Rue Royale, left on the Place de la Madeleine to the Boulevard Malesherbes, past the church at Saint-Augustin to the Rue d'Astorg, then a right on Haussmann to boulevard Malesherbes, all the way to where it changed names and became the Avenue de la Porte d'Asnières, to continue on Rue Victor Hugo, then right onto Rue Pierre Bérégovoy to the Route d'Asnières, another 600 metres to make a left on the Quai du Dr. Dervaux, then right on Rue Normandie, left on Rue Pasteur, left again on Rue de la Station to Rue Denis Papin, to continue for one kilometre on Avenue Henri Barbusse, a left on Rue des Bourguignons and an immediate right on the Route Departmental 13, for one kilometre, where it became the D106, to make a left on Rue Gabriel Péri, continuing to Boulevard Edgar Quinet, then Rue Paul Bert, to finally fetch up at No. 12, Rue François Faber, the entrance to the 45,000-seat stadium. 12.5 kilometres, 2 hours 37 minutes there, on duty from 8.30 in the morning to the end of the last event of the day which could be anywhere between 7pm and 10pm, then 12.5 kilometres, 2 hours 37 minutes, home. 25 kilometres a day, every day for a fortnight, a total distance of 350 kilometres. The distance from Paris to Brussels. Rain or shine. For money.

When they began dismantling the Pavilions of the Arts Décoratifs after the Exposition closed in October 1925, it was closer, since he only had to walk to the Trocadero from the Rue Boissonade, 5.7 kilometres, 1 hour if he hurried down Boulevard Raspail, 1 hour and 15 minutes if he went through the Jardin de Luxembourg. And back. Every day for three months, unskilled labour, 12-hour shifts. Rain, sleet, snow, bitter cold. For money.

Sometimes he wondered why and most of the time his empty belly supplied the answer. But he knew the real reason: activity, any activity to prevent his thoughts returning to the fatal instant he pulled the trigger on his machine-gun all those years ago. Like an indelible stain that no amount of time could fade, that memory of the night in the trenches below

Vauquois would bloom in his mind, his heart would race, and he often found himself short of breath. Why? He had fought in so many battles and yet this was the one relived. Why? No answer. A reflex. Just an excuse. Obliterating the life of his schoolmate. Blasting his face to oblivion under the staccato hammer of the 9mm rounds pouring out of the barrel of the machine-gun as he lay there wounded in the snow and dirt. And? And then…trading places, unforgivable…his mind would shear away. Don't go there. Don't go there. But it always lay in wait.

In December, on the eve of his 30th year, Pyotr and Lucette, making their way home from shopping for groceries in the open air market sprawled along Boulevard Raspail, chanced upon Markus, Anna and Nathalie seated on the terrace of the Café Flore on the Boulevard St. Germain, a meeting that could have been awkward were it not for Anna's delighted smile and gregarious greeting, pointing to two empty chairs and saying, "How very lovely to see you. Please join us." Offering a cheek to be kissed by Pyotr and a warm handshake to Lucette. "Let's have a drink? What about a kir?"

A waiter was summoned, the drinks ordered, crème de Cassis with white wine, served ice-cold in long crystal flutes.

"A toast?" Anna said, holding up her glass, looking at Pyotr.

Inevitably each one had variations of the same thought - 'Le Coq dans son poulailler'/ The Rooster in his henhouse.' (Lucette), 'Il a eu chacun de nous/ He's had each one of us.' (Nathalie), 'Er hatte sie alle und schau bei wem er gelandet ist! He's had 'em all and look who he's ended up with!' (Markus) "On s'est tous fait baiser/ We've all been screwed,' (Anna) 'Funny to think they've all had me.' (Pyotr)

It fell to the youngest, Nathalie, who said, with a grin, 'To the absurd lives we lead!' The glasses clinked. "Who's next?" she added. Pyotr blushed. The women laughed.

"You know whom we should really be toasting today?" Pyotr said, "we should drink to the memory of Monet." Claude Monet had just died at the beginning of the month in Giverny, December 5. "You heard what Clemenceau did at his funeral? No? Let me tell you. They had draped his coffin with a black cloth, which Monsieur le President yanked off and replaced with a colourful tablecloth. 'Il n'y a pas de noir chez Monet!' he said."

"Chapeau!" Anna said. "But surely not a tablecloth?"

"It's what I read in the papers," Pyotr said. "He was my inspiration. Unmixed paint straight from the tube, pale-coloured primers in the under-painting, light and shadow as real objects, broad strokes, everything loose and free."

"Why don't you paint anymore?" Nathalie said. "You were much happier doing that."

"It's what I keep telling him," Lucette said.

"One day, maybe,"Pyotr said.

"But what if that day never comes?" Anna said.

"Maman!" Nathalie said. "Must you always be so morbid?"

"Carpe Diem," Anna said, and Pyotr heard an echo in his head. *Carpe diem*, where had he heard that before?

Dreamland - 13

In a montage of the hellish images of war, cannons belching smoke and flame, flashing swords and pikes, charging cavalry, death vomiting on the shattered bodies of man and beast, blasted walls, burning towns, shot-torn banners mown down by musket-fire, yells and screams of anguish over the bark of command: "Charge!" "Fire!" Stand!" - Petrus relives Lützen, a murderous conflict, everywhere visible and then invisible in the flash of guns, as a Finnish Cuirassier gallops up to make his report to the King. Leaping from his horse, out of breath, he says, "My Liege, General Horn's compliments. He is in pursuit of the enemy's left flank but begs to report that severe gunfire from the enemy cannon posted at the windmills is causing your own left wing to give ground."

Alarmed, Gustavus says, "What say you? How can this be?"

"Look yonder," the Cuirassier says, pointing across the battlefield, "your infantry retreat over the same trenches they took this morning, leaving behind their numberless dead and the batteries captured at such cost!"

"Then must we promptly support them or perish trying," the King said, mounting his charger. "General -" this to the attendant General Steinbeck - "order your squadron to mount! Sound the charge!" - and to Francis Albert, Duke of Saxe-Lauenburg, standing by - "How say you, Francis? Will you and your troop ride with me?"

Not waiting for an answer, the King clapped spurs to his horse and charged to the sound of bugles and the thunder of the battle drums rolling down to where Wallenstein's line of musketeers under the tattered Imperial Flag of the Habsburgs, stood to meet him.

185

"What fool is this?" the Imperial Gefreiter in command said - as Pyotr rolled over. In his sleep, he remembers. The message… *Carpe Diem!* And the King's signature.

Chapter Twenty-seven

On waking up that morning, Pyotr had the distinct smell of dust in his nose, his throat felt sore as if he had been screaming, and there was some elusive thing he could not remember. It was important, but try as he might, he simply could not remember it. He put it out of his mind, determined to enjoy his 30th birthday and not give a thought to the future. Little did he know what fate had in store as a birthday present.

For his birthday dinner party, Lucette invited Delphine Demailly, Pauline Paulin and Alice Guy, and she brought a friend with her, Rouben Mamoulian, a dapper Armenian theatre director, with slicked-back black hair, large round black glasses giving him the look of an inquisitive owl, and a black-and-white jacquard scarf knotted at his throat. Crammed into her tiny lodging, with the men seated at each end of her kitchen table, and the women paired on each side, they had a splendid feast of caramelised fig and goat cheese tart, a roasted shoulder of lamb stuffed with spiced couscous, braised endives, a pomegranate and apple salad and a chocolate birthday cake with crème fraiche and vanilla ice cream. Wisely, Lucette had calculated a bottle of wine per head, and it was as the last drop was being poured, that Alice elaborated the virtues of her friend.

"Rouben is the *enfant terrible* of the theatre," Alice said, "the producer and director of Faust, Carmen, Gilbert and Sullivan, Boris Godunov and God knows how many other operas for the American Opera Company in New York, and now staging plays at the Moscow Art Theatre in London's West End, from where he has just come. He, too, is just 30. Stand up and take a bow, Rouben."

"I can't," he said. "*J'ai trop manger.* I've eaten too much."

Pyotr stared at the man. He was unnerved. They were the same age, but Mamoulian had already accumplished so much. How? And he? What had he done? Nothing.

"And now," Alice continued, "Drum roll, Monsieur is going to direct his first feature film."

"Hope to direct," Mamoulian murmured.

"What's it about," Pauline said.

"The movie is about a girl called Kitty, Kitty Darling. She is an alcoholic, a drunk living in the past when she used to be a famous burlesque star," Mamoulian said in his version of English, his eighth language as he confessed, and not his best. "Kitty sends her young daughter, April, to a convent, to get her away from the sleazy burlesque world in which she lives. Kitty marries a comic named Hitch, who cheats on her and only cares about spending what little money she has. When he finds out she paid for her daughter's convent school for over ten years he goes crazy; he pushes her to bring April home." Mamoulian took off his glasses, inspected them, polished the lenses with his scarf, and put them on again.

"And then?" Delphine said.

"Then when April arrives, she is disgusted with her mother and her sad life. Hitch tries to force April into show business and repeatedly gropes her, at one point forcing a kiss on her."

"*Déguelasse!*" Lucette said.

"*D'accord.*" Mamoulian said. "*Mais ce n'est pas moi, c'est comme ça que c'est écrit.*"

"*Et puis?*" Delphine said.

"Then April walks in the city and meets a lonely young sailor named Tony. They fall in love, agree to marry, and plan for April to move to his home in Wisconsin."

"Really? Wisconsin?" Alice said, deadpan.

"Yes, sailing on the Great Lakes in Wisconsin," Mamoulian said, "April goes to tell her mother about their plans, but overhears Hitch running down Kitty, calling her a has-been. This upsets April who calls off the wedding and joins the chorus line of the burlesque show. She says goodbye to Tony at the subway. Meanwhile, Kitty takes an overdose of sleeping pills. The bottle clearly says, 'For insomnia, one tablet only.' Now it is empty. The Producer of the show finds her half-comatose, draped over a couch, and berates her, mistaking her reaction for delirium tremens. April, not realising what her mother's done, says she will take Kitty's place. Kitty tries to object. April tells Kitty she will take care of her now, like Kitty always did for April. As April goes on stage, Kitty passes away, her head hanging over the edge of the couch. When she finds out her mother is dead, April cannot complete the show and runs off stage where Tony is there to greet her. He says he had a feeling she did not mean what she was saying. She hugs him close and says she wants to go far, far away with him. It is a musical comedy. It's called '*Applause*'." Mamoulian stopped talking.

Silence.

Finally, Alice shook her head. "Whose idea is this?" she said.

"Paramount's."

"What's the budget?"

"It is being discussed."

"What are they paying you?"

"It's also being discussed."

"Until you have a check in your hand, and it doesn't bounce, stick to the theatre," Alice said.

"They want to make the first all-talking picture," Mamoulian said. "It is like a race. Everyone's been trying to do it since the arrival of sound. Warner Brothers are in the lead, but they don't know how to master the new technique."

"And you do?"

"I have some ideas, yes, how to make sound and talk essential, like in the theatre, only better."

"You'll have to be a genius to make it work."

"No. Only lucky."

"With a storyline like that, I agree." Alice said. "Now tell Pyotr about the film you would really like to make."

"Really?" Mamoulian said, looking curiously at Pyotr across the length of the kitchen table. "It takes place in Sweden, at the beginning of the 17th

189

century when the country was ruled by a great queen, Christina. I see Greta Garbo, playing the Queen. Imagine it. The Queen of cinema in such a regal role. She is the same age today as Christina was at the time. She is going to abdicate her throne in favour of her cousin. It will be very dramatic. Very."

"I think he knows more about that than you do, Monsieur, "Pauline said. "Go on, Pyotr, tell him."

Dreamland - 14

6th of June, 1654. As the sun rose over Stockholm to herald a new day's dawning, Petrus was summoned by his master, Count Oxenstierna, still in his bedchamber pulling on his stockings. "What's happening out there?" he said.

"All is quiet, my Lord," Petrus said.

"Karl Gustav?"

"Still not here, my Lord."

"Magnus?"

"Waiting for you in the Auditorium, my Lord."

From where he sat on the edge of his bed, Oxenstierna had a fine view out of his window over the rooftops and church spires of the city. "Ninety-nine percent of them don't know what's going to happen today," he said, as if speaking aloud his thoughts.

"My Lord?" Petrus said.

"The population. Waking up under all those roofs. They have no idea their world will turn upside down if she goes through with this."

"It makes you uneasy?"

"Anything to do with Her Majesty makes me uneasy." Oxenstierna stood up slowly, stretched, squared his shoulders, straightened his ancient spine, fished with his feet to find his shoes, and slipped into them. "Hand me my coat, please, Petrus," he said. Adding, as he put it on, "Now to face the music."

Twenty minutes later, when they entered the Auditorium of the Royal Palace of Stockholm, they found Magnus in the middle of the room studying a tableau of the Royal Crown, Orb and Sceptre, set on a large purple velvet cushion with gold braids, placed on a plinth. "They've been cleaned," he said, by way of introduction.

"Good morning, Lord Magnus," Count Oxenstierna said. "Cleaned, as instructed."

"By whom?"

"Who do you think?"

"She's a strange creature."

"The strangest God ever created. She never stays with anything…if only she had some beliefs to keep her afloat."

"We're not blameless, Axel. We moulded her."

"And look at the result!"

"You think she'll do it?"

"Unfortunately, yes!"

"Do what, My Lords?" Christina said, stepping out of a curtained alcove where she had been standing to see without being seen.

"Your Majesty!" Simultaneously exclaimed by the three men as they bowed.

"I see I surprise you gentlemen," the Queen said.

"With the Crown at stake? Yes, Madame, you do." Count Oxenstierna said.

"It is as well we are in private and can speak frankly," Christina said, looking at the crown on the pillow. "So, which one of you wants to try it on?" She laughed. "It's heavier than you think!"

"Christina, please!" Magnus said. "I think I speak for everyone, please do not do this!"

"Why? In your heart of hearts, it's what you want, isn't it?" She looked around. "What all of you want, a real king, if only you dared speak the truth?"

"The truth? Let me tell it to you," Count Oxenstierna said, his face stern. "The truth is you will betray your mission! You will betray your father, the King! You will betray your Church! Somewhere you are deceiving yourself. This act must stop or one day you will find out what it is like to grow old and be powerless - and alone!"

"But I am alone!" the Queen said, her face darkening in anger. "Don't you understand that? You have directed my every step, beaten into me who I am meant to be, what I am meant to do. Dangling every wretched prince in Europe to be my bedmate so you have an heir. Always watching me, criticising me - there should be a name for men like you!"

"You may call me by whatever name you wish," Oxenstierna said. "I have only done my duty to your great father and the task he entrusted to me in raising you."

"But that's the point. You raised me to be a man. But I am not a man. I am a woman. Is the difference so difficult to comprehend? Let me spell it out. I. Want. To. Be. Who. I. Am. A. Woman!" Christina glared at him. "Enough said."

It was at this moment that the Lord Chamberlain entered the Auditorium to bang his stave on the floor three times to herald the arrival of the Crown Prince, Karl Gustav, who rolled in beaming smiles to one and all. "Just in time," Christina said.

"You look very beautiful when you are angry, Christina," Karl Gustav said. "Am I interrupting something?"

"Only an airing of the truth," Christina said. "It's all yours now -" she waved at the crown, orb and sceptre - "the promise I made you as a girl."

"You promised to marry me - all smoke of course - but do you really want to do this? Give everything up for, for..." he searched for the word.

"Freedom," the Queen said.

Announced, at the stoke of noon, by the peeling of the bells in the city's many church towers, it was the first word she used, seated on the massive throne raised on its dais in the Throne Room, wearing full regalia, the Crown on her head, the Orb and Sceptre in either hand, before the gathered multitude of her Court dressed in all their finery - the Great Officers of State, the Nobles and Councilors, those of the Guilds and the Peasants Estates - a sea of anxious faces looking up to her as she slowly surveyed them. Then a flourish of trumpets from the Court Heralds and the Lord Chamberlain banging his stave on the stone floor again as he cried out: "Pray silence for Her Majesty!"

Silence.

"Freedom," the Queen said, her clear voice carried to the farthest corner of the room. "Man or woman, the birthright of every living Swede, is freedom." Many in her audience nod.

"My people, you know me as I am, a woman brought up as a man to be King. For twenty-two years I have endeavoured to fulfil my role. I know I have not been perfect and acknowledge my faults" – here her audience gasped! - "but it does not become me to make excuses. As a child, living in the long shadow cast by my great father, I learnt the importance of duty. When he died, it was my heritage to serve Sweden and you, and I thank Almighty God who caused me to be born of royal blood that I was called to rule this country." Christina continued her survey, eyes going slowly from left to right. "Now, today, here in this chamber, with God as my witness, I must tell you I am no longer able to fulfil this task -" consternation in the spectators amid a rising clamour of protests, as the Lord Chamberlain repeatedly calls for silence - "and in the absence of an heir of my blood, according to the laws of succession, I am resolved, here and now, to abdicate the throne of Sweden in favour of my elected heir, the -" there is uproar in the chamber, with cries of No! No! Long live Christina! forcing the Queen to raise her voice - "in favour of the Crown Prince of Sweden, Karl Gustav!" Perplexed, the Crown Prince looks on as agitated cries of No! Your Majesty, no! Do not forsake us! No! No! engulf the audience.

In the bedlam the Speaker for the Peasants goes down on his knees, to beg Christina: "Do not abandon us, Madam! Reign over us as long as you may live!"

Followed by the Speaker for the Guilds, also on his knees, "Fie, my Lady, we will help you bear the burden. We beg you, Madam, stay! Rule us as your father wished."

"My good people," Christina said, her cheeks flushed, "as I look on you, my heart fills with the thought of your love and loyalty and I thank all of you who have supported me and defended our country these long years past while I grew up. My decision has not been made lightly but realistically, in all honesty and in the best interests of the state. I recognise within my soul the overriding need to be free, to be myself, in direct contradiction with my obligations to the Crown. In divesting myself of the symbols of power -" at her sign a page steps forward holding the purple velvet cushion onto which Christina placed the orb and sceptre while a deathly hush filled the great room - "My wish is to be like you, free to pursue my dreams, of my life as a woman, true to herself alone."

Pause.

For what seemed an eternity to Petrus, the Queen sat still, saying nothing. Not a sound in the room where the audience held their breath. Then, turning to Count Oxenstierna, she simply said, "My Lord, will you take the crown from my head?"

Stunned, Count Oxenstierna could only stare.

"I am still the Queen," Christina said. "It is not a request. It is an order."

"An order I cannot obey, Your Majesty," the old courtier said. "Did I not swear to your father to keep it there? I will have no part in this, nor -" Oxenstierna glared at the spectators - "nor I think will any other man here today!" There is a growl of approval in the crowd.

"If that be the case," Christina said, "then it is fitting I do it myself!"

Slowly she raised up her hands to take the crown from her head, as anguished cries broke out in the multitude. Slowly, holding the crown before her, she said, "I bid you farewell and ask that Almighty God protect and guide all those who in the future may wear this crown. May their wisdom, duty and loyalty forever be the shield of Sweden." And, turning slowly to give the crown to her cousin, she said, "LONG LIVE PRINCE KARL GUSTAV! LONG LIVE THE KING!"

Chapter Twenty-eight

The echo of her words leave the dinner party stunned. Shortly afterwards, almost forgetting to thank their hosts, the guests leave, and Pyotr finds himself alone with Lucette. Together they clean up. In silence. When the last dish and the last glass had been washed, dried, and put away, with the kitchen once again spotless, Lucette said, "Forgive me for what I am about to tell you. I am superstitious. This may be wrong, it may even be unfair, but the more I hear of your double life the more uncomfortable I feel. I think it would be best if you went home to your room in the Rue des Beaux Arts."

"Je comprends," Pyotr said. "I understand. Thank you." Putting on his coat, he kissed her on both cheeks. "Goodbye, Lucette. *Bonne chance.*"

"Alice will call you," Lucette said, making a helpless gesture with her hands watching him leave. And thought to herself, I have closed a chapter of my life.

Footloose and fancy free, the cliché trundled through Pyotr's mind as he walked, by himself, in and out of the lamplight along the Rue Boissonade. Not for the first time he found himself alone. What a birthday present. Strange that an event from 270 years ago could end a relationship today. Was it just superstition? Or a convenient way to turn the page? At the end of the street, crossing an empty Boulevard Montparnasse, he started to walk around the terrace of the Closerie des Lilas on his way to the Rue d'Assas, when he heard his name called. It was Markus alone at a table on the terrace. "Sit," Markus ordered. "You should see your face. You look like you need a nightcap. What happened?"

Pyotr told him.

Markus laughed. "Join the club," he said. "Anna kicked me out. *Je ne suis pas un homme sérieux,* she said, I am not sérieux, as if that was news. Bloody women. I'm off back to Germany. What will you do?"

Pyotr shrugged. "I'll find something," he said.

"We'll drink to that," Markus said. "I worry about you, my friend. All these little odd jobs don't add up to much. You're thirty now, you need a career. I'm going to America soon. Why don't you come with me?"

Paris Now.

"That was in '27, right, George?"

"Yup. They arrived in New York in February. Their trip took seven days in a ship of the Hamburg-Amerika Line, travelling first class. Markus was a wealthy man by this time, and we know he put up at the Chelsea Hotel and started investing in real estate backed by J.P.Morgan. There is no trace of Pyotr at the hotel and it is unknown what he did or how long he stayed in the city, but we do know he took the train to Chicago from New York's Pennsylvania Station leaving at 2.55 pm on June 14, arriving at Union Station at 9.50 am the following morning, then connecting to the Santa Fe Super Chief, leaving Chicago at 7.30 pm for the 37 hour journey to LA. where he met Mamoulian again. Alice Guy set it up, and Pyotr began at the bottom of the totem pole in Hollywood knocking out screenplays for peanuts. We know these details because he starts to keep a daily journal - a routine he maintained for 70 years - in which he not only records events, the people he meets, and his numerous affairs, but also sticks in found ephemera like ticket stubs, match box covers, and the odd photograph. He moves about the city, living in a doss house downtown behind the Embassy hotel, then in a wooden hunting shack on San Ysidro in Beverly Hills and finally in the hotel on Sunset when it went bust and Bank of America took it over as trustee. He rewrote 'Alias' there but the actual film was made on location here and in Britain. There's a fictional novel about this period in which he is the main protagonist, with real places and people mixed up with the entire screenplay. - well-worth reading; you get a genuine whiff of what it was like back then, right up to the death of the star, Barbara Burns, sadly forgotten today. After the funeral, in '34, he moved back to Europe, ending up - well, you know the answer to that as well as I do."

Chapter Twenty-nine

The journals are kept in a vault in the mansion occupied by Fondazione Szépség, in Genoa. As noted by the resident Librarian, 'They cover the years 1927 to 1997 with two gaps, one of 5 years, 1940 to 1944, held under the Official Secrets' Act, GHQ Auxiliary Units, and one of 9 years, 1962 to 1971, burned by the author in Sicily. The 56 remaining volumes are in relatively good condition, with slight crinkling to paper at the gutters, the pages clean with some foxing to the edges and faint tanning and thumb markings throughout. Heavier tanning to free endpapers, some annotated in pencil. A few show moderate water staining to top and fore edges. Some bindings have slight edge-wear with some rubbing to surfaces and curling to corners. Visible wear marks to the spine of some, some minutely split. Some ephemera unglued, some missing. The "American Years", 1927-1933 and 1982-1994 are intact. At your request, please find selected italicised highlights:'

July 2, 1927 - *It being a Saturday, Mamoulian showed me around the empty Studio Lot in Burbank that Warner Bros hope to acquire: 60+ acres! He told me the original family name was Wonsal, a Polish-Jewish family from Krasnosielc. 'Even if they now call themselves Warner, never forget where they come from. They're all Jewish. The entire industry has been invented by them; Mayor, Goldwyn, Fox, every major studio built from scratch due to their hard work and ingenuity.' Orange groves all around the lot fill what is called the Valley. You can smell them as you come over the hill from the city.*

September 7, 1927 - *Got an offer from Flying A for 'Whiteout Showdown', a Western I pitched, in which a relentless blizzard traps a veteran*

Sheriff, a gang of gold thieves, and his abducted daughter in an abandoned quarry. With the miner's precious gold on the line, the Sheriff must make a gut-wrenching decision: uphold his duty to protect the gold or save his daughter from ruthless outlaws. $800. Told them no: $1250.

September 9, 1927 *- Drove up to Santa Barbara in a borrowed car (well I hope Bernie doesn't think I stole it, ha, ha). Flying A Studios used to occupy two entire city blocks, flattened by the '25 earthquake. They made over 1000 silent movies, mainly Westerns, before moving to LA along with most of a dozen other film companies who operated up here. Small studio lot on Mission, still functioning in all the re-building going on along State Street. Bargained down to $1100. Still, being broke, I now feel I'm rich! Small potatoes compared to the impending visit of Lindbergh, all people can talk about after he flew the Atlantic in his little aeroplane last May.*

September 17, 1927 *- Bernie Dray, my very well-connected roommate, took me to hear Cantor Yossele Rosenblatt chant Kaddish in temple B'nai B'rith on Wilshire, his voice going from contralto to an incredible falsetto seemingly seamlessly from behind a v. big, v. black beard. Bernie says he got a hundred grand for appearing in The Jazz Singer, supposed to be the first talkie if Warner ever gets it released. The way people go on about the importance of what they are doing in the business here, you would never think Fritz Lang has already premiered 'Metropolis' in Berlin and New York, and Abel Gance 'Napoléon' in Paris which I saw at the beginning of the year. Talk about chauvinism, they're not even mentioned at the so-called Oscars! A prize-giving cooked up by Douglas Fairbanks for his Academy of Motion Pictures.*

November 10, 1927 *- Still find it gauche the way everyone says they're AHMURRIKAN! - last guy in saying it the loudest. The town is full of every nation in Europe waving the Stars and Stripes on their doorstep. Magyar in the apartment next to ours on Olive, no visa, has one permanently proclaiming his allegiance stuck on a pole out of his window. His wife and none of his kids speak english, but they're all Amerikai, with the last i said like eee. Gey veys. Go figure, as they say here.*

December 25, 1927 *- v. chilly 44°F this Sunday morning (compared to 92°F two months ago!) Reminds me of 1914 Weinachtsfrieden playing soccer with a tin can between the trenches when we stopped fighting. We're going to Palm Springs, a place in the desert 3 hours to the east, for the holidays with a* *couple of girls Bernie's found. For a city with a population of 750,000, Los Angeles seems to have more girls than Paris with 2 million people.*

***January 27, 1928** - Saw Chaplin's movie 'The Circus' at Grauman's. For all the difficulties he's had making it between the tax authorities, his divorce and his mother dying, the result is a testimony to his courage and sheer balls. As always, the press is banging on about its cost, and delays, and, because it's silent, the probability it will lose money. I'll bet they're wrong. This place - in fact this entire country - is hung up about money. Nothing has value if it doesn't make money. That a movie can make you laugh, or cry is irrelevant if it doesn't 'gross' what the critics think it should. C'est lamentable, mais c'est comme ça.*

Heard from Markus complaining about prohibition. He is well on the way to becoming a millionaire in the property boom in NY.

***March 11, 1928** - Buy car from Bern because he says I use it more than he does. 100 bucks. Not bad for a 3-year-old Chevy Superior sedan. He bought himself the new Ford roadster for just under $400. Get driving licence from DMV. Must remember to renew my visa.*

***April 1, 1928** - Having nothing better to do went to Echo Park to hear the evangelist Aimee Semple McPherson preaching in Angelus Temple, hideous building she's built to praise the Lord and fleece the flock. Cannot fathom the gullibility of the hoi polloi. Scene was more like a circus than a church, with thousands in attendance, the crowd controlled by cops. How to square this with her charitable work? She's more effective than the government. On a bulletin board in the church is an account of McPherson interrupting her radio broadcast to request food, blankets, clothing, and emergency supplies for victims of the earthquake in Santa Barbara, and, after a dam failed leaving 600 dead, leading the relief effort by persuading the fire and police departments to assist in helping children and the elderly!*

***May 4, 1928** - Lunch today with Bernie who brought along Paul Fejos, a director. He couldn't believe I turned down $800 for my Western. He's just made a movie for Universal whose 3-page outline was bought for $25! We talked about the war mainly after Paul said because he had studied medicine in Budapest where he was born, he ended up as a medical orderly on the Italian Front, and I told him about being co-opted into helping one of our surgeons when Manfred and I brought in a wounded soldier, ending up doing a stint in Heidelberg because the surgeon thought I had a doctor's gift. My mistake.*

Sometimes I forget I'm supposed to be a Brit. Fortunately Paul didn't pick up on it. He's a great blagueur and maybe recognises a kindred spirit. Like me he arrived in the States broke and took whatever jobs he could find, including in a funeral parlour! I told him about Alice and was surprised he didn't know her. Asked me if I would work as an extra? For money, of course. We agree to meet again.

July 1, 1928 - *Our lease is up tomorrow. Bern's going off to live with a girlfriend. Et moi? Can't afford Olive on my own. Hunt on for a home. Meanwhile found a cheap room, 2 bucks a night, in the Roosevelt on Hollywood Blvd. Quite grand coming in the front lobby, flea pit when you get to the room on the top floor. From the desk where I'm sitting writing this, without getting up, I can touch the single bed on my left, reach the door to my right and take two steps to the bathroom. Only a year old, it already looks shabby. But, and this is curious, it doesn't matter as long as I write down something of the day's events, today also being the 1st anniversary of my journal. I kick myself that I didn't start sooner. What did I do, think, feel, in all those forgotten moments when I was a kid in China, India? Or when Mummy died? Must remember to write to Alice, thank her for all the introductions.*

October 12, 1928 - *Starting to feel at home in this part of town. Walked down the street a block to Musso & Frank's Grill, la cantine de Hollywood. Lunch is two bucks. Everybody in the business eats here. Drinks too, if you are 'connected' as I am. Louie, a waiter since they opened the 'joint' in 1919, knows me by name but mispronounces it so I am Monsieur Pierre to him. He knows I like to sit in a corner when I'm on my own (which is most of the time since I can't afford to treat a guest) where I can survey the room. Paul was in today with one of his leading ladies from the new movie he's making, Barbara Kent. One look and I was in love. The 'thud of lust' as they write in the penny dreadfuls, plus that je ne sais quoi - a kind of reciprocated electricity of two magnets clamping together. Unfortunately the lady is engaged. Paul could see what was going on the moment he introduced us and judiciously supplied this vital piece of information before I could make an ass of myself and withdraw. Every now and again from my corner table I could feel her glancing over but I pretended not to notice. The advantage of writing screenplays is that you can cook up a story and vicariously put in your every fancy and that is how I will get the lovely lady!*

October 26, 1928 - *Finished 'Engaged'. 96 pages. Pitched it to Bernie. 'So what happened? I'll tell you what happened. Without the fucking fog we would have wiped the floor with them, Martin said, removing his top hat and silk scarf. It was then he noticed Barbara for the first time sitting in the corner watching him, smoking, the smoke curling out of lips he already imagined kissing. Who's the dame? he said. She owns this joint, the answer was whispered. I wouldn't go near her, I was you. That's all he needed to hear, someone telling him what he shouldn't do. Walked over. Buy you a drink? he said. Blue. Her eyes were blue. Laughing at him. My daddy said never drink where you work, she said. Then added, Wiped the floor with whom?'*

Pause.

And then? Bernie said.

Sold! Celebrated at the Beverly Hills Hotel, now owned by an outfit from NY, the Interstate Company.

New Year's Day, 1929 - *The army is going to fly an aeroplane over the city for 10 days starting tomorrow, refuelling in the air, to prove it can be done. They've called the plane the 'Question Mark', whether in irony or as a joke nobody knows. If it works it will prove long distance travel by plane is possible and not just a stunt a la Lindbergh. (Note: plane's name would make a good title) Headache from too much booze last night.*

Tuesday, February 12, 1929 - *Letter from Aunt Tilly: They've chased Trotsky out of Russia! Her family has known his family since Tsar Alexander ruled. Lenin's right-hand man sent into exile to Turkey - of all places! Rumour says Attaturk agreed on condition Stalin would not attempt to murder him there. Unreal seen from Hollywood, like a dark, Grimm fairy tale. At least the old bird's still alive and kicking.*

Receptionist gave me a note from Bern. Apparently Flying A have resold my western to a new outfit, Monogram Pictures. $10 grand! (Hell of a lot for a Poverty Row studio.???) Want to contact me if interested to rewrite some scenes in Santa Barbara where shooting is scheduled to begin March 4. Call them.

March 6, 1929 - *Drove up to meet the director, Bill Day. He confirmed the 10 grand. Told him what I got. His comment; That's show business. Patted me on the shoulder. You'll learn. Wants to change the rape scene in the cave. Apparently a new code is going to be enforced: no profanity, no suggestive nudity, no graphic or realistic violence, no sexual persuasions and no rape. See a problem? No. Will I get paid? Yes - maybe. Maybe? Day's an intelligent man. Over the lunch break he voiced a concern about over-speculation in the economy and the effect it would have on the financing of movies if there was no audience who could afford to go to see them. First time I've ever heard this.*

March 30, 1929 *- On set. They're about halfway through. Met one of the stuntmen, a Crow Indian. Possibly the strangest meeting of my life. We traded details. The man was much older than me, lean, tough, with the physique of a gymnast. I wanted to learn how much time was spent on rehearsal of some of the more dangerous stunts like falling off a galloping horse and making it look real without hurting yourself. He smiled. It's an old trick you learn by falling off for real and getting hurt, he said. Then added, Has anybody told you that you have your Mother's eyes? Before I could answer he was called away to shoot the next scene. When they broke at the end of the day he was gone. How could he have known my mother, or the colour of her eyes?*

April 11, 1929 *- Shooting suspended, crew laid off until further notice. Finance dried up? Not a word out of Monogram, the company still in formation? Went to see a cabin up San Ysidro in Beverly Hills. Used to be a hunting lodge in the days when this part of town was a jungle with mountain lions. Made of wood, sawn-off barn door, painted dark green, outside shower and toilet. 2 acres. Cheap. Agree lease for 3 years after 6 months free trial period. $25 per month.*

September 6, 1929 *- Met Day in town who showed me a copy of the Reporter quoting a Professor in Boston, Roger Babson, who gave a speech yesterday to the National Business Conference at Babson College, in which he proclaimed, "More people are borrowing and speculating today than ever in our history. Sooner or later a crash is coming, and it may be terrific. Wise are those investors who now get out of debt and reef their sails. This does not mean selling all you have, but it does mean paying up your loans and avoiding margin speculation" Here it comes, Day said, just as I told you when we met. Talk about coincidence, letter from Markus saying the same thing. He's bailing out, advised me to sell whatever stocks I had. Made me laugh. What stocks? Tough enough paying my rent.*

October 30, 1969 *- Variety: "WALL ST. LAYS AN EGG. Drop in Stocks Ropes Showmen. Many weep and Call Off Christmas Orders. Legit Shows Hit. Mergers Halted." The headlines smother you in a blizzard. It's* *impossible. How can this happen in America? It's unrelenting. "The most dramatic event in the financial history of America is the collapse of the New York Stock Exchange. The stage was Wall Street, but the onlookers covered the country. Estimates are that 22,600,000 people were in the market at the time. Tragedy, despair and ruination spell the story of countless thousands of marginal traders. Many may remain broke for the rest of their lives..." It doesn't bear reading. You can't help thinking, what about me? Louie says, What's to worry? Look around. This crowd's tough. They've been through worse shit. He may be right. Every table in Frank & Musso's occupied, beautiful women smiling, dining; guys drinking, making deals. What's to worry, right?*

***November 13, 1929** - The Crash has finally bottomed out according to the Journal. Quote: 'Stocks had been driven too low. People throughout the country have become panic stricken and have thrown their sound securities over without regard to values. There is nothing wrong with the country or the business of the country, and just because trade has slumped moderately after an extremely active summer is no reason why first-class securities should be ruthlessly thrown into the market in such fashion as we have seen in the last few trading days.' Jesse Livermore.' Send article to Markus.*

***December 31, 1929** - New Year's Eve on my own in my wooden shack. Rumor Buster Keaton's been badly hurt by the crash, headed for divorce, probably cost him his estate around the corner on Hartford Drive. Saw two deer as I came in. Almost tame. Just looked at me as I got out of the car, then went on nibbling the plants. My letter to Markus returned: addressee unknown???*

***June 4, 1930** - Went to the opening of the Pantages Theater, corner of Hollywood and Vine. Spectacular. Huge, gilded interior. Escorted tiny little Barbara Kent on one of our clandestine dates. 60 to 80 million Americans attended movies each week according to Variety (so much for Day's pessimism) and most of them seemed to be on hand to see the opening program: MGM's "The Floradora Girl" starring Marion Davies; a Metronome News (MGM's newsreel), a Walt Disney cartoon, with Slim Martin conducting the Greater Pantages Orchestra; and also, a Fanchon-and-Marco stage piece, called "The Rose Garden Idea." Wild night.*

***July 10, 1930** - Been here for 3 years already - hard to believe. What have I learned? Write in the vernacular: Gimme not Give me. Friendship doesn't exist in this town - it's like instant coffee; Tasteless and instantly cold. Getting* *laid is easier done than said. Every name is fiction. The business will outlive the Crash. I'm a writing mercenary, quick on the draw, banging out screenplays.*

August 24, 1930 - *Finally got to see 'All Quiet on the Western Front' in which I'm an extra along with a surprisingly large number of German Army vets currently living in LA - recruited as bit players and technical advisers. Around 2,000 were used during production!!!! (Crash? What crash?) The film runs 152 minutes, and Variety had this to say: 'The League of Nations could make no better investment than to buy up the master-print, reproduce it in every language, to be shown in all the nations of the world, until the word "war" is taken out of the dictionaries.' Will see it again because I didn't spot myself.*

September 5, 1930 - *Going out with one of the extras, Lilla. Runs a second-hand bookshop on Sunset when she's not filming. Unlike several girls, she did not freak out when I brought her here, in fact she thought it very original to be living in a wooden shack in the jungle right behind Pickfair, the mansion of Douglas Fairbanks and Mary Pickford. When I told her Fred Astaire was building a house up the hill directly opposite the entrance to our driveway she said I wouldn't trade this for some lousy mansion. Asks if she can put up shelves, bring some books from her shop?*

November 7, 1930 - *1,300 banks have failed so far as depositors hurry to withdraw their life savings. (Variety) The industrial production of the United States has fallen by half, (The Hollywood Reporter) and I saw my first soup kitchen downtown on 6th Street, with bread lines around the block and large numbers of homeless people on the sidewalk. Heard the Beverly Hills Hotel was closing. Trying to clear our backyard, poor Lilla got badly stung by poison ivy. Put baking soda with water on the rash to stop the itching. Go to Schwab's, pick up some colloidal oatmeal ointment for her skin. What a wagonload of negative shit today has been.*

April 15, 1931 - *By chance, down by the pier in Santa Monica, saw a nutter with the wonderful name of Plennie Wingo, set off to walk backwards across the country. Along with other spectators, I tried keeping up with him on the sidewalk but got a crick in my neck looking over my shoulder within two blocks, gave up. Don't forget Monogram meeting tomorrow with Trem Carr, one of the founders, for lunch at their studio on Sunset Drive.*

April 16, 1931 - *Would I like to go to New York? Asked before I could sit down. Said yes before asking why. Carr, who specialises in low-budget features*

(I checked) wants an action-melodrama written about building a skyscraper. 'Throw in a bit of mystery if you can.' Asked what happened to my western? Carr said it will get finished when Day finds the time??? (Wonder how many other half-finished films are lying on a shelf somewhere?) Asked him if he knew the Crow stuntman? No. Casting is not his job.

April 25 - 27, 1931 *- Coast-to-coast via Chicago in the train because Monogram would not spring for airfare for a lousy screenwriter. Arrive, try to find Markus at the Chelsea. No dice. They think he's gone back to Europe. Go over to 34th Street to see them finishing the Empire State Building, the reason I am here. From the street looking up you can't see the top, 102-stories above, 1250 feet, the tallest building in the world. Walked the entire block; v. impressive ArtDeco entrance on 5th. They say the design was changed fifteen times to make sure it would be the world's tallest building. Despite the Crash, construction started on March 17, 1930, with 3500 workmen, working two 12-hour shifts per day, and the building going up ahead of schedule and under budget in just thirteen and a half months. It opens at the end of the week.*

May 1, 1931 *- Bang on time, President Hoover, in Washington, pressed a button and the lights went on in the Empire State Building. Huge crowd at the bottom. Walked up Fifth on the opposite sidewalk to see what it looked like as you got farther and farther uptown. What an extraordinary achievement! Making movies v. small beer in comparison; the one a momentary illusion, the other a reality casting its shadow not only over the city but over the world. Haven't a clue what to write, but God would I be proud if I had been one of those workmen who built it leave alone the architect.*

May 11, 1931 *- Letter from Tilly, destitute. Last of her great fortune gone kaput in the failure of Credit-Anstalt, largest bank in Austria. Can I send her some money? If only she knew. Borrow $250 from Bernie to send. Western Union on La Brea. Lilla going on location to Santa Fe, New Mexico to shoot a movie in which she has a small speaking part, her dream, at last. See her off at Union Station. Back here, in my shack, I realise how much I like being on my own.*

May 14, 1931 *- Pitch to Monogram for 'Skyscraper': 'A meeting is called by the client. It is held in the palatial boardroom before the Chairman and Directors. There is an enormous easel set in front of them. On the easel is a huge drawing covered with a white sheet. The world-famous architect, Goody*

Mulliner, comes in, bows, takes a corner of the white sheet and pulls it off. The audience gasps. They see drawn on parchment, a rectangle sitting on a horizontal line. Next to the rectangle is an arrow. The arrow goes to words written in capital letters: REPEAT UPWARDS UNTIL YOU REACH THE SKY. *Silence. Mulliner bows and leaves the room.' Result? I'm fired.*

June 6, 1931 - *'The Creditanstalt bankruptcy has put the whole of the German banking system on the verge of collapse' (Dr. Heinrich Brüning, the German Chancellor, quoted in the Herald-Tribune today). Markus was right, the dominoes are falling. Add this from the Jewish Telegraphic Agency: 'Berlin, June 4th. "Jews, clear out of Germany!" was the shout kept up uninterruptedly by a crowd of Hitlerists who went marching today through the Kurfuerstendamm, the principal street in the East-end of Berlin, insulting and molesting any Jews they came across.' As if this were not enough drama for one day, a letter from Lilla: 'Don't get upset, please. I love it here in Santa Fe. I am going to stay. Maybe become a potter. Keep the books as a present and memento of me. Your everloving once-upon-a-time soulmate, Lilla.' Shades of Lucette and Nathalie. Gone. Just like that. Wonder if they all sense I want to be on my own?*

July 6, 1931 - *100°F. Woke, sweating, out of a nightmare. Eddy Earnie, Izzy Isaccs, Alex Thompson. Eddy. Edward Earnie. The names came at me out of the blue. Eddy, the boy who sat next to me at school for five years. We won the three-legged race three years running. And the other two, Izzy and Alex, the four of us inseparable, making our own orphan family in that rambling red-brick building on Audley End, Saffron Walden. Then I was Hans. Because my Prussian great-uncle, Graf Otto-Friedrich Habermann von Oldesloe-Schlaffenberg, obliged to adopt me after the death of my mother, (his cousin), choose to change my name to Hans Habermann when he shipped me off to the orphanage in England. And, at 17, it was as Hans that I was enrolled in his regiment and sent to fight the Kaiser's war. And it was Hans who shot Eddy in that trench. Hans. Not me.???? But I am, was, still am, Hans. A tidal wave of interconnected synapses woke me up this morning as these names and memories surged out of the past. Where they have been blacked out in my brain, suppressed for all these years. Why now? As I write this I ask myself, why now? I don't know the answer. Does it matter? What will it change? Nobody knows this except me. Here in my shack I am alone with the thought- nobody knows. Nobody knows. But for one thing. Switching identities. We were so alike in height and build, Eddy and I, right down to our straw-coloured hair, that we could have been* twins. *Legs tied at ankle and knee, my left against his right, arms wrapped around each other's waist, three-legged, we even won the cross-country race in pouring rain. Switching uniforms. Hans became Eddy. No. I did.*

July 8, 1931 *- It's a relief being on my own and admitting who I am. Abou told me Socrates said: 'Know thyself.' C'est vrai.*

August 24, 1931 *- Amongst the books left by Lilla found a Mss by Kurt Gödel published last year "Über formal unentscheidbare Sätze der Principia Mathematica und verwandte Systeme I" ("On Formally Undecidable Propositions of Principia Mathematica and Related Systems I"), a paper in mathematical logic. Hooked by Gödel's use of self-referential sentences. Gödel shows that the classical paradoxes of self-reference, such as 'This statement is false', can be recast as self-referential formal sentences of arithmetic. Witness Epimenides paradox - All Cretans are liars - where he himself is a Cretan. Am I telling the truth when I say I always lie? Consider a member of a club of all clubs who are not members of any club. Not sure that works.*

September 4, 1931 *- Back from Palm Springs. Meeting with the boys from Fleischer Studios, Dave and his brother, Max. 'We pissed ourselves laughing when we heard about the pitch you made for 'Skyscraper' Dave said.*

'Carr was red in the face at the next table when he overheard Rouben telling us the story in Musso's,' Max said.

'Here's a thought for you,' Dave said, 'when we finish "Boop" (Boop-Oop-a-Doop is an animated short they're making about Betty Boop and Koko the Clown), would you consider a re-write entitled 'Alice and the Building That Reached the Sky', with Alice as the Client and the King and Queen of Hearts joint-ChairPersons of the Board of Directors, and the Mad Hatter as Goody Mulliner?'

'Alice says How high is Up?' Max said, 'and the Queen says at least to the top of my Crown and the King says my Crown is taller, each of them standing in front of the drawing on the easel, with the Mad Hatter adding one rectangle on top of another as they speak.'

'They step back to see the result,' Dave said, 'and Alice says That doesn't look tall enough to be Up.'

'Up is higher, the Mad Hatter agrees,' Max said, 'and adds another rectangle.'

'Alice raises her head as far back as she can,' Dave said, 'You'll have to do better to get Up there, she says, pointing at the sky. Up is much higher Up.

'For such a small person she is absolutely right, the King mutters to the Queen,' Max said.

'Of course she is, the Queen mutters back,' Dave said, 'of course she is. Small has nothing to do with it.'

Brilliant. Absolutely, flabbergastingly, brilliant. Of course, I said yes, I'd do it for free. And Hollywood being Hollywood, bloody Trem Carr insisted they owned the rights to the story since I went to New York on their dime. Pay up.

December 28, 1931 *- See where Gandhi has returned to India. In my mind's eye I picture him in his dhoti standing in the path with carrots to feed our ponies when we rode them to the reservoir because the horses liked to swim. As children we thought it was his job. Somewhere there's a photograph of his wife holding hands with me and my sister in the bazaar.*

February 4, 1932 *- Papers full of Sino-Japanese war, with dogfights over Shanghai. Hard to imagine (I was too little) our house on the Bund looking up to see a dogfight. My mother's been dead for over 20 years. Strange thought to come along. God knows what she would think of my life in a wooden shack in Hollywood.*

February 22, 1932 *- Bernie: 'You wont believe this, Goebbels has announced Hitler will challenge Hindenberg for the office of the President of Germany! The little bastard is claiming that his appointment as liaison to Braunschweig gives him citizenship because citizens of that city are considered to be Germans, therefore he, although Austrian born, could now run for the office of President.'*

April 10, 1932 *- Bernie: 'Thank Christ, Hindenburg won the second round of elections getting 53% of the votes to Hitler's 36.8%.' I suggest he's becoming too involved. He tells me to get my head out of the sand.*

April 15, 1932 *- Letter at last from Markus: First, the bad news: Klara, his ex-girlfriend is dead, murdered in Newport, Rhode Island. No other details. Second, worse news if that's possible, Berlin is in chaos, with 400,000 Nazi storm troopers, under Röhm, an ominous presence on every street corner, threatening homos, gipsies, Jews, even the government by force, upsetting Hitler's own plans for a coup to make himself Führer despite his recent loss in the elections. Hitler's clever and knows he must have the backing of the Army and* *the entrenched, powerful industrialists, both groups aware of how dangerous the Brownshirts could be. Bruening has invoked Article 48 of the constitution and issued a decree banning the SA and SS all across Germany. The Nazis are outraged and want Hitler to fight the ban. But Hitler, Goebbels at his elbow, is always a step ahead and knows better. He's sure the republic is on its last legs and that his opportunity will soon come along. Seen from California this all seems remote. Apart from Bern, people just shrug when you bring it up here. All anybody talks about is the upcoming Olympics and the problems getting about town with all the work they've got going.*

July 27, 1932 - I'm becoming as bad as Bernie, and it's interrupting filming. Von Papen, the German Chancellor, has dissolved the Government after the Nazis clashed with the communists and the police in Hamburg, leaving 19 dead and hundreds injured. Hitler is everywhere haranguing huge crowds with new elections scheduled for the 31st. Shown on Movietone News between every A and B feature.

July 30, 1932 - What a day! Opening of the Olympic Games in Los Angeles in the Coliseum downtown. Managed to get tickets with Bernie. Spectacular arena, hard to believe we were a hundred thousand in there, seated in relative comfort, the flags of 41 nations flapping and cracking like so many popguns in the breeze. You would never think the nation was in the middle of what the papers now call the Great Depression. We were lucky to be able to park in the garden of an enterprising negro family living behind the stadium, who, for a couple of bucks, not only looked after the car but washed and polished it while we enjoyed ourselves.

July 31, 1932 - The Nazi's gain 230 seats in The Reichstag and now have a 38% majority! Hitler's going to demand the Chancellorship.

September 14, 1932 *- New letter from Markus shared with Bern over drinks at the Derby. Hitler met with President Hindenberg on August 13th and demanded the Chancellorship with the power to dissolve the Reichstag as he saw fit, Turned down flat! H. furious, gone to Berchtesgaden to plot with Goebbels. Goebbels, back in Berlin, helps elect Hermann Göring president of the Reichstag. Hitler's gang now in place with only Von Papen to defend the republic! On September 12, Von Papen attempted to order the dissolution of the Reichstag, ignored by Göring, who effectively got a vote to nullify Von Papen's order. You can see where this is going - a dictatorship under Herr Hitler.*

November 18, 1932 - *With Bernie to the Ambassador for the Academy Awards - first time for me. A Western, 'Cimarron', wins Best Picture. Since I love westerns I can't wait to see it. Bernie has. His verdict: 'American goulash, garnished in racial caricatures, slow as treacle, that will put you to sleep. Forget it.' Since it also won an Oscar for Best Adapted Screenplay and Best Production Design, maybe he's wrong?*

January 2, 1933 - *Saw 'Cimarron' over the holiday. Bernie was right.*

January 6, 1933 - *Report of a secret meeting between Von Papen and Hitler to undermine the new Chancellor Kurt von Schleicher.*

January 31, 1933 - *It worked! Hitler is appointed German Chancellor, with three of the eleven cabinet posts given to other Nazis. He's made a bogus offer to form a coalition with the Center Party to create a majority in the Reichstag and when that fails, he has Göring approve a re-election scheduled for March 5. When you see the pictures of these guys it's like Central Casting sent over a gang to rival Capone's.*

February 28, 1933 - *Missive from Markus: Reichstag destroyed by fire! Hindenburg's suspended civil liberties and 10,000 opponents of the Nazis have been arrested. Hitler's got the army on his side. He's outlawed any gatherings, meetings or publications against the government, meaning against him! He's dissolved all the elected bodies in Prussia and Germany and control of the police is now his and the Nazis he's put in place. Every day he tightens the screws on free speech. Pretty soon you won't be allowed to think. It's worse than I thought it would ever be, and I fear what is to come.*

May 29, 1933 - *Got home to find a team of surveyors on 'my' property. The landlord from whom I rent is going to start building a house next year and the land must be surveyed. Sorry, no renewal of my lease. No peace for the wicked. Maybe it is my destiny to always move. So far, I've lived in Hawaii, China, India, Prussia, England, Germany, France and America. Where next?*

June 30, 1933 - *Accepted offer from Bernie to write a war movie he is going to direct. Best part of the deal is I get to relocate to a bungalow in the Beverly Hills Hotel now in trusteeship to the Bank of America. The place is not much better than my shack but rent free. Who am I to complain?*

Chapter Thirty

The seven years Pyotr spent in America were not kind to the old building - he could see that from the street, where cracks and fissures in the plaster on the long-unpainted façade and the misaligned shutters on the windows gave the place a drunken look. Marie was still the concierge though, and here time had been kinder, she was the same doughty woman he remembered. When she opened the door to her lodge and saw who had knocked, she recognised him immediately, a smile bloomed on her face as he kissed her on both cheeks, and she said, "Vous voila enfin de retour, Monsieur Pyotr! Bien bronzés, mais je vous ai quand même reconnu. Heureusement vous êtes revenu, la maison a besoin de vos talents. Entrez, que je vous raconte tout."

It was quite a tale she told. Pyotr, seated opposite the picture he had painted all those years ago, was in turn fascinated and appalled. Things were difficult in France, *avec la crise économique en Europe*, but the children, Émile and Marie-France, were both in good health, studying for the *bac*. Mlle. Victorine had died, peacefully, in her sleep, of old age; Mlle. Géraldine was still alive, bedridden, *un peu gaga*, her accounts a shambles, with half the tenants cheating on their rents; your Great-Aunt Tilly and her nephew have moved, no one knows where, and that apartment is vacant, as is the apartment Mme. Steinem and her daughter, Nathalie, used to occupy on the 6th; Mme. Lambert is now a widow, with her daughter, Marie-Claire, living with her, the other siblings still across the landing on the 4th floor, but Gaby, their maid, dismissed, no longer affordable, for the obvious reason, lack of money, since none of them work; Monsieur Zucchi is still on the 3rd, but his mistress, Mlle. Spilimbergo has been replaced by a new

213

one, Mlle. Vanessa von Paraboom, a friend of Mlle. Zoffany, his neighbour, currently in hospital with syphilis; Monsieur Doumeng is still on the 5th, but the American poet has gone and Monsieur Faccini's place is now occupied by a dancer in the Ballet Russe, Monsieur Vladimiroff; your friends, Mlle. Paulin and Mme. Demailly, are still there on the 6th, but Coco, their parrot flew away; only the 2nd floor is unchanged, that woman with her cats and M. and Mme. Descourtis, *vieillissant, mais sans le chien qui est mort, heureusement.* All the *chambres de bonnes* on the top floor are occupied, even your old room, with students from the Beaux Arts, except for Marie-Laure, who is still there because she looks after Géraldine. But it's not like before, no, *malheureusement* people are sad, tired, and dubious about the future…

When the flood of information finally stopped, Marie looked Pyotr anxiously in the face: *"Et vous, Monsieur Pyotr*, will you come back?"

It was the same question asked of him after he climbed the ninety steps to the 6th floor and knocked on the door of Pauline and Delphine. After being smothered in hugs and kisses, hauled in to sit at the kitchen table, glass in hand, repeatedly filled with a fine Beaujolais nouveau it being September, obliged to recount his adventures in America in every tiny detail, punctuated with cries of astonishment when he mentioned meeting Charlie Chaplin or Boris Karloff or Greta Garbo, it was Delphine who finally said: "So now you are here, are you glad you came back?" A simple question, deserving a simple answer, yet Pyotr hesitated for a moment before he said, "Yes."

"Then you will be glad to know the apartment across the landing is empty," Pauline said. "We have the key to show the place since Géraldine is too old to climb up here."

"Not for me. I have found another place to rent," Pyotr said.

"Why?" Delphine said.

"It is a small gallery in the Palais-Royal, where I can paint again and sell my work directly to the public without giving away half what I earn."

"So? Work there and live here. You get three months free rent if you sign a three-year lease. Géraldine needs you; the building needs you; my God, we need you. It has not been the same since you left."

He signed.

Within a month it was as if he had never left. America, California, Hollywood, the 'bizness', a distant mirage. A momentary dream. Reality was Paris, the Rue des Beaux Arts, the building, the hundred and five steps to the top floor, the smell of wood polish, Dettol and cat piss. When he finally saw 'Alias' in the Pagode on the Rue Babylon behind the Bon Marché, it was a revelation and it was only when the credits rolled at the end and he saw Bernie's name as the director and his own as the screenwriter that he recognised the work, acknowledging that strange sense of 'otherness' all artists feel. Of a work done by some other person, not themselves. The same feeling he had when he walked across the landing with Pauline and she opened the door to Anna and Nathalie's apartment and for a moment he felt the urge to call out 'Anna, c'est moi,' the place, the space, even empty of all furniture, still redolent of the two women he had loved there. Géraldine, in her 97th year, propped up in her bed by a mountain of frilly lace pillows, had cackled with glee when he enquired where they had gone. "To Italy," she said. "Somewhere near Lucca. Supposedly to learn Italian, but really for the birth of the child." Child? "Nathalie, the daughter was pregnant. They pretended she wasn't, but she was. By that German…I can't remember his name. It will come to me. Never mind. Sit. Sit down. There is much to be discussed."

There was. Starting with a budget for the façade, then the empty apartments, followed by delayed maintenance on gutters, plumbing, heating, the electric wiring, the boilers and rising damp in the cellar. Henri was called in from Belleville to help with professional advice and labour. Scaffolding soon covered the front and rear elevation, and Pyotr found himself scurrying up and down ladders with tiles for the roof where they had blown off, cement and plaster in buckets hauled up on pulleys for the endless cracks and fissures to be sealed and repainted, using a pickaxe and spade on the cellar floor after chasing out generations of rats who lived down there to get at the clogged drains and replace the broken ones dating back to the Middle Ages, removing, stripping, repairing, sanding, repainting, rehinging and rehanging all 35 pairs of shutters on the front of the building, ditto for the front door and the entrance to the bar, while laying a protective strip of beige canvas down the entrance hall and up all 105 steps and risers, to facilitate the redecoration and relighting of the property's vertical access core and still allow the tenants egress to their apartments side-stepping around the workmen.

The three months free rent period came and went. As did the following three months. When finally, just before Christmas, the job was completed, Géraldine, still in her nightgown covered by a fushia- coloured silk bathrobe knotted at the waist, supported by her maid on one side and Pyotr on the other, tottered downstairs and out to the street to gaze up in admiration at her newly renovated building amidst a crowd of neighbours on hand to congratulate her, the doyenne of the street, as if she personally had done all the work. "J'offre la tournée," she said, steering for the bar and the crowd followed her in for a round of free drinks. Shortly afterwards, a few days into the new year, the old lady died. She was laid to rest next to her sister in the family vault in Montluçon. When her will was opened her sole bequest read as follows: '*Le Bâtiment, situé Rue des Beaux Arts, Paris, et tout son contenu, à Monsieur Pyotr Alexis Belanopek.*'

Pyotr, Landlord in the City of Lights! It was so incongruous for a man who had never owned anything that he sometimes felt it must be another one of his dreams. It took a chance meeting with old Phillipon, standing as usual in the doorway of his shop, to bring him back to earth. Removing the habitual Gitanes dangling from his lower lip, Phillipon waved it at him. "Oh, *l'Artiste*," he said. "My congratulations on your good fortune!"

"*Bonjour, Monsieur Phillipon*," Pyotr said, shrugging his shoulders. "I have no idea why she did it."

"What else could she do," Phillipon said, "leave it to a cat's home? Or the Church? Bah! Impossible. Don't forget she and her sister were not just spinsters, but orphans, like you, with no kin. I've known them since they got here. In her eyes you did all the work, you saved the bar, your pictures are hanging on the walls, the place was as much yours as theirs. They were very proud of you, you know. Every time they walked by they would stop to tell me what you were doing for them. So, enjoy your good fortune while you can."

"What do you mean?" Pyotr said.

"Owning property in France is a poison pill waiting to be swallowed. You now have a very greedy silent partner. You know who that is?"

216

"No."

"The government. They will not do a stroke of work, but good year or bad, they will get their pound of flesh out of you by way of taxes. Taxes on what you inherit. Taxes on what you buy. Taxes on what you sell. Taxes on your rents. Taxes on your salary. Taxes on your profits. Taxes on your wealth. Taxes on liquor. Taxes on water, gas and electricity. The Land Tax. The *Taxe d'Habitation*. And the *Droits de Succession*. Even taxes on what you may own outside France if you happen to be a French resident. Unilaterally, at their sole discretion, they can even tax a loss if they deem your accounts to be false. And if you don't pay, they will impose penalties. And if you can't pay, they will say you have forfeited your property in lieu of payment. Your carefree days are over, my friend. You are no longer a young student or even an impoverished artist without a care in the world other than something to eat and somewhere to sleep. No. You are now a *bourgeois gentilhomme*. Owner of a magnificent property on the Rue des Beaux Arts, to which you are enslaved for life, your every moment accounted in the books you must keep and have verified professionally every year. You will rue the day and dream of the time when you made pictures in the shower in the middle of the night."

Not for a moment did Pyotr believe him. Until the day the postman brought a letter from the *Direction Générale des Finances Publiques* curtly advising him of a '*contrôle et vérification fiscale*' of his books and records, to be conducted on the premises of the Rue des Beaux Arts, with the aim of 'detecting any breaches or infringements of tax law, unintentional or deliberate.'

He was standing in the lobby re-reading the letter for a second time when Pauline and Delphine came in from doing their shopping. "*Mon Dieu*," Delphine said, "are you unwell? You are very pale."

It was true. Under his tan, Pyotr's face was drawn. Without a word he showed them the letter. On reading it, Pauline laughed, and Delphine smiled. "You are in luck," Pauline said. "Do you know who this lady is?" With her thumb, she pointed at Delphine. "She is the nemesis of all tax inspectors. They fear her because they know she knows more about tax law than they do and with her in your corner they will be lucky not to get fired."

"Maybe not fired," Delphine said modestly, "but removed to the colonies. With your permission I will keep this letter and prepare for battle. I used to be one of them when I was young, you know."

"A tax inspector?"

"Yes. One of the few women they had back then. After nearly ten years I realised there was more money to be made in the private sector, and if you were going to lose your eyesight staring at numbers you might as well get properly paid for it. You must be adept at navigating the labyrinthine pathways of our inheritance laws. The rules are complex, and you could be liable for up to 60% of the value of what you've just inherited."

Pyotr nearly fainted. "60%!" he exclaimed. "That's preposterous!"

"Yes," Delphine said, "it is. The Third Estate, which is 97% of the population, has historically been taxed the most. The Church, being 1%, pays no tax, and the hereditary Nobles, just 2% of the population, are taxed fractionally at 0.5%, even though the monarchy has been abolished and we are now a republic."

"You're joking!"

"Alas, no. But don't panic. The tax is only due within six months of the date of death. Mlle. Espinasse died two months ago, which leaves us four months to find a solution. The first thing I will need is your passport and Titre de Séjour. Let's go upstairs, make ourselves comfortable with a glass of wine, and sort this out." And it was upstairs on the 6th floor, after climbing 90 steps, that a most unusual solution was found. Pyotr Alexis Belanopek did not exist.

"So, let me understand, "Delphine said. "You invented this name with Phillipon?"

"Yes."

"And there are no official papers, no passport, no bank account, no document anywhere with this name?"

"No. None."

"What about the lease you signed?"

"I never got it back. I moved in during the free rent period and immediately went to work."

"How did Géraldine pay you for the work you did here?"

"In cash. From the bar."

"Of course. The solution then is simple." And it was. The letter from the Direction Générale des Finances Publiques was returned to them, with an inscription on the envelope: *'Inconnue à cette adresse.'* All subsequent letters from the same source were returned, unopened, with the same inscription, Unknown at this address. After four months the letters ceased.

"And now? Who owns the property?" Pyotr asked.

"That is the question?" Delphine said, a twinkle in her eyes. "Technically, according to the will, the name of a person with no public record is on the title. Leave it like that to gather dust. Just make sure the property taxes are paid."

Paris Now.

"Pretty clever, don't you think, George? She didn't say he doesn't exist, just that he's unknown at that address."

"Wouldn't happen today with computerised records and things."

"You sure? The turf wars of the French bureaucracy being what they are, this is just the kind of situation that would get batted from office to office with claim and counterclaim about jurisdiction. What is crafty is paying the property taxes every year."

"Why?"

"In France, delinquent property taxes are taken very seriously. The State depends on them. Adverse possession is a cornerstone of the law. Don't pay for five years and the property can be sold at public auction. If the taxes are paid nobody comes after you and, get this, anybody can pay the taxes."

"Taxes or not," George said, "even if he got the property for nothing, he never made a dime from owning it. Hanging on by his fingernails he was; if it wasn't for the bar he would have gone bust."

"Well, that, and taking up painting again. The exact date he got his place in the Palais-Royal is unknown, but we know he was there in '35. Doing those academic portraits, à la Sargent or Boldini for money. Right

Bank stuff. Good at it too. I think it was Sickert who persuaded him to switch styles."

Chapter Thirty-one

Locking the gallery, Pyotr made his way to lunch at the Grand Colbert on the Rue Vivienne, his canteen, a block away from the Palais, where the menu fixe was reasonably priced and came with a decent carafe of Bordeaux. It was his habit to read the newspapers when dining on his own and he was immersed in an article in the Journal dated September 17, 1935 about Germany: 'We should recall that Nazi Germany resumed compulsory male military service on March 17, an action directly contravening the Treaty of Versailles, which is flaunted daily by the régime of Herr Hitler, the Führer. On April 1, his government banned Jehovah's Witnesses because of their refusal to swear allegiance to the state as their convictions forbid them to serve in the armed forces of any temporal power. On May 21, the German government issued the so-called *Wehrgesetz,* which mandates that only *"Aryans"* could serve in the army, and that soldiers could only marry *"Aryan"* wives. On June 28, the German Ministry of Justice revised the German criminal code, expanding the range of criminal offences to encompass any contact between men that could be construed as sexual, be it by word or gesture, with severe penalties, facilitating the systematic persecution of homosexuals and broadening the rights of the police to enforce them. Two days ago, September 15, in the Reichstag, the German Government decreed The Reich Citizenship Law and the Law for the Protection of the German Blood and Honour. Adolf Hitler, at the Nazi Party rally in Nuremberg, announced that these *"Race Laws"* make Jews into second-class citizens, and prohibits the intermarriage or sexual union between Jews and persons of German or related blood. Which laws the German Government says includes Communists, Gypsies, Afro-Germans,

221

Jehovah Witnesses and homosexuals…' At which juncture his waiter brought him his first course, hareng Baltique, smothered in dill and fresh cream, served with boiled potatoes, and a chilled glass of Chablis. Hardly had he removed his reading glasses to bend forward to start his meal, when a voice above him said, "Habermann?"

It was a distinguished man in his 60s, trim white beard, receding white hair, beautifully dressed in a pale grey mohair suit with a matching waistcoat, leaning over his table, smiling, holding out his hand. "Hans Habermann, what a pleasure to see you again!" he said, and, turning to speak to an equally elegantly dressed woman standing next to him, he added, "*Ich war mit diesem jungen Mann im Krieg.*"

That momentary aside to the woman gave Pyotr the fraction of time he needed. Fumbling to put on his glasses again, he pretended a bewildered look at the couple, and the extended hand. Blinking, he half rose from his chair without shaking hands and said in impeccable English, "I fear there must be a mistake. The name is Edwards, Ernest Edwards. Have we met?" And sat back down again, his eyebrows raised in query, his face otherwise blank, looking from them to his meal and back at them again.

Pause.

"*Unmöglich,*" the gentleman said, keenly studying Pyotr. "You could be a twin. Please forgive me. I apologise for interrupting your meal." He and the woman then turned away to go to their table but not before Pyotr heard him say under his breath, "*Ich weiss dass ich mich nicht irre.*"

The incident spoiled lunch as Pyotr realised he had been disturbed to the extent of inverting Ernie's name. Edward Ernie, not Ernest Edwards. What could he be thinking? Who was this man? And then it came to him, the surgeon! The surgeon he helped in the trenches 18 years ago! Who got him into Heidelberg. Had the man caught a flash of recognition when their eyes met? For a moment Pyotr doubted it, then said to himself, he knows, and he knows you know he knows. What to do? And just as it had when he was writing 'Alias', he knew what he had to do. He smiled to himself. Took a sip of wine. Talk about life imitating art. Do what Ant would have done. Lie.

In the event it was unnecessary. When he finished lunch, the couple had gone and when he asked for his bill it was given to him with a note:

'Herr Edwards, I never forget a face. It is immaterial to me whether you are Edwards or Habermann today. The young man I knew in the trenches in that dreadful war was someone I valued and trusted. He had a genuine talent for the care and mercy of his fellow men and would have made a great doctor. Fate has taken you down a different path and my only wish is that you fulfil your life's ambitions and leave the world a better place. Respectfully yours, Generalstabsarzt Siegfried von Schülz.'

When Pyotr got home that evening it was to find another note pigeon-holed in his letter box in the Rue des Beaux Arts. It was from Markus and momentarily eclipsed the shock of seeing Von Schülz in the restaurant. Markus wrote:

'I don't know if you know this. I have just learned that Nathalie in Italy has a child, a girl. Anna asked if I knew where you were? I think she thinks you are still in America. I have not written back but leave that to you. Their address is Pensione Lucrezia, Viale Cadorna, Lucca. May I be the first to congratulate you on becoming a father!'

For a moment stunned, Pyotr did the maths, burst out laughing and wrote back: 'Nice try, Markus. I haven't seen Nathalie in eight years and unless the child is older than that I cannot possibly be the father. Worse luck. I quite fancy the idea. But according to the late Mlle. Géraldine, you are the anointed hero of this saga and the reason Anna and her daughter left Paris for Italy. I suggest you get on a train down to Tuscany and shoulder your responsibilities. Lucca, you will find, is a well-preserved Renaissance town, and, since I know you love music, the home of Puccini and Boccherini. Also great wine. Let me know how it goes.' After signing the letter, he added a post scriptum: 'Strange encounter in the Colbert. I'll tell you about it when we next see each other. Hopefully soon.'

223

Chapter Thirty-two

On November 9th of that same year, a woman went into labour in the Martin Luther Krankenhaus in Caspar-Theyss-Strasse, Berlin, at 4 o'clock in the evening and finally gave birth to a healthy boy at 3.38AM November 10th. The mother's name was Ilse. She was exhausted after such a long and difficult delivery and slept for nearly two days afterwards. It therefore fell to the father, an Anglo-Indian shipping agent from Bombay, to register the child at the British Embassy in Wilhelmstrasse. His Majesty's Consul, Mr. G. Lyall, who took down the details to certify the birth, asked an obvious question: the child's name? The father looked perplexed: "We haven't chosen a name yet," he said. "Well, that won't do. I must have a name to register his birth," the Consul said, fidgeting with his Montblanc fountain pen. "What is your name?" "William," the man said.

"Perfect," the Consul said, and the child was registered with his father's name.

Pyotr was 39 at the time of William's birth, and he would be 82 in 1978 when they met for the first time in the photographic studio of Patrick Demarchelier on 43rd Street in New York City on the occasion of William's 43rd birthday - such is the unplanned trajectory of life.

In those intervening years, which saw the doubling of the World's population from 2 billion to 4 billion; the rise and fall of the Nazis; the mindless slaughter of millions in the Second World War; the death of three of history's greatest murderers, Hitler, Stalin and Mao; the splitting of the Atom and it's first tragic use on Hiroshima and Nagasaki; man's first step on the Moon; the Cold War with the relentless expenditure by the industrial-military complex of two countries, America and Russia; the 'hot' wars in Korea, Vietnam, Laos and Cambodia; the coming and going of 8 U.S. Presidents in Franklin Roosevelt, Harry Truman, Dwight Eisenhower, John Kennedy, Lyndon Johnson, Richard Nixon, Gerald Ford and Jimmy Carter; 3 Kings and a Queen in the UK, George V, Edward V111, George V1 and Elizabeth 11; 4 leaders of the Soviet Union, Joseph Stalin, Georgy Malenkov, Nikita Khrushev and Leonid Breznev; 3 Paramount Leaders of the Republic of China, Lin Chen, Chiang Kai-shek and Mao Zedong; 8 Presidents of Germany, Adolf Hitler, Karl Dönitz, Wilhelm Pieck, Johannes Dieckmann, Walter Ulbricht, Friedrich Ebert, Willi Stoph and Erich Hoenecker; 11 Presidents of France, Albert Lebrun, Philippe Pétain, Charles de Gaulle, Félix Gouin, Georges Bidault, Vincent Auriol, Léon Blum, René Coty, Alain Poher, Georges Pompidou and Valéry Giscard d'Estaing; and in Italy, 1Duce, Benito Mussolini, followed by 25 Presidents, Etcetera…a goulash of events, names and faces, some familiar, some obscure, the wine stains of history on the tablecloth of the world.

All of which lay in the future, a distant prospect for Pyotr, fast asleep, dreaming of Sweden.

Dreamland - 15

The Treasury is in the Royal Palace. It is a large, heavily guarded, dimly lit chamber, with iron bars in its two windows, the walls lined with shelves filled with blue and yellow bound folios and stacked bundles of grey paper bound with red ribbons sealed in wax; on the floor, tied with heavy leather cords, sacks of coins and bullion, and a large set of scales. A log fire burns in the hearth of a vast fireplace bracketed by an inglenook in which two wolfhounds are sleeping. The Lord High Chancellor, Axel Oxenstierna, sits at a desk writing in a ledger, its pages lit by a very fat candle, who's flame flickers with each passing eddy of air. Every time he asks for an invoice or bill-of-sale or promissory note, his assistant, Petrus, unearths the required document with practised autonomy. Outside, someone is pounding on the metal-studded door that protects the room. Without looking up, Lord Oxenstierna wearily calls, "Come in!" It is Magnus, shown in by a sergeant-at-arms.

"What do you want, Magnus?" Oxenstierna said.

"How did you know it was me?" Magnus said.

"Most men are intimidated when they come to see me here," Oxenstierna said, still writing, "probably because they owe the Treasury money or want to borrow some." Now he pauses his writing to glance at Magnus. "Only you sound like you are going to break down the door. Sit a minute, I am nearly done..." Petrus watched Magnus fidgeting about the room, unable to sit still, hefting some of the sacks, and, finally, pouring gold coins out of one of them into the scales, running his fingers through them again and again and again. Exasperated, Oxenstierna sighed, put down his pen, and said, "You can't have any. They are all committed. Have you the remotest idea what condition the Kingdom is in?"

"I am Lord High Treasurer, am I not?" Magnus said sarcastically. "I sit on the Council..."

"Yes, yes - and like most of your peers, you can't even read a balance sheet. I know all that. Are you still in disfavour, De la Gardie?"

"Yes," Magnus, said, "in as great disfavour as anyone can be without getting one's head chopped off under Christina."

"Please speak of our ruler with respect!" Lord Oxenstierna snapped.

"Even after that little operetta of hers in church? With those Jesuits and Catholics there to report her every word. Excuse me, Oxenstierna, when the Kingdom is on the verge of ruin..."

"Magnus! Stop! Do not continue!"

"I must! I am just as great a patriot as you, my Lord...," as Oxenstierna turns in his chair to glare at him, "...yes, and love the Queen as much. But what she is doing is reprehensible. She cannot run out and leave Karl Gustav dangling. This is my concern. Have you heard of Messenius's pamphlet? Do you know its contents?"

"No," Oxenstierna said.

"Why lie?" Magnus said, flicking a glance at Petrus. "You're better informed than I am. If you've checked her accounts as I have, you know the slightest audit will reveal that what Messenius alleges is true."

"I will admit I was, in fact I still am, amazed at its accuracy," Oxenstierna said. "Most likely it's hearsay, the author parroting what people are talking about, unaware they are being recorded. But it's treason to publish it."

"So, he writes what we think: the 5 million riksdalers we got from Prague are missing. What are you going to do, hang him? Remember, Old Messenius is nobody's fool and can add with the best. Plus, his son is Karl Gustav's servant, as well-placed as any to hear the truth. Face it, my Lord. Somewhere there is a leak and it's close to her."

"It is distressing, most distressing," Lord Oxenstierna said. "If this is believed and word gets out..." Petrus could see his mentor struggling with what he had to say, "...as you know, De la Gardie, I have always had the greatest reverence for the memory of my King and his heirs. But I love my country more. More than my eyes, more than life itself, more..," Oxenstierna cannot finish the thought. He stands up, shivers, moves across the room to warm his hands at the fire. "I am too old for this. I have to speak. Tell me, is it true she intends to ennoble her tailor, that little man Holm?"

"True!" Magnus said. "Why, she even intends that young Tott become a member of the National Council."

"Good God! That's ridiculous! At twenty-three, he can hardly wipe his own bottom."

"It is not for that part of his anatomy that he is a favourite."

"Magnus!" Oxenstierna is shocked. It shows in his face. Petrus has never seen the old man so disturbed.

"You should get out of this dingy counting house if such news surprises you," Magnus said.

"I would rather be dead! Is it also true...God forgive me...that the Queen..." stooping over, Oxenstierna looks from Magnus to Petrus and back again, "...I can hardly say this...that she voluntarily attends Catholic mass at the French Ambassador's?"

"Yes!" Magnus said. "And makes the sign of the Cross? Yes! And kneels and takes holy communion? Yes! Yes! Yes! The whole town knows this; they can speak of nothing else!"

"God, strike me dead!" Lord Oxenstierna paces the room. "Hear me out. I shall have to throw overboard everything I have respected: reverence, deference, loyalty to the royal house..."

"Now it is for me to say, stop!" Magnus said. "Please, my Lord, do not continue. The walls have ears."

"In Jesus' name, Magnus, let me speak!" Count Oxenstierna drew himself up to his full height. "I have closed my eyes out of reverence; I have closed my ears out of deference; and I have become false from pure loyalty. I have become cowardly - don't shake your head - a servile toady at court. I have respected meanness; accepted compromise to avoid argument; the convenient falsehood over the damaging truth; and I am beginning to despise myself. The kingdom's been ruled by a crazy woman; the accounts look as if a mad child has kept them; all the possessions of the Crown are mortgaged to foreigners; she has ruined us with ballets at thirty thousand crowns a night; the army only exists on paper; and the navy sits rotting outside Karlskrona harbour; the estates of Parliament are treated as a parish council; the National Council recruited with second-class lieutenants; the Palace chapel is a Jesuit meeting place; the Palace is a dance hall; to say nothing of whom she beds. Our people now spy on each other, and if they are not spying, they are slandering. And in the middle of all this she calls it quits. In truth I cannot bear it any longer. I have no stomach for the game. My statesmanship has grown cold, De la Gardie. What must be done?"

"With 5 million riksdalers?" Magnus said. "I could buy Poland with 5 million riksdalers."

Chapter Thirty-three

The letter from Markus was dated 30 March 1936, postmarked Copenhagen.

'I've made it to Denmark, on the run from the Gestapo for aiding the Jews, who lost their right to vote along with the Roma, three weeks ago. Thus rigged, the Nazis claimed all 741 seats in the Reichstag in yesterday's election. And, get this, the only question on the ballot was to approve the reoccupation of the Rhineland in violation of the Treaty of Versailles, which now has more holes in it than a torn lace curtain without a peep from any of the Western powers. Meanwhile Adolph's propaganda machine has been spewing out the usual lies about the tremendous success of the Winter Games in Garmisch-Partenkirchen, blatantly ignoring that they are putting back up the signs saying Jews are unwanted in Germany which were taken down for the duration of the Games to spare Olympic visitors a glimpse of what these bastards are up to. Never forget the quote: 'The only thing necessary for the triumph of evil is for good men to do nothing.' And we still have the Summer games to come! I've said it before, and I'll say it again, I am very, very fearful of the future, not just for Germany, but for Europe and the world. Hopefully by the time you receive this letter I will have found a way to reach France and get to see you again.'

It was unsigned, with no return address. Pyotr found the letter in his box on April 5. As usual he read it standing in the hallway, unmindful of the other tenants having to step around him as they came in or went out. An extraordinary thought had him preoccupied and he did not hear a voice croaking, *"Pardon, Monsieur."* Nor did he register the words until they were repeated: *"Pardon, Monsieur. Je voudrais passer."* The words scarcely audible, said with an accent. He looked at the speaker. Under a mashup of hats with

230

scarves to hold them in place, from deep within a multitude of wrinkles, two blinking, cataracted eyes peeped up at him over multiple layers of shawls. A crabbed, diminutive, anonymous figure in two filthy, threadbare greatcoats fraying at every seam, grey and black, one worn on top of the other, and a smell. The smell was not anonymous, being a mixture of unwashed flesh, rotted socks, faded cologne and cat piss from the unknown number of cats living in her apartment. "Madame Seidenfeld," the voice croaked again. "We have not met." She held out a half-fingered knitted gloved hand, blackened fingernails bitten to the quick. "I am your tenant on the second floor."

To his credit, Pyotr did not flinch, but took the offered hand in his and briefly bent over it to kiss the air. "Madame," he said, with a little bow of the head.

"*Vous avez l'air inquiet, Monsieur?*" the lady said. "You seem worried, Monsieur?"

"Yes," Pyotr said, and for a reason he could not explain to himself, showed her the letter from Markus. This set off a chain reaction in Madame, fishing under her coats to locate a beaded purse in the interior of which she managed to locate her spectacles. After breathing on each lens and giving them a slow deliberate polish on one of the shawls, she hooked them in place behind her ears, adjusted them on her nose and ceremoniously read the proffered letter.

A long pause ensued with the lady nodding her head.

"It begins again," she finally croaked. "To think this little man who was of no importance a few years ago, an Austrian corporal in the German army, a prisoner of war -" it was hard to make out her words the way she croaked, but her meaning was clear - "in and out of trouble, in and out of jail, he should have been squashed like the verminous bug that he is before infecting the world. Now this" - a nod to the letter - "and this." From a pocket she pulled a filthy, old copy of Le Petit Journal manifestly used for wrapping fish and chips given the stains and stench on the front page. Nevertheless the headline could be read: ***98% of Germans vote for Hitler ! 44.3 million say yes! Only 500,000 say no!***

"Hard to believe he has duped them all," she said, clearing her throat and spitting phlegm into a rag. "Pardon, I am losing the use of my voice. I do not often get the chance to speak."

"Madame?" Pyotr said, non-pulsed.

"Do you think they'll come here?"

"Who?"

"The Nazis."

"No. I don't think so. Nobody wants another war."

"You are an optimist, Monsieur. You say one thing, but your face says another. You will excuse me now; I must be going." So Madame Seidenfeld squeezed past Pyotr to the staircase, where, one foot on the first tread, she looked back at him and said, "I fled the pogroms in Russia, in the Ukraine, in Poland and Hungary. I am tired of running, but that's what we Jews do if we want to live. You are a young man with your life ahead of you. Remember that." She turned and went on her slow way up the stairs to the second floor. Pyotr remained in the hall, unmoving, staring after her, until faintly he heard her open and then close the door to her apartment. It was then he realised, try as he might, that he could not remember the extraordinary thought with which he had been preoccupied before she spoke to him. It was important, he knew that. But the more he fished for it in his memory, the more it slipped away. Unwittingly he smelled his hand. It stank. Unwashed flesh, rotted socks, faded cologne and cat piss; his tenant's legacy. Despite himself, he smiled, turned to go to the bathroom to wash his hand, changed his mind, and still smiling walked out into the street, occasionally raising his hand to his nose as he walked along to see how long the smell would last. Down Rue Bonaparte, all the way along the Quai, across the Pont Neuf, through the parterre of the Louvre, across the Rue de Rivoli, to the gallery in the Palais-Royal, where it was finally vanquished by the turpentine with which he cleaned his paint brushes. Yet even with the smell gone, the echo of the old woman's words remained: You are an optimist, Monsieur! Yes, he thought, for better or worse, it is what I am.

Chapter Thirty-four

" $\mathbf{E}$ t l'univers entier ne peut rien voir d'égal aux superbes dehors du Palais Cardinal. Toute une ville entière, avec pompe bâtie, Semble d'un vieux fossé par miracle sortie, Et nous fait présumer à ses superbes toits que tous ses habitants sont des dieux ou des rois. "

You would have to be an optimist to move into the Palais-Royal in 1935, a neglected monument whose cracked pilasters and blackened cloisters stained by the pollution of centuries were a far cry from the enchanted view Corneille had when he wrote his description in 1644 just five years after Cardinal Richelieu completed his palace. No fool the Cardinal, aware of the avarice of the jealous monarch building his own palace across the street, immediately bequeathed both land and building to Louis X111, retaining the right of *usufruit* for the rest of his life, in one stroke ensuring his right of access and possession protected by the sovereign and his right to derive profit from the thing possessed. Richelieu died in 1642, and the King, as is their habit, promptly renamed the place as his - *Le Palais-Royal.* Poor man, he only had it for a year when he in turn died, and it became the home of that scheming woman, the Queen Mother, Anne of Austria, and her two young sons, Louis X1V and Philippe, the Duke of Anjou, along with her advisor, another shrewd cleric, Cardinal Mazarin.

As a distant princely descendant of the Habsburgs, a distinction he shared with Anne, Pyotr wondered what she would have made of his realm, just one-arcade wide, measuring 4M x 8M, with a mezzanine above, giving on the Rue de Montpensier on one side and the Galerie de Montpensier facing the gardens. An added *frisson* coming from the fact that he could also trace a kinship to La Grande Mademoiselle, Duchess of Montpensier, one of the greatest heiresses in history, a woman whose vast fortune was coveted by the Sun King himself and is today only remembered by a narrow street and an even narrower *galerie*. True to what was by now his custom, sleeves rolled up, apron on, climbing ladders, chasing out rats and spiders while scraping off moulding wallpaper and chiselling out termite-infested wood, Pyotr attacked the tiny space he rented with sardonic vigour.

After a month of diligent work and 15-hour days the result was a bright long rectangle, with plastered, whitewashed, 12-foot stone walls, an entrance through a huge storefront window inset with a narrow glass door framed in bronze, facing the gardens; an exit through glazed French doors opening to the street. Daylight at both ends, excellent for painting. In one corner a narrow spiral staircase led to the mezzanine, where there was a toilet, a washroom with a claw-footed bathtub, a small kitchen, kitchen table and chair, set against a hip-high oak room-divider containing double-sided drawers and, beyond that, a boudoir, where, standing on assorted Kilim rugs, was a classic Récamier satinwood couch covered in faded two-tone green and gold velvet, on which Pyotr could lounge, nap, read a book or just look out at the foot traffic below or the children playing in the *Jardin*. Two full-length gilt framed mirrors hung on the walls opposite each other, seemingly enlarging the space, reflecting the couch, and anyone sitting on it. His inspiration was a passage from Diderot:

"Qu'il fasse beau, qu'il fasse laid, c'est mon habitude d'aller sur les cinq heures du soir me promener au Palais-Royal. C'est moi qu'on voit toujours seul. J'abandonne mon esprit à tout son libertinage. Je le laisse maître de suivre la première idée sage ou folle qui se présente, comme on voit nos jeunes dissolus marcher sur les pas d'une courtisane à l'air éventé, au visage riant, à l'œil vif, au nez retroussé, quitter celle-ci pour une autre, les attaquant toutes et ne s'attachant à aucune."

And he loved to quote the philosopher's famous axiom: '*Man will never be free until the last king is strangled with the entrails of the last priest.*' A sentiment he shared exactly.

Entering the gallery, the wall on the left was covered by an exceptional mahogany-framed mirror, fully 6-metres long and 3-metres high, with a very long narrow oak refectory table, set on trestles, standing against it. Sets of drawers were underneath to hold drawings, with shelves above packed with books, and flowerpots and an assortment of flowers needing water. On top of the table were ceramic pots holding dozens of assorted paint brushes, pencils, crayons, charcoal and chalk sticks, jars of turpentine and varnish, rows of paint tubes, pots of watercolours, paint smeared palettes, palette knives, bowls, a pestle and mortar for grinding colours, ink, pens, a jackknife, steel canvas stretching pliers, scissors, rags and a sponge. Two wooden stools stood against the opposite wall in front of stacked canvases and frames and a drawing board, with the floor covered in a mosaic of paint-splattered oriental rugs on which stood a wood-burning stove framed by two large easels; hanging from one, a grey painter's smock; on the other, a tacking hammer with nails and tacks in a child's wooden pencil case screwed to the frame of it. This wall, on the right, was covered in unfinished sketches, some framed, some unframed, done in all kinds of media, reflected in the long mirror opposite, doubling the apparent width of the gallery. It was a spectacle to be enjoyed by any passerby. At first the novelty of watching a painter at work attracted spectators who stared at him through the plate glass window. This only lasted the first few weeks and as the window got dirty and remained uncleaned, Pyotr could paint unobserved. He liked it better that way. In short order it felt as if he had always been there, part of the furniture in a 300-year-old house.

On the day he got back after his encounter with Madame Seidenfeld, he had hardly taken off his coat, put on his smock, picked up a brush, when there was a knock on the window. It was Alphonse, the moustachioed *Gardien* of the *Palais,* in his dark blue uniform, heavy key chain belted at the waist with the myriad keys on a ring that he needed to open the thirty gates in the iron gold-spiked fence around the periphery of the *Jardin* at 7.30AM every morning and close again at 10PM every night, day in, day out, including holidays; Alphonse, complicit smile on his long-boned face, come in for a *coup de rouge* and a chat, a habit he invented, particularly when it was cold and he knew Pyotr would have his stove going. "*Alors, Monsieur le Peintre? Vous allez bien?*" he said, shaking hands, before taking his customary seat on one of the stools.

"*Bonjour, Monsieur Alphonse. Ça va, comme d'hab.*" Pyotr said. "*Un petit coup pour se réchauffer?*"

"Avec le froid qu'il fait? Un plaisir!" And after the wine was poured, sniffed, sipped, the eternal question: *"Qu'est qu'on peint aujourd'hui?"*

What are *we* painting today? Said with a veteran's appreciation. As a *grand mutilé de la guerre,* trying to survive on a minuscule pension, whose infirmity got him his job, with the sleeve of the arm he lost in the Great War carefully tucked into the left-hand pocket of his coat, he went about his duties with the same dedication he had shown in the trenches. He had been one of Pyotr's first models, had he not? Did he not have his portrait hanging in his *loge*? Did he not escort the many beautiful women asking for directions to the painter's quarters? Of course, he did.

From where he sat on his stool, single handedly, without looking, he would fish out his pipe and tobacco pouch from the right hand pocket of his coat, place the pouch on his lap, stab the pipe bowl into the tobacco, tamp down an appropriate amount with his thumb, put the loaded pipe in his mouth, replace the pouch in his pocket, fish out a matchbox, select a match and, seemingly by magic, flick the match head alight to bring the flame to the pipe bowl and, sucking thoughtfully on the pipe stem, start smoking, as evidenced by a first cloud of smoke puffed into the air like a locomotive leaving the station. In no time he would have a cheerful fug going which didn't bother Pyotr since he enjoyed the camaraderie of a fellow smoker even though he preferred cigarettes to a pipe. Neither thought it appropriate to discuss the hell they had been through. So? To the question of what was being painted the answer was the underpainting for a life-size nude, referred to by Alphonse as 'une grande horizontale', a singular commission for a lady who refused to undress, but wanted the artist to imagine what she would look like stretched out in the altogether on the Récamier, given that her gentleman friend (the lucky fellow, who would pay for the picture!) was charmingly jealous to the point of being blind to her profession.

"C'est une pute," as Alphonse succinctly put it.

"With all the hookers this place has seen over the centuries," Pyotr said, "what's one more?"

How true.

Alphonse, enamoured of his work, having accumulated an historian's knowledge of the lives of the denizens who once lived there, loved to recite the names. Starting with Louis X1V who, from 1661 till his death in 1715, stashed one *maîtresse-en-titre* after another in the *Palais*, beginning with Louise de La Vallière, in an apartmènt at one end while secretly carrying on in another with Madame de Montespan, not to mention the Duchess of Fontanges, and the Marquise of Maintenon, interspersed with an entire bedchamber full of *petite maîtresses:* Catherine Bellier, Baronne de Beauvais, between 1652-1654; Olympe Mancini, Comtesse de Soissons, 1654-1657 and again 1660 to1661; Anne-Madeleine de Conty d'Argencourt, a maid of honour, 1658 - (Alphonse, never one for missing a pun, chortling: *'Elle mérite bien son nom, Argencourt! Et Dame d'honneur de surcroît!'*); an unknown gardener's daughter who gave birth to a daughter in 1660 - (*'Bien planté, le Roi, hein?'*); Catherine-Charlotte de Gramont, Princess of Monaco, 1665; Bonne de Pons d'Heudicourt, the wife of the King's Master of the Wolf Hunt, 1665; - (*'Le chasseur, chassée!'*) The Marquise de Thianges, Gabrielle de Rochechouart de Mortemart, sister of Madame de Montespan ! 1666; Anne de Rohan-Chabot, Princesse de Soubise, on-and-off, 1669 to 1675; Claude de Vin des Oeillets, on-and-off, 1670 to 1676; Dame-Gabrielle de Damas de Thianges, the daughter of Gabrielle, two-timing her own mother, 1670 to 1673; the aristocrat, Lydie de Rochefort-Théobon, 1673 to 1677; Isabelle, the Marquess de Ludres, 1675 -1678; Marie Charlotte de Castelnau, Comtesse de Louvigny, 1676-1677; the Marquise de Nogaret, Marie-Madeleine Agnès de Gontaut Biron, 1680 to 1683; Louise-Elisabeth Rouxel, known as Mme de Grancey, 1681; Françoise Thérèse de Voyer de Dorée, 1681; the Marquise de Chevrières, Jeanne de Rouvray, 1681; la Marquise de Châtillon, Marie-Rosalie de Piennes, 1681; Marie-Antoinette de Rouvroy, Comtesse d'Oisy, 1681; - (Alphonse, laughing in admiration: *'Quel sacré année '81, pour un vieux bélier comme lui!)* Mme de Saint-Martin in 1682 and in 1683, the Duchess de Roquelaure, Marie-Louise de Montmorency-Laval !

Not to be outdone, Louis' younger brother, Philippe, Duke d'Orléans, (known officially as *Monsieur,* given to wearing dresses and keeping almost as many male 'friends' in the palace as the King had women), married his first cousin, Princess Henrietta Anne, daughter of Charles 1 of England, in the palace chapel in 1661, and lived there with her, fathering three children, (in addition to four miscarriages and one still-birth), and, when she died in1670 at the age of 26, re-married a year later, Elizabeth Charlotte of the Palatinate, with whom he had three more children, neither marriage nor children interrupting his romantic affairs with handsome young men.

The King finally gave the *Palais* to Philippe in 1692, and since he could not afford its upkeep, he had the bright idea of beginning a career in real estate by starting the construction of 60 uniform houses to border the gardens on three sides, five stories high, above arcaded galleries, an enterprise successfully continued by all the succeeding Dukes of Orléans, so that by 1784, under the reign of Louis Philippe d'Orléans, the arcades and gardens were thrown open to the public to enjoy and spend their money in 145 boutiques, cafés, restaurants, hair salons, bookshops, jewellers, hatters, bootmakers, museums, bowling alleys, an underground circus, a music hall, 2 theatres and 18 casinos, '*rendezvous de tous les crocs, escrocs et filous*' not to mention the accommodation afforded to 1500 '*demoiselle de vertu, fleurs vivantes qui gagnent à être connues'* (with the emphasis on *nues*) plying their trade to such good effect that the Archbishop of Paris ordered a census be taken of the prices for each ladies' *spécialités, heure de travail,* and *cértificat de santé,* as a means of stopping provincials getting scalped and/or catching venereal disease.

From the aristocracy to the lower orders, the Palais Royal became the Parisian centre, indeed the European centre, for every form of shameless debauchery, spirited debate, licentious larceny, gogo gaiety, knees-up dancing, drop dead drinking, eating, playacting, and gambling. All of which made money. And the House of Orléans, rich. So rich that Louis Philippe had to borrow Swiss guards from the Vatican to control the hoi polloi.

"*Dommage que ce n'est pas comme ça aujourd'hui,*" Alphonse said, looking out at the empty arcade. "*On dirait un cimetière.*"

Which was also true, Pyotr thought. Times *had* changed. It was all downhill after the French Revolution. Today you count the rare footsteps in the arcades at night over the rustling of the many rats that come out once it gets dark. The palace was a forgotten relic, unknown to most Parisians other than the theatre crowd attending the Comédie-Française, or the Théâtre Royal, at either end of the Galerie de Montpensier, or dining at Le Grand Véfour in the Colonnade de Joinville, last of the great restaurants to have adorned the place, now revived after years of neglect by Louis

Vaudable, the owner of Maxim's, aided by the support of two neighbours, Colette, who lived in the mezzanine of 9, Rue de Beuajolais, and Jean Cocteau, at 36, Rue de Montpensier. His neighbours too, come to think of it, seen often enough sitting side-by-side in the Jardin.

Just then the little cannon in the garden fired to signal noon.

"*Au turbin.* Time to do the rounds," Alphonse said, getting off his stool. "*À la prochaine!*" He shook hands, and, standing in the doorway, added an afterthought. "You know it's not just because they liked to fuck. *Dans la tête*, built into their deepest subconscious belief, was the knowledge that the only way to secure the future, the heritage of their family and fortune, was to have children, preferably male, and since so many died in childbirth or very young, the more you had the better your chances, even if you were a King."

Chapter Thirty-five

On or about November 30, 1936, Pyotr was 40 years old. Not knowing the exact day he was born made it easy to forget his birthday. Walking home from the gallery that evening, he was preoccupied by the memory of what von Schülz had said in the Grand Colbert months ago. Had he fulfilled his life's ambitions? Would he leave the world a better place? Entering his building, he was surprised Marie was not in her loge, and as he climbed the 90 stairs to his apartment on the 6th floor, he slowly became aware that the usual background noise of people faintly heard behind all the closed doors on each successive floor was missing. It was eerie, as if the building was holding its breath. Arriving on his landing, he instinctively looked to his left to see if his neighbours were in. Silence, with no light under their door. Turning right, with his key ready in his hand to open his door, he saw a message pinned to it: *Your Presence is Urgently Requested in the Bar!* Now what? he thought, as he retraced his 90 steps back down, through the hall, to the street. Another surprise. All the lights of the bar were out! Bizarre. Even more strange, a large printed notice in capital letters was posted across the entrance:

FERMETURE EXCEPTIONNELLE!

How was it possible he had not seen that when he came home? And who had the audacity to order the bar closed? Perplexed, he tried the door. It was locked. Frowning, he knocked on the door, a sharp rat-a-tat-tat with his knuckles. "Qui est là?" came a voice from inside. A young woman's voice. Strangely familiar.

"*C'est moi!*" Pyotr said. And on cue, all the lights came on, the door was thrown open, and there, to his amazement, were all his tenants,

240

grinning, smiling, laughing, glasses of champagne raised in salute, joining in a loud chorus of 'Happy Birthday to You!' - with at their centre, Nathalie, holding the hand of a young girl.

"Claudia, dis bonjour à ton Papa !" Nathalie said.

Paris Now.

Was she his daughter? Nobody knows. She was 8 years old then - so it was theoretically possible. George has a head for numbers, and a nose for scandal. You should ask him.

"Very unlikely," George said. "Markus was there with Nathalie. He had done what Pyotr had suggested, gone to Italy, to Lucca, to find Nathalie and her daughter. They were on their way back to Berlin. Ask yourself why? It can only be because Markus knew he was the father. That they stopped off in Paris to see Pyotr on his birthday is pure coincidence. I think what Nathalie said was meant as a joke, a rather poor joke in my opinion if you consider her daughter. Anyway, the girl looked nothing like Pyotr. Let's not forget he was in a relationship with the concierge in Boissonade for over a year before taking off for America. For him to be the father would suppose that he had a clandestine fling with Nathalie just before he left. There is nothing to suggest this happened. Add in the fact that in subsequent letters from Markus he alludes to how difficult his clandestine life has become with a wife and daughter in tow, even though there is no evidence they married. Nathalie's Jewish heritage must have been a nightmare for him and the child."

Chapter Thirty-six

The envelope is postmarked Zurich, with the date, April 30, 1937, stamped across it. The letter inside is handwritten in pencil with no addressee and no signature:

'There is street fighting every day, not just here but in Berlin, Munich, Dusseldorf, Kiel, with Goebbels' Ministry of Public Enlightenment and Propaganda predictably blaming the Jews. N, who had gone to pick up her daughter from school, was lucky to get back unharmed when they came upon a bunch of Nazi thugs smashing the windows of Brandt's, the watchmaker around the corner from our flat - the poor man's not even a Jew, he just looks like one. Most Germans, particularly the young, are so indoctrinated by all the placards stuck on walls and lampposts with grotesque caricatures of the so-called 'vermin' blamed for all their misery, that they accept the chaos as being part of everyday life, the 'cleansing' Hitler promised them in a Marxist-free country with 'lebensraum' for all - and without the constraints of the Versailles Treaty. The Nazi Party is now so entrenched behind the declarations Hitler made promulgating the Nuremberg Laws in '35, that it no longer bothers to hide how it has taken control of all state and federal institutions, imposed a loyalty oath to Hitler on every party official and soldier with the SS there to enforce it, and openly boasts of the improvements they have made like the Autobahn, while conveniently forgetting to mention how they have stripped the Jews of their wealth, their right to intermarry with non-Jews, and their right to occupy the many fields in which they are expert, medicine, finance, law or education, to name a few. Nor do they mention - whisper it - the concentration camps. People disappear. When you notice it for the first time it's usually because someone says where's so-and-so? No answer. Gone.

242

Disappeared. The denunciation can come from anywhere, anytime, for a reason you will never know. Maybe your neighbour. Your friend. Even your family. It's frightening and pervasive. We move all the time as a precaution, which is hard on C. as she can't make friends.

I must tell you I cannot fathom the gullibility of foreigners coming here on holiday, kowtowing to these lying bastards, giving credence to whatever claptrap comes out of Goebbels' ministry. Don't they read their own newspapers back home? Here you never ever read about the brave people opposed to all this shit, inevitably labelled as degenerates, disloyal traitors or worse.

As for the politicians! You saw what happened last year? Not a peep out of anyone when the Saarland got swallowed. On the back of that Hitler creates an air force, the Reichswehr is increased by 500,000 men, and Britain! BLOODY BRITAIN!!! signs an agreement that allows Germany to build a naval fleet! Talk about appeasement. What does Baldwin think the Führer wants it for, to go fishing? Then, that clown, Mussolini, invades Ethiopia, with hardly a squeak from Britain and France. The result - surprise! surprise! - last month Hitler used the Franco-Soviet Treaty of Mutual Assistance (eh?) as a pretext to order his army to march 3,000 troops into the demilitarised zone in the Rhineland in direct violation of the Versailles Treaty, and, talk about chutzpah, claims the territory was part of Germany anyway, so what's the fuss? Once again, the British and French governments do not feel that attempting to enforce the treaty is worth the risk of war! They really don't get it. This madman wants war! He even practises war. Last year he sent military supplies and assistance to the fascist forces of another of his pals, General Francisco Franco, to use in the Spanish Civil War, with the proviso the German Condor Legion be included, and a range of aircraft, and their crews, as well as a tank contingent! And now - guess what? - the aircraft of the Legion have just destroyed the city of Guernica! Enough said. This is truly fucking frightening for anyone pulling their head out of the sand and willing to look. I could go on a rant like this for pages and pages, but what I really want to do is get N and C out of here. Back to France if it is possible. Could they stay with you?

Pyotr showed the letter to his tenant on the 2nd floor, Madame Seidenfeld, in whom he had an instinctive, if inexplicable, trust. He had knocked on her door and she had shown no surprise to find him there when she opened it. "Come in," she said. "I hope you don't mind cats."

They were everywhere, and the stench of cat piss so overpowering it cancelled the ripe aroma of Madame herself. Pyotr could see her eyeing his reaction as she chased a couple of them off an armchair and invited him to sit down. "A cognac?" she said, and in the time it took for him to nod and for her to pour a drink, an orange tabby cat made itself comfortable on his lap and started purring.

"*C'est bien*," Madame Seidenfeld said and then ignored him as, squinting through a large magnifying glass she kept in a pocket, she slowly read the letter held close to her nose. And then read it again to make sure she understood the contents. "This is the same writer who sent the other letter?" she said.

Pyotr nodded. "My friend, Markus."

"How will you answer?"

"That is my problem," Pyotr said. "Of course I will help, but I have no way to communicate with him, no address, nothing."

"He must be in considerable danger." She tapped the letter which she was still holding. "See how he only uses initials? And there is no mention of the town they're in. Obviously, he has someone he trusts enough to take and post a letter for him in Switzerland. A courier of some sort. You do not know him, but he knows of you since it's your name on the envelope."

"Maybe Markus posted it."

"I don't think so. If he could get to Switzerland to post a letter, he could get his wife and child out. He's using a courier - someone brave enough to risk getting caught."

Chapter Thirty-seven

The courier was a nurse, by name Gertrude Minor, a middle-aged woman of Swiss-German origin, commonplace in appearance, who came and went at regular intervals to visit her aged mother residing in a nursing home in Küsnacht, a suburb of Zurich. She always travelled by train in Germany, arriving at Konstanz on the Bodensee, crossing the town on foot to walk the 1.3 kilometres to the frontier in Kreuzlingen, Switzerland, from where she caught another train to Wil via Weinfelden, catching the Wiler Bahn tramway to Frauenfeld, and from there by bus to Küsnacht. Tedious, time consuming, subject to delays due to weather, but designed to thwart surveillance. With her dual nationality she had no need for entry or exit visas to either country. And she had no idea who deposited the letters she carried, collected by her at a post restante in the old post office building next to the Rathaus in Hamburg. All she had to do on reaching her destination was to put Swiss stamps on the envelopes and post them. In so doing it was inevitable she saw to whom the letters were addressed.

These details were discovered in the first 24 hours of her interrogation by the SD, the *Sicherheitsdienst*, a subdivision of the SS founded by Reinhard Heydrich. They had been lucky. The woman had stumbled getting off the train at Konstanz Bahnhof, pitching forward to strike her head on a metal post supporting the roof over the platform, momentarily losing consciousness and her handbag. In the ensuing confusion, while medical help was fetched, the handbag was taken by a railway guard and given to a policeman on duty for safe keeping. Thinking it necessary to find out the name of the invalid, the policeman checked the contents of the handbag, and discovered not only her two passports, but also three unstamped letters addressed to three different people, one in France and two in Spain. By instruction, anything suspicious had to be reported to the SD officer on duty at the station in his office on the mezzanine. That Tuesday it was a man called, Heinrich Muller, married, two children, a native of Bonn, a diligent clerical worker, who, of necessity, joined the Nazi party in 1933, and found an aptitude in sorting out the credible from the less credible denunciations of his fellow citizens, leading to specialist training in the Security and Counterintelligence Department E1 of the SD in Berlin, and his subsequent appointment as *Inspektor der Sicherheitspolizei* for the states of Baden-Wüttemberg and Bavaria, in which post an early perk was an upgrade from his 2-room flat at home to a lakeside villa on Seestrasse donated gratuitously by (read appropriated from) a Jewish family anxious to escape Germany. It was an easy morning stroll from *his* villa to the station, and he had just arrived in his office when he was made aware of the accident to the nurse and shown the contents of her handbag by the policeman. After examining the two passports and opening and reading the three letters, he said, "Once she's patched up, have her brought to me."

"*Jawohl, so fort,*" the policeman said, saluting with an outstretched arm. "*Sieg heil!*"

One thing Muller found unfathomable in his job was how and why people resisted giving him the information he sought. He was a mild man, who was at heart not given to violence. He always asked his questions, quietly, patiently - unlike many of his colleagues who loved to shout, pull out fingernails and crush limbs with hammers. So it was with a quiet voice that he said to the nurse seated in front of him, head bandaged concealing four stitches in her scalp, "I am so sorry you got hurt. If it is too painful please tell me. I have some pills which may help you, *ja?*" (That 'yes' was one of his little tricks. It always got the same response.)

"*Danke,*" the nurse said, "Thank you."

Thanking *him.* Already. "I will just ask you a few questions, and then you can rest, yes?"

A nod. "*Danke.*"

"These are your papers, yes?" Muller waved a hand at the contents of her handbag spread across his desk.

"Yes."

"I see from your papers you are a nurse, yes?"

Another nod. "Yes."

"In which hospital?"

"In Hamburg."

"Which hospital in Hamburg?"

"The IK"

Was there a slight hesitation there? Muller raised an eyebrow. "I am not familiar with that abbreviation. What does IK stand for?"

The woman dropped her eyes and whispered, "*Israelitisches Krankenhaus.*"

"The Jewish Hospital? I have heard of the Jewish Hospital. It is quite famous, I think. Yes?"

A nod. Eyes down, looking at her hands folded on her lap.

"Please, Frau Minor, you must not just nod. Speak up so that our stenographer can hear you, yes?" Another casual wave of his hand to indicate the stenographer, a young officer in uniform, seated inconspicuously behind her.

"Yes."

"Good." Muller smiled encouragement. "How long have you been employed at the Jewish Hospital?"

"Since 1933."

"I see. Just 4 years? And before that what did you do?"

"I was a schoolteacher."

"Really? So was I once." Muller lied effortlessly. "Proud to belong to the *Nationalsozialistischer Lehrerbund,* even if I thought the League boring with all that business swearing an oath of loyalty and obedience to Hitler, as if that has anything to do with education, *nichtwar,* isn't it so?"

Bemused, Frau Minor nodded again, then caught herself, and said, "Yes."

"How long were you a schoolteacher?"

"Seventeen years."

"Seventeen years! My word! And then, let me guess, you were dismissed because you were Jewish? After they passed that anti-Semitic legislation in '33 to remove all Jews from the education system, yes?"

"No, not Jewish. But through lack of conformity as a so-called foreign atheist."

"An atheist?" Muller's smile broadened. "You, an atheist? How very interesting. Not exactly the Nazi party ideal. Is that why you choose to become a nurse?" Gertrude Minor could not follow the connection and just stared at him.

"Never mind," Muller said. "Who recommended you?" - and over the woman's vacant stare, added - "you don't get a job in an important hospital like the IK just by showing up. Somebody must have recommended you, yes?"

"No. They were short-staffed because so many Jews had been dismissed. They needed auxiliaries."

"I see…and naturally an auxiliary has the right to travel to Konstanz in the middle of the week despite the hospital being 'short-staffed'?" Said with a tinge of sarcasm.

"I got leave to see my mother in Zurich. She is not well."

"Your mother? Yes, of course; it is only natural." Muller smiled. Then tapped the two passports. "But from the entrance and exit stamps in your passports you do this on a regular basis. Is it a policy of the hospital to let auxiliary staff leave whenever they feel it necessary?" - and before the woman could answer - "Who pays for the tickets?"

Bewildered by the sudden blizzard of sharp questions, Frau Minor blinked, her lower lip trembled, and she felt a sudden urge to urinate such that she pressed her folded hands down in her lap lest she soil herself.

"It is a simple question, Frau Minor, yes?" Muller was still smiling. "Who pays?"

"I..I have some savings…" the woman stammered, squirming in her seat. "*Entschuldigung bitte*, excuse me please, I really must use the toilet."

"Of course! Of course!" Muller said, ever the jovial host. "Fritz," he said to the stenographer, "kindly show the lady to the bathroom."

While patiently waiting for their return, Heinrich Muller stood up from behind his desk to go over to the large window of his office, from where, hands behind his back, he could enjoy the almost hypnotic view down onto endless trains, wisps of steam coming from their engines, coming and going on a crisscross of multiple train tracks leading in and out of the station all day long. He could not help but think how fortunate he was to have such a job in such a city, the natural focus of the wealthy seeking safety across the border in Switzerland. He became so lost in his thoughts it took him a moment to realise that Fritz, the stenographer, was clearing his throat to attract his attention as he ushered Frau Minor back to her seat.

Silence.

Muller let the silence build before turning round and walking back to sit at his desk. Silently he lined up the three envelopes in front of Frau Minor. Silently he watched her eyes dart from the envelopes to her handbag, to her hands again folded in her lap, and back to the envelopes. What could she be thinking, Muller wondered, silently enjoying himself. He let a long moment pass. Then he said, tapping the envelopes, "These are yours, yes?" The question was deliberately ambiguous.

"I..I do not understand."

"They were in your handbag. I am sure you recognise them. What is there to understand, Frau Minor?" Pause. "Unless they are not yours, yes?" Silence. The woman's lip was trembling again.

"I will make it simple," Muller said. "If these are yours and you wrote them then you know to whom you were writing and what is written in each envelope, yes?" He picked up the first envelope. "Do you know what is in this envelope? It is addressed to the abbot of the Benedictine monastery in Montserrat. Do you know the abbot?"

Silence.

He picked up the second envelope. "This one is addressed to a numbered Poste Restante in Barcelona. Do you know what is written in here? And the name of the person behind the number?"

Silence.

He picked up the third envelope. "And this one, addressed to a Monsieur Belanopek, in a building on the Rue des Beaux Arts in Paris. What could it contain, eh?"

Silence.

"By your silence I take it to mean you do not know what is in any of these envelopes. Which leads to the obvious: you did not write them. Which leads to the question: who did? Tell me, Frau Minor, do you know who wrote them?"

Silence.

"If you don't know who wrote them, that only leaves one thing that you most definitely do know - who gave them to you to post?"

Silence.

"I do not think your silence will be of any benefit to you, Frau Minor. I am a very patient man, and sooner or later you will tell me what I want to know. Now it is getting late, and I must be going. Think about these matters tonight and we will meet again in the morning." And to Fritz he said, "*Nimm sie weg.*"

Before going home that night, Heinrich Muller telegraphed a verbatim copy of the interrogation (suitably edited to remove any criticism of Hitler and the Nazis) to Gestapo headquarters in Prinz-Albrecht-Straße, Berlin, with a request to expedite information on Minor's employment as a schoolteacher and nurse in Hamburg, focusing on any personnel with whom she may have had contact, specifically a married couple with one child. Wife's name begins with the letter N. Maybe French. He then instructed Fritz, "Tomorrow, I want you to go over the way to buy some chocolates," his euphemism for Switzerland. "When you get to Zurich, buy some stamps, and post these letters. If anybody asks, say you're a tourist. *Stehts?*" Off his stenographer's blank look he explained, "There is nothing in any of these letters of particular importance, just the usual bitching about the Nazis and the Gestapo, nothing you can't read in the foreign press. What is interesting is the recipients. With luck we may have stumbled upon an escape network. We'll set up surveillance; see if we can identify both ends, eh? Wouldn't that be a coup?" Then, satisfied with his day, he stepped out of his office to stroll along to his favourite *bierkeller* for a *schnapps* before dinner with his wife and children, never once giving thought to Gertrude

Minor, shivering in a prison cell, with no idea who deposited the letters she carried, collected by her at the post restante in the old post office building next to the Rathaus in Hamburg.

Chapter Thirty-eight

Marie smelled a rat as soon as she saw the stranger in the hallway checking the names of tenants on the letter boxes. *Her* hallway. Without a moment's hesitation, she put down the mop she was holding, flung open the door to her *loge* and loudly said: *"Monsieur?"*

"Bonjour, Madame. Je cherche Monsieur Belanopek." The man spoke perfect French.

Marie frowned. *"Connais pas,"* she said, shrugging her shoulders.

"Oh? How curious," the man said. "I was told he lived here."

"By whom?"

"The postman when I saw him in the street just now. He told me he sometimes delivered letters with that name here."

"Ce vieux con? I suppose you tipped him? When you see him again ask him why so much mail is returned *'Inconnue à cette adresse.'"* Arms akimbo, Marie stared the man down. "If that is all, I have things to do. Good day to you, Monsieur." She watched him leave, muttered *'Sale Boche'* to herself, and went to warn Pyotr. She found him taking inventory in the bar.

"You know who just came looking for you?" she said. *"Un sale Boche!* I threw him out."

"Calme-toi, Marie," Pyotr said. It was rare to see the concierge upset. "Are you sure? Maybe it was someone from the tax office?"

"Non! Non! A German. A spy. I can always smell them out, it doesn't matter how well they speak French," Marie said. Why would a German come looking for you? she wanted to add but held her tongue. It was not

her place to question Monsieur Pyotr, who had gone up in her estimation since inheriting the building.

"What did he look like?" Pyotr said.

"Not as tall as you," Marie said. "Grey suit, black coat, black Homburg hat, blue eyes, *maigre*, skinny face, bad breath. Oh, and brown shoes, real leather ones."

"Well, unless you see him again, let's not worry about him," Pyotr said, attempting a nonchalance he did not really feel. There were plenty of Germans in Paris, businessmen and tourists, but why would one come asking after Belanopek? What could be the connection? Which is when he remembered what Mme. Seidenfeld had said, 'You do not know him, but he knows of you since it's your name on the envelope.' Maybe Marie was right. And Pyotr again felt the familiar *frisson* of fear that he had always felt when leaving the safety of the trenches for no man's land. Game on.

But there were no further letters from Markus and the man Marie saw did not reappear. 1937 inexorably became 1938. The weave of time, the warp of uncounted hours, the humdrum routine of work managing the building and walking to the gallery to paint, overlaid his fears, putting a patina of everyday life like a bandage on a festering wound. You know it's there and should be disinfected but choose to ignore it in the hope it will go away. Reading the papers made the wound itch, so he stopped reading the papers. His amorous life was in the doldrums; his libido switched off. He ate and drank of necessity, by preference alone. The conversation of others? Unheard vocal clouds carried away into a penumbra of silence. Even his nights were untroubled by dreams. Adrift in homeostatic comfort, Pyotr forgot an essential factor of life: with or without his participation, the outside world was changing.

Paris Now.

"Funny how things happen. It's not just chance or luck. It's..it's..what's the word I'm looking for, George, begins with an s?"

"Serendipity," George said.

"That's it. Thank you. Hard to believe that a serendipitous meeting in April 1914 in Dar-es-Salaam, of two Prussian aristocrats, Paul Emil von Lettow-Vorbeck and Pyotr's Great-Uncle, Graf Otto-Friedrich Habermann von Oldesloe-Schlaffenberg, posted to German East Africa just before the Great War started, would lead to both acquiring vast plantations in between the exceptional guerilla campaign conducted by Lettow-Vorbeck as commander of the Imperial German Army's forces. For four years, his guerilla army of only 3,000 Germans and 11,000 African Askaris, held in check the combined might of 300,000 British, Indian, Belgian, and Portuguese troops. He is not known as the Lion of Africa for nothing, having never been defeated or captured in battle. In all that time he only lost twelve German officers, Von Oldesloe-Schlaffenberg being one of them. His 18,000 acre estate south of Usumbura on Lake Tanganyika, was conveyed to a trust set up in Luxembourg and thus escaped confiscation with the defeat of Germany and the Treaty of Versailles, which gave the 750,000 square miles of German East Africa to be divided between Britain, Belgium and Portugal. And it was a trustee who tracked down Pyotr in Paris in 1938 to tell him he was the last known survivor of his Great-Uncle, and it was by this happenstance that Pyotr first left France for Africa to visit his new possessions, take up a new calling with a wonderful woman, ugly as sin, then a marriage with his gardener's daughter who gave birth to twin girls, one white, one black, one to become a famous model, the other enslaved to a guerrilla leader of the RPF, the dreaded Rwandan Patriotic Front. So much for homeostasis. Of course it didn't all happen overnight. Over the years, even decades, would be a better description - particularly with the advent of the 2nd World War."

Chapter Thirty-nine

On Christmas Eve, 1938, two officers met for dinner in 'The Rag', the nickname of their club on Pall Mall, The Army and Navy Club. They sat in a discreet corner of the dining room on the first floor overlooking St. James's Square, the heart of all the men's clubs in London. They ordered Madras beef curry, served with basmati rice, naan bread, mint and cucumber yoghurt and mango chutney, recalling the heady days of the British Raj in India. Neither wore a uniform. To the uninformed they looked like two minor bank officials, although somewhat better dressed. No one in the general public, or even in the highest echelons of the military, would know that these two anonymous men would one day head the most secret spy-and-counterintelligence operations in Britain and abroad: the dour-faced man, Mr. Hollis, of MI5 and the Etonian, Mr. Menzies, of MI6. Having eaten, they spoke. There was no love lost between the two; they were there on business.

"By this time next year Winston thinks we'll be at war with Jerry," Hollis said. "He's concerned we won't be ready."

Menzies nodded. "So does Beaumont-Nesbitt in Paris. As military attaché he probably has better info than Churchill."

"After the Anschluss in Austria in March, giving up the Sudeten in September is insane, with Chamberlain ditching the Czechs, twisting Benes' arm to force him to surrender their border regions and defenses to appease that bastard, Hitler - '*Peace in our time*', my arse." Hollis said. "It's taken the Nazis, what, two weeks and their troops already occupy the region. Next thing he'll offer them the Home Counties."

"That's a bit harsh, don't you think?" Menzies raised an eyebrow. "He means well. With three million Germans living there and after Hitler's speech at Nuremberg, the writing was already on the wall. You know that. You saw what Henderson wrote?"

"The bit about President Benes never going far enough till he is made to do so. Just because he's our ambassador in Berlin doesn't mean he has to take his trousers down for Neville."

"No. It means you play the cards you are dealt. Did you get my memo on Kristallnacht?"

"What memo?"

"The one I sent to Grand. You were copied on it."

"Grand?"

"Laurence Grand, over at the Foreign Office. Head of Section D of the S.I.S. Chap who fought with Lawrence in the Middle East. Outfit's set up to figure out how to fight an enemy without the use of regular military forces, behind the lines with sabotage, blowing things up, crippling the adversary by all means, fair and foul. Surely you know all this?"

"No, I don't. I sit behind a desk sifting mounds of paper looking for traitors here at home." Hollis sniffed, took out a packet of Player's, lit one up. "So? What was in your memo?"

"A review of Hitler's radicalization of the Nazis' Jewish policy, and the crackdown on Jews. They're really cranking this up. Goebbels wants us to believe it's a spontaneous public outburst. It's been planned and implemented by the highest echelons of the Nazi leadership and carried out by members of the Nazi regime. Two months ago, beginning of October, all Jews' passports were invalidated, and those who needed a passport for emigration were given one marked with the letter J, you know, Jude for Jew. Then, October 27, the Nazis carried out the first mass deportation of Jews with the brutal eviction of resident Jews with Polish citizenship. SS men have driven children, the old, the sick across the Polish border; most of them concentrated into abandoned stables - and they're still there without any permission from the Poles. This deportation is directly connected with what happened last month, Kristallnacht, the night of November 9 -10, with the murder of nearly a hundred Jews, more than

1,400 synagogues across Germany and Austria torched, and Jewish-owned shops and businesses plundered and destroyed. In addition, get this, the Jews are being forced to pay 'compensation' for the damage that's been caused and approximately 30,000 of them have been arrested and sent to concentration camps. To top it all, can you imagine Funk, their Minister of Economics, publicly boasting that the Nazis have managed to steal Jewish property worth two million marks?"

"You sound like an editorial in The Times," Hollis said.

"Well, here's something you won't find in The Times. Have you heard of the Auxiliary Units?"

Hollis frowned. "No. What about them?"

"Very hush-hush. Seeing how the dominoes are falling in Europe, the idea is to create an all-volunteer, specially trained, highly secret, quasi-military unit with the aim of using irregular warfare in response to a possible invasion of Britain. Essentially duplicating what Grand's setting up abroad but here, a guerilla force, independent of the Home Guard, in fact independent of any command, with no uniforms, no official records of their activities, designed to inflict maximum mayhem and violent disruption on the invader. Service in the Units is expected to be highly dangerous, with a projected life expectancy of just twelve days for its members. It's got Winston's blessing."

"Christ!"

"I'm telling you this because your outfit will be tasked with vetting the volunteers. Starting with a rum one, recommended by Fleming. Have you heard of someone called Pyotr Szépség?"

"No."

"42. Bit old for this sort of lark. Austro-Hungarian aristocrat, born in Hawaii, raised in China and India, speaks God knows how many languages fluently, English boarding school, fights for the Huns in the Great War, survives 4 years of trench warfare with minor injuries, is invalided out as a Brit!, ends up as a painter in Paris until he inherits a bloody great plantation on Lake Tanganyika from his Prussian Grand-Uncle, from whose former Askari warriors he learns the bushcraft that allows him, and I quote, 'to live off a country which offers no apparent sustenance; to run in conditions when most men barely have the strength to walk; to condition the body to go without food or water; and, most important of all, how to become so much a part of an unfriendly wilderness that survival is possible, just as snakes and land crabs and lizards survive.'"

"Christ!" Hollis said, again.

"That's not all," Menzies said, taking a folder from his briefcase. "When he turned up to enlist, he was asked why he wanted to volunteer? He said he was good at two things: killing the enemy and blowing stuff up! Here's his dossier. Let me know what you think."

Paris Now.

"'There is nothing remotely heroic about killing people and destroying things.' This a rare quote from a man who has always refused to be interviewed on what he did in the war -"

"Not that he could have said much," George said, "seeing he'd signed the Official Secrets Act covering the activities of the Auxiliary Units."

"Right. Oddly enough at his first evaluation Pyotr was turned down. The reason given was that he was too old and there was a question mark on his patriotism. All that changed in '39 after Hitler invaded Poland, overran Belgium, flattened France, trapped the British Forces at Dunkirk and looked poised to invade Britain but for two obstacles, the Royal Air Force and Stalin. Without air cover there could be no invasion - the Battle of Britain, where *'the Few'* shot down Göring's Luftwaffe, saw to that. Then Hitler's insane decision to open a second front by invading Russia, tearing up the Molotov-Ribbentrop non-aggression pact with its Secret Protocol dividing Eastern Europe, guaranteed to infuriate Stalin, who had used it to also invade Poland, start a war with Finland, annex Estonia, Latvia, Lithuania, and parts of Romania.

Not needed at home, the Auxiliary Units were reassigned abroad and absorbed into the SOE, the Special Ops Executive, created to 'set Europe ablaze' (dixit Churchill), and the army reserve lists were combed for executives, writers, explorers, linguists and experts on foreign countries who might be put to good use by military intelligence. Pyotr was a shoe-in at his second interview. We know he was trained by a Gurkha demolition specialist in Beaulieu, the SOE headquarters in the New Forest, and then parachuted into Austria. Numerous other missions followed as alluded to in a curious book about an Old Man fighting the Mafia in Sicily in the '70s. But, as you know, history is written by 'winners', a trope served up by the media to vindicate the people in power who don't like to admit they committed the same atrocities as losers. Hence the anonymity of the Auxiliaries, no medals, no heroes, no parades, no thanks for a job well done. No one wants to read about murder and mayhem done in their name.

Today it's easy to forget that post-war, after the fall of Nazi Germany, and after the atomic bomb was dropped on Hiroshima and Nagasaki to end the Empire of Japan, much of Europe and Asia lay in ruins. Demobbed, unsung, Pyotr made a deal with Monsieur Doumeng to manage the old building on the Rue des Beaux Arts, and returned to Africa, to find Rwanda-Burundi recovering from the worst famine in its history, where 10% of the population died of starvation, with people selling leaves off trees to the hungry. Luckily for him, the numerous staff of his plantation and their even more numerous families had ample fish from Lake Tanganyika on which to feed. That, and the cultivation of cotton and sisal, insured the prosperity of the estate in a colony fretting under colonial rule with just four independent African countries: Egypt, Ethiopia, Liberia, and South Africa."

Chapter Forty

Pyotr did not translate into any African tongue, and it fell to
Nsengiyumva, his Estate Steward, a tall Tutsi who spoke Swahili to
find the nearest approximation: *Bwana Petro Mtakatifu* - Saint Peter
in English. Since Nsengiyumva's own name in Kinyarwanda, the chief
language of Rwanda, meant *God hears our prayers,* he considered his
translation to be perfectly legitimate.

"Trouble is coming, Bwana Petro Mtakatifu," Nsengiyumva said upon
Pyotr's return, when they met in the Trophy Room of his vast farmhouse,
on the walls of which hung the heads of virtually every wild animal known
to exist in Africa, all seemingly intent on hearing the steward as he made his
report. "If I may speak freely, when you went to the war you asked me to
oversee our plantation and all who live here, whether Hutu, Tutsi or Twa.
We have been blessed with the many children God has given to our families,
many, as you know, of mixed marriages between the different races, with
no distinctions, because for us we are all the same people, we speak the same
language, share the same culture and religion, like myself with my Hutu
wife and our six Hutu/Tutsi children. Many, many moons ago, despite no
European ever having even visited the country, the Kingdom of Rwanda
was incorporated into the so-called German East Africa protectorate. While
the Germans ruled they understood that we had lived in peace with one
another since before time, but when the Belgian Colonial Authorities came
to rule after the Great War, they changed the name of our country to
Ruanda-Urundi and forced us to say who we are, with mandatory identity
cards marking a difference between Hutu, Twa and Tutsi, calling the Hutu
indigenous "Bantu" people, and the Tutsi "Hamitic" invaders and

260

relegating the Twa to hunting and living in the forest. Their Catholic missionaries have taken over all primary schooling in the country, and today Tutsi children are told that they are better than Hutu, and the education for Hutu children is only meant to prepare them for work in the fields and herding cattle, with children of the Twa getting no schooling at all. Our King, the Mwami, is toothless, his authority gone, and with it the power of the old aristocrats who served him. We Tutsi are favoured by the Belgians for the most prestigious work in government. You know why? Because we are taller, and now superintend the Hutu, as if being taller makes it right. This is what I fear…"

Pyotr nodded. "Go on," he said.

"Do not be offended, Bwana, when I say the white man wants to teach us lessons on how to live by his rules," Nsengiyumva said, "ignoring our customs and our Gods. The white man sees the black man as uniformly ignorant. You do not see and never ask how we Africans see you. Because what we see is that you are blind to your own faults, which is how a small white man, a lowly corporal in the Great War, writes a book in prison which attracts so many to follow him that he strikes fear in the world and commits unspeakable crimes on his own people and his neighbours if they are of a different tribe, like the Jews, or do not have blonde hair and blue eyes, like the Gypsies, and ends with the death of millions and millions of innocent people. We could see this from here. If you cannot see this, you cannot have peace in your own house, and you cannot be surprised at what is happening outside your front door."

He was right, his fear well placed. Wherever he went, Pyotr had a ringside seat to watch the dissolution of European Colonial rule; the end of the exploitation of the vast natural resources of the continent by a few thousand white men. In its wake came an uncontrolled hunger for power of people long subjugated, now polarised into ethnic groups seeking their place in the sun. It was a slow process, slow but unrelenting, a small cloud on a distant horizon.

In 1946, to celebrate his 50th birthday, Pyotr chose to travel from Usumbura, the capital on the north-eastern shore of Lake Tanganyika, upstream on the Ruzizi River to Lake Kivu, a distance of 117 kilometres, ascending from 770 metres altitude above sea level to 1500 metres. It was December, the nights cold and rainy. It took him five days. He saw hippopotami, elephants, warthogs, buffalo and man-eating crocodiles. On reaching the fresh water of Lake Kivu, crocodile free because of the altitude, the rain stopped, the sun came out. Sweaty and hot, on an unnaturally muggy day, he went for a swim. And got bitten by a mosquito. Unfortunately, not any mosquito, but an infected female Anopheles mosquito carrying single-celled microorganisms introduced into Pyotr's blood from the mosquito's saliva, travelling from the bite to his liver where they matured and reproduced, a narrative that culminated two weeks later after his return home when he developed a fever, and chills. His muscles ached; his sheets were soaked in sweat. Then nausea, vomiting and diarrhea. For a man who had never been seriously ill, it was an agonising revelation of just how devastating acute pain could be, and, when his temperature went over 104° F, he became delirious, and his servants sent for the doctor to be fetched from her villa on the waterfront in Ubuntu.

The doctor was a tall, angular, bony-faced Finnish woman of 60, grey hair pulled back into a knot, who had spent her career in Africa after graduate studies in St. Pancras Hospital for Tropical Diseases in London. It took her three hours on dirt roads to arrive at the plantation and be taken into the high-ceilinged bedroom where Pyotr lay semi-conscious under a mosquito net. One glance at his tortured body made her diagnosis easy: Malaria! "How long has he been like this?" she said.

"It started one week ago," Nala said. Nala was Nsengiyumva's wife, in charge of the plantation's infirmary. "We gave him quinine as soon as we were sure it was malaria. Two tablets a day, but his fever won't come down."

"Is he drinking enough water?"

"When he is able, yes, Doctor."

"He must stay hydrated. And rested. We'll put him on an IV for 24 hours. Increase the Quinine to three times a day, every eight hours. I will have to take a blood sample to find out what kind of malaria we are dealing with here." The doctor looked out of a window as night fell. "It's getting late. I must be getting back to town."

"Perhaps, Doctor, you could stay until morning?" Nala said. "Just in case? We have many bedrooms. May I prepare one for you?"

The doctor stayed, and when Pyotr opened his eyes the following morning, he found himself looking up into the craggy face of a stranger. "I am Doctor Essi Heikkilä," the tall woman said. "We have not met. Your people called me because you are very sick. Do you understand me?" Pyotr could only stare.

"You have malaria," the doctor continued, "and I have put you on an IV to rehydrate your body. Your temperature has been abnormally high for an adult, but it is slowly coming down. You must drink as much as possible, and you must rest. Understand?"

Pyotr moved his head a fraction to nod, his face contorting in pain.

"Try not to move," the doctor said. "Just blink your eyes if you understand me."

Pyotr blinked.

"The pain will lessen in the next twenty-four hours. In a few days you will feel better, but you will be very tired. Very, very tired. Do not jump out of bed and imagine you are cured. This will take time. You understand?"

Blink.

"Good. I must get back to my practice in town now. I have taken a blood sample and as soon as I have the result I will be back. I have put a mild sedative in the saline solution to help you sleep. Sleep and rest and your fever will break." Even as she said the words the doctor could see her patient had drifted off to sleep. She turned to Nala standing next to her. "I hope." She shrugged. "He looks very strong. Fingers crossed this works. Keep his bedding as dry as you can while he sweats it out. Call me if his temperature rises."

One week later, a very tired Pyotr lay on a couch in the shade of the broad verandah outside his bedroom overlooking the manicured gardens and lawns that surrounded the farm, when the doctor returned. "So? Feeling better?" she said.

"Yes, Doctor, much better, thanks to you." Pyotr said, struggling to sit up.

"No, no. Lie down," the doctor said, taking a seat in a bamboo pavilion chair next to his couch, lighting up a cigarette, studying him. "Your analysis came back. It is very unfortunate that the mosquito that bit you carried the deadliest species of plasmodium, falciparum, which is responsible for 90% of the cases here. It is a parasite that lingers in the blood, causing recrudescence of the cycle you have just been through, fever, chills, sweating, acute pain, etcetera, even after successful antimalarial medication, and it can come and go for years. It's also responsible for 95% of all malaria deaths. I prefer you know this so you take it seriously. We will continue with quinine, but if that proves ineffective I may also want to try a derivative drug developed by the Germans for their colonies, chloroquine. We'll see. For now, no panic. Rest and sleep. Clear?"

Pyotr nodded. "I like 'no panic'," he said.

The doctor smiled. "I've had it, and I am cured. It just takes time. You were delirious when I came here last week. In some strange dream world, shouting in Swedish."

"Oh God, not again!" Pyotr said and told her of his recurring dream.

Dreamland - 16

On the highest tower of Stockholm Castle, Christina sits alone with her pet falcon on her gloved wrist. It is a beautiful summer day, and she is in a pretty summer dress, with a laced bodice and small silk waistcoat. Overhead her personal banner floats gently in the breeze. She kicks off her shoes and starts to undo the falcon's hood, when, behind her she hears someone laboriously climbing the stairs. It is the Catholic priest, her advisor, Father Silva, crucifix hanging down the front of his brown robe, puffing as he emerges on the battlement, bobbing his head in embarrassment. "Forgive me, your Majesty," he says.

"What would you have me forgive, Father?" the Queen says.

"I am disturbing your sport."

"Not at all. She loves an audience. Don't you my pet?" The Queen stroked the bird's head as it emerged from under the hood, its stern yellow eyes fixed on the priest. "Say hello to Father Silva."

The falcon ignores the priest, flexes its wings, preparatory to soaring into the sky, followed by two pairs of eyes.

"Would that I were so free," Christina said, as Father Silva sat, hands folded in his lap, apprehension written across his face. "What troubles you, Father?"

"The Pope," Father Silva said.

"Of course. Tell me, can anyone annul what the pope has decreed?"

"No. Nobody!"

"Then how is it that we hear of papal judgements rescinded on the ground that popes were misinformed?"

"Ignorance about a person or a fact can occur in a pope as it can in any man. But what proceeds from the authority of a universal council is a heavenly oracle and carries weight equal to that of the Gospels."

"Then you believe a group of elderly men dressed up in elaborate robes speak in the name of our Lord?"

"Does not Paul say: 'Obey them that have the rule over you if you seek salvation'? Outside the habitation of the Holy Catholic Church there is no salvation!"

"Says who? Are we not all Christians?" The Queen cannot sit still and strides across the battlements the better to air her thoughts. "Catholic! Protestant! These are but labels we inflict on ourselves to justify our bitter quarrels. Whole worlds are shaken by the supposed reasoning of these deadly disputes between Rome, Luther, Calvin and Zwingli. We hear them and are asked to believe that the way they eat, fast, gesture and chant are the essence of their religion and the basis for judging their neighbours - contrary to the command of the Gospels! Thus it is, that in the name of faith and Christian love, whole peoples are destroyed, cities fired, the very art and culture of mankind obliterated. If we could rid ourselves of these petty ceremonies -"

"Petty ceremonies!" Father Silva is shocked.

"Yes, petty ceremonies," the Queen was adamant. "That divide us where we should be united! Straining only for those essential things Christ taught! In so doing, it is our firm conviction all peoples of all races would more readily embrace a religion joined with freedom."

"That is not for us to say!" Father Silva said. "Whoever does not recognize the Roman Pontiff is outside the Church! Beware, your Majesty. He who disregards the Pope's ordinances does not recognize him and is not recognized!"

"And for that very reason we send this message," the Queen stood stock still to glare at the priest. "Let your ambassador convey to this pope, that for the purpose of attracting all races into the fellowship of Christ, he must mitigate his making of conditions that estrange the Christian flock; that he should prefer the word of the Gospel to carrying out his own prerogative in everything! Instead of burdening the people with annates, pardons, dispensations, and other taxes to support his distant wars, let him at once proclaim a universal truce and demobilise his armies and those of his allies. Let him set an example, demonstrate that the only Christian rivalry is that we strive to outdo the other in good faith, duty and generosity. Let each of us try *not* to rule a larger kingdom than we have, but to govern his own dominion more righteously and *unransom* our people from dogma and prejudice! What nation, I ask you, would not willingly follow the ruler of a Church which longed for nothing other than the Glory of Christ and the salvation of all mankind?"

"Amen," Father Silva said, (but could not help himself wondering if Gustavus was now rolling over in his grave - a thought best left unspoken), so he diplomatically added: "Would that all monarchs thought the same!"

Which is when, in the sky above them, they heard a far-off, high-pitched screech, and looked up to see the falcon in a steep dive aimed straight at an unsuspecting dove flying innocently below. The falcon held its dive until the last second when its talons struck, and, in a small puff of white feathers, instantly killed its prey. Then it swooped to land on the battlement to eat. "Take note, Father Silva," the Queen said.

Chapter Forty-one

Pulling on her cigarette, Essi Heikkilä listened patiently without comment. Then she said something which opened Pyotr's eyes and recalled to him an important long-forgotten thought.

"Do you not think," she said, "that Gustavus was no better than Hitler?"

"What!"

"Think about it. He waged unmerciful war on neighbouring states for no other reason than a difference in religious belief. And did it for 30 years! Protestant against Catholic, ostensibly believing in the same God, and" - in a sudden insight where Pyotr felt as if his couch had moved - "and, if you get down to it, the same could be said of every venerated hero of the past, Alexander, Caesar, Genghis Khan, Hannibal, Napoleon, Foch, Haig, Bismarck, even Augustus, all of them, with all their marble busts decorating the hallways of Academia, fundamentally inhumane warlords, always in the name of God, taking the lives of their fellow men as their divine right. Nothing. Nothing has changed. Why do we venerate them? Man's inhumanity to man is as constant as water flowing downhill."

"Yes! Yes, I agree. You have put in words a thought I had months ago. It slipped my mind and try as I might I could not recall it. How extraordinary!" In his excitement, Pyotr tried to sit up.

"No, no. Rest," Essi said. "Enough for now. You need to rest, try to sleep. I'm staying the night. We'll talk tomorrow."

Over breakfast the following morning, like friends who have known each other for years, they exchanged mundanities - How are you? Better, thank you. Fever? I think it's gone. Sleep well? Off and on. You? Very comfortable. Your Nala is a gem. Yes, she is. Where did you find her? She came with the farm. I see. - followed by a comfortable silence. And then another. Finally, Essi said, "It's strange we haven't met before. I thought I knew all the expats out here. You married?"

"No. Never found the right one."

"Me, neither. When did you get this place?"

"In '38; inherited from my Great-Uncle, Graf von Schlaffenberg."

"The Prussian? I think I met him when I first came out. Randy old goat, chased anything in a petticoat. Must be 35 - 40 years ago, before the Great War. You were in that, I believe."

"Yes," Pyotr said, wondering who could have told her.

As if reading his mind, she said, "It's your wounds. When we were cleaning you up between bouts of delirium, I couldn't help but notice how old some were and asked Nala. She told me they are the marks of a great warrior."

Pyotr made a face, shrugged. "I don't like to talk about it," he said.

Essi nodded in understanding, then changed the subject. "Have you heard of *ubuhake*?" she said.

"No."

"What about *umuganda*?"

"No."

"*Uburetwa*?"

"No."

"If you are to live here it's important you know how the country works. For hundreds of years, Rwanda has been run through what is really a feudal system. Through a contract known as *ubuhake*, the Hutu farmers pledged their services and those of their descendants to a Tutsi lord in return for the loan of cattle and use of pastures and arable land. Thus, the Tutsi reduced the Hutu to virtual serfdom. To make the system fair, a diligent Hutu could become a Tutsi by breeding the cattle and selling any excess produce from his agricultural labour to his Tutsi overlord until his debt was expunged. In their language, Kinyarwanda, they have a proverb, '*Umuntu ngumutu ngabantu*', which means 'a person is a person through other persons', from

269

which root you get *umuganda,* the notion of communal work. Communities came together to help people who were unable to do physical work and protect not just their security but also to create economic opportunities. With the arrival of the Belgians this coalesced into *uburetwa,* communal labour, forced on the male population of every family to participate in 60 days of community labour per year. Doesn't sound like much, but that's 5 working days per month, leaving precious little time to provide for themselves or their families. You must have noticed your male servants slipping off at regular intervals?"

"Not really," Pyotr said, embarrassed. "I don't exactly know how many work here; there are always new faces turning up saying they are a cousin or uncle just visiting and then my steward says they've been taken on to help with whatever he says needs doing."

"Typical. To run a place this big I bet you have more than 30 servants," Esssi said, "plus their families. You are the *Bwana* who provides. No wonder they venerate you."

"What do you mean?"

"Nala told me that when you went off to enlist in 1940 you left her husband in charge of the plantation, something practically unheard of in this country where no white man ever leaves a black man in control."

Pyotr blushed. "Truth be told, he knew far more than I did about how to make this place work. Still does."

"Of course he does," Essi said. "He's a Tutsi, brought up to govern. But the Belgians have taken a leaf out of the British colonial playbook, divide and rule. And they can count. The Hutu make up 70% of the population and insidiously they are backed by the Belgians, giving them more authority, levelling the field with the Tutsi, polarising the natives. This is going to end badly, mark my words. I have to get back to town now. Take your quinine and rest. If you keep improving, come and visit me and we can continue our conversation. Thank you for your hospitality." Without further ado, she got up to leave, hesitated, then added, "I too have a spare bedroom. Perhaps you will stay overnight?"

Thus began a romance that slowly bloomed, indifferent to the 10 years in age that separated them, and the inevitable gossip that followed wherever they went amongst the expats. Within a matter of months some of Essi's dresses were in a cupboard in 'her' bedroom on the farm, and some of Pyotr's kit in 'his' bedroom in her house in town. They wined and dined at every opportunity, their heads together in animated talk, she sharing her 40 years of experience living in Africa and he the avid pupil.

"In Kinyarwanda," Essi said, "you say *Mwaramutse* to greet someone, both a question and a wish, literally meaning, 'Have you woken up alive?' And if the person hasn't seen you for a day they may answer '*Muraho*,' meaning 'are you alive?' or '*Murayama?*' which means 'are you still moving.' To say *au revoir* when leaving someone, they say '*Hrubeho*, Stay alive!' or '*Urakarama!* Live long!' There is a deep existential concern for life here, an acute awareness of how precarious it can be, and it's reflected in their language and the drums."

"Drums?" Pyotr said.

"Yes," Essi said. "Listen. They use drums to talk." Silence. Somewhere in the distance there is a wireless playing, a couple argue, a dog barks, faintly the voices of children and the sound of traffic on the esplanade can be heard. Then, deep in the background, a far-off throbbing, a muffled beat - to which an ear must be tuned. After a moment, Pyotr nods.

"What does it mean?" he said.

"You have to be an African to know," Essi said.

When she learned about him being co-opted into helping one of the surgeons in the trenches at Verdun, ending up doing a stint in Heidelberg because the surgeon thought he had a doctor's gift, she immediately suggested he accompany her on her rounds and in her clinic, where he learned first-hand about measles, polio, diphtheria, cholera, hepatitis, meningitis, rabies, typhoid, yellow fever, leptospirosis, schistosomiasis, and how bug bites by mosquitoes, ticks, fleas and flies led to African sleeping sickness, African tick-bite fever, Chikungunya, Dengue, Zika and malaria, the entire laundry list seen in the long lines of patients, old, young, rich, poor, waiting patiently every morning outside the office for their chance to see the doctor. "I know a lot about this stuff," Doctor Essi Heikkilä said, "because as a small-town doctor I see it five days a week, 52 weeks a year. The point is to stop the dying, particularly children. Almost all of it comes from contaminated water or food, with the risk for infection highest in the poorest segment of the population."

271

"Aren't you scared you might catch something?" Pyotr said.

"Just about as scared as a soldier in battle. He knows there's a bullet with his name that will get him one day. Until that day comes, why worry about all the bullets that miss?"

The clinic, a simple one-story structure made of mud bricks painted white with a tin roof, one ward, 4 beds, staffed by two nurses, Kampire, a Tutsi, and Keza, a Hutu, was at the bottom of the Doctor's property where it backed onto the dusty service road that ran parallel to the Avenue de la Plage on the esplanade overlooking the lake. It opened at 7 every morning, but patients arrived long before that, some even camping out overnight. None had appointments. All came with relatives. They brought their ailments to the Doctor after all home remedies had failed, these delays often being fatal. Few could pay for the cost of treatment, and fewer still in cash. The rest paid in kind, a chicken, a goat, a sack of maize, whatever, very often nothing. These '*payments*' were returned by way of the food prepared in the canteen adjacent to the clinic and served every day at noon by Essi's cook to all the waiting multitude. "How can you afford this?" Pyotr asked.

"By myself, I can't," Effi said. "Various charities here and back home help out. I also have grants and some of the pharmaceutical companies give us the drugs we need. I also steal" - said with a laugh - "It's never enough, but we manage."

Once a week, the Doctor made house calls to the surrounding villages in a dilapidated lorry painted white with a red cross on the driver's door. Pyotr was given a knee-length white cotton gown to wear and became the designated driver and mechanic.

"Just be thankful for the truck," Essi said on their first trip, with Pyotr swearing at the gearbox, "in the old days we had a mule and a cart. It took a week to do the rounds and another week of showers to get the dirt and dust out of your hair when you got back."

In every village their reception was the same - a gaggle of laughing children running to greet them and accompany them to a given station, usually in the shade under a tree where the sick gathered beneath the stern gaze of the headman. The tail of the lorry was dropped and became the counter for a makeshift dispensary, every jar of pills, box of bandages, phial of drugs, flask of ointment, cause for comment and enquiry. "Look, listen, learn," was the Doctor's mantra, as she examined her patients, whether it be a distended belly, a broken limb, a pustule, a cataract, a weeping wound that would not heal, a fever, a cough, the shivers, a bite. "If you say *amakuru*, how are you? They always say *Ndarwaye buke*, I'm a bit sick. Only a bit. Even close to death they say *Ndarwaye buke. Yego*. Rwandans like to have the last word in any conversation. *Yego* means yes, got it?"

"Yego," Pyotr said.

Beyond driving the lorry, Pyotr's role was to take notes, shut up and learn. Essi gave him a spiral bound medical journal, 31 pages, one page for each day of the month, each page with headings: Date & Time, Location, Name of Patient, Age, Reason for visit, Diagnosis, Prescription, Questions/Observations, Next appointment (if any). A typical day read:

Jan.4, 1947

- 7.10am; Clinic; Mrs.Uwimbabazi Kwizera; 55; Chest pain; Heart arrhythmia; Rest/Cardiac monitoring; Has had 9 children (4 dead) obese, high blood fats, family trait; None.

- 7.30am; Clinic; Gasimba (no family name); 47; deep infected cut (machete?) left leg below knee; Wash, Disinfect, Seventeen sutures, Bandage; Accident? Won't say; Keep clean; Come back next week.

- 8am; Clinic; Mugabo Niyodusenga (5 years old); multiple 2nd degree burns, kerosene lamp explosion; blistered skin, washed gently, pat dry, keep patient warm; brought by Grandmother to clinic in a wheelbarrow (parents dead); stay overnight.

- 8.45am; Clinic; Mrs. Ingabire Poweri and teenage daughter (15?) no name; rape victim; test for pregnancy; negative; DO NOT REPORT.

- 9.30am; Clinic; Gahigi Ganza; claims to be 90+; UN (undernourished), severe headache, severe eye pain; chronic glaucoma, blind in left eye; no cure, remain hydrated at all time, eye drops. None.

- 9.50am; Clinic; Mihigo Kayumba; 37; swelling in lymph nodes armpits and groyne; infected abscess in mouth; fever; bacterial infection probable; penicillin and rest; return if condition worsens.

- 10.20am; Clinic; Neza Kayumba (no relation to above); 19; ringworm, arms, buttocks, back of thighs; antifungal cream, extract of garlic, apply twice daily for one week; return if not better.
- 10.45am; Clinic; Shema Imanzi, 28; UN; multiple tick bites around ankles; fever 102°, comes and goes every 3 days; shivering; penicillin and rest; will subside - but probable recurrence in future.
- 11.15am; Clinic; Bisangwa (no family name); 25; high fever, chills, blood in stool, diarrhoea; Typhoid? Paratyphoid? Quarantine. Warn 4 family members accompanying him it is highly contagious. Must not touch feces or urine.
- 11.45am; Clinic; Niriniri Shumbusho, 24; repeat patient (prostitute?); chlamydia; penicillin; caution: advice must follow treatment, warn partners.

LUNCH BREAK - As always, cooked in a large pot, *Igisafuria*, fried chicken thighs with some spinach and green plantains blended together with celery, green peppers and hot chilli peppers to make the dish spicy. Essi and the two nurses eat with the patients.

- 1.00pm; Clinic; Nshuti (no family name); 30? dog bite marks on hands and right leg; when? 'A few days ago'; tingling, itching around bites; Rabies? wounds washed with soap and water and iodine solution; saliva and blood samples for lab; stay overnight for results.
- 1.35pm; Clinic; Mrs. Mutesi Belysi; 51; fever; Malaria, repeat patient, 3rd incident over past 2 years. Quinine. Rest.
- 2.00pm; Clinic; Mugwaneza Kamanzi and sister, Mitaako; 13 & 14; jaundice, nausea, stomach pain, diarrhea, dark urine; Hepatitis; blood samples to determine type A,B, or C?; keep

hydrated; accompanied by mother, told to wash hands and cook food thoroughly, children immune for life after recovering.

- 2.30pm; Clinic; Gasore Iyakaremye; 60+; repeat patient, impotent; cannot 'honour' his wife and mistress; has been drinking watermelon and pomegranate juice to diminishing effect; trying herbal ginseng, maca and ginkgo; also chewing Ubangalala roots. Heard there is a 'Whiteman's magic pill'? No. Sent home.

- 2.50pm; Clinic; Gatete Ntare; 30; skin rash, slight fever, red eye; mosquito bites; Zika; not dangerous, no vaccine. Rest.

- 3.15pm; Clinic; Ntwali Tumusiime; age ?; mosquito bite; high temperature, fever, shivering. Malaria. Course of Quinine and rest. Stay hydrated.

- 3.45pm; Clinic; family of 5, Mr. & Mrs. Niyoyita, children aged 3, 5 and 7; victims of recent famine; thin, bloated, listless; bones protruding; loss of muscle mass; parents report children always feeling cold and tired, getting sick easily. 'No matter how much we feed them they remain thin'. Water? From the village well. Must be contaminated. Test. Until the result is known, drink only from another source. Where? Stay overnight. Small snacks every two hours. Fresh water.

- 4.30pm; Clinic; Uwamahoro Mwine; 32; pain in bladder when urinating; Cystitis. Short course penicillin. Avoid having sex; drink plenty of water. Should clear up in 2/3 days. If not, return.

- 4.50pm; Clinic; Uwase Alheri; 13; swollen glands, sore throat, difficulty breathing; Diphtheria; highly contagious in crowded living conditions; child has had no previous vaccination; Pertussis vaccine; return in 1 week for follow-up examination.

- 5.15pm; Clinic; Nkurunziza Mukami; 60s; pain from hip, left side, after fall; x-ray from hospital no fracture; has tried willow bark tea to alleviate pain; prescribe Laudanum/opium powder in 10% alcohol solution; report back in one week.

- 5.45pm; Clinic; Neza Mutoni; multiple mosquito bites; high temp., chills, shivers; Malaria recurrence; Quinine; rest.

Impossible - only working member of large family dependent on her (four of whom are present- Uncle in charge, taken aside for severe lecture from Doctor about non-cooperation!)

6.00pm; CLINIC CLOSED

They never closed on time. There was always another patient waiting. 22 patients treated on an average day, with as many lined up for the morrow. It showed in Essi's face, a story of stress, and grief.

"I worry about you, you know," Pyotr said, over dinner one evening.

"Do you, Doctor?" Essi said, smiling.

"Out of curiosity I did the maths," Pyotr said. "Roughly speaking, if you have 20 patients a day for 300 days a year, that's 6000; times 40 years, equals 240,000!"

"So? You've left out house calls, and hospital visits. That probably doubles the number." Essi said.

"Must you work so hard? Surely you have done enough?"

"What is enough? I doubt there is a doctor in the world who knows that word. Anyway, it's not work, it's love." Pyotr sat up, surprised.

"You know Eliot's poem?" Essi said.

'We *shall not cease from exploration,*
And the end of all our exploring,
Will be to arrive where we started,
And know the place for the first time.'

It ends: '*And the children in the apple-tree,*
Not known, because not looked for,
But heard, half-heard in the stillness,
Between two waves of the sea.'

In the stillness of Africa I half-hear all I haven't done."

Pyotr was speechless, trying to understand.

"Give it a few years," Essi said, still smiling, "you'll see what I mean."

Five years later, the bullet with Essi's name arrived in the shape of cholera, its origin unknown, but possibly vegetables washed in contaminated water. She self-diagnosed her own 'rice-water stool' with its fishy smell, vomiting and dehydration. Pyotr, attended by the two nurses,

Kampire and Keza, administered a subcutaneous parenteral cholera vaccine to Essi under her instruction, and inserted an IV to rehydrate her body, with morphine in the solution to alleviate her suffering. To no avail. Her kidneys failed. Within hours, helpless, he held her hand as the dehydration reached a critical stage, with excruciating cramps that had Essi writhing in pain. Her skin went dark and started to turn blue, her eyes sank into her skull, her mouth pulled back in a rictus exposing her teeth, and she died in agony in her own bed. He had not heard the drums carrying the message, but seemingly the entire black population of Usumbura had, and they came in their silent thousands, tearing their clothes in grief, to attend her funeral, with a tiny minority of expats, white dots in the crowd. A month after her burial, Pyotr left Africa for Europe.

Paris Now.

"Heartbroken," George said. "Poor bloke. In the six years they had together, she taught him everything she knew about tropical diseases, enough to get himself a doctorate. Life can be so fucking cruel. Then he goes off to hide in Sicily, and look what happened to him there, more heartbreak."

"Dunno about that," I said. "He gets a young wife."

"A widow, you mean, plus two stepchildren. Can you imagine being lumbered with two kids?"

"I can actually. We'd make perfect parents."

"Us two poofters? What a load of bollocks."

No point in arguing. Particularly if you're standing on a ladder as I was, trying to hang some posters in a new display on the back wall of the shop.

"Left hand down a bit on the middle one," George said.

"What do you make of the rumour he had a second wife in Africa?"

"Don't believe it for a moment."

"Why not? He was going backwards and forwards between Europe and Africa before that second long stretch in the States. Bit like an old pirate, one in every port."

Little did he know.

FLASHBACK

An old man, hair cut short, wearing a black shirt, black pants and a black fedora pulled down on his brow, carrying a child fast asleep against his shoulder and a suitcase, stepped off the night ferry from Messina to Naples, looked around to make sure he was not surveilled, and quickly nodded to a woman, carrying another small child and another suitcase, to disembark. They followed the hoard of passengers out of the Molo Beverello terminal, deliberately lagging behind them, until, in the shadow of the port's gloomy fortress, Maschio Angioino, they were alone, and he stopped, put down the suitcase he was carrying and turned to her.

"We have never had the chance to talk," he said.

"Yes?" she said, putting down her suitcase.

"You are free now," he said.

"Free?" she said.

"Yes," he said. "You are free now to live your life, to go where you will."

"I see," she said. "But am I free to be with you?"

For the longest time he just looked at her. Then he said, "If that is your choice?"

"Isn't that why I am here?"

"I must warn you, I am an old man. I get up to pee at night."

"Maybe it is so," she smiled, taking his hand, "but you are my old man. I knew it the first day I saw you in that café."

He nodded.

"There is one thing though, if we are to be together," she said. "You must swear to me you will never, ever, ask me any questions about my life with him."

Him. The Capo. Lividiani. The name unspoken.

"*Capire?* Understood?"

"Yes."

"This you must promise. *Giammai!* Never!"

Again, he nodded. "I promise."

"And I must *warn* you," - another smile - "I am a young woman, with two small children who will need a father."

Now it was his turn to smile. "Let's get married, then" he said.

"But I don't know your name?" she said, now laughing. "We have never been introduced."

It was true.

"Pyotr," Pyotr said.

"Pyotr," she said, kissing him. "I am called Serafina."

Pause.

"Where will we go?" she said.

Chapter Forty-two

To Genoa, to the Palazzo Szépség, a rather grand designation for the huge old dilapidated mansion, measuring close to 1500 square metres, set back in a cul de sac off Via Giorgio Byron in the hills of Albaro, overlooking the seafront, Corso Italia, the beach at Boccadasse, and, in the distance, the Porto Antico.

Seen through an archway, set in the middle of an overgrown walled Italian garden, the entire palace dominated the town from its balconies, its eclectic past evident in a decor of ribbed vaults, randomly-matched flooring, Lecce stone, terrazzo inlaid with a wealth of motifs, coats-of-arms, and sinuous, intricate plasterwork, the building dating from the beginning of the 18th century when Rococo was all the rage, a Grande Dame of the period, now sadly showing her age. The mansion was built over two vaulted cellars, with a faded pink facade, fourteen tall windows on the ground floor, and the first floor, featuring arched pediments, including windowsills on corbels, two string courses and a cornice, as well as molded window surrounds, spandrel panels and corner quoins. Fourteen square windows on the second floor with simple stone sills; an attic topped by a hipped monk-and-nun tiled, Roman roof.

Up three terraced steps, a porch gave access to a vast reception hall, with, on the right, a wide, elegant dressed stone staircase leading to the *piano nobile*. Opposite, an endless enfilade of rooms, bigger and smaller depending on their use: a bright study/atelier with two corner windows, paint splattered floorboards, a ceiling 7-metres above; a dining room that could easily seat twenty, with wainscoting and a marble fireplace topped by an ornamental overmantel gilded mirror; a butler's pantry, (the kitchens and staff dining room, below stairs); an immense ballroom, with Versailles parquet flooring and mirrored walls; a large ceremonial reception room of 105m², accessed through tall doors, wainscoting, painted cornices, decorative moldings, arched corners and another marble fireplace, followed by three reception rooms of decreasing size (one of which had been turned into a playroom for children); a sculpture gallery; a library; the billiard room; a nursery, continuing on to a suite of temporary bedrooms, boudoirs, powder rooms and bathrooms pending their permanent location to the upper floors; and, across the entire rear, a conservatory with a riot of plants. A total of 500m² just on the ground floor.

When they arrived, unannounced, to the consternation of the family living there in bohemian squalor, caretakers of the property for so long they thought they owned it, an *avvocato* had to be called. The lawyer explained the matter to the family. Compensation was agreed. The family left. Finally taking possession, Pyotr did what he always did, rolled up his sleeves and got to work. "When it's done, we'll get married," he told Serafina. It took a year. Just to do the ground floor.

To pay for its renovation, Pyotr, with the help of old Monsieur Doumeng, sold the tenement on the Rue des Beaux Arts in Paris to a *Marchand de Bien*, a Monsieur Azzan, who flipped it to a colleague, Monsieur Banon, who sold it to an English company, the Raglan Property Trust, who hardly had time to close on the transaction before going bankrupt in the aftermath of the '74 Sterling crisis, with the receiver selling it on to the GAN, a French insurance company, who converted the building into a *copropriété* of 12 apartments at great cost and substantial gain. Of the original tenants, only the ancient Mme. Seidenfeld, *2eme Gauche*, could afford to remain, paying for her apartment in gold. Even Marie, the concierge, had retired, and it was her successor, her daughter, Marie-France, who, after the sale, forwarded to Pyotr those things he had left in storage, plus a string-tied dusty packet of letters, accumulated in his 29-year absence. One was from Markus enclosing another envelope in which was a single sheet of paper. From Great-Aunt Tilly. It read:

'*Liebe Pyotr, wherever you are, greetings!*

281

At long last, thank God, I am dying. Nothing will give me greater pleasure than to depart this dreadful world. Alles ist arrangiert. Cousin István will bury me. Like Erasmus, I have nothing, I owe much, the rest I leave to the poor. As you are in this category, and the last of our line, I bequeath to you whatever remains of our once vast family estates and fortune. Cast your seed far and wide in any woman seeing merit in your scrofulous self - Ha! Ha! - and may you sire many, many progeny in the preservation of our bloodline. Carpe Diem! L'Chaim! Adieu,

    Tilly.'

An obituary notice, bordered in black, from the Gazette de Lausanne dated ll.6.1971, was attached to the letter. It read:

Caux-sur-Montreux, Canton de Vaud
'There is a time to live and a time to die.'
In silent mourning on behalf of all relatives, it is with the greatest sadness that we say farewell to the doyenne of the Ancien Régime in Switzerland,
Aged 107 years.
Augustine, Grand Duchess of Austria-Hungary, Princess of Romania-Bukovina, Baroness of Reichenau, Countess of Saxe-Meiningen, Princess of Neuchâtel
R.I.P
(1864 - 1971)

Markus' letter bore the date Berlin, July 2, 1971. It read:

'Cher Ami - Not having heard from you for so long, I imagine you are still in Africa - hopefully this letter will be forwarded to you. As you can see from the attached, the old lady passed away. What a life! We met occasionally for drinks in the Adler since it reopened. She was much taken by Nathalie and Claudia - who is now 43! - hard to believe my daughter is nearly as old as I was when I met her mother. She has lived with us since her divorce. Teaches music and ballet.

Did you know Anna died? Car accident on a skiing holiday in Gstaad three years ago. Nat took it badly. Still does. Knocked the impulsive nuttiness out of her that I love so much. You did too if I remember. It's been ten years since they built the bloody wall splitting this city in two, and surrounding us with barbed wire, tank traps and minefields for 155 kilometres with manned observation towers and soldiers ordered to shoot anyone trying to escape, making sure we know we are trapped in the middle of East Germany. I still can't believe that after we defeated the Nazis we've ended up in such a shit heap. The Four Powers - three really, the French are a joke - responsible (another joke) for running the show have just concluded yet another conference - read blah, blah - about mutual cooperation and détente. Can you believe the agreement they reached has only been published in English, French and Russian? There is not even an official German translation - supposedly to leave wriggle room for interpretation between the two German States, a guaranteed formula for disaster which the Commies will use to their full advantage while we dither around with a thumb up our ass listening to Douglas-Home and Schumann telling the world how clever they've been, and that ignoramus Rogers, chosen by Nixon solely because he knows fuck all about foreign affairs, pushed to the sidelines by Nixon's eminence grise, Kissinger. Where are the people who had the balls to put up the Airlift which saved the city when the Russians had us by the throat?

I'm 80 in December and can see the finish line. Apart from when I was a very small child, my entire life has been tainted by war - overt, covert, on the front page, buried in the back, from 1914 to today. It's like a stain on me. Nathalie, whose intuition I am sure you also remember, thinks this explains my endless Priapic conquest of women. Something I can do, to offset what I can't. Me giving her the freedom to do the same is just a ploy to salve my conscience, she says. Qui sait? She is 65 now, dealing with breast cancer, with never a murmur of complaint or self-pity. What a marvel; God alone knows how she puts up with me. Other than her, I have few friends. Please write, M.

"Is that what you're going to do, cast your seed in me?" Serafina said, when she had finished reading.

"At my age?" Pyotr laughed. "You should be so lucky."

Serafina stuck out her tongue at him. "Your friend's letter is four years old, are you going to write back?"

"I would," Pyotr said, "but as you can see, there's no return address. Just like Markus, on the dodge from someone or something." Even as he said it, Pyotr knew what the 'something' was: death. The fnish line. To change the subject, he added, "You'd like them." Which earned him a shrewd look from Serafina.

"You mean the women?" she said.

Silence.

They were sitting opposite each other at a desk in the library which had become an architect's office, with plans strewn around, drawings pinned to the walls, quotes, bills, change orders, fabric samples, spilling out of every cupboard and drawer. Far of they could hear the children calling "*Dove sei? Dove sei?*" in their endless game of hide-and-seek in the many rooms. As always, with a project of this scope, the year so optimistically forecast for completion had come and gone, as had almost all the money from the sale of the property in Paris. Dressed in faded dungarees, working gloves dangling from a back pocket, Pyotr said, "What?"

"You know what," Serafina said. "It will never be finished." She waved a hand to indicate the house, the plans, the endless work…

"So, pick a date," Pyotr said, knowing where this was going.

"June 8," Serafina said promptly. A Sunday, three months away. "For us Italians getting married on a Sunday signifies a day of good fortune for our future prosperity - and fertility!" She laughed. "Your Great-Aunt would approve." Pause. Then, seriously, she said, "But first you have to serenade me."

"What?"

"On your knees. It's a tradition. You have to sing to me."

"Me? Sing?"

"Yes."

"But I'm a hopeless singer."

"No, you're not. I've heard you in the shower."

And so it was that Pyotr, watched by his fiancée and her two giggling children, knelt under the shower and did his best imitation of Edith Piaf singing all six verses of '*Non, je ne regrette rien.*'

Soaking wet, as he sang his eyes never left hers, and at the end he pulled her in under the shower, followed by Allegra and Guido clutching onto their mother, all four screaming hysterically. There, under the pouring water, a bond was formed, an enchanted family bond. And on Sunday, June

8, 1975, they were duly married in the private chapel attached to the mansion in a ceremony solemnised by a priest from their parish church on Via Giorgio Byron, the Chiesa Delle Adoratrici Perpetue Del SS. Sacramento, attended only by the children, and two witnesses, one a carpenter, the other a plumber, part of the crew working on the renovation.

As for the letters from Tilly and Markus, they ended up in the attic, stored away in a Victorian roll-top desk crammed with other papers and a locked central drawer, buried among furniture, filing cabinets, rolled carpets, boxes of books, shelves of pottery and kitchen implements, paintings with and without frames, easels, ladders - everything laced in spiderwebs and dust, the accumulated bric-a-brac of Pyotr's past lives. Surveying it all one day, Serafina said, "How strange? There is not a single thing of mine in here."

"No," Pyotr said, "but all this and the house are now yours."

He had made the decision on receipt of another letter which he had not yet shown her. From Africa.

Bujumbura, Burundi, December 30, 1975

Bwana Petro Mtakatifu,

May this letter find you in good health. It has been many, many moons since we last saw you. I am grown old now and I have grey hair and I have buried my beloved, Nala, taken from me by the yellow fever. My youngest daughter, Amahoro, looks after me, as the other three are now married, all to good men working on the Estate. And it is Amahoro who has corrected the language in this letter I am proud to say, for she has been a diligent student in school, admired by her teachers and school friends. She blushes to hear this.

I, Nsengiyumva, your Estate Steward, feel I must write to you today to urge you to return as I am deeply afraid of not being able to carry out the duties entrusted to me by you. You may remember what I told you when you came back from the war, that trouble was coming to our country because the Belgians forced us to say we are Hutu or Tutsi or Twa, favouring one group over the other. Like a sickness, this has spread, with more and more violence, each group seeking power, killing one another without mercy, even to women and children, and when the Belgians could no longer control it, they ran away in 1962, leaving the country split in two, Rwanda and Burundi, with our city as the Burundi capital, changing its name from Usumbura to Bujumbura and Kigali the capital of Rwanda. The Hutu now rule in Rwanda with half the Tutsi population fleeing from there to here and to neighbouring countries to escape the massacres. Perhaps this is reported in the papers you read? You can see the unrest and mistrust on the faces of our own people on the plantation, some of whom refuse to work with a neighbour because he is of a different tribe. It is all I can do to prevent them coming to blows.

Now news comes that the army chief of staff, General Juvenal Habyarimana, a Hutu, has taken power and become President of Rwanda, saying he will restore order. His party, the MRND (Mouvement Révolutionnaire National pour le Développement) is formed mainly of Hutus from the president's home area of northern Rwanda who are given overwhelming preference in public service and military jobs. The first thing he's done is limit Tutsis to nine percent of available jobs and then he's purged Tutsis from the universities. He thinks he is the new Mwami but he is in fact a tyrant. For the first time I hear the whisper that I am to be targeted as a Tutsi in charge of a large foreign plantation.

This is the situation. I do not fear for myself, but I fear for the people under my care. I leave it to you, Bwana Petro Mtakatifu, in the hope that you will be able to come back to your African home.

Nsengiyumva.

On the long journey to Africa, via Alitalia from Genoa to Fiumicino, Rome, with a connection onto a DC-9 of Air Zaire for the 14 hour flight to M'Poko in Bangui, Central African Republic, then half-a-day waiting to connect with Transafricair's Twin Otter into Kigali, Rwanda, Pyotr had more than enough time to sleep and dream, to awake to what he had done, and sleep again, to dream.

Dreamland - 17

A panorama of open sea with no discernable horizon against which a tiny dot is slowly moving from left to right. It is a small sailing boat seen through the eyes of a falcon flying far overhead. In the stern a lonely figure steers, Christina, her hair pinned up, her face drawn, her gaze vacant. There is an infinite sadness about her lonely figure bundled up against the cold, her mind cast back to when she sat in the saddle of a black pony, a 6-year old Prince of the House of Vasa...on the battlefield...at Lützen...holding a lighted taper to a huge cannon...where in the roar and smoke of the guns...a line of beautiful painted wooden toy soldiers are blown to pieces –

(the plane drones on; What had Serafina said after reading the letter from Nsengiyumva? You have just married me and become stepfather to my children and now you must leave me to go to Africa, but we can't go with you because it may be too dangerous, and if it is, and something happens to you, I will be a widow again; to which he had said that is why the house is now yours; and she had said, what would a peasant girl from Sicily do in a Palazzo in Genoa? To which he said, it is all I have to give you)

- At dusk the sailing boat is drawn up on a snow-covered beach. Footsteps trace a path across a dune, a small meadow, and into a forest, to a small wooden cottage, smoke from a chimney streaming away in an early winter breeze. Inside, a fire burns in the hearth where Christina is cooking a stew in a large black pot: simmering in chicken stock are onions, carrot slices, diced potatoes, chopped celery, beans, peppers, tomatoes, shallots and mushrooms, with garlic and ginger, herbs and spices, seasoned with salt and pepper. She is waiting for someone to arrive and while she waits she occasionally stirs the stew, sipping the broth, adding a pinch of salt. Finally, footsteps crunch snow, there is a knock on the

cottage door, it is Magnus, followed by Petrus and two small children, strangely dressed. This is Allegra, Petrus says, and this is her brother, Guido. The children have never seen a Queen before. They stare. And the Queen cannot help herself, but stares back at them. Where have they come from, the Queen says. We found them on the way here, Magnus says. It was snowing, they were cold, so we brought them along knowing you wouldn't mind. He sniffs. That smells delicious. And from a sack carried under his arm produces two bottles of wine. Glasses are brought. A toast is drunk. They sit on crude benches around the kitchen table. They eat. Guido falls asleep, his head on the Queen's lap. She strokes his hair as she would pet a cat. So, what did he have to say? She asks Magnus. Oxenstierna? What you expect no doubt, that the kingdom's ruled by a crazy woman; the accounts kept by a dimwit; the Crown mortgaged to foreigners; we are ruined by ballets at thirty thousand a night; the army exists on paper while the navy sits and rots; the estates of Parliament are a parish council; the National Council is stuffed with second-class pantaloons; the Palace chapel is a Jesuit meeting place; the Palace itself is a dance hall; to say nothing of whom she beds. Our people now spy on each other, and if they are not spying they are slandering. And in the middle of all this she calls it quits. Have I left anything out, Petrus? No, my Lord, Petrus says –

(the plane suddenly drops, and with it his stomach, waking him momentarily to what Serafina had said about the time it would take for the children to get used to him as their father and as the turbulence subsides he stretches to ease his back and thought of their last night together with the children in bed in the room they shared waiting for him to continue the story about the one-eyed girl, Wonderful, and her Sun machine, their mother watching him a slight smile on her face, she wonders what I am thinking he thought, and, as if reading his mind, she said, I know)

- He says I robbed the country, Christina said. What he doesn't understand is I wanted the country to be great in areas less perishable than the booty brought home from war. I have tried to educate this crude nation in art and literature, in architecture and music - and he calls me a thief! For the price of a ballet? And a heretic because I am curious about other religions? What does he know of me who pretends to know everything? Do you understand? Magnus says nothing. Do you? The Queen says to Petrus, who is struck dumb. I, me, I could not be. I had to be the Queen! Christina said. As the Queen my life was a lie, marching to his persistent drumbeat: duty, dominion, distinction, devoir, a debt

demanded by this identity of the Monarch, un-sexed, un-loved, raised up to be revered, respected, expecting all to kowtow, cringe and grovel. Isolated from my own people. Magnus raises his eyebrows. You query me? Christina said. Me? She looked at Allegra, 10-years old, listening with wide-eyed attention, Men! The Queen said. Never believe a word they say, or you end up like that - and she points to a glass showcase of exotic butterflies pinned to a black velvet background - admired for the brilliant colour of a dress for every occasion, but only to look at, not to touch! Nor feel, or kiss, or hug! Oh no! God forbid such human failings. No! Nothing human. There is always this clear unbreakable glass through which this creature, with these beautiful wings made to fly, looks out at freedom! A freedom all enjoy but her. Now the Queen stands, holds out her hand to Allegra, and says, Come!

(I know, Serafina said. You haven't really thought this through, have you, adopting two children, never mind a wife? A man of your experience! Quiet witch, he said, I have dreamt of this from the moment I set eyes on you. If I must leave now it is only to hurry back. With an ellipse in his thoughts to the boxes of medicine he had brought on board for the clinic.)

The Queen led the girl down musty corridors to a part of the Palace no longer used. She opened a door into a nursery, its windows shuttered, a bare bed, furniture shrouded in dust sheets, broken toys littering the floor. This used to be my room, she said. I would lie on that couch with my mother next to me...Christina stretches out on the couch using Maria Elenora's lap as a cushion. Maria Eleonora is old, an old, dignified woman, now ignored. Her voice is warm though, tender, as she says, Christina, you are upsetting everyone. Are you really going to do this thing? Why? What have you been up to? Stroking Christina's hair. What's wrong with my little girl? You should know, Mother, Christina said. You were Queen...once. Yes, Maria Eleonora said. And well satisfied to be the great King's wife...and your mother for as long as they would let me. They raised you to be a man. Now look at what they have! There, do that again, Christina said. I like your hand on my forehead. I'll close my eyes for a minute...to be a child again...One candle sheds light on Queen Maria Eleonora resplendent in her youth as she caresses the golden locks of her six-year old daughter. When you go away, Mama, Christina says, will they still let me play with Karl Gustav? Of course they will - you are now the King, her mother says. You are a bright girl, Christina, in many ways too bright for your age. How many languages do you already speak? Five, Christina says with pride, if you include Swedish. Well, you must watch what you say. People don't like clever-cleversticks. Then I'll just say stupid things five different ways, Christina said. I was a horrid little girl, the Queen said to Allegra, and couldn't wait to grow up.

(And then what happened? Allegra said. It's late, Pyotr said. Time for you to sleep. I'll tell you when I get back.)

High above Africa the plane droned on and on and the man slept.

Chapter Forty-three

The pilot woke up the passengers with the laconic announcement they were crossing the Equator, to buckle up as they would be landing in 25 minutes in M'Poko, 135 miles south, the weather chilly, with some mist and rain, normal for the time of year. Disembarking, Pyotr was one of the last people to clear customs with all his boxes and the last to embark for the short hop to Kigali. Nsengiyumva had sent the Head Gardener, Nshuti, to pick him up at the airport for the 9-hour drive home in the gardener's truck.

"He is sorry he could not come himself, Bwana," the gardener said, "but he is too old, and it is too dangerous for him. I am Hutu. They will do nothing to me. But Nsengiyumva says you should wear this." This was his old white doctor's coat from the clinic, two pens still in the breast pocket. Pyotr put it on. Then they waited in a line of traffic at a roadblock leaving the airport with heavily armed militia in a variety of uniforms verifying the identity of drivers and passengers. At an altitude of 1500 metres above sea level, the windscreen soon fogged up. Nshuti's 3-year-old daughter, Uwase, who had come along for the ride to keep her father company, stood on the bench seat between them drawing pictures with her fingertip on the misted glass. A house, a tree, a rabbit with big ears chewing grass. When a guard tapped the driver's window with the butt of his machine pistol it startled all of them. Nshuti lowered the window letting in the rain. The guard looked in, looked at them, saw what the little girl had drawn, laughed, waved them on. They were through. On the highway out of town, the two men exchanged glances. "That was lucky," Nshuti said. "On this highway there are many more roadblocks and checkpoints. It is

291

dangerous to trust in luck. If they saw what you have in your boxes…" He didn't finish the thought but turned off onto a dirt road. Which joined another and then another, snaking across the hills, often no more than a muddy track. They went a hundred miles before they saw the vultures. A distant column, high in the sky, riding a vortex of warm air, circling, their wings almost motionless. "Trouble, Bwana," Nshuti said.

Five miles on, the road empty of all traffic, they saw what the vultures saw. A burnt-out village, the site of a massacre. The strike marks of machetes, vivid testimony to mindless slaughter. In the still-smoking ruins, bodies without heads or limbs. Hacked, butchered. Lying on the road, in the ditches, in the encroaching jungle. Feasted on by hyenas who scarcely looked up at the passing truck. Not a living soul, neither victor nor vanquished. Fortunately, Uwase was asleep and saw nothing. At the next crossroads her father turned off again. "It is longer," Nshuti said, "but hopefully safer."

Safer? They had hardly driven a further ten miles before they heard the unmistakable sound of rifle fire and the staccato of machine guns. With nowhere to turn off and unwilling to turn back, Nshuti slowed the truck to a crawl as they approached a bend. As the firing grew louder, he stopped. "Wait here, Bwana. I will go and see," he said. But Pyotr was already getting out. "You wait, Nshuti. I was a soldier. I'll see," he said, taking off his white coat and disappearing into the surrounding jungle. As naturally as riding a bicycle, all the skills developed as a guerilla fighter brought him undetected to the edge of a firefight between a small detachment of blue-helmeted UN troops defending an outpost of *Médecin sans Frontières* against a ragtag Hutu paramilitary force. What exactly transpired then is undocumented. The UN soldiers were under strict orders to defend. They had modest equipment and no mandate to stop a slaughter. But it is a fact the Hutu were routed when an unseen assailant attacked their flank, killed their commander, and destroyed their ammunition depot. Reappearing out of the jungle, Pyotr put on his white coat again before climbing back into the truck. "The road's clear," he told Nshuti. "Move out." When they finally arrived home, what was meant to have been a 9-hour trip took two days.

Welcome to Africa, Pyotr thought.

Around the native's campfire, over dinner, after work had ceased on the plantation, Nshuti's retelling of those 48 hours became part of the Bwana Doctor's legend. "We hear the shooting. Bwana says stop. I stop. Bwana takes off his doctor's coat. Gets out. With no weapons, he disappears into the jungle like magic. Shooting stops. Bwana comes back, puts on coat, gets in truck. Go now, Nshuti, he says. He smells of gunpowder, blood on his shirt and hands. We arrive at the Lake. Stop here, Nshuti, he says. I stop. He goes swimming. Put on a clean shirt, no smell. No word about how the shooting stopped. He smiles when I ask. A secret, he says. Is it magic? I say. Yes, he says, a magical secret." And his daughter, Uwase, peering around to make sure there were no listeners, wisely says, "Shh!" putting a finger to her lips.

In a similar fashion, the day Nsengiyumva accompanied him to the clinic, insisting he wore his white coat, his appearance with boxes and boxes of medicine was akin to a magician pulling a rabbit out of an empty hat. Both nurses, Kampire and Keza, a Tutsi and a Hutu, now 25 years older, were still on duty. After Essi's death, a letter was found giving her house and clinic to Pyotr for the care of the native population, which, in the case of Usumbura, now Bujumbura, had gone from 22,000 in 1952 to 135,00 in 1976. As he had done for the plantation, Pyotr had left Nsengiyumva in charge and he in turn delegated the two nurses to run the clinic. They in turn turned the Doctor's house into a nursing home, using the ward in the clinic for emergency patients. On Pyotr's arrival, with great fanfare and no small dose of pride, the two women showed Bwana Doctor all they had done to honour the name of Bibi Essi. Nsengiyumva explained he had used any surplus money from the plantation to support the clinic. It was never enough, but they survived, even if the buildings looked rundown and what had been a flourishing garden now a dirt yard. Every spare penny went on medicine, which had become harder and harder to find in direct proportion to the massacres.

"Today most patients are Tutsi," Kampire said. "They are attacked in so-called safe areas and even in refugee camps. Those not slaughtered come to us with limbs hacked off, open wounds festering, gangrene..." she stopped, tears in her eyes.

"We do what we can for them," Keza said, "but we are not equipped to handle major trauma victims. Even when we refer them to the big hospital, the Prince Regent Charles, most are turned away because they cannot afford treatment and it is administered by Hutus, so for Tutsi…"she shrugged. "It is good you have come back, Bwana Doctor. The authorities ignore us. They need to see a man in charge."

Nsengiyumva nodded his support. "Particularly a white man," he said. And it was in this way that the former soldier, student, painter, *plongeur*, jailbird, screenwriter, property developer, plantation owner became a fully-fledged doctor in charge of his own clinic, 7.00am to 7.00pm, inexorably linked to a taxing routine: consult, examine, diagnose, prescribe; consult, examine, diagnose, prescribe; rinse and repeat, the endless quartet of a doctor's duty to a never-ending stream of patients filling each day's Medical Journal as he had been so carefully taught to do by Essi Heikkilä so long ago. Day after day. Days, which became months - months, years.

No matter how tired, every Sunday he wrote to Serafina, an account of each week. It was his gospel. *'Night duty, today,'* he wrote one Sunday. *'The nurses are exhausted and need the time off to see their families. Oddly, I find the night familiar and the quiet in the wards as you make the rounds a little like the quiet in church, where the odd congregant might cough or shift in a pew. All the intimate things you do for the bedridden are akin to the ritual of communion, be it a bedpan in which to urinate or changing fouled bed sheets or resupplying an intravenous IV drip, making the adjustments you need to make in their treatment dependent on their progress. There is a Tutsi here with both feet cut off and tongue cut out. A teenager, he thanks me by blinking his eyes when I turn him over to treat his bedsores. My mind cannot imagine his suffering or his thoughts, or what possible future there is for him. It is the same for so many. The Hutu are even turning on their own tribesmen if they are thought to be sympathetic to the Tutsi.*

I don't write this to frighten you, Serafina. It is a feeble attempt to explain to you why, despite my promises, I have not yet come home. Our beds overflow and we have patients sleeping in the corridors. I have guards protecting all the entrances to our compound for fear of what a mob of renegades might do if they could get in. This Wednesday there was a vote in the Security Council of the United Nations to send more troops with a rider ruling they must ask for, quote,

'Permission to engage,' even as they are attacked. Can you imagine calling from Rwanda to New York, six time zones away, to say we are under fire, have we permission to fire back? How can supposedly intelligent men condone this? I am becoming incoherent with anger and rage and apologise for spewing all this up on paper. You are my rock. The only person to whom I can confess my fear of failing in my mission here. We need more medicine - what am I saying, we need more of everything - above all compassion for our fellows to stop this senseless genocide. I really will come home, I promise you and the children. Your ever loving husband. P.

He always signed with his initial P. Serafina kept the letters bundled up, tied with string, in the attic with all the others.

In the Fall of 1978 Pyotr flew to New York as part of a delegation from Rwanda/Burundi invited to speak at the United Nations. *'The crowds and traffic in the streets make it hard to believe nearly a million people have left the city during the past decade,'* he wrote to Serafina, *'supposedly due to a combination of crime, the financial crisis, and the newspaper strike which just ended after a total of 88 days. You can imagine how this has affected coverage of our mission, which is basically nill. Quite literally, no one is interested in what is happening in a country most people couldn't find on the map. If I mention Rwanda, even to people who are supposedly intelligent, I get a blank look. When you think back to when I was last here 50 years ago - yes, 50! You've married an OLD, OLD codger, mia cara - nothing has really changed even if there are more taller buildings. You know the maxim, money isn't everything, it's the only thing? The entire focus of the population is on self- gratification in every way possible: food, money, sex, money, drugs, money. Drugs, sex and rock 'n roll! Take as much as you can; give as little as possible. More is better; big is better; rich is better still. I saw it full blast this weekend when we were taken to a place called Studio 54, an old theatre turned into a nightclub for every hedonist on earth. The noise! It felt like my blood was being whipped up like egg white, getting thicker and thicker. Exhilarating, yes, but it was a relief to go outside and breathe fresh air. Later, trying to sleep back at the hotel, the music was still thumping in my head.*

Last night we went to a movie called 'Saturday Night Fever'. The lyrics of its theme song perfectly reflect this - 'Listen to the ground, there is movement all around, there is something goin' down, And I can feel it' - and you can, feel 'it'. The impatience of wanting to get 'it' (wherever 'it' is) trampling over anyone who gets in the way. Afterwards we went to see the work of a photographer, Patrick Demarchelier, in his studio near Times Square, where I met a young Brit, William Beale, born in Berlin in 1935 when I was there visiting Markus. He's a property developer and his birthday is tomorrow, November 10, when he'll be 43 and in a few days I'll be 82. We trade war stories. He's in America to buy property. With debt. 'You buy the money, like you buy cement. The cost is in equity and interest. The art of the deal is to have little or no skin in the game. The banker you borrow from is not lending you a penny out of his own pocket. He's making a spread on his cost of funds which is the amount he pays to depositors for banking with him, and it is their money he is lending you. No one will lend you a penny for Africa if you can't show them how they will benefit.' I feel like a Neanderthal listening to him. This whole modern world is unimaginably distant from what I've been living in Africa.'

On the way back from America, Pyotr came home to Serafina after an absence of nearly three years. He stayed for two months. On the eve of returning to Bujumbura, following lunch and a vigorous siesta - *una partita di gambe all'aria* - sipping an aperitif together out on the terrace overlooking Genoa in surprisingly balmy weather for the time of year, Serafina said, "I'm 27 and I'm exhausted. You sit there smiling, ready to go another three rounds. How do you do it?"

"*Jamais deux sans trois,*" Pyotr said, taking his time, studying his wife lying there on her chaise-longue, wearing just a black kaftan, naked underneath. "Something to remember and something to look forward to."

"Me to remember and you to look forward to?"

"Yes. Near enough."

"I never thought it would be like this."

"Neither did I." Pause. "You know you've changed."

"In what way?"

"I used to feel I was in charge. Now I realise it's always been you. From the moment Guido knocked over Allegra's chocolate…"

Serafina nodded, then changed the subject. "It's too bad you have to go. We miss you, you know. Nothing's the same when you're not here."

"What can I do? One day, perhaps…" Pyotr left the thought dangling.

"Haven't you done enough? Must you work so hard?" Serafina said.

The echo of his question to Essi all those years ago. Pyotr smiled again, and he repeated her answer, "What is enough? I doubt there is a doctor in the world who knows that word. Anyway, it's not work, it's love."

"As long as it doesn't take another three years for you to get back," Serafina said. "Promise?"

"I promise," Pyotr said.

"By the way, we have a guest for dinner tonight, your great-nephew, Fortunato."

"Fortunato?"

"Remember the caretakers, the family you kicked out when we got here…"

"Kicked out? Handsomely paid off, you mean, after living rent free for the best part of 25 years!"

"Whatever. Their boy was 7 then and he's now 13, an orphan since his parents died."

"I didn't know that. When did it happen?"

"You'd know if you read the letters I sent you."

"Read them? I read them so often I know most of them by heart."

A blatant lie. Serafina laughed. "You're such a bad liar," she said. Silence. She watched a parade of ants coming and going along a trail they had made through the grass under her chaise. "Anyway, however distant, he's part of your family and the children adore him. He's an older brother to them. I thought you should see him before you go."

"Whatever for?"

"He thinks you don't like him."

"How can I not like him? I don't even know him."

Serafina shrugged. "Try and be nice."

The phrase stayed with him. Back in Bujumbura, in the clinic, doing his rounds in his white coat, stethoscope around his neck, diaphragm on a patient's chest listening for any little abnormality, the slightest murmur in a valve instead of the thud of a healthy heartbeat, it would pop into his head: 'Be nice.' Be nice? Wasn't he always nice? Nice to his staff, nice to the nurses, nice to the patients, nice to the cook and nice to all the servants.

What did she mean? He was always nice. Night after night, under the mosquito net, the thought would carry him off to sleep. And in the morning, he was no wiser.

Time passes. 1979 became 1980, then 1981. A roof tile is blown off. Half a million Rwandans live in exile in Uganda, Burundi, Tanzania. They are marginalised refugees, existing precariously with few rights or guarantees. The rainy seasons come and go. War rages between Uganda and Tanzania. The roof leaks. Roads are washed out, rebuilt. The Shah is driven out of Iran. Nsengiyumva falls sick, prostate cancer, metastasising. Conferences are held in Washington, Brussels, Geneva, affirming the rights of the refugees to return to their homeland. Burundi wants them to go. President Juvenal Habyarimana declares that his country was too overpopulated to permit their return. Bugs and insects bite. The doctor sees 20, 25, 30 patients a day, too tired to dream. Margaret Thatcher is the first woman to be elected Prime Minister of Britain. There is drought. Then famine. Emperor Bokassa is overthrown. Illness, grief, loss. The Soviet Union covertly invades Afghanistan. Mount St. Helens erupts. Iraq invades Iran. A letter from Serafina asks if he has forgotten his promise to come home. An actor, Ronald Regan, is elected President of the United States. A singer, John Lennon, is murdered. Regan is shot. The Pope is shot. Power and wealth accumulate to President Juvenal Habyarimana and his henchmen. Hutus slaughter Tutsis. Weeds block the drains to the septic tank. Everything is imperfect, in flux. Except for the never-ending line of patients always there, rain or shine, uncomplaining, waiting for him.

On impulse one day, Pyotr drove to the plantation to sit at the bedside of Nsengiyumva. The old man was asleep when he arrived. His daughter, Amahoro, rose from where she sat by a window, surprised to see Bwana Doctor arrive unannounced into the servant's quarters. "*Mwaramutse?*" Pyotr said.

"*Murayama?*" Amahoro answered, her voice pitched low so as not to disturb her father. "It is an honour to see you, Bwana Petro Mtakatifu." She dropped her eyes, bowed her head. "If I had been told I would have prepared your room for you."

"That is very kind, but it won't be necessary. I must get back to the clinic as soon as I can," Pyotr said, quietly walking to the head of the bed to look down at the old man who lay there. "How is he?"

"*Ndarwaye buke, Bwana Petro Mtakatifu,*" the old man said without opening his eyes. "I am a bit sick."

"*Yego,*" Pyotr said, "yes, you are."

A small, tired smile illuminated the patient's face and with an effort he slowly opened his eyes to look up at the doctor. "Thank you for coming," he said. "It will not be long now." He struggled to sit up.

"No," Pyotr said, "rest easy. Please." Nsengiyumva sank back into his pillows. "Are you in pain?" Pyotr said.

Nsengiyumva shrugged. "I am a Tutsi lying in his own bed instead of being hunted down. I am attended by my loved ones. The only pain I feel is for them. Where I am going I can no longer protect them." The words came slowly, a long pause between each sentence. He closed his eyes. His brow furrowed. His lips moved as if to say something. His daughter stepped closer to hold her father's hand. Without opening his eyes, he said, "How old are you now, Bwana Doctor?"

"Eighty-five," Pyotr said.

The eyes open, a gleam of amusement, another smile. "You have ten years on me and look ten years younger," Nsengiyumva said, sounding almost normal. "It is well. I fear for my people. Fear for what lies ahead. *Gutsembatsemba,* they say, to exterminate us radically, and *inyenzi,* as if we are cockroaches. Even in your clinic they will come for us. Only the strong will survive..." his voice quavered. He looked from the doctor to his daughter and back again. "Amahoro here has all the plantation accounts. They are prepared for the next steward you appoint. If you would permit a word of advice, you would be wise to choose a Hutu...someone from Nala's tribe...they are powerful..." the voice fades, the eyes close, he drifts away. Like pieces on a chessboard, Amahoro and Pyotr remain silent, immobile, unsure of their next move. What was there to say? Slowly, slowly, Nsengiyumva lets go of his daughter's hand, his mouth falls open, there is a smell of morphine, some birds are chattering in the bushes outside, in the distance a door bangs shut. He dies. All that can be heard is the odd ticking sound the corrugated tin roof makes as the sun beats down.

Pyotr stayed that night. Over breakfast, before leaving for the three-hour drive back to the clinic in Bujumbura, he studied the plantation's accounts. Then he asked for a meeting with Amahoro on the broad shaded verandah surrounding the farmhouse. She came dressed in mourning in a black pagne and black hijab. In her sadness, a madonna. Beautiful.

"*Mwaramutse?*" Pyotr said.

"*Murayama?*" Amahoro answered.

"How old are you?" Pyotr said.

"I am twenty-three," Amahoro answered.

"Hutu or Tutsi?"

"We are descended from our mother. My mother was Hutu. I am Hutu."

"What will you do now?"

"Arrangements have been made to take my father home to our village. My sisters are there with their families. After the funeral I will live with one of them. They will find me a husband."

"And all this -" Pyotr waved his hand in the air to include the account books, the farmhouse and the distant lands belonging to it, "- will be forgotten?"

"Yes."

Pause.

"Will you not regret all your father taught you in running this place?"

"Yes."

"Do you know why your father devoted all his life to this?"

"Yes. For you."

"I think for all of us, white, black, Hutu, Tutsi. He set the example of how we can live together."

"He did it for you, Bwana."

"Would you do the same? For me?"

The question was so astonishing that Amahoro could only stare. Pyotr smiled. "Your wise father said to choose a Hutu. I choose you."

Silence. Finally, blushing, Amahoro said, "I am a single woman, Bwana. It would not be proper."

"Well, that's easily solved," Pyotr said. "Let's get married. And stop calling me bwana. My name is Pyotr."

Predictably the expat community were horrified, even more so when it was learned Pyotr had given title to all his vast possessions in Rwanda-Burundi to Amahoro, making her one of the richest women in Africa. Shortly afterwards he returned alone to Europe and then to America, no one the wiser he was a bigamist.

Paris Now.

"That woman asking questions about Belanopek came in again; claims to be a journalist -"

"Journalist, my arse," George muttered, nose down at his desk trying to reconcile our accounts with our tax declaration. "Bloody nosey parker."

"What was that, George?"

"Woman writes a gossip column. She doesn't give a shit about him. Just looking for dirt to juice up her blog on social media...she fancies herself as one of these influencer gurus - fucking internet."

"I see."

Chapter Forty-four

'God knows why I've come back.' It is the first line in a letter to his wife, Serafina, dated 24/12/1982 (but unsent) found in the back of the journal for 1983. 'Between 20 and 30 everything is an adventure, good or bad. I honestly cannot remember ever being afraid of taking on whatever life offered by way of work or personal relationships. Time was on my side. Whatever happened, happened. There was no soul-searching introspection back then - well, none on my part, I can tell you. (Not sure what my many partners would say today if you asked them.) You didn't have a dime but felt rich just the same. Every blank canvas was an opportunity. Today I hesitate to make the first mark, just as I am reluctant to go out without a wallet full of dollars. Time is rationed; it's the only thing you have that you don't own. All you can do is spend it and there's no bank manager to tell you when your purse is empty, or your account overdrawn. The conservatism of old age with the walls closing in, I guess. What an appalling thought.

I found another flat on Beekman overlooking the East River, two doors down from the Rudolf Building where I stayed with Sofia. Well, more loft than flat, great light for painting, with two bedrooms so you and the kids can visit me here. Never mind about their school. They'll learn more by travelling than in any scuola secondaria whatever indirizzo they pursue - or you push them into. Allegra's what, 14 now? Guido, 13? They need to get out of the family nest, sniff about, flap their wings. Your thoughts?

That English fellow I met, the property developer, has bought a couple of brownstones in Boston and commissioned me to paint a few of what he calls 'heirloom' pictures to go over the fireplaces. Asked me if I'd heard of Tom Keating. I told him I don't do fakes. Fakes? he said. Who's talking about fakes?

302

In the manner of...Stubbs, Turner, Reynolds. Ye Olde Masters. (I think he's reacting to Sotheby's selling a Turner for $10 million.) All a bit boring, but the money's good.

I had to get away, you know that, right? There's a limit to the number of awful things you see about which you can do nothing. I am haunted by the unrelenting line of patients waiting in the dust, the rain, the heat, always, always there no matter how hard we worked. I was exhausted - no, I am exhausted. Just writing these few words and I hear the mosquitoes and feel feverish. What do they say, the only constant is change? I must - or go crazy. And then I think of Essi and feel guilty. Of course, I know I'll go back. It's inevitable. Africa is not a place; it is a state of mind.

Unless you've been there you cannot remotely comprehend the sheer scale of the continent. All those Eurocentric maps we were brought up with make you think it's this pear shape on the other side of the Med just below Algeria and Morocco and the Sahara, about the size of Greenland, whereas it is actually 14 times larger. You could fit China, India, the USA, Japan and most of Europe into it. Rwanda is right in the middle, so poor there are individuals here in America richer than the entire country. The very idea I could make a difference is a joke. Sometimes when I walk to the deli on the corner of 51st Street I do not recognise the Bwana Doctor that I used to be, and I cannot connect my life here with my life there.'

Letter ends. It is not known why it was not sent. As requested, here are further excerpts from the extant journals:

February 11, 1983 - *Mother & father of all snow storms has buried the city. People on skis going down 5th Avenue. The blizzard has winds so powerful that entire skyscrapers are coated in ice top to bottom, with ropes cordoning off danger zones. What will happen when this lot melts?*

April 16, 1983 - *Lunch at Barbetta's W. 46th - Lasagna + v.good Montepulciano. Pissing down outside, so took my time reading Variety on the Oscars. Ben Kingsley wins best actor for 'Gandhi', which also wins best picture and best director (despite 'E.T.' - my bet). Couldn't help thinking I had met the Mahatma when I was a child, certainly the only person in the restaurant, maybe even in the city, to have done so.*

July 4, 1983 - *Yellow cab to meet Ivan Karp at his gallery in Soho on W.Broadway: the OK Harris Gallery, which includes a cigar store! Think he* *was surprised to see how old I was. My stuff is not at all like the photorealism he has on his walls. But we hit it off and repaired to the Cafe des Artistes on West 67th for an early dinner.*

September 12, 1983 *- Fly to Boston to meet Beale and his American partner. Drive to Newport, Rhode Island where they are redeveloping one of the mansions on Bellevue Ave. Asked to quote for a variety of pictures to 'decorate' the various condominiums. Told them I don't do decorations. Town effervescent with upcoming America's Cup, US v. Australia. Found time to sneak off in search of Planetree House where Markus's girlfriend, Karla, was murdered 54 years ago and my portrait of her slashed to pieces. House demolished; replaced by retirement home.*

September 26, 1983 *- In Dave's Deli where news of the US losing the Cup 4-3 to Australia after leading 3-1 is considered a disaster having won the thing for the previous 132 years! Since no Aussies were having breakfast, I was scowled at for cheering.*

December 27, 1983 *- Letter from Kampire bringing news of the Clinic and the recent elections. Habyarimana has been re-elected President of Rwanda with 99.97% of the votes - not surprising since he was the only candidate. The vote consolidates his position as dictator and the Hutus as absolute rulers. Being a Tutsi, her position is precarious and Amahoro advises closing the clinic in town temporarily and moving it to the plantation even if this means a longer journey for patients. They want my blessing to move. Done.*

January 22, 1984 *- In PJ Clark's for a drink. Super Bowl on TV. Extraordinary ad for a computer called Mackintosh by Apple based on Orwel's '1984'. The thing is you never see a computer! Like the man said, 'Sell the sizzle, not the steak.' Extraordinary!*

March 12, 1984 *- New York is one of the best 'walking' towns. It just seems natural to walk a few blocks here and there and by the evening you've done 10/12 miles. Spent the afternoon at the Mary Boone Gallery, 420 West Broadway—right below Leo Castelli's, where a painter called Jean-Michel Basquiat was showing his graffiti-inspired stuff. Certainly challenges convention, but it's a bit pompous to invite viewers to 'confront the complexities of race, identity, and society' as suggested by the gallery notes, as if that's how artists think in front of a canvas. Everything is a hype by the galleristas intent on only one thing: moolah!*

In the evening, strolled over to Broadway to catch a performance of 'Cats', Andrew Lloyd Webber's musical adaptation of T.S. Eliot's whimsical poems. The choreography and melodies brought the jolly jingling Jellicle cats to life in a splendid spectacle. V. clever.

May 8, 1984 *- Since I was in midtown planning to lunch at Delmonico's, popped into the Argosy on E. 59th Street to browse the books. One of the girls there (Marjorie Maxwellington according to her name tag) suggested I might like Salman Rushdie's "Midnight's Children," According to her "the magical realism of India's tumultuous history unfolds in a mesmerising narrative. Rushdie's prose and intricate storytelling opens a window into the soul of a nation in flux." Try saying that. Instead, I asked her if she'd had lunch. She blushed and dashed off. Picked up Milan Kundera's "The Unbearable Lightness of Being,". Looks like my kind of thing: existential philosophy and political turmoil colliding in a tale of love and longing. We'll see. Back home, letter from Serafina confirming her arrival with the kids in time for the Los Angeles Games.*

July 24, 1984 *- Out to Kennedy to meet the gang. Allegra has metamorphosed into a dazzling young creature, nearly as tall as me, leaving her brother in the shade. She wants to be a nun!!!! Quite extraordinary. I explained I'd been invited to take part in the Olympic Arts Festival, scheduled to open on August 4 in a rehabilitated ArtDeco building downtown. We fly out on the 30th, but first a week in the Big Apple. Serafina holds hands in the cab into town.*

July 30, 1984 *- LA. Slept, exhausted, on the plane getting here. All this touristy running around showing the sights of NYC, c'est pas moi, mais noblesse oblige. What's interesting is Serafina. At 35, una bella donna, whom you would never imagine was once a 17-year-old Sicilian peasant girl. She takes everything in stride. She has our rooms changed at the Chateau because she doesn't like the noise on Sunset. This, after the man on Reception said there were no rooms available because of the Olympics, etc! Chats up the Manager, bingo! Got tickets for Athletics, Gymnastics and Rowing out on Lake Casitas near Ojai.*

August 2, 1984 *- Allegra AWOL after Men's coxed four repechage. I panicked. Serafina v. cool. "Correre la cavallina, we say. She's just sowing her wild oats." Me: "She's only sixteen!" Serafina: "Look on the bright side. Maybe it will change her mind about becoming a nun?"*

August 5, 1984 - *A. turns up. Confers with her mother. Both give me that mind-your-own-business look! Serafina winks.*

August 8, 1984 - *Le Dôme for dinner on Sunset. As luck would have it, our table was next to a very large rowdy crowd at a table reserved to celebrate the French pole vault team. According to Eddy, (owner of the restaurant), the pole vaulters had been heavily criticised because they refused to live in the Olympic Village, preferring to be housed by the Marquess of Montaigu in his villa above the Strip where they had been photographed - supposedly training - in his jacuzzi carousing with some very pretty girls. The Gods of Sport must have a fine sense of humour with Pierre Quinon winning the gold medal and Thierry Vigneron, the bronze. The dinner concluded with a rousing version of La Marseillaise, the two athletes standing on the table wearing nothing but their medals solemnly belting out the song.*

September 1, 1984 - *S & Co off back to Italy. Nice to be on my own again. Like the pressure to keep up is off, and I can dawdle around being my selfish self. Être mariée, ce n'est pas vraiment moi. Which is why I legged it round to the Argosy to chat up Mlle. Marjorie Maxwellington. At lunch all she could talk about was her boyfriend!*

September 20, 1984 - *Delivered a couple of pictures for a bank downtown. Walking back through Times Square saw on TV what remained of the US Embassy in Beirut bombed by a group called Hezbollah using a van. 23 dead! With a banner reading "Shockwaves through Wall Street." Typical of the news here that a tragedy is transmuted financially, as if the only way to understand a calamity is to count its $ cost. Walked off when two talking heads started debating the knock-on effects this would have on leveraged buyouts and hostile takeovers 'reshaping the landscape of American capitalism.' Talk about 'unfettered corporate greed.'*

November 6, 1984 - *Reagan wins reelection by a landslide. Public bought into his vision of American exceptionalism and his confrontational stance towards the Soviet Union. Cranks up the budget on military spending. How this reshapes the geopolitical landscape of the current Cold War, makes me wonder what he thinks when he looks at himself in the mirror. What's it to me, really? Do I care? Should I?*

February 10, 1985 - *Picture of Basquiat on the front cover of the New York Times Magazine, with a long 11-page story inside basically valuing art purely in terms of money (like everything else in this country.) Quite a contrast with the Met's show of Caravaggio's chiaroscuro masterpieces. Impossible to imagine a Basquiat capable of the drama and emotion of Baroque painting. C's revolutionary use of light and shadow are an inspiration. Most of this modern stuff will not last the test of time.*

April 9, 1985 *- Mlle. M brought over a copy of Gabriel García Márquez's "Love in the Time of Cholera," All about lust and longing unfolding against a backdrop of tropical paradise. I think she came because she was curious and wanted to see what living on Beekman was like. Cooked us a stew while she rabbited on about magical realism and passion and desire knowing no bounds. At breakfast this morning she was still banging away on the nature of love and commitment, the boyfriend forgotten, wearing nothing but one of my T-shirts.*

June 13, 1985 *- Marj insists we listen to a broadcast: Live Aid concert from London and Philadelphia tonight, with Queen, U2, the Beach Boys and David Bowie, to raise funds for famine relief in Ethiopia. Can't help wondering how much they will raise. Marj in tears, says it shows the power of music to unite people across the globe. Afterwards, in the shower (she's always in the shower with me) she said 'Of course you don't understand. How can you? You're older than my grandfather!!!!!!' God knows what Marj thinks she's doing here. I certainly don't. Even when you think you know someone, you know sweet fuck all. Now and then, everybody wants to be someone else, so who knows with her?*

June 17, 1985 *- Incredible. They raised over £70 million!!!!*

September 1, 1985 *- Not sure how these two are related: Margaret Thatcher acclaims the reelection of Reagan and they've found the wreck of the 'Titanic' on the floor of the ocean. She's so closely aligned with Reagan that it's sink or swim for her if his Cold War stance gets challenged. The belligerence of the US and the UK is difficult to explain and always finessed by the politicos with the old bromide about being the gendarme for the free world. What is it about power that politicians find so attractive? The hubris involved in their self-importance is mind boggling. Don't they know they will be forgotten as soon as they leave the stage?*

January 14, 1986 *- Walked over to 945 Madison to revisit the Whitney, Marcel Breuer's fantastic, stepped box of a building now 20 years old but as jarring to view as anything in NY. Georgia O'Keeffe expo inside is almost classical in comparison. Rumour has it that they're going to remodel the building* *because they need more space. A bit like saying you're going to remodel the Taj Mahal because there's a housing shortage.*

January 28, 1986: Extraordinary how everything is different but the same. They knock a building down because it's forty years old and build a new one slightly taller, yet the street stays the same, familiar. The real difference, compared to when I was a working stiff in Hollywood fifty years ago, is that then I was part of something, part of the 'bizness', the movie bizness. I belonged. Now, as a painter, on me jack-jones, I don't. If I dropped down dead right now, I doubt there's a person in the city who would blink. This morning the Challenger rocket blew up and they're already telling jokes on the radio: 'Where's the Challenger crew? All over Florida! You know what NASA stands for? Not A Soul Alive!' Sick. This country's sick.

February 2, 1986 - Dep. Pan Am Fl. 188 747 JFK 3 PM - Dakar - Monrovia - Lagos - Nairobi - Kigali. Dead beat. So many delays. Fucking sandstorm! And then drive in an armed convoy to Bujumbura. 3 days travelling! Surprised Amahoro - more beautiful than ever.

March 29, 1986 - Return: Pan Am 189. Enormous Nigerian ladies travelling with 8 to 10 trunks and me with a shoulder bag and one suitcase. There's a symbol - of what I'm not sure.

April 23, 1986 - Minor earthquake 20 miles north of here, in Westchester County. Felt it in my feet walking home from PJ's. Marj shrugged. Still pissed at me going off to Africa without telling her.

April 27, 1986 - Nuclear reactor blew up in Chernobyl, USSR yesterday, with fallout going all over Europe!!!!

June 16, 1986 - Times picks up news thread: 'Pravda announces that high-level Chernobyl staff have been fired for stupidity.' No shit. Soviet scientists estimate the land around Chernobyl's 'exclusion zone' will not be habitable for 20,000 years! Say again? TWENTY THOUSAND YEARS!!!!

October 11, 1986 - Tripped on a paving stone outside Bloomingdale's. Bashed in front teeth. Carted off to the French Hospital down in Chelsea. Probably have to extract five. Bloody difficult speaking properly. No insurance of course, God knows what this will end up costing but at least they patched me up. In the emergency waiting room on TV they had the high-stakes drama of the Reykjavik Summit, Reagan and Gorbachev going to the mat over nuclear disarmament and the terms for 'peace and security in a rapidly changing world.'

Why on earth chose Iceland for a meeting? I mean why not the Cap d'Antibes? Wonder who negotiates this sort of thing - I can already see a hilarious sketch of two undersecretaries ordered to make the necessary arrangements.

October 13, 1986 *- I look like a gargoyle. Invited to tea in Murray Hill by Marj's Mum, v. eccentric lady who used to make ballet costumes. Straight off she said, 'If you're sleeping with my daughter I hope you're being careful - we can't afford another pregnancy!' And when I took my leave she said, 'I am reminded of something I read about Byron: 'I shall always remember the wild originality of your countenance.' (Not sure why I keep these notes. Maybe to make sure I'm still alive? Does it matter? No, of course not if nobody reads them. The future will decide. I'll be in a hole, and it won't matter to me and probably not to the future either.)*

January 13, 1987 *- In Pete's having b'fast, overhear three men discussing seven of the top New York City Mafia bosses sentenced to 100 years each in prison! The indictments and arrests date from February 1985, including narcotics trafficking, prostitution, loansharking, gambling, labour racketeering and extortion against construction companies. The Post had a laundry list of names:*

Paul "Big Paul" Castellano, boss of the Gambino crime family Anthony "Fat Tony" Salerno, boss of the Genovese crime family
Anthony "Tony Ducks" Corallo, boss of the Lucchese crime family
Philip "Rusty" Rastelli, boss of the Bonanno crime family
Carmine "Junior" Persico, boss of the Colombo crime family
Aniello Dellacroce, Gambino family underboss
Gennaro "Jerry Lang" Langella, Colombo family acting boss/underboss
Salvatore "Tom Mix" Santoro, Lucchese family underboss
Christopher "Christy Tick" Furnari, Lucchese family consigliere
Ralph "Little Ralphie" Scopo, Colombo family soldier
Stefano Canone, Bonanno family consigliere Anthony "Bruno" Indelicato, Bonanno family capo

Fancy being called Indelicato in that lineup. Shades of Lividiani and his 'suggerimento dolce'!!!!!!!! Too bad Verdi's not alive with that cast.

March 15 , 1987 - *Marj to Broadway for a performance of "Les Misérables" - Knockout tale of love, redemption, and revolution. Schönberg's score and Alain Boublil's lyrics actually bring Hugo's novel to life, and you forget you're in NY in the 20th century. M. ecstatic.*

April 21, 1987 - *Marj lugs over Umberto Eco's "Foucault's Pendulum," where conspiracy theories and historical intrigue collide in a dizzying whirlwind of ideas. She reads to me in bed. Eco's erudite prose and intricate narrative get tangled up with our naked legs but I'm captivated from beginning to end, her's and the book's.*

September 3, 1987 - *In Pete's they're talking about the tangled web of the Iran-Contra scandal, covert arms deals, clandestine operations, government corruption and illegal activity - as if any of this has anything to do with any of them. Why? What gets under their skin while having breakfast? Troubling questions about the rule of law and accountability and the leaders they've elected? Or is it regret that they live such boring mundane lives?*

October 19, 1987 - *Shades of '29. Absolute chaos on Wall Street this morning. Predictably labelled 'Black Monday', the DOW plummets down 23% in a day. A frenzy of panic selling and investor fear, shaking the 'foundations of the global economy' according to the press. I don't own a single share so why am I concerned? On the back of this, I bought Tom Wolfe's "Bonfire of the Vanities." Spot on depiction of greed, ambition, and race in today's Manhattan, skewering the excesses of Wall Street and our so-called social elite.*

October 27, 1987 - *At Karp's invitation, walked 44 blocks over to the Guggenheim on 5th (Gotta love FLW's meisterwerk) to attend a symposium of art collectors and dealers to discuss the risks and benefits of buying and promoting 'New Art'. Make notes, Karp said. GILBERT E: The topic for our panel tonight is, "Embracing New Art, Pleasures, Perils and Profits." "Embracing" is an interesting word, full of connotation, and all sorts of thoughts, some Freudian come to mind; when one thinks of a pleasurable embrace, a perilous embrace, and a profitable embrace. We have five embracers here tonight to talk about their love affair with new art, and how true love never runs smooth. HOLLY S : Sure, I don't think any dealer - I guess I can say this - I don't think a dealer who doesn't buy what he sells is a real dealer. GENE S: The Hofmann, the Avery and the Noland were all wet when we bought them; we could smell them. They were new...It became clear to us as the years went*

310

along that the thing that attracted us most was the wet art, the art that you could smell as you brought it into the house, RONALD F: I made the discovery that art was about ideas, like good literature, I was hooked. DOUGLAS C: I was born acquisitive. By the time I was a year old, I had the largest collection of teddy bears in town. GILBERT E Are you buying wet, as Gene is? DOUGLAS C Yes, I buy wet often. As some people today are doing, I don't buy from the bill of sale or an invoice. But when the painting is finished, I'll buy. GILBERT E You see it first. DOUGLAS C I see it first. RONALD F: One of the perils involved in this is that somewhere along the way, in many cases, when you see a new work with something that's touted as new, you have to erase from your memory anything you knew about art history. HOLLY S I mean, you know, our big expression is, 'Wow!' RONALD F: Ivan Karp sent out this wonderful letter one day, absolutely classic: "I am looking at X-thousands of artists a week," it said. And then it said, "Please don't recommend me. Enough people find me on their own."

Walk 44 blocks back, feet burning. Neuropathy? Re-reading my notes I'm not sure it was such a good idea to only have famously successful dealers and collectors airing their opinions. The questions from the audience were juvenile. As was the topic. Pleasures, Perils and Profits, my arse. Making marks on paper or canvas is work. Bloody hard work. Broch spells it out: 'He knew of the innermost danger of all artists, he knew the utter loneliness of the man destined to be an artist, he knew the inherent loneliness which drove such a one into the still deeper loneliness of art and into the beauty that cannot be articulated, and he knew that for the most part such men were shattered by this immolation, that it made them blind'); Too chicken to yell it out.

__November 22, 1987__ - Pan Am 188 6PM Dep. JFK - Frankfurt - Lagos - Nairobi - Kigali. Lorry to Bujumbura.

__November 30, 1987__ - Amahoro gives birth to twin girls - astonishingly one is black, and one is white. According to Kampire this is less rare than one imagines in a mixed marriage. Anyway, and most importantly, both are healthy and so is the mother. I get to name the white one and call her Sydney, and Amahoro names the black one, Habimana. Of all the strange things to happen to me this takes the cake. Twins. Imagine - at my age!!!!!!!!

__December 30, 1987__ - Kigali - Frankfurt - Milan. Quickie to Genoa for New Year to see Serafina and the kids. All good. S has got the Palazzo in *immaculate shape, remarkable on the little money I can afford to send her. She wants to know if I approve of Allegra using the watchtower in Sicily as a hermitage!!!! Keeping all these balls in the air sometimes makes me wonder.*

January 29, 1988 *- Genoa's not exactly clean but NY's a shitheap: graffiti, dog turds, crack available everywhere. Saw a stoned couple in the Park, needle still in the arm of one. Not sure how long I can bear this even if this is where my pictures have a market.*

June 22, 1988 *- M up in arms. She's been reading "The Satanic Verses" by Salman Rushdie, and those idiot ayatollahs in Iran who have now put out a 'fatwa' against him for blasphemy. M: "What is it about men - and it's always men - using the cloak of religion to warp reality since all religion is fiction? And they call it blasphemous! They couldn't tell a metaphor from a traffic light (great image!). Hard to imagine Reagan issuing a fatwa against Isaac Singer or any other writer.*

October 18, 1988 *- Paid 8 bucks for lecture at MOMA on Anselm Kiefer's show that just opened. Looked really, really, closely at the small photographs. Think I understand where his enormous paintings come from. No, not understand, intuit. Because I share the same scars of war and what's epic about his work: its complexity - he doesn't make it simple or dumb it down because it isn't. But would I want to live with one of those huge things hanging on the wall? No, I think not. This is stuff made for public display. Otherwise, it would haunt my dreams and I already sleep badly enough without help.*

October 30, 1988 *- Piece in the Post about 414 homicides in the City since March, mainly due to the explosion of crack, with the dealers and users knocking each other off in disputes over territory and/or money. This, in one city in the USA, is more than all of England or France in a year. Plus the filth, the homeless, graffiti everywhere - everyone bitches, nobody does anything from the Mayor on down.*

November 10, 1988 *- Union Square Cafe on East 16th for my 92nd b'day. M loves the place and took charge of ordering for her 'Grandfather' (this to Danny Meyer, the owner, who gave me a knowing look) Duck liver mousse to kickoff, then rigatoni alla cacciatore, and a main course of trout with apples sprinkled with caviar. As good as it gets, helped down with a favourite Bordeaux, Château Beychevelle 1970. What a life, eh? Sometimes I have to*

312

pinch myself. Afterwards headed over to Harlem for some jazz at the Lenox Lounge.

December 22, 1988 - *How to equate George H.W. Bush becoming President a month ago on the promise of a 'kinder, gentler America' with the bombing of Pan Am's flight over Scotland, killing everyone, including 190 Americans? Somebody somewhere deliberately sits down and plans to put a bomb on a civilian aeroplane. Just writing that down shows how mad it is. What possible justification can there be to do such a thing? As if on cue a letter from Africa confirms the fear that Rwandan Tutsis in exile are determined to return, by force if necessary, just as a flood of 50,000 Hutus are expelled from Burundi. "I know you are far away, and I trouble you with this news. I am doing my best, but I am fearful it may not be enough. There is a simmering hatred, growing daily, in a population that is so polarised that even here on the plantation you feel the tension in the way people speak and the way they look at each other. If it is possible, please come home. Your daughters need you, as does your wife, Amahoro." Makes me feel guilty. Talk about a fucked-up world!*

February 15, 1989 - *My bread is buttered here. God knows why people buy my stuff, but they do and for that I am grateful and it keeps the good ship Lollipop afloat. Over to the New Museum on the Bowery for the installations of Barbara Kruger. Not really my thing, all this comment on consumerism and gender. There's something facile and 'so what?' about it all. From there to Louise Bourgeois's sculptures at MOMA where I feel at home with her monsters and spiders which I like. The bigger the better, although - as – usual - the curator's notes about the 'visceral exploration of the human experience' etc is enough to throw up on. Met the artist; traded stories of when we were both young and broke in Paris. She remembers meeting ee cummings in my building. Our paths must have crossed so many times... What makes her tick? "I transfer hate into love." Small world. Soaked getting home in freak rain shower. Couldn't stop grinning.*

April 19,1989 - *Woke up feeling I had missed something momentous. Most peculiar. Obviously, part of a dream or my recollection of it. Funny how they used to be so vivid that they seemed more real than life itself. Don't have those anymore, worse luck. Important not to be a victim of the past. What's her name...Paulin...my God, I can still remember her after 50 years, more, Pauline, that's it. What had she said? 'It's not given to everyone to live two lives.'*

One floor down from my room with one of my paintings over her bed, instructing me on the meaning of astrology. Pauline Paulin.

Librarian's note: Queen Christina died in Rome on April 19, 1689, 300 years ago to the day.

April 22, 1989 *- "You've gotta read this!" M busting in with Amy Tan's "The Joy Luck Club," about Chinese immigrant women and their American-born daughters. Talk about other people's lives! For some reason made me think of the Tsar and his daughters whom we met when I was a child in Sylt on one of my mother's forays back to Europe. They were on their yacht and for a moment I see the face of Tatiana, vivid in my mind's eye, an image from 90 years ago. And to think they were shot and bayoneted to death by the Bolsheviks in Yekaterinburg where Great Aunt Tilly had a house. How do you bayonet women, girls?*

April 27, 1989 *- Woke up drenched in sweat. Recurrent malaria back, temperature 103+F. Send M out to pick up some quinine. Comes back with another book by Eco, with a labyrinthine plot: "The Name of the Rose."*

Murder and mystery against the backdrop of a mediaeval monastery, a world of secret codes, hidden truths, where the pursuit of knowledge is deadly. Right up my street. What is it about books that makes you forget you're sick?

May 18, 1989 *- To Africa tomorrow.*

May 26, 1989 *- Back in hospital scrubs, like putting on old gloves. The clinic, set up in an annex of the farm, is an integral part of the plantation now and the way it is swarmed by patients you'd think it had always been there. Greatest benefit for me is not having to yo-yo between here and town.*

June 6, 1989 *- Staff conference to review our position viz insurrection. Apart from the political angle our terrain is hopeless being mostly flat agricultural land down by the lake with the only feasible defensive position the hills to the east (maybe withdraw there if we're attacked?) We number 31 adults (24 male, 7 female). 26 are married with children. 70% are Hutu. The gamekeepers agree with me it is impossible to physically defend the plantation. "The RPF are coming, Bwana," Mugabo, our headman said. "They are burning and killing everyone, even each other," Nshuti said.*

July 4, 1989 *- So far so good. Things have quieted down with Habyarimana's offer to share power with the Tutsi. Need to get back to NY to*

314

fill up the coffers - no patrons for art here. Amahoro understands (or says she does) and the girls are too little to care - not even sure they know who I am?

September 22, 1989 - *Seen from NY it is like a dystopian nightmare: Tanks flattening kids holding flowers on TV! Chinese government's brutal crackdown on pro-democracy demonstrators in Tiananmen Square! Rolling through the streets against unarmed students made me throw up, quite literally. In the face of opposition, the knee jerk reaction of these bastards is to kill. Talk about leaving 'an indelible mark on the collective consciousness'. Of course, they don't give a shit, while our government feebly calls for 'justice and freedom around the globe.' I should just turn it all off, no TV, no newspapers. If you don't know, did it happen?*

October 4, 1989 - *M's treat along with her mother = surprise visit to Carnegie Hall for Stéphane Grapelli Trio concert + Yo-Yo Ma + Dave Grisman's Jazz Quartet! Auditory overload in spades, finished up in the Russian Tea Room next door stuffing ourselves on borscht, caviar and vodka.*

Mother talked to me as if I was already a son-in-law, while M knows me for the old fart I am. WTF - what the fuck, as they say here.

November 11, 1989 - *Unreal! The Wall comes down. Crowds on either side tear it apart. Berlin is once again whole. East and West Germans going nuts celebrating the end of decades of division and separation. Rushed over to Lüchows to commemorate with schnitzel, sauerbraten and German beer!!!*

December 15, 1989 - Letter from Nathalie! Bounced from Italy to Africa to Italy to here. Dated Nov. 13 - 'You'll have heard the news. Thank the gods I'm still alive to enjoy this. It is so sad Markus missed the fun. Claudia and I got drunk celebrating tearing the fucking thing down with pickaxes, can you imagine? Two old birds, with hundreds like us on either side, lobbing chunks of concrete in the air while the stupid Stasi look on, their bloody machine-guns limp impotent dicks in their hands. Reunification is next and then this lot will be out of a job and on the breadline.' Extraordinary! 85 and still alive despite cancer. And Markus? Obviously gone, but why wasn't I told?

December 25, 1989 - On TV Bernstein's performance of Beethoven's 9th from the Schauspielhaus in East Berlin with a joint orchestra from East and West and substituting 'freiheit' for 'freude' in the chorus to celebrate the fall of the Wall. Exhilarating goosebump time! Tears streamed down my face as they sang.

February 11, 1990 - *After spending 27 years in prison, Nelson Mandela is released. 27 YEARS!!!!! And he thanks his guards!*

March 8, 1990 - *Imagine adapting 'Madame Butterfly' against the backdrop of the Vietnam War? Puccini would turn somersaults. M got tickets for us to a performance of "Miss Saigon" on Broadway. Knockout score by Claude-Michel Schönberg and Alain Boublil. Supercharges M's erotic inventiveness. No sleep for the wicked.*

April 28, 1990 - *Letter from Amahoro, sounding so adult: 'Coffee prices have collapsed! Severe economic hardship in Rwanda and Burundi, with our crop unsold!!! Under pressure from Western aid donors, Habyarimana has conceded the principle of multi-party democracy. The man's such a liar it's too soon to tell if he will keep his promises.' Not a word about herself or the children???.*

May 19, 1990 - *Philip Glass's opera "Satyagraha," at the Met. Deep bow to Gandhi and India's struggle for independence. Music both mesmerising and hypnotic. Over drinks in the bar hear a man say 'music is the only language that needs no translation.' Why do I note this stuff? Who's going to read it and in what context? Just habit? Or superstition? (Like saying prayers at night even if you don't believe.) If I'm honest - and even if I'm not - it makes me wonder what's the connection?*

August 14, 1990 - *They're going to start another war in the Persian Gulf! Iraq and Iran have just finished slaughtering each other and now this mad bastard Hussein has gone for Kuwait! Everyone in Pete's has an opinion. 'America's most profitable export: 'War!' 'The more tensions escalate in the Middle East, the more the global oil markets wobble, the greater the spectre of conflict, the better for the military-industrial complex!' They've obviously forgotten Eisenhower's warning: 'We must guard against the acquisition of unwarranted influence, whether sought or unsought' by the military-industrial complex.' What's it to me? Really? Fuck all if I'm truthful. They game the system. Cousin's has it right when he says 'Were the Soviet Union to sink tomorrow, the American military-industrial complex would have to remain, substantially unchanged, until some other adversary could be invented. Anything else would be an unacceptable shock to the American economy.' Of course, the same fuckers are monitoring the diplomatic efforts to end apartheid in South Africa after Mandela's release! Cheney simply can't keep his nose out of anything.*

October 3, 1990 - At long last Germany is reunified! Following decades of division, Berlin is the capital again - hard to believe, but about bloody time. Remember what Abou said about invisible lines drawn by blind politicians. Must try to get over there while Nat is still alive. Walk 30 blocks over to Broadway to celebrate at Zabar's with a wine tasting tour of the Rhine/Rhone region, introducing M into the mysteries of terroir and tradition that defines these wines - at a price! When we got home, good news: lawyer in LA wants to buy my triptych - $70 grand! Real money! Have to pinch myself.

January 17, 1991 - Nearly a million troops, led by the US, flatten Saddam's army in Kuwait. The barbarity of it all ends up in the retreating Iraquis firing 600 oil wells and a highway of death killing thousands. And here in NY it's freezing, I have the flu and trying to grope my way to the pharmacy on 2nd, I was rescued by a kind passerby, taken into the nearest pub and given a live-saving shot of Fernet Branca and rum to kill the bugs!!

February 10, 1991 - Brâncuși at the Guggenheim - it all seems effortless, form, movement, the sheer elegance of the stone. For once the curatorial notes have it right, it is transformational. A minimalist stiptease, baring rock, mineral rock, transmogrified into sculpture (just saw the pun). Don't know how the guy does it. There's wizardry afoot. Makes me feel small.

April 22, 1991 - M buried in the pages of Arundhati Roy's "The God of Small Things," tells me to shush when I query dinner. Family secrets and social hierarchies in the lush landscape of Kerala trump eating. (I think she nicks all these books from the shop, but she says they are just borrowed.) Leave her with Roy and leg it round to PJ's. M's presence makes me feel secure, so why do I feel guilty when I skip off on my own? He asks himself, age 94. Schmuck.

July 8, 1991 - The Soviet Union on the skids, going bust! Independence for the 15 constituent republics. The direct cause being Gorbachev's introduction of perestroika and glasnost and Reagan outspending them in the arms race. He got that right. Hard to believe, as, one after the other, the Baltic states declare their freedom. End of the line for the Commies. All change on the geopolitical landscape for sure; doesn't justify the chest thumping of Western leaders climbing on the bandwagon boasting about the merits of democracy and global security. Cable from Serafina: Fortunato coming to NY to see me?????

August 20, 1991 - Restitution?

Paris Now.

"He was 26 or 27 years old."

"Fortunato? No. 25." (George was always a stickler for details.) "Just finished law at Sciences Po, in the Rue Saint-Guillaume, after his double-first from Oxford and that silver medal he got in the LA Olympics. Rowing or something. An athlete, but clever beneath all that bohemian long-haired, weed-smoking je-ne-sais-quoi-je-m'en-foutisme attitude he trailed around the Quartier. First one to spot the opportunity in Yeltsin's courting of the West and the wild west show that then led to the oligarchs ripping off anything they could in the collapse of the Soviet Union. Restitution was the name of the game, and it was Fortunato who showed the old man how to play it, did the research for him on what he could claim, and lined up Oxbridge to do the funding and divide the loot. Bloody clever, if you ask me. Simply put, restitution was defined as *returning to the proper owner property or the monetary value of its loss.* It consisted in proving that what was once yours had been nicked by the state. Didn't matter which state or when, whether in a time of war or peace, if you could prove it had been yours and it had been illegally taken by duress or decree or revolutionary zeal, it had to be returned to you. Saying it and proving it, of course, being at polar opposites. All the old Soviet states were essentially bust and only too glad to unload property falling into ruin which they couldn't even afford to insure leave alone repair or restore. (Once George gets going there's no stopping him.) But the contents - the art works, books, jewellery, tapestries, furniture, rugs, you name it - the whole laundry list of stuff plundered, stolen and/or confiscated from said properties, now stashed in museums or flogged off to private collections around the world, another order of magnitude to recover. Theoretically, all the *Ancien Régime* families with their vast land holdings qualified, provided there was a legitimate living heir. Notice the qualifiers: *legitimate* and *living.* Enter the old man…

Chapter Forty-five

"You know Gorby, right?"

"Gorby?"

"Gorbachev. You know him, right?" They were lunching in Tavern on the Green, having walked across Central Park on Fortunato's first day in New York. Grilled asparagus to start, then rainbow trout with a walnut caper sauce and shoestring fries, and cheesecake and coffee to finish. A Pouilly Fuissé to help it down, a glass of which Pyotr was sipping before he replied.

"No. I met him a couple of times when he was touring France back in '77 with his wife," Pyotr said. "The French Commies wanted me to do his portrait, but it doesn't mean I know him. Anyway, I...hang on, isn't he under house arrest in his dacha? Those plotters, what do they call themselves, the *Gang of Eight,* Baklanov, Boldin, General Varennikov, that lot, they've got him."

"Not anymore," Fortunato said. For a moment he looked serious. "Yeltsin bailed him out. What do you remember about him?"

"How hard it was to look at him because of that port-wine birthmark on top of his head. If you were going to paint him, how would you handle that? I think he was surprised I spoke Russian so well. Why? Is it important?"

"It may get us to the head of the queue. Once the big law firms cotton on, there's going to be an avalanche of applications and we need to get in ahead of the crowd."

"I don't understand."

"Right now, everything's in a state of flux, the regulations are a shambles and there's a revolving door of civil servants with no masters to tell them what to do. They're all crooks grabbing what they can." Despite his youth, Fortunato sounded very sure of himself. "From Riga to Budapest to Kyiv and Prague and all points in between, including Moscow, with the correct credentials - which we have - and sponsors - which we don't have yet - all you have to do is fill out a form to make your claim, get it stamped, and bingo! you're in. Just rattling off the titles of your Great-Aunt Augustine will be like gold dust to the bureaucrats: Grand Duchess of Austria-Hungary, Princess of Romania-Bukovina, Baroness of Reichenau, Countess of Saxe-Meiningen, Princess of Neuchâtel. Her only survivor, Pyotr Alexis Szépség. Nearly 100 years old. Claiming title to - Christ! Going back ten generations the list of stuff she owned would fill a book. And that's just a start. Add in your family tree and you'll end up owning half of Mittel Europa."

"To what purpose?" Pyotr said.

Fortunato looked surprised. "Don't you want to be rich?" he said.

Pyotr laughed. "You remind me of myself when I was your age - always optimistic, even in the trenches." Which is when Marjorie Maxwellington chose to swoop into the restaurant with a conversation of giggling girlfriends having a bridal shower. She spotted him, legged on over to roost in his lap, and kissed him to the goggling astonishment of Fortunato. Coming up for air, she said, "Who's this?"

"My Great-Nephew, Fortunato."

"Doesn't he know it's rude to stare?"

Fortunato blinked. "She's yours?" he said to Pyotr.

"No. He's mine," Marjorie Maxwellington said.

"But.." Fortunato struggled. Pyotr smiled.

"And here I was, feeling sorry for you," Fortunato said. "What about Serafina?"

"Serafina?" Miss Maxwellington came alert.

"His wife," Fortunato said

"Wife?!" Marjorie Maxwellington said, springing up from where she sat, slapping Pyotr and storming off, seemingly in one seamless motion, to the startled stares of several diners.

"Oh, my God!" Fortunato said, red-faced with embarrassment. "Sorry!"

"Sorry? Really Fortunato?" Pyotr said, the imprint of Marjorie's hand vivid on his cheek. "Extraordinary, coming from a hedonist like you."

That night Pyotr wrote in his journal: *September 1, 1991 - Fortunato back to Europe. Ego to Africa. I signed all the papers - now it's up to him.*

Chapter Forty-six

S erafina is sitting on the terrace overlooking Genoa, bundled up in a quilted coat, long silk scarf around her neck, mittens, woollen stockings, thankful for her thick black hair and cashmere beret to fight against the tramontana, the north-easterly wind blasting in off the cold plains of the Po. She is reading a letter posted three weeks before.

Bujumbura,

Sunday, December 29, 1991

Cara Serafina,

Hard to believe four months have gone by. I'm exhausted. We all are - afraid and exhausted, the house full, the clinic jam packed. I think we're feeding over a hundred people a day. The staff are brave and stoic. The RPF invasion, supplied by arms and ammunition from Uganda for over a year now, is turning into a flood, with Tutsis murdered daily. Habyarimana does nothing but dither, making promises he has no intention to keep. The cease-fire signed back in March doesn't mean a thing today, with the creation and training of civilian militias called Interahamwe ('Those who stand together') which are really squads of killers going after anybody opposed to them. When will men learn that war is not a solution? I think of all the long years of strife behind me and then remember what you said: stop looking in the rearview mirror, look at the road ahead. You're right. The past is just that, past, and here is now…sorry, had to break off, just another emergency - water coming in one of the many holes in our roof from this never-ending monsoon. My brain's in a bit of a muddle. I had to tell you something but it's gone. Never mind; if it's important it will come back.

I'm not sure why I mentioned it, the rain, I mean, which gurgles and splashes about in such abundance that when it stops you think you've gone deaf. There are always emergencies going on in this kind of clinic, the drumbeat of living - not to say dying - in Africa. To tell the truth I'm tired of all the drama and I'm looking forward to getting home to you and the children and some decent pasta. Il tuo amorevole marito, P.

P.S. What I forgot was about Fortunato, but on reflection I think it better I tell you when I see you.

Serafina puts the letter down in her lap, where it flaps in the wind. She looks out at the distant panorama of Genoa without consciously seeing it, her thoughts far away with her distant husband. Somehow, she has married a ghost who comes and goes with no explanation, a chance meteorological frequency, an air current, huffing and puffing, now a zephyr, now a gale, a hurricane, a gentle breeze. She sniffs, rubs her nose. She should be resentful, even angry. Instead, at the thought of his arrival, she feels her heart quicken. She smiles. What a rogue! A servant comes out to tell her something, but she isn't listening. There were four servants, all female, two inherited with the Palazzo, both ancient, one bed-ridden, Nanny Ursula, the other suffering, Alzheimer's or Parkinson's. Nobody knew which. Of the two new ones, originally taken on as nurses for the children, only one could cook on those days Cook had the day off. Seven women, counting Cook, Allegra and herself. Not good for Guido to be surrounded by so many. Which brought her back to her husband. His hopes and aspirations. Now Fortunato's.

Fortunato is in a waiting room in Old Kyiv, sitting, wondering how long it would take the Minister to return from lunch, what the bribe would be, how and by whom it would be handled. The room is on the first floor of what had been a vast 4-storey Maison-de-Maître, midway between the Golden Gates and the church of Saint Sophia, part of a 40-hectare estate the old man's uncle had inherited in 1903, the grounds and gardens of which had been taken by compulsory order of a succession of regimes to build roads, tramways, government offices, a public library, and two museums, until, today, there was nothing left but the building itself, now an embassy. How to put a value on what had been appropriated was an interesting problem. Sitting with Fortunato are two professors from his college in Oxford, bearded dons, experts on Volodymyr the Great and Yaroslav the Wise, Grand Prince of Kyiv, who ruled the city from 1019 until his death in 1054, an extraordinary span of 35 years. Yaroslav had married the King of Sweden's daughter, Ingegerd Olofsdotter, and their issue gave birth to three Queens, Elisiv of Norway, Anastasia of Hungary and Anne, Queen of the Franks; plus six sons, four of whom ruled Kyiv in succession to their father. The second son, Iziaslav, ruled from 1054 to 1068. He married Gertrude-Olisava, a Polish princess, the great-granddaughter of Otto the 2nd, the Holy Roman Emperor. The old man's uncle was a direct descendant of this union, hence the claim.

The Minister is a young man. He is lunching with a Swiss banker in the Matisse, seated at a window overlooking Old Kyiv. The banker knows the Minister is out of his depth and simply obeying orders. Nepotism is the name of the game. Back in Zurich, off a corner where the Bahnhofstrasse transects Parade Platz, on one of the most expensive pieces of real estate in the world, is a private merchant bank adjacent to the Hotel Baur, where the father of the Minister has a numbered bank account in the name of a Cayman Island limited company. This is where the finder's 'fee' will go. The Minister does not need to know the details.

"Are you quite satisfied as to this man's provenance?" the banker said.

"Absolutely," the Minister said. "Everything has been verified. The man's related to half the families in the Almanach de Gotha. His claim is bullet proof. His people didn't just own all this -" here the Minister waves his hand at the window as if he meant the entire city - "they built it. He's nearly a hundred years old now, but apparently fit as a fiddle. As to the legitimacy of such a retroactive claim?" the Minister shrugged, "It is not for me to say."

"Quite," the banker said. Sometimes it was best to leave certain things unsaid. "At what time do we meet him?"

"Oh, we don't. He's not here but on his estate, a plantation in some black African country, trying to save his staff from getting chopped to pieces. A great-nephew has been delegated to negotiate on his behalf. He's waiting in my office." The Minister pinches his nose, clears his throat. "If it's all the same to you, I would rather not be there when you meet him."

"Yes," the banker said. "That would probably be the best."

The banker finds Fortunato in good humour, chatting with a pretty secretary, taking in stride the phoney excuse for the Minister's absence, introducing his two companions as experts in the myriad details of the old man's claim and, after spending a couple of hours expounding on just what had been filched, plundered, nicked, stolen, bombed, burned, and lost, ending the conversation with a smile and a total. Cash. For compensation. A figure so fantastical, in US dollars, it makes the banker blink.

"That is out of the question," the banker said. "It would bankrupt the entire country."

"So?"

"Surely you are not serious?"

Fortunato smiles. "Just because I smile doesn't mean I'm not serious. The number I have given you is conservative. Just the value of the rare books and manuscripts that have disappeared, not to mention the pictures, furniture, and jewellery, comes to far more. Far, far more. Then there is the land. The centre of the city. What price do you put on that? Not to mention the compounded value of all this over time. How do you compensate us for the years, not to say centuries, that this abuse has gone on?" The banker looks lost.

"You look lost," Fortunato said, still smiling. "I suggest you return to your clients, remind them of every little clause, all the definitions in their treaty of restitution, and come back with a counter-offer. Yes?" Then turns to the pretty secretary and asks if she is free for dinner that evening.

This same scenario is played out in Yerevan, the capital of Armenia, Tbilisi, the capital of Georgia, Tallinn, the capital of Estonia, Minsk, the capital of Belarus, Riga, the capital of Latvia, Vilnius, the capital of Lithuania, Pristina, the capital of Kosovo, Prague, the capital of Czechia, Warsaw, the capital of Poland, and Budapest, the capital of Hungary. All the countries where the old man's ancestors had their estates. It takes time. A year. And then another year. There is reluctance. There's resistance. Even obstruction. But in the end a deal is made, property handed over, a few bribes paid. The old man becomes rich. Obscenely rich. And Fortunato dines out with a lot of pretty secretaries.

One day, returning to Genoa, Pyotr suffered the same disbelief as winners of 'El Gordo' - The Fat One - the name given to the Christmas Lottery in Spain and its outlandish first prize. You buy a ticket never really believing you will win. When you do, the surprising reaction is to say why? Why me? And like many, you suffer the multiple demands of people and charities, even friends, assuming that your luck is theirs to share. Tainting a refusal with the indelible mark of ingratitude. Pyotr blamed Fortunato for not keeping his name out of the press. Which was unjust given that restitution was a matter of public record, transparency the declared aim of all the municipal bodies involved. None of which anticipated the flood of mail pouring into Palazzo Szépség; hands begging for a share of his new-found wealth. Serafina contemplated her disgruntled husband scowling at the postman lugging in sacks of letters, interrupting brunch, and expecting a healthy tip for his efforts. Seeing the man off fell to her. Resuming her place at the table, she said, "Instead of being upset, you should be grateful."

"Grateful?" Pyotr said. "The whole thing's become ridiculous. I am not going to go to Prague to get a medal, nor am I going to Budapest to shake hands with a bunch of pseudo-monarchists who want me crowned. All I want is to be left in peace to paint. If I can't paint, I can't earn any money."

Serafina laughed. She turned in her chair to face Fortunato seated at the far end of the table. "It still hasn't sunk in," she said.

"He'll get used to it," Fortunato said, helping himself to more rashers of crispy bacon to go with his scrambled eggs on toast.

They both spoke as if he wasn't there, which only served to rile up Pyotr. He had been poor, bankrupt, shot, jailed, and broke. Yet never once doubted himself. Never felt life was unfair, but, like the Chinese, believed in his joss, that the gods were always on his side. Why then was he feeling guilty? His good fortune should be a relief. But? That word again. But power corrupts, he reminded himself. Yes. And absolute power corrupts absolutely. In today's world money is power. A windfall like this will completely change our lives if we let it, he thought. Is that what we want? Looking from his wife to his nephew the answer was obvious.

"I may be getting on and hard of hearing," he said, "but I refuse to allow the roll of dice to change me and the way I live." Pause. "I speak for myself. The scale of what you've achieved, Fortunato, is beyond anything I'd imagined. If it cannot be used for the public good, I want no part of it."

Eyes wide open, Fortunato gaped, a forkful of food halfway to his mouth. "I only did as you instructed," he said.

Paris Now.

"That's when he set up his private foundation, right George?"

"Yes," George said. "It was another suggestion of Fortunato's, seeing as they were already in partnership with Oxbridge. Bundling their interests together made sense and the stewardship of the colleges guaranteed legitimacy and custodial longevity, plus a shrewd use of certain tax havens - the whole thing overseen by his wife, Serafina, as board chair and chief executive. She focused on the rights of women and children. The old boy lapped it up and took off for New York."

"And Fortunato?"

"No nine-to-five for him; he bums around, ends up as professor of adventure at UCLA, if you can believe there is such a post, his chair endowed by the foundation of course."

"And then the tragedy."

"Yes."

Chapter Forty-seven

December 19, 1993 - *Go with Abraham, one of our doormen, to The Schomburg Center for Research in Black Culture at 515 Malcolm X Blvd, over in Harlem, a block from the river. Panel discussions and film screenings on the aftermath of the Los Angeles riots last year. Pouring light on why social and economic disparity are like dousing fire with jet fuel. When we leave Abraham says: "Could happen here, the way things are. You scared?" I say, no. "You should be," Abraham says. "Underneath this city's hot, ready to blow. You whites don't see the tensions, the unfairness, the systemic racism we have to put up with long's it's someplace else. But it's here, right under your feet. Same injustice those guys felt blew up the parking structure under the World Trade Center back in February."*

December 29,1993 - Marj marries a Senator's son on a vineyard in the Finger Lakes in upstate New York. Gave the happy couple a picture and escaped the reception sampling local varietals as I don't give a twopenny fig for 'crisp' Rieslings or 'velvety' Gewürztraminers, supposedly offering a 'glimpse' into the terroir of the region and 'tantalising' the palate. Who writes this stuff? Just before the event Marj sneaked into my bedroom in the inn where I was staying in Cooperstown for old times sake 'so you remember what you'll be missing!'

January 17, 1994 - Northridge earthquake in LA, 57 dead, damage estimated between $20-50 billion. Still not 'the Big One' the newspapers warn.

February 15, 1994 - Ai Weiwei exhibition over at the Brooklyn Museum, in Prospect Heights. He's challenging human rights and some uncomfortable truths about censorship, surveillance, and freedom of expression. 'For me, my personal response is a personal struggle - it is for a totally selfish purpose - a way I test myself - I have strong curiosity about who I am - it is not about courage,

328

but about how an individual can react to a situation.' For which he ends up detained in Beijing on charges of 'economic crimes' for 81 days!

March 9, 1994 - *Can't believe the weather. Since the 3rd we've had, snow, ice pellets, light snow, drizzle and fog; on the 4th, fog; the 5th, rain on ice sheets; yesterday, thunderstorms, light rain and fog; today, more snow, freezing rain and ice pellets denting car bodies; and tomorrow they're predicting over an inch of rain. What the fuck, right! Am safe in bed with Annie Proulx's "The Shipping News," and Khaled Hosseini's "The Kite Runner," both a world of love, loss, and redemption in a landscape torn apart by conflict.*

March 25, 1994 - *Letter from Keza in Bujumbura: 'Bwana Doctor, Sorry, I bring bad news. Nurse Kampire is sick so I write her words. The RPF has launched a fresh offensive and the guerillas have reached the outskirts of Kigali. French forces are again called in to help the government.*

Fighting has been going on for several months despite the negotiations and the supposed peace accord between Habyarimana and the RPF allowing the return of refugees and a coalition Hutu-RPF government. But Habyarimana is still stalling on setting up a power-sharing government. The extremist station, Radio Mille Collines, is broadcasting incitements to attack Tutsis and warning the international community of impending calamity if they stand in the way. Many Rwandan human rights activists are evacuating their families from Kigali believing massacres are imminent. Many are leaving the plantation to go back to their villages to protect their families.

Your wife is well and so are your children. She does not know I am writing to you because she does not want you to worry. But I feel I must tell you these things!'

April 6, 1994 - *Headline in NY Times:*

Rwanda President Habyarimana and the president of Burundi, Cyprien Ntaryamira, are killed when their plane is shot down near Kigali Airport.

April 7, 1994 - Telegram:

Amahoro and Habimana missing Stop. We have hidden Sydney Stop. Urgent you come Stop. Keza.

April 8, 1994 - *Delta Flight 188 6PM Dep. JFK - Frankfurt - Nairobi - Kigali. Despite warnings from the State Department not to travel to Rwanda, made it on time, to find the airport jammed with UN troops doing nothing as they are forbidden to intervene because this would breach their "monitoring"* *mandate!!! - while the Forces Armées Rwandaises, (convinced Habyarimana was murdered,) and the Interahamwe have roadblocks set up and are going from house to house killing Tutsis and moderate Hutu politicians, and the RPF has launched a major offensive to rescue 600 of its troops surrounded in Kigali. Thousands are dying, the slaughter goes on, and the international community twiddles its thumbs over questions of accountability and justice. Put on my old white doctor's coat from the clinic, two pens still in the breast pocket. Bribe an ambulance driver to take me to Bujumbura...*

Pyotr sat back, looked down at what he was trying to record in his journal, his handwriting shaky. Lack of sleep since getting the telegram, the adrenaline spike worn off, with cramp in his lower back, stressed, running on fumes, he feels his age. He has had a desk moved into his bedroom. From where he sits his eyes constantly dart across the room to his bed where his 7-year old daughter, Sydney, is sleeping. No news of Amahoro, only rumours, her village cut off, overrun by gunmen taking all children found alive into the bush. His mind freezes at the thought they may have Habimana. There is a gentle knock on the door and Keza comes in with a clean white coat for him to put on in exchange for the blood-stained one he is wearing. "Anything?" he asked. Keza shook her head, no. No news. The clinic is jammed with the wounded, the dying and the dead. There are armed staff at all the doors. In the distance the chatter of small arms, an occasional explosion, the pin-pon, pin-pon of an ambulance. On his desk is a photograph taken five years previously. In it he is standing on the front terrace of his farmhouse, with some of his staff, his infant twins playing in the foreground. They look so intent as they try to dam a rivulet of water seeping from under the terrace with pebbles and mud. They are almost identical but for their skin. Black and white. His gardener had warned him of what was coming, the RPF. And now? They are here. Racing through the streets. Half-naked youths, crammed into Toyota pick-ups, festooned with bandoliers of bullets, manning machine-guns, brandishing AKs and machetes, masked with every fashionable brand of sunglasses and headgear, drunk, stoned, murderous. Killers. His atavistic reaction is a thickening of blood, an acceleration of pulse, a miosis of pupils, a surge of aggression. Nostrils pinched, he's ready to go over the top. Which is when Keza says, "Bwana?" her voice pitched in panic. She is staring at his face. She has never seen the Doctor like this. It takes a moment for him to remember he is no longer 18 in the trenches at Verdun. No. He is an old man in a white coat. Responsible for many. Particularly his wife and children. Again, he looks at Sydney innocently asleep in his bed. Save her. At the very least, he must save her.

Paris Now.

"He did," George said. "Took her with him to New York after it was confirmed his wife, Amahoro, was dead, raped, murdered, and his daughter, Habimana, abducted with hundreds of other children. The slaughter in Rwanda grew to the point no one was safe. The U.N. cut its forces from 2,500 to 250 following the death of ten Belgian soldiers assigned to guard the moderate Hutu prime minister, Agathe Uwiliyingimana. Surprise, surprise, the prime minister was murdered, and the Belgians disarmed, tortured, shot and then hacked to death. Incredibly, they had been told not to resist violently by the U.N. force commander, as this would have breached their mandate!

The wimps in the U.N. Security Council spent eight hours discussing the Rwandan crisis and ended up condemning the killing, but carefully omitted to use the word "genocide." Had the term been used, the U.N. would have been legally obliged to act to "prevent and punish" the perpetrators. Meanwhile, through May, tens of thousands of refugees poured into Burundi and Zaire and in just one day 250,000 Rwandans, fled the advance of the RPF, and crossed the border into Tanzania. As the slaughter of the Tutsis continued, the U.N. agreed to send 6,800 troops and policemen to Rwanda with powers to defend civilians, but the deployment of this force was delayed because of arguments over who would pay the bill and provide the equipment!

Even the deployment of French forces in south-west Rwanda to create a so-called 'safe area' in territory controlled by the government didn't stop the killing of Tutsis. Inevitably, the RPF captured Kigali, the Hutu government fled to Zaire, followed by a further tidal wave of refugees. The French bailed out and were replaced by Ethiopian U.N. troops. The RPF set up an interim government of 'national unity' in Kigali, while different

U.N. agencies clashed over reports that RPF troops had carried out a series of reprisal killings all over Rwanda with hundreds of civilians executed. Say it slowly, in just 100 days, from the 7th of April to the 16th of July, 1994, more than 800,000 human beings were hacked to death by the Hutu-led government of Théoneste Bagosora, mastermind of the genocide, and his senior cohorts, Robert Kajuga, of the Interahamwe, Jean-Bosco Barayagwiza, of the Impuzamugambi, and gangs financed by Félicien Kabuga. A mind-boggling, monumental, unmitigated disaster, almost totally ignored in the West, where Clinton was getting blowjobs in the White House, John Major was dealing with 'sleaze' and being asked in Parliament how he could defend the fact that the chairman of the North West Water Board received £47,000 a year before privatization and now got £338,000 for doing exactly the same job, Mitterand was defending France's role in supplying arms to the FAR and the Catholic Church affirmed genocide did take place but those who took part in it did so without the permission of the Church!"

(George hates politicians and at the drop of a hat loves to misquote e.e. cummings: *a politician is an arse, upon which no man ever sat.*)

"Through it all, year-after-year, back and forth to Africa, the old man never quit in his determination to find Habimana even though it was more than likely she was dead. Who would have thought it was the chance remark of a limo driver in New York that would lead to him tracking her down?"

Chapter Forty-eight

The driver's name was Patrice, originally from Haiti, a long-time limo driver with his own car, a well-maintained stretch Lincoln Continental, black-on-black, with the usual dings for a vehicle that had done 400,000 miles over the potholes of the poorly maintained streets of the five boroughs that composed New York City, the Bronx, Brooklyn, Manhattan, Queens and Staten Island - particularly Queens, the location of both JFK and LGA, the City's major airports, his preferred local to pick up passengers flying in from overseas. It had taken an hour and forty minutes slowly inching up the endless lines of taxis and limos waiting for a fare, during which time he did what he always did, polish his car and the worn leather interior. He was second in line when the cab in front turned down a grandfather and a young girl, skinny, braces, face covered in spots and pimples. They came to his open window, and he said, "Problem?"

"This time of night, he" - pointing at the cab - "doesn't want to go back into Manhattan," the grandfather said.

"No worries," Patrice said. "I'll take you."

"What'll it cost?" the old man said.

To which Patrice smiled and gave his idiosyncratic answer for which he was justly famous: "Whatever you think is fair." Then opened his door, stepped out to open the rear door, ushered the couple in after putting their luggage in the trunk, and got back behind the wheel. "Address?" he said.

"Beekman Place," the old man said. "You know it?"

Is the Pope a Catholic, Patrice thought, firing up the engine, but instead he said, "You think, after driving the city for thirty years?"

"Scuzi," the old man said in Italian, trading glances in the rearview mirror attached to the upper centre of the limo's windshield from where the driver could see both of his passengers. "I didn't mean to be rude. So many drivers today don't know the streets."

"Relax," Patrice said. "There are soft drinks and snacks in the bar back there. Enjoy." He eased out into the traffic. "Fancy some music?" The young girl said something to the old man. "I didn't catch that," Patrice said.

"She wants to know if you have anything by Samputu?" the old man said.

"Samputu? Never heard of him."

"From Rwanda. He's famous there. Sings in six languages."

"Rwanda?" Patrice said, heading south on I-678. "You got me. Where's Rwanda?" The girl giggled. He looked up in the rearview mirror. "She know where Haiti is?"

"Mbabarira," the girl said, flustered. "Mpole. Mbabajwe cyane n'ibyo nakoze."

"Come again?" Patrice said, swinging through two traffic circles and then merging onto I-678 north, tucked into the stream of traffic headed into town.

"It's Kinyarwanda for sorry," the old man said, trading glances again in the rearview mirror. "My daughter's English is not so good. She says she's sorry."

"Kinyarwanda?" Patrice tried the word as if he were tasting it. "New one on me. Is that where you're from, Rwanda?" He moved to the right lane to take the exit for the Long Island Expressway and the Midtown Tunnel.

"Yes. It's in the middle of Africa, next to Burundi and the Congo," the old man said.

Patrice filed the information away with all the other eclectic tidbits he'd picked up from the many passengers who'd ridden in his car. How could a man so old have such a young daughter? He drove on in silence for 5 miles and swung the wheel over for the right lane exit onto Van Dam.

"You wanna know something?" he said, his eyes big in the rearview mirror.

"What?" the old man said.

"I used to be a photographer before I became a limo driver. Good one too, even if I say so myself. I had an eye." He slowed to make the right hand turn onto Borden Avenue. "I'm sure you've heard this before, but I gotta tell you, and don't get me wrong..." he stopped speaking as the vehicle in front of them braked hard, forcing him to do the same... "Opps. Sorry. You guys okay?" No harm done, they drove on in silence, through Queens to the Midtown Tunnel, through the Tunnel to where it emptied onto 34th Street, a left on 3rd Avenue, a left on 51st and a left on Beekman. Door-to-door 38 minutes, par for that time of night. He parked where directed, got out and helped his fares disembark. Then he opened the trunk to give them their luggage and the old man opened his wallet, took out a $50 bill, and gave it to him. "Fair?" the old man said.

Smiling, without even looking, Patrice put the note in his pocket. "Fair," he said. "Enjoy your stay in the City." And went to get back in his car.

"A moment," the old man said, bending to pick up his suitcase. "What were you going to tell me back there?"

Patrice hesitated, glanced at the girl holding her suitcase, nodded to himself. "What I was going to tell you was that if I was still a photographer, I would ask your permission to photograph your daughter. I have never seen anyone so beautiful in my life."

The old man looked blank, glanced at his daughter. Not at all put out, Sydney, 10-years old, giggled, smiled to show her braces, batted her eyes like Betty Boop. "Spots and all?" she said, her English quite perfect.

Patrice laughed, took out a business card from the breast pocket of his coat and gave it to her. "You ever need a ride, give me a call," he said. At the end of his graveyard shift, he drove home to Yonkers, his tiny house on Herriot two blocks from the Hudson and a block from Riverside - where his wife, a mulatto stripper and pole-dancer in a dago joint between a muffler discount shop and a church, was asleep, a Glock-22 semiautomatic pistol under her pillow. He took a shower before climbing into bed and woke her up to give her the news.

"You woke me up to tell me you had a pretty girl in the limo?" she said. "You want that I shoot you now or can it wait till the morning?"

"No," Patrice said, "I woke you up to tell you won't have to work for them fucking goombas no more. Ma petite Zuzu, I have found us a gold mine. I have the eye. When those braces come off, she'll be on the cover of every fashion magazine in town." And she was.

By the time Sydney was 15 her face was on Elle, Vogue, Glamour, Harper's Bazaar, Cosmopolitan, Marie Claire, Grazia, and countless others. She had been photographed by all the greats, Lindbergh, Demarchelier, Boudin, Weber, Alice Springs, an endless list. She was a millionaire, with her modelling fees going up and up. (Patrice, now her agent, taking 20% of all she made.) At 16, she lost her virginity to a slimebag called Louie-Louie, another agent, who introduced her to coke, then raped her. At 17 she had her own apartment in the Delmonico on 59th. At 18, the paparazzi's favourite swinger, her affairs with famous and infamous men and women filled the gossip columns of the Mail, Express, Post, Variety, Hollywood Reporter, Hola, Tatler and even the Times. At 19 she took over the old man's flat on Beekman which he could no longer afford as he spent more and more of his time in Africa.

And it was in Africa that the story came full circle when an Amnesty International search party looking for any trace of the children abducted so many years before came across an abandoned guerrilla encampment in the jungle on the contiguous border between the Kibira and Nyungwe Forests. There, glued, taped, and stapled on the walls of a ruined hut, were pictures of Sydney torn from dozens of magazines. Hundreds and hundreds of pictures, so many it posed the question: Why? Who could have done this? A Hutu reporter of The New Times' Kinyarwanda subsidiary, the Izuba Rirashe, mentioned this to the Doctor when he interviewed him in his clinic in Bujumbura about his work as a surgeon in the field.

"Where did you hear this?" the Doctor said.

"It was on Radio Rwanda," the reporter said.

Habimana. Who else could it be? 13 years after her abduction? Was it possible? Goosebumps on his arms, the Doctor intuitively knew it must be. His daughter. Alive!

Chapter Forty-nine

The last days of May are the end of the rainy season in Rwanda and Burundi. Every shade of green is in the foliage and leaves of the trees covering the hills receding like so many frozen waves to a distant horizon. Water drips everywhere, off everything, and turns into a fine mist as the sun rises over miles and miles of trackless forest heaving with unseen life, big and small, swarming in ancestral cycles. As Pyotr leaves the clinic, he is surrounded by the children of his patients, touching his trousers and pulling his shirt, their bright teeth in their black faces smiling up at him like so many sunflowers They follow him to the truck, pressing against the door and windows, only falling back when Nshuti starts the engine and makes off along the muddy potholed road whose deep corrugations and unseen rocks bang against the chassis and suspension. In no time the sun will turn the mud into dust and the green of the trees will be mixed with shades of wilting greys and browns. There, somewhere in the jungle, is Habimana.

The Nyungwe is the largest expanse of forest in Rwanda, and one of the oldest rainforests in Africa. It covers over 1000 km2 of dense tropical jungle, with more than 1000 species of trees standing in serried ranks up to 1900 metres above the sea, some being over 60 metres tall and 500 years old, surrounded by bamboo-covered slopes, grasslands, swamps and bogs. Adjoining it to the south is the Kibira Forest, another 400 km2. Together, fed by the countless streams flowing through their hills and ravines, these forests are the true source of Africa's two largest rivers, the Congo and the Nile. 70% of the water supply for millions of people comes from here. Where the two forests meet is a line on a foreign map, with few roads and trails, laced with the hidden tracks of animals, infested by hunters and poachers who killed the last buffalo in 1974 and the last elephant in 1999, but still the habitat of 11 different species of monkeys and 250 different kinds of birds. On the fringes, eating away at the boundaries, are hundreds of villages, home to countless thousands, many opposed to the government, happy to hide a few insurgents in exchange for food and protection.

From the New Times reporter Pyotr had the coordinates of the guerrilla camp but having it and finding it were two different things. For days Nshuti tried one track after another, only to find most petered out against a cliff face or a raging river and they would have to trace their way back to start the search again. When they eventually found it, it was not just abandoned but burned to the ground, smoking embers, with no trace of a hut with Sydney's pictures. Seeing the dejected look on the face of his boss, Nsuti said, "If she is alive, Bwana, she knows you are looking for her. The drums, they tell her." The bush telegraph - felt - there in the background like a heartbeat, Africans talking to Africans in a language that needed no translation. Nshuti did not add that the drums also spoke to the guerrillas.

Paris Now.

"And here's the strangest thing. The old boy is over 110 years old - 111 to be exact - and it never occurs to him that hacking through the jungle to look for his daughter was insane," George said. "And of course, it was the guerillas who found him when they needed him. The exact details are unclear. Apparently, the son of one of their leaders was badly hurt, so it was logical to send a messenger to the Bwana Doctor asking for his aid. In this long and terrible genocidal tragedy his impartial treatment of all the sick and wounded, of whatever tribe, was known to all, even the witch doctors and shamans with their fatalistic creed that when something ends, it ends. So he follows the messenger to a makeshift field hospital in the jungle, walks under a tented canopy where the smell of gangrene in the leg of the wounded boy lying there naked is so overpowering he wonders why they have fetched him. 'Make better,' the messenger said. And a nurse comes forward with a few medical implements on a metal tray, a dog's collar around her neck, with a long chain attached to it held in the fist of a heavily-armed, half-stoned, half-drunk guerilla. The nurse is black, wearing torn camouflage fatigues. It is his daughter. Habimana. 'Say nothing,' she mutters in English."

November 10, 2096
45.4158° N, 141.6732° E
E HOKKAIDO, JAPAN

The monastery is built above a rocky promontory on the northernmost tip of Japan. It has been there for over one thousand years. It is a place of solitude and hardship. Access is difficult, visitors rare. None of the monks, not even the oldest, have any idea when or how the old man arrived. Only the fish know. The jellyfish, turritopsis dohrnii, are always waiting for him. They are said to be immortal, capable of an endless cycle from their birth as a bottom-living polyp in the parent hydroid colony, to their liberation to swim free in plankton, growing in size from a tiny medusa of 1 mm with eight tentacles to an adult measuring 4.5 mm with 80 or 90 tentacles, and which, if exposed to stress, attacked or sick, can revert to being a polyp again. Over and over, forever. They hover there, in the cold waters of the Sea of Okhotsk which lap the old man's rock, sometimes just one or two widely separated, sometimes in a curtain with their tentacles drifting in the current like lace in a breeze, difficult to swim through. He is stung often, so often he develops an immunity to them. They taught him how to drift, his body vertically suspended under the sea, moving to the same subtle currents with scarcely a twitch of his fingers to alter course, rising to the surface to breathe every five minutes or so, the sea more familiar to him then the monk's cell he so rarely visited.

Every day, in all weather, there he sits, cross-legged, motionless, on his rock, a netsuke carved and folded into itself, scarcely the image of an old man, more of a compact fossil, wisps of long white hair stirring in the wind, an endless wind combing the sea, the sea at his feet in which float a bloom of ageless jellyfish. A

Greenland shark, always the same one, itself three hundred and sixty years old, dank, black eyes glancing up to confirm the presence of the antique fossil sitting on his rock as it swam by shadowed by an ancient bowhead whale. It was always so. In the monastery for the past fifty years, in which time the oldest monks, none of whom were there when he first arrived, told the novice monks the story of the two-hundred-year-old living legend out on his rock one hundred and seventy-five feet from the shore with the fish who came to visit him. Nobody knew how he got to the rock. By levitation some said. What could he be thinking . . .Nothing. Nada. Zero.

Paris Now.

On Thursday evenings in the Quartier, it is traditional for galleries to hold a *vernissage* - the word meaning a last-minute varnishing of the pictures to be displayed of the latest work by one or other of their accredited Artists, or, more rarely, the introduction of a new talent they are promoting. Of course, George and I are invited to all the important events and it's natural to dress up for the occasion. One evening, going by Alexander's place on Boulevard St. Germain, we saw an enormous Agathangelou triptych in the window, ignored as usual by the fashionista crowd clutching champagne glasses while they gossiped on the pavement outside. We went in to greet the Queen of galleristas, dressed in a splendid muumuu with huge pink polka dots that he got from Marimekko in Finland, offset nicely by George's boho linen kaftan in pale peach, and my outfit, a dark blue silk robe with white embroidery depicting the strategic details of a woman's body. While we kissed each other and cooed over how marvelous we looked, I could see the artist, Alekos Agathangelou, slowly going bald, watching us, amusement in his eyes.

"You'll never guess who was in here last week when we were preparing for Alekos's show?" Alexander said. "We were hanging that big piece in the window watched by an old man out in the street. When it was up, he came in to ask if it was for sale. I said yes and told him the price, 280,000. 'So much?' he said. 'I am prepared to offer you half.' We laughed and carried on with what we were doing while he pottered around the gallery looking at this and that. On a stand in the middle of the gallery was a very large portfolio bound in black linen, standing on its spine, full of drawings, watercolours, etchings, lithographs and woodcuts, through which the old man was slowly fingering his way, occasionally lifting out a piece for a better look. After a few minutes, he suddenly stopped and almost with reverence pulled out a thick parchment sheet and stared at it as if mesmerised. 'And how much is this?' he said.

'23,000,' I said.

'So much for a gouache?'

'Yes. That's a Belanopek. Signed and dated. You don't see many around nowadays. In fact, they are quite rare.'

'I offer you half,' he said, and when I smiled and shook my head, he put it back and walked out the door. On Saturday he came back to say he had reconsidered and was prepared to pay what I wanted for the Agathangelou.

'I regret, it is sold,' I said.

He looked at the portfolio on its stand. 'And the Belanopek?'

'I am sorry, that too is sold,' I said. 'You know - may I speak frankly? - it is my experience in this business, if you hesitate over the price of something unique, inevitably it will go to a person who is more, how shall we say...more *appassionato, impulsivo*, more passionate, more impulsive, than yourself. A bit crazy, eh?"

He nodded and left. On Monday a messenger delivered another portfolio. In it were 10 Belanopeks accompanied by a simple card, signed:

'*Complimenti ! Belanopek.*'

It took a moment for the significance to sink in.

"Holy Christ!" I said, "The man himself? He really is alive, then?"

"How's that possible?" George said. "He must be nearly 200. When's he coming back?"

"I have no idea," Alexander said. "Can you believe he left no address, no telephone number?"

"Can we at least see the pictures, maybe buy one?" I said.

Alexander shook his head. "Alas. They're gone. Sold. Alekos here impulsively bought the lot."

The Greek artist smiled. Made a little bow. "Sono un uomo appassionato," he said in fluent Italian, "un po' pazzo."

Acknowledgements

My thanks

To my children for their everlasting help and encouragement.
To the influence of the life and work of August Strindberg.
To the astute comments of my editor, Kamilya Kuspan.
To Walt (polarbear19325@Fiverr) for designing this book.
To my readers for buying it.

Printed in Poland
by Amazon Fulfillment
Poland Sp. z o.o., Wrocław

40571173R00198